EXILE

ALSO BY PETER WEISS

THE PERSECUTION AND ASSASSINATION
OF JEAN-PAUL MARAT AS PERFORMED BY
THE INMATES OF THE ASYLUM OF
CHARENTON UNDER THE DIRECTION OF
THE MARQUIS DE SADE

THE INVESTIGATION

SONG OF THE LUSITANIAN BOGEY

EXILE

A NOVEL BY
PETER WEISS

Translators: E. B. GARSIDE • ALASTAIR HAMILTON • CHRISTOPHER LEVENSON

A SEYMOUR LAWRENCE BOOK
DELACORTE PRESS / NEW YORK

Contents

I. Leavetaking

I have often tried to come to an understanding of the images of my father and my mother, to take bearings and steer a course between rebellion and submission. But I have never been able to grasp and interpret the essential being of these two figures standing at either side of the gateway of my life. Both died almost at the same time and it was then I saw how deeply estranged I was from them. The grief that overcame me was not for them, for I hardly knew them, the grief was for what had been missed, for the yawning emptiness that surrounded my childhood and youth. Grief sprang from the recognition that the attempt at togetherness in which the members of the family had persisted to the end for two whole decades had completely failed. My sorrow was for the sense of too-lateness that lay on us, brothers and sister, at the graveside, that afterward again drove us apart, each off into his own existence. After my mother's death, my father, whose whole life had been given over to working tirelessly, once again tried to evoke the appearance of a fresh start. He set out on a trip to Belgium, to establish business connections there, as he said, but really to die like a wounded animal in its lair. He went as a broken man, able to move only with difficulty, helped by two canes. When, after learning in Ghent of his death, I had landed at the Brussels airport, with heavy heart I retraced the long trek my father must have had to make, upstairs, downstairs, through hall and corridors on legs enfeebled by poor circulation. It was early March, clear sky, sharp sunlight, a cold wind over Ghent. I went along the street by the railroad embankment, on to the hospital and its chapel where my father had been laid out. Freight-cars were being shunted on the tracks behind bare, lopped trees. The cars were rolling and clanking up on the embankment as I stood before the chapel, which looked like a garage, and whose double-door a nun opened for me. Inside, next to a coffin covered with flowers and wreaths, lay my father on a cloth-draped bier, dressed in a black suit now too large for him, in black socks, and with his arms folded across his chest, embracing the framed photograph of my mother. His gaunt face was relaxed, the thin hair, hardly gray at all, curling in one soft lock over his brow, and something of pride, boldness I had never noticed in him before stamped on his features. His hands were perfect, the fingernails symmetrical, bluishly shimmering mussel shells. I stroked the cold, yellowish, taut skin of his hands, while the Sister waited out in the sun a few steps behind me. I recalled my father as I had last seen him, lying on the living-room sofa under a blanket after my mother's burial, his face gray and blurry, blotted out by tears, his mouth stammering and whispering the name of the deceased. I stood there frozen, felt the cold wind, heard the whistles and puffs of steam coming from the railroad embankment, and there before me a life become a completely closed account, an enormous outlay of energy dissolved into nothingness. Before me lay the corpse of a man in an alien land, no longer reachable, a corpse in a shed by the railroad embankment, a man in whose life there had been office spaces and hotel rooms, and always large dwellings, big houses with many rooms filled with furniture, and in this man's life there had always been the wife who waited for him in the house they shared, and there had been children in this man's life, children whom he always shied away from and with whom he could never talk, but when he was away from the house he could perhaps feel tenderness for his children and longing for them, and always he carried pictures of them with him and certainly looked at them, all worn out, creased from so much handling, nights in hotel rooms when he was away on his trips, certainly believing that this time on his return he would find trust, but when he got back there was always disappointment and the impossibility of mutual understanding. In this man's life there had been ceaseless effort to support home and family, amid worries and sickness, together with his wife, and he had stuck fast to owning his own home, without ever experiencing happiness in it. This man, who now lay lost before me, had never given up believing in the ideal of a permanent home, but he had suffered death far away from this home alone in a sickroom, and if at his last breath he had stretched out his hand to the bell, it would have been, perhaps, to call for something, for some kind of help, some kind of relief, in the face of suddenly rising coldness and emptiness. I looked into my father's face, I still alive and preserving within me the knowledge of my father's existence, into a face in shadow grown strange to me. With an expression of contentment he lay in his remoteness, and somewhere his last large house was still standing, piled high with carpets, furniture, potted plants and pictures, a home that could no longer breathe, a home that he had kept intact throughout the years of emigration, through the constant resettlements and difficulties in adapting to new environments and through the war. Later that day my father was laid in a plain brown coffin that I had bought at the undertaker's and the nun took care that the picture of his wife stayed in his arms and after the lid had been screwed tight two hospital porters to the accompaniment of continuous rumbling and clattering of freight trains carried the coffin to the hearse which I followed in a hired car. Here and there at the side of the road to Brussels, farm laborers and workmen, lit up by the afternoon sun, took off their caps to the black car in which my father, for the last time, journeyed through a foreign country. The cemetery with the crematorium lay on a rise outside the city and the gravestones and bare trees were besieged by a cold wind. In the circular chapel the coffin was placed on a pedestal, I stood next to it and waited, and at a harmonium in an alcove sat an elderly man with the face of a drinker playing a psalm tune, and then in the middle section of the wall a sliding door suddenly opened and imperceptibly the pedestal with the coffin set itself in motion and slid slowly on almost invisible rails sunk in the floor into the bare, rectangular chamber behind the door, which noiselessly shut again. Two hours later I collected the urn with the ashes of my father's body. I carried the urn container, which had a crown on it and widened out at top, amid looks of consternation past hotel staff and guests up to my room, where I placed it first on the table, then on the windowsill, then on the floor, then on the dressing-table and finally in the wardrobe. I went down into town to buy paper and string in a department store, then wrapped the box in it and spent the night in the hotel with the remains of my father hidden in the wardrobe. Next day I reached my parents' house, where my step-brothers and their wives, my brother and his wife, my sister and her husband awaited me for the burial, the reading of the will and the apportioning of property. In the days that followed the final disintegration of the family was completed. A desecration and crushing underfoot took place, full of the undertones of envy and avarice although outwardly we tried to preserve a friendly and considerate tone of cordial agreement. Even for us, although we had long since become alienated from them, all the articles collected there had their value, and suddenly a wealth of recollections attached itself to each item. The grandfather clock with the sun face had ticked its way into my earliest dreams, in the mirror of the huge wardrobe I had caught sight of myself in the moonlight during my nocturnal excursions, in the diagonal supports beneath the dining-room table I had built dens and dugouts, and had crept behind the rotting velvet curtains to escape the savage pine marten, and many of the books on the high, wide bookshelves contained secret, forbidden things to read. We pushed and shoved around the chairs, sofas, and tables, violently we disrupted the order that had always been unassailable, and soon the house resembled a furniture warehouse and the objects that had been afforded a lifetime's care and protection at my mother's hand lay piled up in various rooms in five huge heaps, some to be taken away, some to be sold. The carpets were rolled up, the pictures lifted down from the walls, the curtains torn from the windows, the cupboards ransacked of crockery and clothes, and the women ran up and down between the attic and the cellar, seizing here an apron, there a wooden spoon, here a box with wornout dusty shoes, there a coal bucket or a rake. The urns of Father and Mother stood side by side in wet, black cemetery earth and we brothers and sisters crouched among the fragments of a dismembered home, we drained the bottles from my father's wine cellar and broke open his bureau to sort out his correspondence and documents. In accordance with his last will mountains of paper were piled up to be burned. Secretly I took some yellowed pages in my father's hand and a few diaries with notes by my mother. The naked bulbs shone harshly in all the rooms and were reflected in the black windowpanes. I had a feeling that the door opened, that my mother had appeared, to stare open-mouthed at her children's ghostly activity. Something died in each of us during these days. Now, after the plundering, we saw that this home, from which we had been thrust out, had nevertheless embodied a security for us, and that with its going the last symbol of our unity disappeared. At the deepest level of the changes this house had gone through lay rooms, spaces in which I had emerged from mythic darkness into first consciousness. I stood in the first floor vestibule looking first through one of the red, then through one of the blue panes of the glass door into the garden, so making the bushes, the pear tree, the gravel path, the lawn, and the summerhouse appear first in a fiery glow and then in subdued, submarine tones. At the time of this viewing my basic nature had already been formed, and only when the observing, controlling part of me wearies and my consciousness loses its hold, do impulses arise in me out of my earliest life, and it is in half-sleep, in dreams, in periods of depression that I re-experience the helplessness, the feeling of having been handed over and the blind rebellion of the time when strange hands tamed, kneaded and did violence to my being. When my mother once told me the first words I ever said were, what a nice life I have, what a nice life, in it I heard the ring of something that had been drummed into my head, parrot-taught, something with which I had wanted to amuse or mock those around me. Like an evil spirit I came into this house, lying in a tin box carried by my mother, received by wild tom-tom beats and my stepbrothers' exorcismal cries. My mother had found me at the edge of a pond among the rushes and storks. The first house has large blind spots in it. I can't find my way through this house, can only dimly remember the steps of a staircase, the corner of a floor on which I built little red-brown houses with blocks grown greasy from so much handling and green redoubts, dimly recall a little toy truck filled with miniature boxes, and the thought of those boxes brings back a thick, heavy sensation in the roof of my mouth. I vaguely recall postage stamps spread out before me, rose-colored and light green stamps with the face of a king with twirled mustaches and my older brothers rushing in and shouting, and my mother sweeping the stamps together and throwing them into the stove. And there is the edge of a tiled stove and the arms of a sofa and I sit on one arm of the sofa and one of my brothers tickles me and I fall backward on to the edge of the stove and knock a hole into my head and some liquid is poured out of a bottle into the hole in my head and my head froths and all the sense runs out of my head. I see a room that is green, the floor green, the curtains green, the wallpaper green, and I am sitting on a raised porcelain vessel shaped like a guitar and my mother stands in back of me and shoves her forefinger into my bum just above the anus, and I push and she pushes and everything is green, and the street outside is green, and the street is called Green Street, the street in the green twilight was full of the trundling of drays laden high with barrels. The hoofs of the heavy shaggy horses struck sparks from the cobblestones, the coachmen clicked their tongues and cracked their whips and a heavy, sweet smell swelled in waves from the breweries. Our house, with its high gables on whose ridge I rode a race against the moon and from whose chimney I sprang with a leap into the sky, lay narrow and squashed between warehouses and the wall of a factory yard. Once a man climbed over our roof, there was commotion in the streets and shots rang out, and my brothers stormed through the house and shouted that someone had fled onto our roof and men rushed in from the street into our house, and the men carried guns in their hands, and they all ran into the garden and switched on their flashlights and shot up at the roof and the wounded man fell from the roof down to the men in the garden below. The house remains strange to me, I cannot find my way around its interior, but I take the garden for my own, I lie stretched out on the ground under the bushes, feel the dry earth between my hands, put the earth into my mouth, crunch the earth between my teeth, feel the white, round pebbles, put the pebbles in my mouth, feel on my tongue their roundness and the warmth of the sun. Closeness, a shut-in feeling reigned in the house, and my senses were trapped. Here out of doors my senses could expand and when I entered the summer house I entered a kingdom that belonged only to me, my self-chosen place of exile. In the narrow bands of sunlight that slanted down through a high, ivy-mantled window, I steered my vehicle, a little handcart with its upright shaft, between stacked garden chairs, baskets and tools, I drove with it, swam with it, flew with it, humming and murmuring to myself. This is like a picture from an old book of fairy tales; something sunken wells up out of the picture, something fraught with expectancy. The secluded and the secretive, the hiding away with myself and my games, this is still with me and stirs at this very hour, it is to be felt every time I get lost in my work. I was my own master, I created the world for myself. But somewhere lurked the foresense of a calling out for me, of a call about to ring out, which would come rolling toward me across the garden. The anticipation of this summons was always lurking somewhere, to this very day the anticipation persists, to this day the fear that all can end suddenly. When it called for me the first time I pretended to be deaf, I kept the calling at arm's length, through being alone I had forgotten my name, I behaved as if it was not meant for me. But then the name was hurled into me again and again until it filled me completely, until I almost burst with it, and I had to answer, I had to confess that the name had found me. I often tried to call myself something else, but when the calling of my only true name whirred toward me, I started, it stuck into me like a harpoon, and I could not avoid it. In a whisper I call to myself with my own name, and frighten myself with it, as if the name came up to me from far outside me from a time in which I was still without form. And then I feel a raving, impotent rage, a storming against the impregnable, and then my stammering is stifled by an invisible hand. There is my mother's face. I flew upward to this face, lifted by her arms, which could enfold all spaces. The face took me up and thrust me from itself. The large, warm mass of the face, with its dark eyes, suddenly became a wolfish grimace with menacing teeth. Out of the hot, white breasts, where drippy milk glands had been a moment before, darted the licking tongues of little snakeheads. Hands had been there earlier than the face. They grabbed me, ripped me up into the air, shook me, sprang at my ears and into my hair. Everything roared and surged about my mother's form. I tried to escape her power by closing my eyes and pressing my lips together over my voice. But then I could no longer endure it, and had to open my eyes wide to cry for my mother's face, and have it proved to me that it was still there. Around my mother everything was unstable, seething, swirling. But next to her stood Augusta, clearly outlined, mild and permanent. From the very first Augusta was old, old as time. In her black, tightly laced dress, her hands softened by dish-water, red and swollen, Augusta stood clearly outlined in space, and everything that came near her increased its radiance. In my mother reigned the wild and unbridled, in Augusta sufferance, humility. When my mother shouted at her, Augusta bent deep over the white potato basin with the blue rim and the potato peel-ings curled over her hands. When my mother's fury was spent Augusta hit herself in the face as punishment or beat her own head with a coat hanger. Mother disappeared but Augusta re-mained there, and with tears in her eyes gazed at me and stroked my hands as if it were I who had to be consoled and from a drawer in the kitchen table she took a dish of dessert, saved from mealtime. I went out into the street holding on to Augusta's hand. My exploration of the city is connected for me with the pressure of Augusta's hand. The streets rise in front of me with their creak-ing iron-rimmed wheels, with their haze of tar and malt and wet dust, with their warehouses at whose façades the chains of the hoists rattled, and in whose storerooms shapes moved about in the uncertain light between packing cases and sacks. We penetrated ever deeper into the alleyways, arcades, and tucked-away squares, past the soot-blackened, scaly, bescribbled masonry walls, until through gateway arches and down worn-out flights of steps we came to the dikes and onto the docks where the masts of ships stood out against the smoky sky, where watery reflections flick-ered on ships' sides, where black and yellow faces peered out of the round portholes and shouted out strange words, where the pennants buffeted on the taut rigging and screaking cargo cranes swung long necks around. Sometimes scenes from these wanderings suddenly surface in my dreams, first impressions which have preserved their glassy transparence and sharpness of focus, they show places, often without any recognizable happening, motionless and still, where I had suddenly become aware of my own existence. There is a broad, sandy avenue, the houses that flank it lie far back from the road, with steep steps leading up to the doors, and in the sand there are wheel tracks. Perhaps a car has just passed, but now the avenue is still and empty, and broods in the noonday warmth and is saturated with the momentousness and uniqueness of my existence. There is a street that slopes down from a rise; it is toward evening, colors shine out of the pinkly shimmering dusk. With long, high leaps I go soaring down the street. Behind the redly lustrous shutters I can make out carved figures of gods and elaborate model ships, chests with chased-silver locks, caskets inlaid with shells and pearls, silk handkerchiefs adorned with firebreathing dragons, lacquered fans, reddish-gold bird feathers and deep-blue butterflies, daggers with waved blades and ivory handles, a rusty pirate musket, nail-studded belts and riding boots with spurs, a white swan with outstretched neck, a horse's head with streaming mane, a naked blackwoman's body, pearl necklaces, bracelets, sawfish, alligators, and monkeys, and in the depths of a workshop, amid his leather stuff, Master Stahlhut at his last, mouth full of nails, hammering on a shoe sole with his hammer, warty face lit up by the glow from a crystal ball. I stood with Augusta on the bank of the river, a train of barges passed by, wash fluttering on one of the barges, and a small white, barking dog, and Augusta took a piece of chocolate from inside the crumbly black leather of her handbag and put it into my mouth. It tasted soapy from the inside of her bag. We stood in a tunnel, and over us rumbled a train and on the deep camber of the wall were stuck yellowed posters, blistered by paste, which Augusta murmuringly deciphered. We looked from all sides at the stone giant Roland in the marketplace and wondered what the dwarf might mean whose head and arms lay crushed between the giant's feet. Mother knew everything, could

do everything, decided everything, but Augusta knew no more
than I did and we looked at things with the same astonishment.
We tried to explain to each other the snake gargoyles along the
tops of the drainpipes, the figures of saints on the cathedral façade, the inscriptions on the doorways and the kings and knights
mounted on their green-smudged horses, we puzzled and felt our
way along passages and clumsily built-over courtyards, we saw
the pigeons flying around the towers and followed the marching
soldiers, keeping in time with their flashing, crashing instruments.
Once we found ourselves caught up in a crowd that had assembled in a square. All eyes were directed upward to a large house.
High up on the walls a man was climbing. Someone said, human
fly. I asked Augusta what that was, a human fly. She did not
know. It seemed to me some sort of profession, a rare and unusu-
ally difficult task to which one would have to devote the whole of
one's life. I felt my palms beginning to sweat, I felt a fluttering in
my stomach and in the bend of my knees, and a tickling on the
soles of my feet, and I knew that this was all part of it. I realized
that fear was the real motive for this performance, that one tried
to overcome fear by the exertion of climbing. My encounter with
the climber awakened in me the premonition of a vocation, it was
as if I was looking ahead into my own future as, breathless and
with fingers and toes tensed, I followed the movements of the
man on the wall. At this moment, under a clear blue sky, out of
which came the droning of a plane, light and metallic, the
groundwork was laid of a longing to do something on my own.
And so there was I, already involved in existence, already in the
middle of life's committedness and so pushed on toward the barrel organ pipings and the uproar of the fair, in a growing throng.
The ground was soft with confetti and paper streamers, in the
booths hot sausages, pretzels and spun honey were being offered
for sale, trumpet blares, shots and runs on the barrel organ became ever more piercing, elbows jogged me, feet brushed against
mine, and then everything was one rotating movement of bodies,
one vast bawling and bubbling of voices, and I was part of it, was
carried along between the faces, hats and arms, between the
swaying grape bunches of multicolored balloons, between the

large flopping streamers, between the wonderfully painted whir-ring merry-go-rounds, and to the hoarse question from the Punch and Judy show, Are you all there, I answered yes in the chorus of countless voices, and as Punch whacked at the policeman with his club, I joined the collective shrieks of laughter, and I saw the lady snakecharmer on the platform in her tights of scintillating black scales and the largest man in the world and the magician out of whose tail coat pigeons flew and everything was fleeting, every-thing changed form, and the canvas of the tents billowed and whispered mysteriously in the wind, and the masks in the shoot-ing galleries jerked open their mouths and on black cushions lay golden medals, and over the rotating merry-go-round hung clack-ing rings to be caught while in circling flight, and in a miniature mine jerky little figures hacked at tunnel walls and cars drawn by stiff-legged horses moved nearer along rails, and shovels were raised over the cars, and away went the cars, and baskets sank down through shafts, and cars inclined over baskets and up went the baskets and hung swinging over approaching trains and everything rattled and jerked until the mechanism suddenly fell silent and everything stopped in mid-motion, cars stuck in the air with picks raised high, horses frozen, baskets hanging still in the shaft, until with a jerk everything got underway again, everything moved along again, shook again, bobbed again, dragged along again, hacked again, cracked again. And nearby on a campstool sat an old man with a white beard and a broad-brimmed slouch hat, motionless and preoccupied he leaned against his mechanical box, deaf to all the questions one put to him. Amid a tangle of supporting beams I climbed into a little rollercoaster car and the wild gay surge of life fell away behind me, ever farther I drew away from the roar and the bustle, until all I could hear was the rolling of the small, sturdy wheels on the rails and I was taken higher and higher till the highest point was reached, from which I could look out far and wide over the whole of the fairground and the city. The car rested only a moment at its peak before it plunged into the depths, but this moment was enough to transfix me with an ecstatic feeling of liberty. There below me lay the sea of roofs, with their smoking chimneys, there lay the glittering water of the river, there lay the ships in the harbor, the freighters and the great liners, there arched the bridges with steaming trains, and on the towers the light green copper shone and the golden weather vanes flashed. Then came the downward plunge, down steep run after run, around breathtaking curves, to the last chasm with the pool where the water sprayed up around the car as it shot through it. When it was dusk I drifted through the streets with the fair-day throng, swam slowly down the avenue with the crowd, saw above me the foliage of the trees glide back in autumnal gold, felt the wind on my perspiring forehead, held up before me the stick with the Chinese lantern in which a candle burned, and joined in the song that was always welling up in waves before and behind me, Lantern, lantern, sun, moon, and stars. And underneath the circus cupola a creature of the air lunged from trapeze to trapeze, turned a somersault, let out shrill, reckless cries, dived out of the heights at me with outspread arms, a precipitously flying mane of black hair, close in front of me she pulled herself out of her dive and drew herself up again, a breath of wind, filled with a curiously drugging fragrance, rushed past me. Her ecstatic smile in her golden-brown, slant-eyed face, her piercing bird cry, burned themselves into me forever. Soon, soon I would travel after her, would fly back and forth across the circus arena, soon, soon, only a short time off, I will belong to you, only first I have to learn to read and write, to get through school quickly, soon, soon, I shall be with you, and see your ecstatic smile again, and hear your wild cry. I learned writing with Berthold Merz in the shed next door in the courtyard of the slate factory, we scratched our first letters on black flat pieces from the scrap pile and the sun shimmered through the cracks in the planks. Berthold's figure is fluid and fading, like dream figures in the morning shortly before waking, only his hand with the short stubby fingers and the bitten fingernails is clear. This hand grips the bow and shoots the arrow, the arrow with the feathered shaft, and the arrow rises high into the sky, so high that it disappears from our view and the arrow never returns. And Berthold Merz disappeared and Friederle took his place. A few years ago I stood in front of the house we had moved into at the time I was starting

school. I had not seen the avenue for years and now, seeing it
again, I felt my childhood within me like the dull ache of an ulcer.
The trunks of the trees at the side of the road had become strong
and tall, the boughs spread far out over the road and their foliage
closed together to form a thick canopy. Like someone entranced
in an evil fairy tale I went toward the park to which the avenue
led and in which our house lay hidden. On the pond at the edge of
the avenue a few white swans were swimming as before and in
the hedge with the prickly leaves the white sweet peas bloomed as
before. From the stream that separated the park from the avenue,
I could see the house glinting bright red between the trees, it was
intact, and in the adjoining garden lay the yellow villa in which
Friederle had lived. Profound silence reigned, everything was
steeped in its long past. In the muddy water of the brook a shoal
of sticklebacks was flashing, tadpoles rowed with their tails
around the algae, a frog with gaping eyes sat on the bank, a blue
dragonfly whirred past. I went down the park path and stood still
at the white posts of the garden gate in front of our house. The
garden with its thicket of fir trees, its spreading copper beech
and tall grass run wild extended to the elder bush at the edge of
the fields. Beside the garden path lay the green henhouse, low and
shrunken, and once we had jumped down from the dizzying
heights of its skylight. The fenced-in hen yard was deserted but a
few white feathers still shone out of the dust. I asked a woman
who came out of the house if she knew anything about the neighbors. She told me that out of the whole large family only one son
was still alive, Freidrich, he had been an outstanding officer and
had won the highest honors. He still lived in the town and she
gave me his address. But I did not look him up, I knew what he
was like. There stood Friederle at the fence of the neighboring
garden, it was the day we moved in. He folded his arms and asked
me imperiously what my name was. Are you going to live here, he
asked, and I nodded and with my gaze followed the men who
were carrying our furniture out of the moving van and into the
house. Your house belongs to my father, Friederle said, you are
only renting it. My father is a president, he said, what is your
father. I did not know. What, you don't even know what your

father is, he said. I sought for an answer that would overpower him, or win his favor, but I found none. Then he asked again. What's that you've got on your hat. I took the hat off. It was a sailor's hat with golden lettering on the headband. What is that, he asked again. I did not know. Can't you even read what's written on your own hat, he said. It says, I am stupid. And with that he took the hat from my hand and threw it high up into a tree. The hat stuck in the branches, the long blue ribbons fluttered in the wind. My mother came out on to the terrace of our house and saw us standing there side by side. Have you found a new playmate already, she cried. Are you having fun. Friederle pulled me with him into the depths of the garden, past the henhouse, from which we could hear a scratching and clucking, past the pump and the strawberry beds, through grass that grew up to our shoulders, through the shrubbery to the wet ditch that ran in a wide arc around our lot. There in front of us were the fields, the vast plain, over which the sun was burning down, the wind rushed toward us out of the open spaces and showered us with its pregnant odors of growing grain and clover and cow dung. Like a thin mist the pictures of my old world were scattered and everything was clothed in blinding brightness. With the help of a stick Friederle jumped over the ditch and signaled impatiently for me to follow. I threw myself across onto the bushy slope, skidded in the mud, pulled myself up by juicy, damp grasses, staggered out into the weight of a sea of air in which green plover were whistling past. And everything belonged to Friederle, he showed me the speckled birds' eggs in the dry, brittle sand, the bittercress with toad spit on it, molehills, field mice runs, foxholes, and then the hare. Do you see him, there, there, and I saw his white undertail disappearing in rapid zigzag leaps. He was always taking me into his domain, up to the marsh where the ground squished under our feet and where we sucked at the poisonous stalks of marsh marigolds. I went back by the avenue in the white dust of the roadway, my childhood lay decades behind me, I can depict it now with well-chosen words, I can take it apart and spread it out in front of me, but as I experienced it there was no thinking out and no dissecting, there was no controlling reason then, I was walking down the avenue and my

black laced boots were whitened by the dust of the avenue and
Friederle walked beside me, and the white swans swam in the
pond and in one garden a peacock strutted and opened up his
scintillating fan of feathers, and it was the first day of school, from
all directions children were streaming into school and each of
them carried a little bag of candy to console him, and fear of the
school was sticky and sickly with the taste of raspberry sweets.
But in front of the school entrance I fled back, I raced back over
the black cinders—trampled hard—of the playground, I ran back
along the white dusty avenue, past the peacock and the swans,
over the little bridge that led from the avenue into the park, into
the overgrown depths of the park up to the edge of the fields, I
can depict it now, see it all now, my first day at school, the beginning of my panic, I did not want to get caught, I fled, gasping, I
struggled for breath, my throat and chest burned like fire, and so I
stand at the edge of the fields and gradually my breathing grows
calmer and I feel safe and for a while am free and away from all
threats. Before me a wild rose bush grows, and in the thorns of
the bush trembles a woolly tuft of hare's fur. Later that day, however, I was led back to school by my mother, later that day I stood
with my mother in the corridor in front of the classroom door, and
my mother knocked at the classroom door and the teacher opened
the door from within and inside all faces were turned toward me,
all within had formed a community together and I was the one
who had come too late. And every day I went down the avenue
with Friederle and Friederle pressed against me, dug his elbow
into my side, shoved me to sidewalk edge. I avoided him and
walked in the road. Why don't you walk here beside me, Friederle
asked, and made room for me. Hardly had I started walking next
to him when he rammed his elbow into my ribs again. I began to
run, but he held me back by my satchel. We came to the square
where the street to school forked off and Friederle stuck his leg
between mine so that I fell, my satchel sprang open, books spilled
out, the slate and the box of chalk clattered out, the box with my
sponge in it rolled far away over the cobbles up to the tramcar
conductors who here, at the end of the line, were sitting on the
trolley car steps, eating their breakfast and laughing and munch-

ing their sandwiches, the conductors threw the box across to me, it
was a box made of black lacquered wood, with a red rose painted
on it. Here at the square where the road to school branched off, a
whole enchanting world began, walls of fortresslike buildings
pushed close together, with glimpses of courtyards and stables, a
church tower built of rough stone rose up out of the shingled
roofs, in a wheel at the top of the spire storks had made their nest
and struck out at one another with their long sharp beaks. Behind
the leaded panes of a window sat an aged man in a rocking chair
and out of a gatehouse came two men with knives, their faces taut
and reddish and silkily shining like the thin skin over healing
wounds, and behind them on a heap of brushwood lay a pig, its
four legs bound together, and on a red-tiled wall a butterfly trembled with outspread wings that had black and yellow markings,
and a hand holding a needle thrust out between its fingers approached the butterfly and the needle pierced it through. On the
school playground rose a small stone building with an arched,
shabby doorway and when one pressed one's eyes to the windowpanes and shielded them from the sides with one's hands, one
could see inside in the half-dark the carriage with its high turned
doorposts and black canopy and it sometimes happened that the
coachman came in a long frock coat with his big black horse, cautiously opened the door, backed the horse into the shafts and
drove the creaking carriage out. The piercing bell summoned us
to the classrooms. Here was a whirring and stirring up of dust
around the splintery desks that smelled of ink and cold sweat. I
unpacked the slate and the broken chalk. Friederle turned around
in his place and threatened me with his fist. The teacher called me
out to the front. I had not understood his question, I never understood his questions. His bloated face rocked close in front of me,
his eyes bulged at me, his thick lips opened. Now, what was it I
wanted, he asked, and rubbed my ear with the knuckles of his
clenched fist, and white threads of saliva trembled on his opened
lips. From the benches all around me came a tittering. Even the
teacher's face was distorted into a grin. That they all laughed at
me was proof that I was funny, and so I too grinned, and this
ability to amuse others was a valuable gift. But, the teacher

screamed, you're still laughing, and his grin had only been a bar-
ing of his teeth, and the laughter around me from the benches
oozed away. I was hauled up by the ear onto the podium and
placed in front of the blackboard, and what I had to demonstrate
to the teacher and class was how one kept one's palm held out
under the raised cane. It was a difficult exercise, for my hand
would not stay still under the cane, it always jerked back. The
class was one, single, thick, blood-thirsty silence. The teacher took
aim and swished the cane down and my hand drew back, and the
stroke whistled through the air. And the teacher shouted, What,
trying to duck your punishment, are you, and snatched my hand
up again and once more swished the cane down at me, again my
hand drew back and again it was held up, and the cane came
down again, and again my hand drew back, and again it was held
up, and again the cane whistled down until finally it caught my
hand and the smarting weal spread out over my palm. Blinded by
welling tears, gripping the wrist of my aching hand with the other
hand, I stumbled back to my place. Thus it was that I learned in
school how to hold out my hand for the teacher's cane. And after
school I tried to evade Friederle but with his gang of cronies he
hunted me out everywhere. When I ran they ran along beside me.
When I walked slowly they walked slowly beside me. When I
dodged suddenly to the other side of the street they threw stones
at me. These small whistling stones, and the mocking voices over
there, how well they knew that I was a fugitive, that I was in their
power. And my little subterfuges, suddenly I bent double and
raised my hand to my forehead, screaming as if I had been hit.
That alarmed my pursuers and they cravenly slunk away, but I
was more cowardly for I knew that if they now felt guilty they
would later only punish me the more so I shouted after them, You
didn't mean me, it was a mistake, you meant someone else. After
lunch, between two and three, as I lay on my bed resting, a lostness came over me. I lay motionless and held my breath. If I only
lay long enough without breathing, I could forget the breathing
altogether. Then, like a stone in water, I sank and soft, black rings
spread out above me. But suddenly I hit the ground and, shaken
by the jolt, was wrenched back to the surface. Now everything in

me became large and swollen and inflated, I became a giant, an all-powerful being, stretched out on the yellow desert of the blankets I played with little colored grains of sugar that I had scraped off a piece of chocolate. The grains trickled around under my hands, grains like heaps of people seen from a vast distance. I blew into the motley heap of people and they scattered in wild flight. The giant is coming, the giant is coming, they shouted below in the desert, and the earth rumbled under the giant's steps, the giant appeared on the horizon, the ingeniously constructed giant, a thousand stories high, populated by workers who serviced the heating system and the machinery, the electricity circuits and switchboards in the interior, and controlled by technicians and officers in the center of the globe of the head, in the eye chambers, the brain halls, the canals of the nostrils, the eardrums. I myself was the commander in chief over this metallic structure in human form, I issued my orders through megaphones, and I was responsible for seeing that all the joints and limbs moved according to plan and that balance was kept at the vast speed at which it jerked itself forward. Jungles crumpled like stubble under the robot's feet, with a single leap he sprang over the widest rivers, the highest mountains, the oceans were puddles to him, and his head disappeared in the clouds. Then I heard Tarmina outside in the garden calling my sisters. I ran to the window, saw Tarmina with upturned face among the rhododendron bushes, Tarmina Nebeltau in her pink dress with the silk ribbon in her hair. I ran downstairs, Margit and Irene came too, we fluttered around the garden, to the swing, the sandpit, the ditch, we trampled the tall grass down into paths, hid ourselves from each other, looked for each other. Then in the wood, to the witches and the will-o'-the-wisps. Ran on the soft springy carpet of pine needles, looked into the hollow trunk where the owl lived, started up rabbits in their runs, chased after the dragonflies by the pond, heard the cuckoo calling from the trees how many years we still had to live. Found in the grass the blue and white feather of a jay and gave it to Tarmina, who stroked herself with it on her closed eyelids. In a clearing I saw Tarmina dancing with Margit, Irene called after them and they rushed towards her, the branches they brushed past in their haste still swung as their steps faded away into the rustling foliage. This clearing, reached by a grass path, lies there in its glittering insistence, a milky blue light hovers over the green green grass that has been stamped down by the dancers' feet. Then back to the garden. Friederle, with a flushed face, called me over to the copper beech at the top of which he had built a lookout. We clambered up and saw far away on the horizon a factory erupt in flames and smoke, then we let ourselves drop backward, stretched out flat, springing from bough to bough. Friederle and my sisters disappeared in the tall grass. Alone with Tarmina beside the swing. Tarmina in front of me on the seat of the swing, swaying lightly away from me, towards me, the air heavy with the scent of lilac. Then suddenly she bends forward as she comes towards me, and kisses me on the mouth. She glides back again, jumps off the swing, and runs away. The kiss on my lips, the empty swing, swinging to and fro, Tarmina near me a moment ago, now with the others, did not again turn around to me. She disappeared with Friederle in the tall grass. Instead of going after her, instead of winning her for myself, I crept back into the house. The kitchen was empty, all the rooms were empty. Only Augusta was upstairs in her attic room. I went over to Augusta's chest of drawers and took in my hand the round, white sea-smoothed and polished stone that she kept there, folded my hand over it, held it, felt the inside of my hand quite filled with it, and asked Augusta if she would put a disk in the music box. Augusta wound up the machine with the key. While the brittle, cracked melody trickled out of the indented tin plate, Augusta with the veined hands folded sat in her violet slip at the edge of the bed and through the open window I heard from afar the rolling of the trains and the voices of the children playing in the garden. From Augusta's room it was only a few steps to the attic, a large room supported by wooden posts where the warmth pressed down on one, sultry and motionless, while beneath its round gable windows the floor lay full of dead wasps. The place of exile that I had found in the summerhouse continued in this attic. In the sensual pleasure of a secret search, I opened suitcases and chests in which things out of my parents' past were kept, I lifted out a light gray uniform that my father had worn during the war, I spread out the uniform on the floor, laid the saber next to it, the saber with the silver tassel at the handle and the field glasses he had carried in the battle in which he was wounded. They were said to have saved his life, for the focusing screw was smashed flat and had softened the impact of the bullet that had penetrated his body. Black-rimmed bullet holes could still be seen in the leather case. Next to my father's uniform I laid out an expensive dress of my mother's, a fan of ostrich feathers, a pearl-inlaid diadem. This was the reconstruction of a prehistoric moment. Full of uneasiness and suspense I tried to find out something about my origins. About my father I knew nothing. The strongest impression he made was his always being away somewhere. I had heard only a few words about his past. My grandfather had a long white beard, he used to say. Or, I went into business when I was very young and supported my family. In the rare hours of mutual understanding, on a Sunday or on Christmas Eve, he used to tell me how when I was still small he used to let me ride on his knee and how I always wanted to hear the story that he told me then, and now, playing with his saber in the loft, I sang this story to myself, Once there was a little boy, who climbed an apple tree, along came a man with a big sword, and the man shouted, you better get right down out of that apple tree, and the boy fell out of the tree. I could still remember how in that dark earlier time the knee pulled away from under me to one side, and I slid into the depths, held back by my father's hands. Of my mother I knew that before she married my father she had been an actress. The costumes in the suitcases derived from that period and little boxes were filled with photographs on which she could be seen as an Egyptian princess, an abbess, a gypsy woman and a Greek priestess. Another picture showed her with my stepbrothers and her first husband, who wore a big, bristly mustache. On the basis of vague hints that I had heard about him, I imagined him as a thug and a sex maniac. He looked like my mother's father, who appeared on another picture. At the dinner table this father used to keep a dog whip beside him with which he gave his six daughters cracks over the head, and made them, as they sat, keep newspapers tucked under their arms to learn perfect posture. I am grateful to him for this strict bringing-up, my mother said, it has made me strong. From the fragments I found in the attic I was able to piece together a family history. There were photos of my father at an equator-crossing ceremony on board a ship going to South America, there was the engagement photograph with my father in uniform, arm in arm with my mother. He was lean, delicately built, my mother large and stately in a dress that reached to the ground. My mother liked telling us the story of their first meeting, it was the romance of the little lieutenant who wooed the celebrated actress and showered her with flowers and finally won her. It was a story not to be fathomed, quite as impenetrable as it is today as I brood over those personal documents of my parents that had been saved from destruction. Why did my mother give up the theater. Did not her later lack of stability come from her having forsaken the career she was naturally cut out for. She did not like the world of the theater any more, she said, it was too free and easy, life in it too makeshift. She created the elegant and the grand in her own home, the large receptions, the extravagance, the expensive clothes, all these became her substitute for the roles she might have played on the stage. My researches in the attic are supplemented today by a letter that my father wrote my mother before the battle in which he received his stomach wound. The contents of the letter are as follows, Zaklikow, 5th July 1915. In the event of my being killed in battle, I request whoever finds me to send the enclosed letter to Frau XX by the quickest possible way, and furthermore to inform the same by telegram of my death. Please also send the ring on my finger, together with all my papers, to the same Frau XX. All other objects, such as my linen, clothing, and equipment, may be disposed of among such of my comrades as need them. Any cash remaining after deductions for postage expenses may likewise be distributed among my companions. If possible also inform the aforementioned person where I am buried. With many thanks for any trouble the carrying out of my requests may have caused you. Then the letter to my mother, My dearest wish was to return home once more from the war, to return to you, my beloved. If it is not granted me to see you again,

these lines that I write before going into battle will greet you for
the last time. It is difficult for me to imagine that I shall no longer
see your dear eyes nor feel your lips, that your arms will no longer
enfold me. If I were still alive your life would only just have begun, I should have arranged everything more beautifully than you
could have ever dreamed of, my life too would only just be beginning. The will, of which you have a copy, is deposited with the
lawyer. See to it also, please, that the balance sheet is audited at
M's, and then I wanted to say to you that my, that is my heirs',
profit-sharing in the business continues for another year. The articles in my apartment are all at your disposal. And the ring you
gave me that I am now wearing, I hope you get it back. Never
give it to anyone else. And now farewell, my beloved, I shall kiss
you to my last breath. Reading this letter brings back to me my
eavesdropping in the nights of my childhood when I lay awake
with my ear pressed to the wall to catch something of the distant,
murmuring voices of my parents. This eavesdropping, this grop-
ing, this concealment upstairs in the sultry attic. The battlefield.
The shots of the machine gun. My father in a foxhole. My father
with a bleeding stomach, moaning among other wounded in the
field hospital. And then my mother appearing. She finds him in
this field hospital, in this overcrowded, stinking ward where he
lies bleeding. She carries him out in order to look after him herself. In the picture world of my mythology she holds him in her
arms, she carries him along a sodden and rutted track, above her
the torn, low-flying clouds. Columns of soldiers, cannons come toward her, the wind rushes through the willows. This retrospective
brooding and fantasy-making, this expectant eavesdropping, this
suspense came before the secret games that were the real reason
for my visits to the attic. Filled with the certainty of being completely secluded and forgotten by everyone, I stole away to my
model countryside which I had built on a plank from clay and
sand and stones and moss. When I lowered my face to the edge of
the countryside it was as if I were there myself, reconnoitering,
and my watchful gaze lit upon hills, woodlands, ditches and gullies and trenches and drawn-up cannons and the General Staff in
a council of war and everything held its breath, everything waited

for the explosion. With a cold passion I marked off the countryside, arranged the positions of the troops, built up the fortresses,
made a gully steeper, put in another thicket, and only when I was
finished with every detail and the total impact of the work satisfied me did I move on to the actual combat. The battle broke out.
Soldiers stormed out of their trenches, the cannons opened up
their bombardment. After every hurricane of annihilation that I
let loose over the landscape, I scrutinised the resulting situation
from all angles, in close-up I saw the dead and wounded half
buried in shell craters and uprooted woods, the fallen horses and
smashed cannons in the ruins of castles, saw soldiers lying on top
of each other in a cruel wrestling match, saw troops lurking in
ambush. Again new waves of attacks broke loose, crowned by the
holocaust. The copse, the fences, the bridges, the melting dugouts
turned to charcoal, soldiers collapsed, the colors ran off them like
blood and mud, and I drank in the visions of my passing world,
breathed in the stench of molten tin and burned wood until nothing existed any longer but one single smoldering desolation. After
the great battles when the mangled corpses had been buried and
the wounded had been brought to the field hospitals, I made little
expeditions, in which only a few specially privileged figures took
part. These expeditions were marked by a sense of relief and a
desire to explore. With these figures I crossed the broad sweep of
the floor, landed with them on foreign shores, reached inacces-
sible mountain peaks or distant planets. But always I had to return to my battleground on the board and had to recompose my
landscape and populate it with troops. High up in our house I
spread death and destruction all about me. Something incomprehensible had begun within me. I sought release. But in the evenings the incomprehensible came and paralyzed me. I hid my
hands under the blanket. But my mother would come and lift out
my hands again. Imperiously she pressed my hands down on to
the blanket. My hands had to lie outside in the cold, exposed to
ghostly attackers. Cramped in fear I lay, abandoned to visions of
giants and huge animals. I stared into the twilight of the room
that became ever more inky until the objects in it began to dissolve into black floating patches, I strained my eyes to the utmost

to find something recognizable and things moved everywhere in
the shadows, in the shadows the figures squatted and lurked, they
crept out from behind the curtain, they rose up from the floor
with a soft crackling and whistling. Sweat streamed down over
me. The attacks had hardly begun but I was already annihilated. I
did not move, so as not to attract the attention of the ghosts. I
held my breath, only my heart hammered, and now it came toward me from all sides, I pretended to be dead, if only my heart
would not thud so, I lay amid crouching nameless things that
were plotting to murder me. I could not scream, I tried frantically
to force out some sound but I didn't succeed, it was as if I no
longer knew my own voice, how I could ever make it come out
again, only after complete exhaustion did a strangled sound come
out, which hung in the room and balled itself together, to come at
me again. Every night I died, strangled, suffocated. Still, sometimes, after reaching insensibility, I succeeded in getting beyond
fear, in breaking through horror once it had reached its utmost
power, whereupon I got out of bed, the horror having changed
into a voluptuous weightlessness, on tiptoe I glided through the
room, opened the door, jumped over the large yellow lion that lay
in front of my door and with floating steps, which seemed nevertheless to be held back by some tough, slimy resistance, moved
along the corridor to the door of my parents' bedroom. It was an
endlessly long corridor, behind me loomed the stairs up to the
attic and beside me stretched the banisters, below which lay the
dark shaft of the stairway down to the entrance hall, in front of
me, in the niche next to my parents' bedroom, a few wicker chairs
stood softly creaking and crackling, the white parts of their flower-
patterned cushions standing out sharply in the darkness. From
below came the slow, heavy ticking of the grandfather clock,
slow, heavy steps came up the stairs, it was the Sandman coming
with his sack of sand. Beyond the window lay the garden plunged
in deepest violet, the window was open, the garden stretched and
breathed, and from the ditch I caught the half-extinguished cries
of a drowning child. The door to my parents' bedroom stood ajar,
I cautiously pushed it open and entered. In their double bed,
which stood at right angles to the wall and protruded into the

middle of the room, lay my parents, on the left my father snoring softly and on the right my mother, her face framed by the darkness of her hair. Both lay on their backs, and above them, on the wall at the head of the bed, hung three pictures, on the left a painting of my father's face, the head, in the oval of the cardboard mount, looking like a head cut off, to the right a reproduction of a picture of a naked youth, seen in profile, who with his arms around his knees and his face resting on his knees sat high up above a desolate mountain landscape, and in the middle the picture of the naked goddess, who, surrounded by foam, bent stiffly forward, without ever losing her balance, covering her breasts with one hand and with the other clasping a strand of her long, flowing hair in front of her genitals, stood on the rim of a huge shell. The clothes lay carefully folded on the chairs next to the bedside tables on my father's side and on my mother's side, and beneath the chairs the shoes stayed close together like patiently waiting animals. In the mirror of the large wardrobe on the wall opposite the bed, I saw myself, saw myself in the violet moonlight in the depths of the transfigured room. My parents tried, on our family doctor's advice, to put an end to my nocturnal wanderings, they surrounded my bed with large basins of water that were to wake me from my somnambulant state when I stepped into them. This treatment resulted in my learning to fly. I increased the horror and the creepiness by artificially induced cold shivers that had the property of making me weightless and with their help, stretched out stiff, I hovered up out of bed, to fly, feet first and flying on my back, straight across the room, through the open window and over the garden. I steered myself with light movements of my hands and toes, feeling triumphantly happy, lowering and raising myself according to the varying degrees of my cold shivers. I passed so close by the top of the copper beech that its soft warm leaves brushed me. These nocturnal excursions were the preliminaries to severe attacks of fever which for a long while, at intervals of two weeks or so, overcame me for some days at a time. A committee of doctors stood around my bed, removed their glittering pince-nez, tugged thoughtfully at their beards, tested my pulse, pressed hairy middle fingers into my stomach, knocked with bent index fingers on my chest, telephoned to my heart, hit my knee with little silver hammers, and could find nothing to explain my symptoms. Finally the theory was put forward that a fly had carried bacilli to me from the malaria cultures of a nearby mental hospital. The chain of thought that attributed the origins of my illness to a mental hospital made me think that I must be near to madness, I studied my face in the mirror, made faces, babbled foolishness and let my spittle drip out of my mouth as I had seen happen at times with the mental defectives I had watched on their walks in the park. I learned to live in that way, I know that something is missing, I fumble about and search, I whimper and scream and I don't find it, I grow, I develop, and my freedom of movement is ever more restricted, I scarcely dare look any longer, everywhere I knock against boundaries, and creep off to hide. I learn to fly and I learn how to catch fevers. I make myself at home in the great lack, in the disease of disappointment, of impotence and mistrust. And deep down in me the unsatisfied wish lived on. When my mother, summoned by my scream, came to my bed and set me upright and enclosed me in her arms, the sinister atmosphere to which her own appearance had contributed vanished. It was she who threatened me, but at the same time she was my savior. She took away with one hand and gave back with the other, and thus kept me in continual suspense, almost as if I longed for the eerie, as if I found a certain enjoyment in its torments because I could afterward savor the relief. Only once in my childhood had I experienced a foretaste of bodily freedom. I was with my parents and brothers and sisters on a visit to a family with whom we were on friendly terms, Fritz W., our host, was in every way my father's opposite. He was strong and lively, he had a witty and direct way of speaking, he was comradely in the way he treated his children and intimate and demanding in his approach to my mother, who blossomed in his company. I perceived clearly the rivalry that arose between him and my father, with Fritz the contest was relaxed and self-confident whereas with my father it expressed itself in strained self-control. Fritz's children jumped around the garden naked, two girls and a boy, the same age as I and my two younger sisters. We were in our Sunday best and looked on in embarrassment at the naked, sun-burned bodies at their play. My sisters wore white frocks with starched collars, white knee stockings, and buckled shoes. I had on my dark blue sailor suit, with the thickly knotted tie, also white stockings and black laced boots. It was midsummer. Then Fritz suddenly leaped at us, and in a few tugs ripped my sisters' clothes off, I myself crept under the low branches of a fir tree, but he pulled me out into the open, stripped off my trousers and blouse and shoved me together with my sisters into the circle of his own children. In dismay we fumbled off the remainder of our clothing and felt the warm air on the whole of our skin. My parents had got up from their garden chairs and were completely overcome by what was happening. And we now found out what we could have found out any day that summer, though it never returned, how alive we became in our nakedness. We felt the grass, leaves, earth, and stones with all our pores and nerves, romping and shouting with joy, we lost ourselves in a brief dream of unsuspected potentialities. On one other occasion Fritz W. intervened in my life. It was years later. I came home with my school report, which contained one terrible sentence, in face of which my whole being seemed to crumble. I made great detours with this sentence, did not dare go home with it, always looked to see if it had not suddenly disappeared, but it was still there, clear and distinct. When I finally reached home, because I did not have the courage to ship out as cabin boy to America, Fritz W. was sitting with my parents. What's that glum face for, he called out to me. Is it a bad report card, my mother asked in her concerned voice and my father looked toward me as if he saw all the troubles of the world piling up behind me. I passed the report to my mother, but Fritz snatched it out of my hand and read it and broke into peals of laughter. Not promoted, he cried, and slapped himself on the thighs with his powerful hand. Not promoted, he shouted again, while my parents looked in consternation first at him, then at me, then he drew me to him and slapped me on the shoulder. Not promoted, just like me, he said, I stayed in the same class four times, all gifted men have had to repeat classes at school. With that my deathly anxiety dissolved, all danger passed. No longer could my parents' shocked faces work themselves into a rage, no longer could they reproach me with anything, for after all Fritz W., this hard-working and successful man, had removed all stigma from me and even thought me worthy of special honor. These two encounters with Fritz W. were the highlights of my childhood; for they showed me how different the course of my life could have been under other circumstances, and they showed me the wealth of unexpended happiness that was in me and still lies within me beneath the boils and matted hair. When my puberty began, my mother again forced me on to the white guitar-shaped sacrificial bowl on which I had already sat in Green Street, this time to clean my penis. With soap, warm water, and cotton wool my mother tried to force back the foreskin, one hand holding my genitals, while the other pressed and urged the all too tight skin. I had half fainted with pain and humiliation by the time the tip of my penis was laid bare and my mother had washed away the smegma that had collected under the foreskin. Later I asked her what it was, the white slime that sometimes leaked out of me at night, I knew well enough, but I wanted to provoke her, by pretending ignorance I taunted her, and she answered, that's dirt, you must keep yourself clean, absolutely clean, the dirt comes from all those dirty thoughts you have. For a long time I could not rid myself of the feel of her hand grasping my penis. In bed of an evening it twitched and reared up, it throbbed and swelled up and burned. A furious hatred of this organ seized me, I would have liked to chop it off, but the voluptuousness that accompanied these painful movements increased and I gave way to them even if as a result of this surrender my hair and my teeth should fall out and my face be covered with boils. This alloy of pain and pleasure set its stamp on the fantasies of my dissipations. I imagined myself imprisoned by violent, barbaric women who bound me and overwhelmed me with their cruel caresses. You need more fresh air, people said, when they noticed my hollow eyes, you need exercise and company. And so I was given a uniform, a neckerchief, a shirt with a fleur-de-lis badge on the breast pocket, a peaked hat, a knapsack and a jackknife, and I was sent off with marching groups into the countryside. In the evenings Abi, the leader, crept under the blanket with me at the hostel and asked me if I wanted to be his adjutant. He embraced me with his hairy arms and legs, his bristly chin roamed over my face and his thick, red lips tried to kiss my mouth. I turned away from him but the voluptuous nauseating dream continued. We climbed naked in the trees, not in free, animal-like nakedness, but in a frantic feverish nakedness, we emptied our semen into the rough bark of the trees, we whipped each other with switches and wrestled with one another in burning lasciviousness in the moist warm earth, we burrowed our way through the woods, built shelters, stayed overnight in barracks where we learned to handle machine guns, and in the realization of my old war games I took part in an attack on the camp of an enemy group, we rushed out of our ambush over to their tents, plundered and sacked them, then as quick as lightning disappeared again into the woods. Close in front of me I still see the frightened face of a boy from whom, despite his pleadings, I wrested a carved staff, and then possessed with the flush of victory rushed off with my loot. Like an evil omen this crying terror-stricken face now rose up in front of me, I felt that somewhere I was doing violence to myself, but I did not perceive it, I was caught up by a whirling hurricane. Everything was inflated and swollen. As I had myself been courted so now I courted another, moodily he let himself be kissed by me, then deceived me, looked from his embracing smilingly over to me, threw back his head with its long black hair and shut his eyes. Everything was filled with furtive enticements, advances, jealousies, and slanderings. Favorites were played off one against the other, and ingenious punishments devised for the scapegoats. All the destructiveness and lust for power in us was allowed to unfold. I became Friederle. I was there when a weak one was dragged to the stove and made to kiss the hot iron, I was there when we pushed a prisoner off on a raft on a flooded building site and pelted it with lumps of clay, I was filled with brief happiness to be able to be one of the strong ones, although I knew that my place was among the weaklings. As the sly and treacherous and sinister elements within us grew, we began to throw our weight about in the streets, fires were started, shop windows smashed, passersby were knocked down and flags were borne past to sarcastic cries of Hats off. Contorted in a cramp of reverence we sang the national anthem and heaven help him who did not bare his head. In the evenings in the blossoming avenues I swept out on my bicycle after the girls. But it seemed impossible ever to touch these shrinking figures with their darkly giggling voices. Unattainable, I saw the brightness of their dresses dissolve into the depths of the leaf-shaded streets, dazed by the heavy scent of the blossom I heard soft steps beside me, heard the whispering of a tender voice in my ear, and ever more deeply I gave myself up to the hallucinations of the night till a dream being rose at my side, until I saw a face next to me, a face without features, a face that was a conglomeration of my own feelings, and I caressed this face, this face of self-love, no other face existed, thus I had to invent one, I kissed this face, I kissed the air, I kissed myself reeling under my need for love, and everything sank from me, the pressure of school, the threats and warnings, and I heard the demands of the world now only as a distant eternal surge. And I changed even this surge to my own purposes. In the evenings, alone in my room, a wild sea surrounded the island on which I lived with my beloved, here the waves had tossed us up on to the beach, and here we dwelt between the cliffs in a tumbledown hut, entirely given up to our mad love. It was complete love, hermaphroditic love, enclosed in itself, and self-consuming. My beloved was part of me, she was the female element in me, I knew every one of her movements, and she responded to every one of my movements. When I embraced her I embraced myself, offered myself, pressed into myself. And then, after the spilled happiness, the room resumed its shape, the terribly same old room, and destroyed my imaginings. The dream scattered like ashes and I lay and listened to the ticking of the clock in the hall. This wakeful loneliness was part of our encounters, this was the price, that I had to lie awake a long time, with aching eyes, in a slow dying, in a slow inward decay. But next morning my longing for a new meeting made itself felt again and I waited impatiently for the evening. In the lethargic hour between two and three I lay on the sofa in the living room, with my hands folded under my head, staring up at the color print of Hannibal's Tomb on the wall. Beneath a grayish brown, massive, many-branched tree there rose a heap of stones, next to which stood an old shepherd, leaning contemplatively on his crook, while before him a flock of sheep grazed in the wild, dry grass. The window on to the street stood open, outside motes of white sunlight danced, and from the tennis court on the opposite side of the road sounded the heavy, dull thuds of the ball being hit. Occasionally right beneath my window a car hummed past, or a bicycle bell rang. The thought of the city outside put new life into me, I saw in front of me the long, broad blocks of streets, the giant houses borne up by bent stone slaves, the castles, museums, monuments, and towers, the overhead railways on their viaducts and the underground railways with their bustling crowds and their rattling advertisement boards. I was about to get up when I saw my mother standing in front of me, I never noticed how she got into the room, she always appeared suddenly in the middle of the room as if she had grown out of the ground, dominating the room with her omnipotence. Have you done your homework, she asked, and I sank back into my weariness. Once again she asked, Have you already finished your homework. Out of my indifference I answered, I'll do it later. But she shouted, You'll do it now. I'll do it afterward, I said in a feeble attempt at defiance. Now she raised her fist, as in a coat of arms, and shouted her heraldic motto: I won't put up with contradiction. She stepped up close to me and her words fell on to me like stones. You must plug and plug away, you will have a few years, then you'll go out into life and for that you've got to be able to do something, otherwise you'll go to rack and ruin. She pulled me to the desk, to the schoolbooks. You are not to let me down, she said, I suffer sleepless nights because of you, I'm responsible for you and if you're a failure, it will reflect on me. Life means working, working, and then more working. Then she left me alone, next to me on a board stood a model city that I had constructed out of paper and cellophane, wires and rods. After my destructive games this was the first attempt to be constructive. It was a city of the future, a utopian metropolis, but it was incomplete, a mere skeleton, and I suddenly knew that I would not build at it any further, I saw only crumpled and glue-cracked paper, and everything was bent out of shape and fragile, one could blow it over with a single breath. I had to look for other means of expression. While I was brooding over my diary the door opened and my father entered. He saw me crouching over my desk busy with something in which he was never allowed to share, he saw how something quickly disappeared into the drawer. What are you up to over there, he asked. I'm doing my homework, I said. Yes, that is what I wanted to discuss with you, he said. There was an embarrassing tension, as always with such discussions. You are old enough now, he said, for me to be able to discuss the problem of a career with you. What do you think you'd really like to do. I could not answer this painful question. With a voice that was meant to sound understanding, and had something of the man-to-man chat about it, he said, I suggest you go to Commerce High and then come into my office. I murmured something about wanting first to finish school, in this way I could at least gain time. My father said now with growing impatience, You don't seem capable of doing that. I don't believe you are talented enough for that, and as for studying you haven't got the stamina, no, you ought to be doing some practical work. His face was gray and careworn. When one talks about life, one has to be gray and careworn. Life means seriousness, effort, responsibilities. My face, the face of a dunce and a loafer, twisted into an embarrassed stereotyped grin. In a hurt voice my father said, You don't need to laugh, life's not a laughing matter and it's about time that you learned how to work properly. Perhaps he felt a twinge of tenderness for me, but when he saw my averted, hostile look, he had to make himself hard and show me how firm his will. With the palm of his hand he hit the table and cried out, When this school year is over, we'll put an end to your daydreaming, then you'll have to come to terms with the realities of life. The realities of life. On my father's lips, these realities became a term for all that was sterile and petrified. I had already lost a decade in this reality, in the domain of school, where during endless hours my senses had been deadened. The threat that I should have to go out into life meant merely a continuation of my long wandering through classrooms and echoing corridors. There, after all, we had been prepared, for proficiency and responsibility, as it was called, by teachers whose spirits had given out. These long stony passages, in which rows of animal-smelling raincoats hung, while from within behind the doors I heard the litany of the school children from which occasionally one single voice would ring out high and clear, these stony passages, paced by the all-seeing Headmaster under whose annihilating gaze I sank on to my knees, these stony passages, among the flagstones of which fossils were interspersed, millions of years old, shaped like comets. From here I was supposed to go on into the corridors of office blocks, to the filing cabinets, the clatter of typewriters, into the rooms where the business affairs of this world were handled. But I had found other things in my search for nourishment for my expanding needs, things that gave me answers to my questions, words of poetry that suddenly stilled my restlessness, pictures that took me up into them, music that touched an answering chord within me. In books I encountered the life that school had kept hidden from me. In books I was shown another reality of life than that into which my parents and teachers wanted to force me. The voices of books demanded my collaboration, the voices of books demanded that I open myself up and reflect upon myself. I hunted through my parents' library. I was forbidden to read these books, so I had to remove them secretly and carefully even out the gaps, my reading took place at night under the blankets by flashlight, or on the toilet seat, or camouflaged behind schoolbooks. The chaos within me of half-baked longings, of romantic extravagances, of terrors and wild dreams of adventure, was reflected back at me in countless mirrors, I preferred the seamy, the suggestive, the lurid, I sought after sexual descriptions, devoured the stories of courtesans and clairvoyants, of vampires, criminals, and libertines, and like a medium I found my way to the seducers and fantasts and listened raptly to them in my inner confusion and melancholy. But the more I became aware of myself, and the less I shrank back from myself, the stronger became my desire for the voice of the book to speak to me in the plainest terms and conceal nothing from me. Soon I could tell the character of the narration from the first words of a book. I wanted it to excite me straight-away, I wanted to feel its glow and inner conviction at once. Long descriptive passages made me impatient. I wanted to be drawn into the middle of things right from the very start, and to know at once what it was about. I read poems only rarely, for here everything was too highly wrought, too much subject to a formal framework. I distrusted well-rounded and perfected things and I found it tiresome to search for the hidden meaning beneath all the artistry and polish. Often the well-planned work of art left me cold while the raw and only half-formed caught hold of me. My logical thinking was underdeveloped. When I tried to counteract this lack by reading scientific or philosophic works, the letters blurred before my eyes, I could not piece them together into living words, I felt no breath in them. What I retained belonged less to the realm of general knowledge than to that of sensations, my knowledge was composed of picturelike experiences, of memories of sounds, voices, noises, movements, gestures, rhythms, of what I had fingered or sniffed, of glimpses into rooms, streets, courtyards, gardens, harbors, workshops, of vibrations in the air, of the play of light and shadow, of the movements of eyes, mouths, and hands. I learned that beneath logic there was another form of consistency, the consistency of inexplicable impulses; here I discovered my own nature, here in what was apparently unorganized, in a world that did not obey the laws of the external order. My thinking allowed no particular goal, but drove me from one to the other, tolerated no superimposed guidelines, often threw me into pitfalls and abysses from which no explanations but only secret, unexpectedly discovered paths could guide me out again. In the course of years the dialogue I sought for in books, in ever more decisive and immediate form, turned ever more deeply toward the personal sphere, and thus it became an ever rarer experience, for only a few could express some part of the things that touched the roots of being. All stages of my development have their own books. In Green Street there was a big book bound in yellow hardboard with the corners all nicked off and in it the adventures of little Mucki were reported. Mucki is a great hero, it said, he knocks off the heads of thistles in the field. I see him before me, Mucki in his baggy cowboy trousers with leather fringes, with a broad-brimmed sombrero and a lasso, surrounded by cacti and rattlesnakes. Mucki was my first alter ego, in the malicious expression on his face was revealed what had been so well covered up in my own appearance, in him I could give full vent to my suppressed aggressiveness, Mucki the adventurer and gangster who was much more myself than the carefully groomed boy in the lace-collared blouse taken for Sunday strolls. Struwelpeter, Dirty Peter, with his bushy forest of hair and his long fingernails, with his pals, for me stood for all my own weaknesses, fears and longings. The naïve, strong-colored pictures were like the scenery of my own dream. There were the cut-off bleeding thumbs and the big gaping shears ready to cut off more if they could, and there was Suppenkasper, the boy who just wouldn't eat when he was told, with his strict, gaunt father and his plump mother, and his words, I won't eat my supper, no, I won't, were my own words, and it was myself who rocked back and forth on the chair and who, when he fell, dragged down with him the tablecloth with all the plates and dishes full of food. That was my revenge. That was what they got for all their scolding and admonishments. And then the idealization of dying. Starving was my retaliation, with this starvation I punished them, the lean man, the fat woman, sweet was the vengeance in which I myself was devoured. To see all this in pictures relieved me, part of the inward pressure had been conjured into externals. And others too could fly through the air, just look at the boy under the umbrella. My childhood is etched in the glossy clarity of this picture, high in the air the flying boy with the little red umbrella, blown along over the trees and the green field and the white church, and behind him the black cloud with the slantwise bursting squall of rain. Struwelpeter and then the wicked, sad fairy tales, these were part and parcel of the world in which I grew up, in them was expressed a distressing, suffocating truth. These clearly displayed terrors and cruelties were better than uncertainty. It was better to stand quite close in front of the danger and look it in the eyes, it was better to see that it was really there than to lie painfully in the dark and only to guess at it. My feeling of abandonment also decreased as I saw that others too were subjected to similar experiences, so that I was no longer quite so lost, I belonged to a community of the bewitched, for whom everything was strange and phantomlike. I belonged to a group of wanderers who had gone into the land of horror. The gruesome was my special province. Protectedness and snug peacefulness repelled me, I felt downcast when I heard about lovely children, kind parents, rich rewards. Depictions of protectedness, of warmth and content evoked in me a searching pain. Perhaps somewhere this security did exist, these rooms that smelled of freshly baked pretzels and in which a friendly old grandmother sat in the rocking chair and a cat played with the ball of wool, but for me it was old Aunty Lenelies, out there in the wavy, headily scented fields, the spooky Corn Witch who suddenly ran out to the edge of the path and kidnapped the child, for me there was losing my way in the forest, the morass with the will-o'-the-wisps and the witches' cabins. I knew what it felt like to crouch in a cage and to hold out through the bars to the witch a bone instead of a finger. I knew the fearful suspense when, right in front of me, she felt out the bone, when I heard her bleating that she wanted pretty, fat little children, nice juicy morsels, to slaughter. The parkland around our house assimilated all the fairy tales, it was enchanted, and amid its mosses, its thick bushy places, its gnarly roots like cartilage, lived animals that talked, gnomes, robbers and fairies. Here I saw the red-bearded dwarf Rumpelstiltskin dancing, saw how he split himself in two, and here in a tumbledown farmyard at the edge of the wood, the head of the horse Falada was nailed to the wall and I heard a hollow voice within him call out, If your mother knew, if your mother knew, her heart would break. In one of these books there was a picture of two children, a boy and a girl, sitting high up in the branches of a large tree. They had lost their way in the forest and had climbed up the tree to keep a lookout. But all around there was nothing to see but green impenetrability and so they had fallen asleep, snuggled up next to each other. The picture expressed that there was no longer a way back, the lostness of the two children was so absolute that all their fear somehow vanished. Their clothes were ragged from their long wanderings, their faces showed signs of their privations, but now they were completely given up to sleep, completely shut off from the world. In this picture I found something that lay beyond witches, ghosts and monsters, complete stillness, quiet and solitude, comfort and strength. I remember another book, with bendy, gray-green covers, a child's Bible with illustrations in the style of the Old Masters. I see before me a picture that depicted the princess on the banks of the Nile finding the basket in which Moses lay. The princess is clad in a veil through whose transparence the shape of her body may be guessed, a female slave holds a protective fan of palm branches over her. In my sketchbook I drew a copy of the princess, originally her whole figure with her sexual features strongly emphasized. Then just her face, a face that became ever more immense until finally the whole sheet was filled with her dark profile and her huge, spying eyes. Next to the first page, which reveals that I had given much attention to the structure of the female body, was a pair of scissors wide open in readiness to cut, and, as if to soothe my fear of the menace, I had painted a jumping jack head between the gaping blades of the scissors and on the sprawled out puppet legs put long boots. It was as if my own knowledge was frightening me, and then the princess' face began to look like my mother's, the domineering dark eye, that was my mother's eye, the eye that missed nothing. On another page of the Bible was depicted the building of a pyramid. Amid whiplashings by the guards the slaves lugged massive stones up the sloping ramps, here and there one broke down and perished in the dust. My fantasy was nourished by this picture's emanations, I lived among guards whose thongs lashed me to pieces, I savored all the sorrows of humiliation and later, when I found *Ben Hur*, I experienced as a chained galley slave the pleasures of direst distress. There was the captive warrior, who, bound naked to the back of a stag, was driven into the thorn thicket. There were the gladiators who wrestled with lions in the arena, there was the Foreign Legionary who lay wounded in desert sand, beset by prowling hyenas. The pictures that I found in the Bible, all these pictures of persecutions and tortures, of plunderings and murders, of slanders and penances, all these formed the groundwork for new visions which blended with my destructive games. I read of steel warships blown to pieces by grenades, of torpedoes launched from a U-boat in which the crew listened with baited breath as it steered toward the enemy ship's side, leaving behind it a telltale trail of foam on the water's surface, I read of the bloody bodies of the wounded, of comrades rescuing each other from the flames, of heroic captains who stuck to their posts on the bridges of their sinking ships and allowed themselves to be sucked down with the wreck into the depths of the ocean, I read of adventurous pirateering expeditions that landed on distant shores, I read of fights in snowstorms on high and rocky mountain peaks, of troops who charged out of their trenches at night in downpours of rain, to butcher each other in close combat in the mud, I saw the picture of the Lancers who rode out in the pallidly luminous dawn, and in brief doubt I asked myself where these Lancers were riding to, and why, as the song said, they rode to an early death, and I foresaw their folly, I felt something of the intangible horror that was the purpose of all my reading, when I saw the picture of the Indian prisoners brought to execution bound to the mouths of cannons and read the caption underneath that said that with such a death not only the body but also the soul is destroyed. There are scenes in a book of which I hardly know the title or author, scenes that are as unforgettable to me as scenes from *The Red and The Black, Hunger, Pan,* and *The Idiot.* There is a river in a jungle and from one bough that stretches far out over the river hangs an Indian, ready to throw himself onto the approaching canoe, a moment of extreme suspense. There is a room in a house in a provincial town, I do not know what happened in this room, nor who is in this room, there is only this room with a cupboard, a bed, and closed shutters, perhaps it is Sunday and everyone in the house is sleeping, and someone is eavesdropping here in this muffled room and is planning something and is full of expectation. There is the island on which the shipwrecked of the Pacific have landed, their reed huts rise, clearly outlined between the tall slender palm trunks. My thought of flight to far-off lands was concentrated in this picture. The curious thing was that, considering the out-of-the-way places and sights, something like recognition arose in me, nothing was so surprising and exotic that it did not find an

understanding echo somewhere within me. My reading was not
selective. I was attracted or repelled according to hidden laws.
Countless books I merely skimmed through, I had scarcely
thumbed through their pages before I knew that they were nothing for me, many that were later to be of value to me passed meaningless through my hand. Others captivated me with a single word.
*The Possessed, The Insulted and Injured, The House of the Dead,
The Devil's Elixir, Black Flags, Inferno*—these were the titles that
suddenly flared up in front of me and lit up something within
me. There was something magical about these titles, they went
straight to my heart. Reading them, the fumbling and searching that I had experienced in front of the door with the red
and blue panes and upstairs in the loft matured. My whole life
was a fumbling and searching. I penetrated into music, into the
architecture of fugues, into the tortuous labyrinths of symphonies,
into the hard structure of jazz, into Oriental chimes, nothing was
unfamiliar to me. I understood the wailing of Chinese flutes and the
solemnity of medieval songs, I was filled to bursting with music,
when I moved it was as if a veil of sound jingled within me, my
steps evoked throbbing drumbeats, interior instruments played
continuously. At home I lived like someone besieged. My room
was like a fortress. I had filled its walls with pictures of masks and
demons, and with my own drawings whose shrieking figures
frightened off the intruder. I felt the explosive force within me
and knew that I had to devote my life to the expression of this
explosive force, but at home my attempts were regarded as aber-
rations of which one did not have to take serious account. Driven
by imperious inner urge I left my room at night, naked and in
nameless excitement. I heard the mattresses creaking under my
parents' bodies, heard their heavy breathing, perhaps they were
lying sleeplessly, thinking of my misery. I, however, crept naked
into the room where my sister Margit lay. She saw me come in, sat
up in bed, a street lamp projected the broken image of the window and the filigree work of the pattern on the curtains, across
the wall and ceiling. Noiselessly I came to Margit's bed, sat next
to her, and noiselessly we explored each other with baited breath,
and Margit too stripped off her nightdress and my hands glided

over the small swellings of her breasts, passed over her soft but slowly hardening nipples, spread over her belly and the childlike smoothness of her genitals, and then we lay side by side, pressed ourselves close to one another and my penis stiffened and pressed itself against the warm part between her thighs, and so we lay, mouth to mouth, while our parents in their bedroom breathed and groaned. On other evenings, when our parents had gone out, I approached Elfriede, who had been hired by our parents to take care of us. In my room we practiced something we called gymnastic exercises. Gymnastics is useful and strengthens the muscles, gymnastics refreshes the mind, no one can object to it if we place ourselves side by side and bend backward and forward or if we lean back to back with our arms linked and hoist each other into the air. That is sport. That I only wore a towel about my hips was to allow the body to breathe more freely. And Elfriede took off her dress only in order that it should not get rumpled in the course of our exertions. If we placed our hands on each other's belly or thigh, this was only for support, and if Elfriede stripped off her slip and rolled down her stockings she did so only for the sake of greater freedom of movement. She was still decently dressed, in brassiere and panties. Kissing was out of the question, I was not allowed to touch her breasts, though she felt my chest to test the beating of my heart. Once when I was bending over backward my loincloth came loose and Elfriede rushed out with a shriek, I ran after her through the dark corridor, the towel hanging over the stiff-out phallus, followed her into her room, which was situated next to the hall leading to the door of the flat, but just as I had leaped over the threshold of her room, I heard the sound of a key being turned in the door and I turned about, fled back through the corridor, back into my room, slipped on a dressing gown, then on a sudden inspiration charged into the sitting room, switched on the radio and was sitting there, subduing my panting with difficulty, when my mother entered in a rustling evening gown and in glittering jewelry. It seemed to me that my flight must still be visible in the hall outside, the imprint of one single great leap transfixed in timelessness. This period of my existence, full of bottled-up disaster, seems to lie endlessly far back, further back than the earliest days of childhood. I look at that time as if from another life, a stranger before the I from which I have emerged. I see the endless columns, hear the monotonous march beat, the clatter of nailed boots, the jingling of daggers on their belts. Again and again came the flags and the standards, the extinguished anonymous faces, the mouths opened in song, again and again came the drums, and above the city a vast fire seemed to glower. Ceaselessly the march beat throbbed, like a pulse in the city's intestines, something was being charged and gained ground, seized me, seized all of us, a force that had throbbed for as long as I could remember, and even earlier, at the time of my birth and of the mythical years when the bombardments lay dully muffled along the horizons, when the wounded bled to death in field hospitals. I too was trapped in a merciless development, and even if I was one of those who fled, I too was melted down into this ceaseless marching, it was as if I had stood here from the beginning at the curb and had seen the mass pass by, linked together and grim, my brothers were with them, armed with knotty sticks, with a look of entrancement on their faces, with steel helmets and the emblems of a new and terrible crusade. Even if, in secret, I sought after other truths, the compulsiveness of a feeling of solidarity with this marching got hold of me, the compulsiveness of the crazy idea of a common destiny. The voices of dream were suppressed by the shouted commands of reality. My anxious protests, my tiny attempts at rebellion were nipped in the bud. I could not recognize my position. Recognition only comes later when it's all over. Later I could understand and assess, but at the time I was blindly drawn along by the current. At that time I thought only of my poetry, my painting, my music. Had I not suddenly been faced with a drastic change I would have been borne along in the torrent of marching columns, into my destruction. This sudden change took place after hearing one of the speeches which in those days spewed out of the loudspeakers and which before my realization possessed an inconceivable power over me, but which afterward seemed like an incoherent screaming from hell. Next to me sat Gottfried, my half brother, and we listened to the hoarse screaming, we were overcome by this screaming, felt only that we were overpowered, we did not grasp its content, indeed there was no content, only emptiness of unprecedented dimension, emptiness filled with screaming. So overpowering was this emptiness that we completely lost ourselves in it, it was as if we were hearing God speaking in oracles. And when the hurricane of jubilant summons to death and self-sacrifice, which at the time seemed like so much cheering for a gold-gleaming future, had run its course, Gottfried said, What a pity you can't be with us. I felt neither surprise nor fear at these words. And when Gottfried then explained that my father was a Jew, this came to me like the confirmation of something I had long suspected. Disclaimed awareness came to life in me, I began to understand my past, I thought of the gang of persecutors who had jeered at me in the streets and had thrown stones in instinctive obedience to a tradition of persecution of those who were different and had inherited contempt for certain facial features and essential characteristics. I thought of Friederle, who was one day to become a model of the heroic defender of the Fatherland, and at once I was entirely on the side of the underdog and the outcast, though I still did not understand that this was my salvation. I still only grasped my lostness, my uprootedness, I was still far from taking my fate into my own hands, and making the fact of my not belonging a source of power for a new independence. Before we left the country and began our journeyings across many frontiers Margit died. On the day her dying began our house was like a greenhouse in the muggy heat before a thunderstorm. My brothers and sisters squabbled and fought among themselves, my mother, tormented by headaches, lay on her bed in the darkened bedroom and shouted for quiet. Entangled in each other like a pack of foxes my sisters and my younger brother rolled into the corridor and my mother stormed out of her room with a tennis racket in her raised hand, her face crimson and her disheveled hair streaming. The combatants scattered, I heard their footsteps fleeing along the stifling corridor and heard Margit calling, Mama's got cramps, Mama's got cramps. Those were the last words I ever heard her speak. The door of the flat was wrenched open, the footsteps died away in the echoing well of the staircase and all was quiet again. After a while I too went outside. My sisters had disappeared, my brother was gliding slowly up and down the white-hot avenue on his roller skates. In glum boredom I slouched through the streets and arrived back later in front of our house, leaned against the porch underneath our balcony, drummed out a rumba rhythm on the rough crumbling surface of the masonry and hummed la cucaracha, la cucaracha. Suddenly I heard my name being called, a soundless cry, yet I had heard it, not so much a cry as an atmospheric disturbance, a breath of cold, and I looked up to the balustrade of the balcony where Irene was leaning out, her face white and her mouth strangely twisted as if laughing, on the yellow wall between us. Then I heard Irene whispering, Margit has been run over. I rushed into the house, the door of our flat was wide open, I saw my mother standing in the depths of the hall. Ceaselessly she rubbed her hand across her face, which seemed to have gone to pieces, and without pause from her mouth came a stammering, everything's all blood, everything's all blood, everything's all blood. Lined up before her in the hallway stood my younger brother, Elfriede, and Irene, turned to stone while in flight, like playing statues, Irene still half-flying, just back from the balcony, Elfriede canted sideways and looking up at me, my brother crouched down, staring up at my mother. And all the time my mother was brushing her hand across her face and her eyes were shut and her lips murmured, Everything's all blood, all blood, all blood. From out of her numbness Elfriede whispered to me that Margit was in the hospital and that they were waiting for my father to arrive. From outdoors came the sound of a car braking to a stop, right afterward my father's hurrying steps on the stairs, he ran past us, leaning forward with his coat flapping, put his arm around my mother, supported her and propelled her at his side out on to the landing. Her face was unrecognizable. We held our breath as they went out. That evening my two elder brothers came and we went together to the hospital, I walking between them. Silently we walked through the dusk, saturated with exhaust fumes, and showers of coldness ran over me. In silence we crossed the broad tree-planted forecourt of the hospital and up in the tall red façade nurses were leaning out of windows and shak-

ing blankets and beating mattresses. In silence we approached
Margit's bed and the shuddering coldness gave way to a trembling that ran right through me. My sister's head was tightly
swathed in bandages, plaster concealed her cheeks and her
squashed nose was stretched in a wire frame. Her grazed hands
opened and contracted. A groan escaped her mouth but it
sounded as if muffled by a gag. She's unconscious, whispered a
nurse in a wide black robe. Her words were meant to console us
but what comfort was there in the face of the frightful convulsion
which suddenly brought Margit's body rearing up into a high arc,
what was the use of such consolation when I could see my sister
arching upward resting only on her head and toes as if stretching
out in an ecstasy of voluptuousness to receive a lover, constructing
a bridge between life and death. The blankets slid off her and I
saw the bright smooth belly that I had felt against my body, I saw
the tiny breasts I had caressed, I saw the soft curve of her womb
which I had pressed with my body. The trembling came upon me,
next day as I stood before the easel in my room and painted my
first large picture. Three figures in white costumes, doctors or
judges, loomed up out of the black background, their faces were
bowed in an oppressive severity, their lowered glances refused all
mercy. I painted on the following day also, still shaking with cold,
and when Gottfried came into my room I had just finished the
final strokes. In silence Gottfried looked at me and I knew that it
was at an end. We went through the warm, dark streets. In the
sickroom my parents were sitting hand in hand at the death bed.
In the background the Catholic nurse moved about like a large
black bird. A candle was burning on the bedside table. Trembling, I stood in front of the immovable, the extinguished. I felt as
if I were floating a few inches above the floor. The bandages and
the wire frame had been removed from the grazed face. It was a
yellowed, squashed, completely strange face. The eyes had sunk
deep into their hollows. The dead hands were folded over her
chest, they were like the tapering, carved hands of a Gothic sculpture. A black crucifix, huge and incongruous, lay beneath the
stiffened fingers. My parents too were like statues submerged in
the half-dark. My mother lay back completely exhausted in the

open car as we slowly drove home. Home. There was no home any longer. The journey into the unknown had begun. Like survivors of a shipwreck in a boat we drove through the gently surging ocean of the city. Next morning I saw Margit once again. She was laid out on a slab in the hospital mortuary. Her eye sockets were covered with cotton batting. Her neatly brushed hair had lost its sheen. A fly crawled over her brow. I shooed the fly away and in doing so brushed against Margit's hair. My hand jerked back, her hair was so cold. I had never imagined that hair could be so cold. In the days that followed when the windows of our flat were draped and the curtains lifted like dark sails in the slightest breeze one could hear only now and then a whispering and a tapping of footsteps on tiptoe on the landing. My mother sat motionless in a chair, with limply drooping arms like a clay figure. Once the pastor came. My father carried on an almost inaudible discussion with him about the memorial sermon that the unknown pastor was to read over the finished life of someone he had not known. My brothers, my sister and I, the survivors, stood around the room and did not dare to look at each other, I noticed how Irene's face sometimes sought mine, but I avoided her glance for I knew that I would have to laugh if our eyes had met. The pastor and my father sat in the deep armchairs, the pastor leaned over toward my father, my father's voice murmured, the pastor jotted down a few notes, wanted him to name some typical quality, a phrase that would sum up the essence of Margit's being, and I caught the word sunshine. She was a ray of sunshine to us all, the pastor said, and he tried out the sentence on his tongue. My father nodded dumbly. Gottfried had taken charge of negotiating with the undertakers. The coffin, the tombstone, the flowers had been chosen, the musical program to accompany the ceremony had been decided. I followed Gottfried to the funeral parlor. Margit's body was already hidden in the coffin and the top screwed down over her. The coffin was lifted into the hearse, the hearse drove off to the graveyard with Margit shut into her coffin and with Gottfried and myself sitting next to the driver. Through the glass window of the hearse behind me I could see the white coffin laden with wreaths and bunches of flowers. The vibrations of the mov-

ing vehicle made the coffin shake, and inside the coffin my dead
sister's body shook in concert. At the funeral service we sat packed
closely together in the narrow chapel pews. When the pastor's
voice had died away and the sound of the word sunshine thrust
into me like a knife for the last time, and when the last prayer had
evaporated into the rotting scent of the flowers and wreaths and
we had all dazedly worked our way out of the pews, my mother
got stuck between the hassock and the armrest. My father and
Gottfried rushed to her rescue and pulled her out sideways. Outside spots of sunlight were dancing. With strong bending and
stretching out of arms, with arched backs and muscle-play beneath jackets, with their tensed thighs thrust forward the black-
coated men lowered the white coffin down on ropes into the black
hole in the earth. The pastor filled a shovel with sand, it was a
little green shovel like the one we had to play with in the sandpit.
My mother stood hidden behind a thick black veil supported by
my father and Gottfried. From the ranks of the mourners a girl of
Margit's age stepped forward, shook my mothers' hand, curtsied
to her and withdrew into the background, whereupon a second
girl stepped forward, shook my mother's hand, curtsied to her and
withdrew into the background, whereupon a third girl stepped
forward, shook my mother's hand, curtsied and withdrew, whereupon a fourth girl stepped forward, shook my mother's hand,
curtsied and withdrew, whereupon a fifth and a sixth girl and
more girls and even more girls stepped forward, shook my
mother's hand, curtsied before her and withdrew, until all the
girls from Margit's class had come forward, shaken hands with my
mother, curtsied to her and returned again to their places. On the
way back we sat squashed together in one car. I crouched on the
floor, Irene half lay over me, my younger brother almost disappeared between my father and my mother, my father's knees dug
into my chest and Gottfried's knees were thrust into my back.
My face was streaming with sweat. Outside the summery streets
flew past and there someone stood in the dust, looking after us.
This was the beginning of the break-up of our family. Soon this
trip in which once again we clung together was at an end, soon
my stepbrothers got out and left us, soon the city lay behind us,

and after that the country in which I had grown up, and a new life in a foreign country began. For many years still the outward structure of the family was to be kept intact in the carefully preserved home. Among silver-green willow trees of an English landscape home was set up in a red brick house; in the mean-natured narrowness of a Bohemian industrial city home was set up in a dirty, yellow-colored villa; the last time home was set up, it was in a large dark brown wooden house on the shores of a Swedish lake, and there the decline that had begun with my sister's death reached its conclusion. Our home was kept going by my parents but even their dying had begun, even their dying had begun with my sister's death. My sister's death was the beginning of my attempts to free myself from my past. There were periods when I raged and stormed about, the suppressed revolt flared up and cursed the old forces that had dominated me and lashed out, but the blows fell wide of their aim and the insults reached no one's ears. Hatred and violence were no longer of any use, the opportunities had been missed, the enemies were no longer tangible. I did not know where the enemy was concealed. I did not know what had happened to me. I was furious with myself for only in myself were there unprotected flanks to attack, only in myself was the past contained and I was the custodian of the past. Past events rose up in me like a gasping for breath, like the pressure of a straitjacket, the past would hem me around in a slow, black seepage of hours, and then suddenly recede and become nothing and allow a brief glimpse of freedom. Then I saw my parents and was full of sympathy and compassion. They had given us all that they had to give, they had given us food and clothing and a civilized home, they had given us their security and their orderliness and they could not understand why we did not thank them for it. They could never understand why we drifted away from them. In the confused knowledge of having made mistakes they bought themselves off with expensive presents, birthdays and bank holidays were the days fixed for paying out their unconscious guilt. And the presents were always wrong, however much we received we always stood there with dissatisfied faces asking for more. We never got what we wanted to have and we did not know what we

wanted to have. Thus we confronted each other, children dissatisfied, parents insulted. And we were unable to explain ourselves to
each other. And this obstacle I took over into myself. I took over
my parents' misunderstanding. My parents' embarrassment became my embarrassment. Their voices live on in me. I chastized
and beat myself and drove myself to forced labor. Again and
again the swamp fever of inadequacy gripped me. There I was
again, a failure at school, sitting locked into my room, and the
warm seething life outside was unattainable. There sat my mother
next to me and heard me repeat my lessons and I could get nothing right. Schwein is pig, pig comes from to pick—pick, pick, pick,
and she took hold of me by the scruff of the neck and pressed my
nose into the vocabulary book, pick, pick, pick, so now perhaps
you'll remember it. I remembered it. At times I could be startled
out of my dream, still feeling the grip of my mother's hand on my
neck, still feel the slap of my mother's hand on my cheek, and
hear her furious voice, see her index finger next to me travel down
the keys of the piano, to point out to me the correct note, the note
that I was unable to find, and she did not find it either, her finger
missed its mark, the dissonance still shrills in my ears. And I take
my mother's hands and put them aside and my hand strokes her
hands and I see my mother sitting under the floor lamp, her hands
busy with pieces of clothing, her hands active, a whole lifetime
at our torn stockings, shirts, and trousers, her hands, devoted a
whole lifetime to caring for us, her hands a whole lifetime holding
us, cleaning us, disciplining us, and suddenly these hands lie down
tired, suddenly they have served their time, and her face, lit up by
the floor lamp, stared in front of her, and her mouth opened and
the hard lines of her face relaxed, and the face listened for the
incomprehensible, and the face's listening is so intense that it
takes on a look of nameless astonishment. This had always been a
part of her, the fear of being stricken dumb, of becoming paralyzed, a fear that she resisted with all her energy, and which made
her domineering and angry, and which at times overcame her
with sudden fainting attacks. As if struck by a terrible blow she
would sink to the ground, where she then lay, a ghastly sight, like
a mountain, and as she aged these states came slowly and

stiflingly, lay across her chest, encased her joints with lead, dead-ened the power of her voice. In her diary I found the following entry, Had a dreadful dream. Mamma took me by the hand and proudly introduced me to all the people in a large room. Then we came into a hall, where on a raised dais a bluish-red eagle sat. Everyone shut into the room was led up to it and the eagle slowly forced its talons into his mouth and ripped out his tongue. I too was led there. I woke with a loud scream. My mother once said to me, you've always been a stranger to me, I'll never be able to understand you. To hear this was harder than to suffer her blows. The need to be embraced by her was not yet dead. There was one event that revealed the nervous tension in our relationship. After the period we had spent in the house in the park, we had moved to a new house. Friends of my parents had decided to celebrate our moving by a surprise party and on the evening for which this was arranged, my mother, who knew nothing of the preparation, was invited to the house of other people in the know. In ghostly haste the friends took over the house, and while they covered themselves in white sheets, bowls of various foods were produced and servants laid the table and when everything was ready some-one called my mother on the phone and informed her in a dark, mysteriously disguised voice that I, who had lain that evening feverish in bed, needed her help. My mother told me later she had believed at that moment that in a feverish fit I had leaped out of the window. A terrifyingly altered reality presented itself to her as she burst into our house and through the wide opened door of the dining room saw a party gathered by candlelight around the table, all deathly still and hidden under their tall peaked hoods, and in the hall Augusta was standing and grinning and gesticulating with her arms as if she were out of her wits and my mother pushed her aside and leaped with a yell into my room, ran to the open win-dow, leaned far out and shouted my name. Here I am, I called and sat up in bed. She spun around and, putting her arms around me, broke down before me weeping. But the heart of our relation-ship was touched on much earlier on our short, extraordinary journey. The doctor had advised my mother, because of my fre-quent illnesses, to take me to a convalescent home on an island in the sea. There I stand in this Home, a broad, smooth parquet flooring stretches out in front of me, my mother has left me alone, my mother has cast me out, and my life is finished. I run over the mirrorlike smoothness of the parquet floor and land up on a path, it is a path of white sand, and in the white sand black patches occur, and the black patches become ever closer and tears stream down onto me, and I run along down the path to the beach, and in front of me lies the vast gray-green body of the sea and the body breathes with rushing noises and lifts itself toward me and calls to me, and I run to this body and I want to go into this body, and then arms enfold me and hold me back and my mother holds me and leads me back, but not back into the Home, not back into exile, she elopes with me to her room in the hotel, and in this room we sit by night, my mother in a wicker chair beneath the window, I at her feet, and at dawn our ship is to leave and I am alone with my mother, have her entirely to myself, and she has given me bank notes to play with, bank notes whose figures promise vast riches, bank notes that will be devalued by tomorrow, and the bank notes rustle in my hands and the searchlight of a lighthouse flits at regular intervals through the room and illuminates a white chest of drawers, a mirror, and the large flowers of the carpet. And then the coach brought us to the landing-stage and in the coach a man sat opposite us with a broad black slouch hat, and his face lay in deep shadows. On board ship I stood on the companionway near the bows and my senses were wide open, and I sang into the fierce wind, and salty foam sprayed over my face and dark snatches of cloud raced adventurously across the lightening sky. Even if I knew nothing about my mother, her body was tangibly there, in forceful encounters. I had become aware of her presence, in the sounds of her voice, in the sweaty exhalations of her sex. But my father was unapproachable and withdrawn. In the mornings when I washed myself next to him in the bathroom I watched him with a searching excitement. Thin, colorless hair spread around his large flat nipples and the middle of his chest. His skin had a white sponginess about it. Below the navel the beginning of a scar was visible. His genitals remained hidden, he had never been naked in my presence. When I washed I took off my nightshirt and bound it around my hips by the sleeves, so that the shirt hung down over my legs like an apron. My father surveyed my washing. Whenever he saw that I shrank from the cold water, he would seize the washcloth and rub down my face and neck with it. My father's relationship to me at home was forced. At my mother's insistence he made himself at times a disciplining authority, which was out of keeping with his retiring nature. When he came home after work, it sometimes happened that my mother worked him up with a report of my misdoings. What these misdoings really were usually remained uncertain—perhaps it was an attack I had made on my younger brother or sister, or a reprimand I had had from a teacher. In the case of exceptionally grievous offenses, my mother waited for my father at the garden gate, I could see her there from the room in which I had been locked for punishment. She paced uneasily up and down and when my father appeared rushed toward him. I pressed my face to the pane and followed their violent gestures with my eyes. The suspense in the pit of my stomach was like a tickle to make one laugh. My parents came along the garden path toward the house, then my father's steps approached on the stairs. I remained glued to the window and listened to the manipulations of the door handle and key. My waiting for the punishment to begin was extended by the difficulties my father had to overcome to unlock the door. While he fumbled away at the door he shouted threatening words to me in order to work himself up into a fury. Finally he came rushing into the room, ran up to me, took hold of me, and bent me over his knee. As he was not strong, his blows did not hurt. But the humiliating communion in which we found ourselves was painful to the point of nausea. He beating me, I moaning, we lay over one another in a terrible embrace. I shouted for forgiveness and he shouted disconnected words, and he no more knew why he was beating me than I knew why I was being beaten, it was a ritual process forced upon us by unknown higher powers. Breathless and covered in perspiration, my father sat there, having spent his strength, and now he had to be consoled and nursed, he had done his duty, now came the reconciliation, now came the artificial family peace, my mother ran to join us, and like a single block we lay entwined in one another, sobbing tears of relief. Together we now went down into the house we inhabited together and we ate cakes and drank chocolate with whipped cream. Only on Sundays, on which I sometimes accompanied my father to his office, did the beginnings of opportunities occur for some other sort of being together. These beginnings were never allowed to develop. In the entrance hall, right next to the stairs that led up to the office, was a peepshow whose vaulted entrance was surmounted by the mask of a boy's face with empty eye-hollows and half open downcast mouth. In passing I glanced anxiously up to the white visage that had wept all its tears and had turned to stone over its pain. The office smelled of tobacco and cold ashes, and on the smoke-stained paneling of the wall hung framed pictures of factories and chubby, bewhiskered faces, and a map of the world with shipping routes marked on the blue of the oceans. Three deep leather armchairs surrounded the smoking table, on the round hammered brass top of which stood blackly mottled ash trays and a white porcelain elephant and wooden cigar boxes which when their lids were raised revealed on the inside colorful pictures of sailing ships, dark-skinned women, anchors, crossed flags and golden coins. The tall brown bookshelves were filled with rows of files and pattern catalogues. My father sat at his desk in front of the catalogues and opened his mail with an ivory paper knife. I sat opposite him and in a bowl of water loosened the stamps from letters and spread them out to dry on a large piece of green blotting paper. Surreptitiously I watched my father as he sat with his letters, with a grave expression on his face, making his notes and holding in his pale, well-manicured hands with their bluish veins standing out a cigarette whose smoke spiraled upward. The silence was broken only now and then by my father clearing his throat and perhaps he looked up once and met my gaze and smiled at me and from time to time there was a feeble humming in the yard below where underneath the peepshow cupola of glass protected by wire netting a picture-drum jerkily rotated. Sometimes I went down into the theater, the proprietress of which sat in corner darkness in a rocking chair, a toy-size dog asthmatically snoring in her lap. Usually I was the only visitor, and the proprietress let me attend several showings, I sat on a chair in front of the big black drum and pressed my eyes against the greasy glass behind which stereoscopic scenes appeared in glaringly lit stiffness. There were herds of buffalo, fleeing a prairie fire, huntsmen under the northern lights of a polar landscape being attacked by polar bears, condemned men bound fast to the block, the executioner holding the ax in readiness to let it fall, a city vanishing in an earthquake, a moon rocket just landed on a distant planet. With smarting eyes and benumbed by a feeling of dizziness, I stared at the panoramas as they hove into view, paused briefly, and then turned on again. Most impressive was the room in which the thief crouched in front of the bureau drawer he had just broken open. It was a refined, well-cared-for room. The cushions on the sofa were squashed down as if someone had just sat in them, a book lay open on the table under the lamplight, and the fire was burning in the grate, the only disturbing thing was the dog, who lay with legs outstretched on the floor. The thief's hands were sunk deep in the drawer, and his face, concealed up to the eyes by a black cloth, was peering toward the open door, as if he had heard some sound in the darkened hall outside. And now I am in London, standing in the storerooms of my father's office, between the samples table and shelves filled with rolls of cloth, and a rankling uneasiness wells up in me, I lean forward and hold my breath and look through the glass window of the door into the office where my father, slim and erect, sits at his desk and his partner, spongy and flabby, leans on the table next to him and bends over it. The partner's clucking voice jabs insistently at my father, who glances up at him with his head on one side. At the back of the room, a Miss Gray sits and hits the typewriter keys with her fingers. I sit down at the samples table, press myself close to the edge and pull a book out of my pocket. I set the book down in front of me at the edge of the table under the cover of a voluminous storeroom catalogue. I open the book and begin to read while a tiny guard on my shoulders is watching and keeps an eye on the door and while my hand lies on the alert with raised pencil in the lists of the catalogue. The words of the book penetrate into me, while I feel the stone floor on the soles of my feet, while above the thick glass squares set into the ceiling, a ceiling covered with maplike stains, there was a rolling of cartwheels and a darkness of shoe clickings, while in the outer office there was whispering and stirring, while unease radiated from my stomach into chest and bowels. "It was during the time I wandered about and starved in Christiania: Christiania, this singular city, from which no man departs without carrying away the traces of his sojourn there." Then the guard clapped me on the shoulder, his other small, hard, flat hand at my throat, the door opened, and the warehouse clerk entered with wheezing breath and heavy, creaking tread. Disheveled gray hair fluttered about his head, the bristles of his beard shone silver. I slid the book down on to my lap and back into my pocket. The warehouse clerk sat down opposite me at the other end of the long table. Between us ran the thick lines of the grain of the table-top, cut across here and there by knife marks. The warehouse clerk dug a flat green flask out of his pocket, uncorked it, raised it to his mouth, took a couple of gurgling swallows, wiped the back of his hand across his lips, and thrust the flask back into his pocket. My gaze fastened on to his emptily staring but powerful face with its big, dirty pores. His jacket was threadbare, his shirt greasy, his trembling stubby hands were busy with a bundle of gray dog-eared papers. To his mouth he lifted an indelible pencil, short and thick as if crushed between his fingers, and moistened the tip with his tongue, leaving a violet dot on it like a pearl. Miss Gray appeared in the doorway and called to me. My father wanted to speak to me. I went into the adjoining room. My father was still sitting at his desk, he was leaning far back in his swivel chair into the yielding back rest, while the partner sat on the desk in front of him and bent over him, bubbling over with talk, his sausage-like hands folded on his stomach, his face with its fatty double chin and bushy eyebrows rocking up and down. I stood next to Miss Gray and smelled the dry, stale odor of her body. She smiled nervously with her faulty teeth, and a slight blush spread over her downy skin. I saw my face in her pupils, my image had penetrated into her head and stared dully back at me from her eyes. My father turned to me, drawing away to one side from his partner's advancing bulk. The face my father turned to me was of a sickly yellowish hue, and I saw a few beads of sweat stand out on his brow. His face was pleading, I could see that his partner had the advantage over him, he was the native here, not only a partner in the firm, he was its founder and owner and had taken my father on out of charity. My father's hand felt its way down to the handle of the leather samplecase. He said that he had to visit the manager of a department store and asked me to go along. I took the case from him and we went out into the alleyway. Dark, shaggy horses, the muscles in their haunches rippling with every step, stamped past us, their hoofs striking sparks from the cobbles, and rays of light flickered through the rotating spokes of the cart-wheels. A booming of bells tumbled down from the dome of St. Paul's. I went with my father through the surge of bells and my father described the manager of the department store to me. From his voice I could feel how he was trying to give himself courage, how he wanted to make himself and me believe that the manager was waiting for him with friendly feelings and that the visit to him was bound to be a great success. Surrounded on all sides by the clangor of the bells and the aggressive cries of the newspaper vendors, I felt how my father was trying to win me for his occupation, how he was trying to paint a rosy future for me in business. For a few paces I forgot where I was, the roaring surf of bells and the rushing of automobiles on whose hoods burned white jets of flame and the rattling and ringing of the red double-decker buses, behind whose windows huddled rows of faces, became lost in the soughing and the brooding of my shapeless world of thought. Before we entered the office of the department store manager, I had crossed a sunken Vineta. We waited on an upright wooden bench. My father had opened the leather case and taken out a few patterns. He pointed out the quality of material to me. His voice was uncertain and strained. A girl with platinum blonde hair came and led us along a corridor, as she walked her hand with its red-varnished fingernails pressed and remolded the bun of hair on her neck. She opened a door for us and out of the blinding brightness of the room the manager of the store came towards us, with elegantly cut suit and broadly jutting, padded shoulders, gold glittering, effervescent, laughing. He patted my father with his hand as one pats a horse, led him to a table as if to a crib, and helped him to empty out the case of samples. My father, with delicately testing fingers, spread out the pieces of material on the table. The manager's hands swooped with sprinkling gestures on to the material, rubbed and tugged at it and flipped it over. Quipping as he picked at it with sharp fingers he made his selection, while my father every now and then winked at me confidentially and his pale hands with their narrow knuckles and the evenly manicured polished fingernails lay expectantly on the edge of the table. The room was a block of light with glittering windows. In this block of light hovered the reflecting surfaces of the table tops. At times figures with dissolved contours went through the room. Above the gleaming surface with the multicolored scraps of material, my father and the store manager were coming to a business agreement. With a friendly gesture, the store manager consented to my entering his firm as an unpaid assistant. I hardly realized what they were saying and immediately afterward forgot it, my father and the manager stood dark blue in front of me with curiously gleaming shirts. On the way back to my father's office I slipped off into side-streets. I went among old-fashioned houses and tall castle walls, crossed a courtyard with a well, and entered a workshop. Inside a spacious room, borne up by high pillars, my pictures hang on the walls. For a few moments I interrupted myself and moved between the shelves filled with bales of material and the samples table in my father's office, and compared the data on a list with the goods actually on the shelves. Then I went out in my yard, saddled a horse and rode over furrowed fields towards a rugged mountain ridge, at the border of a copse sat ragged figures armed with knives and halberds, slowly I rode past them, the bridle jingled, the typewriter clattered, the voice of the partner in the firm murmured at my father, and between the bare birch trunks shimmered large horned animals and the white torso of a woman. Toward evening I stood at the window of my room. Against the sloping gray walls leaned the few pictures I had managed to produce in my spare time. In the depths of the house lived my parents and my brother and sister. Blue dusk enveloped the garden. The striking of golf balls resounded from the links. The windowpane tasted bitter. A figure appeared from the shrubbery in green hunting clothes, with a game bag and a gun on his shoulder. With springy strides the figure crossed the meadow and disappeared in the hedge on the other side of the garden. A soft warm terror arose in me. It was as if a hand had reached into myself. I sat down at the desk on which my manuscripts lay, lit the lamp and thumbed through the pages in which in monkish script I informed the world of my long past life. I had lived centuries ago, here at my desk I conjured up pictures and words that told of my lost existence. Steps that sounded on the stairs woke me from my otherness. They were Elfriede's steps. Elfriede had moved with us, her room was next to mine. She did not close the door behind her. I heard her lighting a cigarette, brushing her hair, shedding her clothes. I got up and went on tiptoe to the door of my room. Below, my father was locking the house up for the night. My mother's footsteps approached. Now she was coming up the stairs to the attic floor, the stairs creaked under the weight of her body and she was breathing heavily. I retreated into the middle of the room. The latch of my door was pressed down and my mother entered. Are you still up, she asked, what are you doing. I'm working, I said. She glanced around the room. She saw the papers on my desk and asked, What's that you're writing there. Nothing special, I murmured evasively. Don't stay up too long, she said, and took the blanket off my bed. She turned back the top sheet and smoothed the pillow, then came toward me, took me in her arms and kissed me. When she had left the room, I went to the door again. I heard my mother let herself down the stairs step by step, in slow, heavy treads. Doors were opened and doors were shut, my mother went from room to room making her evening rounds. Quietly I pressed down my door latch. I went to the next door that stood ajar and pushed it open, Elfriede sat in a short nightdress on the edge of her bed. I slid my hands over her shoulders and hair and she drew herself toward me, and clasped me in her arms and her mouth sucked at my mouth. I pulled her nightgown up above her outspread thighs. Elfriede undid my trousers and I had trapped myself in the obligation to perform an unintelligible task. Elfriede, breathing excitedly, put her hand around my penis and pulled it near the opening between her legs. Form and content of the task facing me were disconnected, made no sense. Elfriede, awaiting my penetration, closed her eyes, and when she opened her eyes again I had disappeared. I was in my room and had locked the door behind me. I paced up and down in my room. I had taken off my shoes so that my steps could not be heard. I imagined myself packing my pictures together and leaving the house. But I did not know where I could go with my pictures. Wherever I set them up in my thoughts, someone always came and moved them on. Finally I saw myself spreading them out on the road and lying down next to them and the tall red buses driving over us. Next day I was in the department store. The perfect clerk always carries a pair of scissors with him, said the floor manager, and thrust a pair of scissors in my breast pocket. Through his pince-nez he inspected my suit and my stiff white collar. Here everyone has to wear a stiff collar, no one dares say No to a stiff collar. He twirled his little waxed mustache and showed me around my new place of work. In the interior of the storage rooms the rank growth of a primeval tropical world had been turned to stone. Lianas, roots, and fern fronds twined around the pillars, the vaulting and the balustrades. The walls and ceilings of the rooms were overgrown with mushrooms, fungi, and moss. The merchandise lay piled up in stalactite caverns. Among gritty rocks, thorns, and gnawed bones lay handles and sandals, blazers and razors, chests and vests, towels and trowels, cradles and ladles, pulleys and woollies, books and hooks, prongs and tongs, pins and bins. In the subdued light of the jungle orange-yellow salesgirls fluttered around like butterflies. In the depths of a white-tiled cellar I took up my first station. Behind the narrow table that stretched the whole length of the disproportionately long room, I bent with other condemned ones over the opened sample books. The city seamstresses came down to us, carrying between the fingers of their raised hands scraps of silk and velvet, linen and damask, spiked on needles, our fingers stretched out toward them, took hold of the needles with the many-colored bits of material and wandered with them across the pages of the book, to find a piece of material that corresponded to the sample. And when a suitable item had been found, numbers, letters and names were noted down on labels, and with these the seamstresses began their journey up into the higher reaches of the building. Our faces approached each other across the table, we whispered questions in their ears under the tickling blonde, black, red, or brown hair, breathed in the skin fragrance of violet and snowdrop, drew the points of our needles scratchily over nipples that stood out from under their thin blouses. To avoid the stifling air of the cellar, we went many times a day to the washrooms, where the slamming metal doors of the clothes lockers clashed like cymbals. We sat in the toilets, whose walls were scratched full of fertility symbols and whose floors were smeared with spittle, urine and trodden butts. Here we sat, bent forward, and from the cubicles all around came a groaning and an inarticulated stammering, in a trance we sat amid the rush and drip of the plumbing, and on our shoulders we carried the burden of the vast, over-laden building. At midday we bounded up the sloping corridors to the street, past the time clock whose teeth hacked into our cards with a ping. Outside we forced our way through the solid ranks of vehicles, played toreador with the cars, beat our fists on the growling metallic beasts, hurtled into the crashing and whirling of the feeding places, gobbled down potatoes in congealed fat, beans, and pieces of stringy bacon. A tightness under the collar, a retching feeling in one's stomach. Back through the throng. Briefcases and braces, pin stripes and pipes, wheels and squeals, seams and hair creams, tires and wires, hoofs and tubes, suitings and hootings, tie pins and pink gins. In the jungle of the store I was given the task of helping the window decorator collect material for his displays. On a piece of paper he wrote me out a list of the goods he needed, and I glided and skidded to and fro between the display window that was to be decorated, and the various departments that were to provide the necessary material. I soon lost the list, the mass of goods filled me with hectic enthusiasm, blindly I hurtled back to the showcases and snatched up whatever came to hand. I piled up a mountain of goods inside the display window and, as the decorator had disappeared, I myself decorated the display window. In the hot glass terrarium I vaunted the surplus of the department store, surrounded myself with matches and hatchets, sandpapers and capers, guns and buns, ash trays and hair sprays, rubber boots and canned fruits, nails and pails, pliers and wires, envelopes and soaps, utensils and stencils, and I myself adopted the pose of an entranced tailor's dummy exposing itself. And outside, beyond the glass, the passersby applauded me, a little sea of faces rocked and laughed, the whole street laughed, the cars tittered, the buses held their sides with laughter; policemen thrust themselves in between, their faces like red balloons, swollen with laughter. But hands grabbed me from behind and pulled me up and a yellow blind banged down at the window, and sharp eyeglasses flashed at me, and the scissors were pulled out of my breast pocket, I had proved unworthy of them. After this attempt I went on strike. But despite my strike I was subject to the laws of our household. After the grandfather clock in the hall below had struck seven, the day began. At the bottom of the stairs my father cleared his throat and called to me. I did not reply. He came up the stairs, opened the door of my room and said, it's time to get up. I got out of bed and dragged my feet down to the bathroom and washed myself next to my father. We did not speak to one another. I dressed myself and went down to the breakfast table. My place was here at table at the family meal. My disease was still regarded as merely temporary. My father asked, Don't you want to go with me to the office. I did not reply. Without saying good-bye, wounded by my silence, my father left the table. I could not make my parents realize that for me painting and writing were work. The accusation from outside had steeped me in profound listlessness. Every day I began my work with a feeling of absolute uselessness. I painted with the colors of entrails, the colors of feces, urine, gall, pus and blood. After a few hours I succeeded in working myself into forgetfulness. I painted until the dusk rose up from the garden and turned all the colors to black. When I had finished a picture, some urge compelled me to call my mother over. I knew how incomprehensible my pictures were to her, but I could not prevent myself from showing my pictures to her each time. I stood next to her and watched her looking at my picture. I showed her a picture of myself. I wanted her to stand a long time in front of this picture. She uttered a few non-committal words. You must move closer to it, I said, so that you can see the details. I can see it very well, she said, and turned away. I knew that I had only a short term of grace. I knew that I could not live here much longer on their charity. I lived like an obedient dog. I snapped up the scraps that I was thrown. I crept away and waited for the moment of an ultimatum. This moment came one green evening in the green garden room. My parents had called me to them. They sat sunk in the green armchairs, my progenitors who had brought me up for seventeen years. What happened in this hour before I ran to the telephone and got myself caught up in the cord. Today I see my father and my mother after a year in a foreign country tired and lost. I see the shadows in their ailing faces, I see my mother's hands pressed into her lap as if holding back some pain, I see my father's shoulders drooping after the day's exertions. They sat here in their home that they had preserved, they sat in their green chairs in front of the tall green curtains and outside dusk settled on the green garden and their postures expressed their uprootedness, they were frightened of the future, and when they glanced at me their faces were full of concern on my account. I see myself today as they saw me then, I did not understand what unimaginable effort it had cost them to keep this home with all its inhabitants alive. You can't keep on living like this, said my father, you can't keep on being a burden to me in the situation we're in now, can't spend all your time daydreaming, the world isn't the way you think, you can never exist in it with your pictures and poems. I see myself as they saw me then, there I stood in front of them in the half-dark, greenish room, I said nothing, I never said anything, just stood there tight-lipped and frozen, with my hands helplessly hanging down, perhaps I was really ill, mentally ill, and then my mother began to groan, she got up from the chair and raised her arm, made a few lurching steps toward the window, and her groaning became worse, and she sought for a grip with her hand and the hand gripped tightly into the curtain and then she crumpled at the knees, tore the curtains down with her, and fell backward on to the carpet, pressing the curtains protectively around her waist.

My father jumped up and shouted to me to call the doctor, and while I was rushing to the telephone my mother groaned, No, not the doctor, not the doctor, it's just this always being upset. And I stood at the telephone, receiver in hand, the cord coiled about my arm and in the receiver buzzed the voice of the exchange and I saw a dark patch spread in the curtain, where my mother had held it pressed over her pelvic region. Just put me in bed, my mother said, then it will be all right again, don't get a doctor, I don't want a doctor, and I replaced the receiver and freed my arm from the cord. And then we dragged Mother between us to the stairs and blood dripped from her womb onto the floor, and on the narrow stairway my mother lay like a mountain between us, and my father's back rubbed along the wall and at my back the banisters creaked and bent and the grandfather clock with the sun face ticked, and behind us the shapeless shadow of the Sandman panted up the stairs. Later, when my mother had calmed down in bed, I went out into the garden, and my younger brother came to me with the small models of his racing cars. It was already almost dark in the garden and light fell on us from the kitchen, where Elfriede was preparing the evening meal. On the path that led around the meadow, we let our model cars take off in a race, and we urged on our favorites, which we had given fantastic names, with shouts of encouragement, and as the darkness thickened it swallowed up the last of my childhood. Now every day for many months I followed my father to the office. After office hours I often sat in a small Russian café near Hyde Park, half a story below street level. Here I met Jacques for the first time. I lent him my coat when he wanted to go out into the rain with his jacket collar turned up. He left his tattered attaché case as a pledge. I looked into the case and saw that it contained a few carpenter's tools, I had rather expected to find leaves of notepaper in it. His face was small and finely chiseled, with a jutting chin and a sharp, hooked nose, his hair was bushy and tousled and his eyes, with their steely gray lustre, lay deep in their hollows. When he came back he sat down by me at table. He informed me that he had spent the last few weeks as a construction laborer in the country. He laughed at my questioning glance and, pretending to hold a violin under his chin, described fingerings with one hand and moved the other through the air as if holding a violin bow, at the same time whistling Bach's concerto for two violins. I joined in with the second violin. After the concerto I told him about my pictures, which in the last few months had been quite extinguished in me, and as I talked about them, they came alive again and regained their colors, and I noticed that my customary way of talking had disappeared, that with these words I was learning how to speak in a new way. By evoking my pictures for Jacques I was reminded that I possessed another life, a different life from my life between sample catalogues and rolls of material, and gasped for breath. I painted for Jacques my visions of apocalyptic landscapes with rustling fires, fleeing animals, drowning and vanishing cities, my visions of the crucified and scourged, of terribly distorted masks and seductive women's faces. The pictures that arose spread out before us and took us up into their depth, we wandered through the antique cities and rocky wildernesses, the ruined halls and enchanted gardens. Jacques built even more into these landscapes. Everywhere we found forms, sounds, concordances. At times we were caught up in wild laughter, it was a laughter that burst out as if a spell had been broken. We sat next to one another at a table in a café in a basement in a rain-sodden street in a vast city in a strange land in the endless world and laughed so much that tears streamed down our faces. Shaken by laughter I talked of my existence at the office, of my existence at home, the life I led there was so improbable that I could only laugh about it. In my conversation with Jacques I suddenly lost all fear of life, everything was possible to me. Jacques had already fought himself free, he had already conquered his consuming freedom. He had exposed himself to unprotectedness and wounds. In his life there was the wildness and unruliness that I had sought, but also the hunger and the distress. In his presence I crept out of my cocoon and hoisted my colors and made my thoughts scintillating and extravagant and thus we unwound our worlds to each other and gave each other rebuslike glimpses into our past, our dreams, our hopes for the future. I saw scaffolding on which Jacques balanced, I saw him playing the violin at a night club, I saw the violin disappear into the pawnbroker's. Jacques showed me the house where he had grown up, the wide entrance hall through which he fled, at its side doors of carved oak, mirrors, tinted, lead-framed windows. In his past an old, gray servant in red livery, in the park dogs who bounded after him up to the door. The wrought-iron latticework, the iron roses, the heavy latch, then the country roads. Surrounded by our images we went through the city, the rain had petered out, the sinking sun shone through the smoke, and our cataracts of laughter continually broke loose, everything grew wavy, as in the mirrors of a fun-house. A nimbus of glorious perspective surrounded us, our future lay open, I saw wide walls hung with my pictures and Jacques directing the orchestra. In the train on our way to the suburb where I lived with my parents we changed the basic elements of our being into music, we were the sounding instruments in the rhythms of the wheels and above in my room under the sloping roof we built a fugue with our voices from the raw material of our hopes. From the unpatterned and as yet unspoken arose transparent blocks of sound, grew, split up, towered one above the other. Later this edifice dissolved in darkness, we listened to the vanishing melodic lines, we returned again to the realm of words and pictures, lay among the drawings and the painted panels, among the manuscripts and books, until we no longer understood our words and each of us sank into the shaft of sleep. Next morning my mother stood beside me in the kitchen and began to attack my friendship with him. I don't like the look of him, she said, he has dangerous eyes. Next to her on the kitchen table sat a cockroach, its front legs crossed and rubbing each other, and looked at my mother. The floor was covered with cockroaches, they swarmed up the walls and disappeared, one after another, head first and rowing with their back legs into the crevices. The cat walked among them with high, disgusted steps and bit one of the cracking bodies, drew back its mouth from the slime that oozed out of it. My father shouted, Hurry up, I'm going now. I answered, I'm going later today, my friend Jacques is here, we are going to give an exhibition of my pictures in town. What did you say, he called, an exhibition. Yes, I replied, an exhibition,

Jacques knows someone who has an empty room where we want to hang up the pictures. My mother stamped her foot on the floor, the cockroach on the table started moving, ran around in a circle several times and then stopped at the edge, shaking its tiny head and quivering with its feelers. My mother swept off the roach with a brush, it fell hard and dry on to the floor and scrambled quickly up the wall where it forced its way into a crack, its pointed hindquarters with the crooked, bristly legs rocked up and down for a while before it disappeared. Upstairs in my room Jacques stood ready with my pictures. Jacques. A thirteen-days' conversation. A thirteen-days' dream we had shared in which everything within us that sought for expression was discussed. Far away stood the totem poles of my father and my mother. Their words ran off me. They stared at me full of horror as at a condemned man. While we were lighting up layer after layer of our inner being, with energy unpent we roamed the city. We hung my pictures up in a room over a garage in a courtyard in a concealed mews in the vast city in the strange land in the endless world. We sent out cards announcing my exhibition. No one came. We did not care. The pictures were there for us, they grew for us, they developed for us. For thirteen days every breath was fruitful, everything we touched unfolded itself and put forth blossom. Silent courtyards saw our pantomimes. Archways heard our oratorios. Dockside pubs were recipients of our thoughts' genius. But then suddenly a gray shadow fell. We felt tired. What would happen now. Now I had either to break loose entirely from the old or sink back into it. On the thirteenth day I accompanied Jacques, who had stayed overnight with us, to the station. I don't know why he wanted to go to town, perhaps some chance of a job had turned up, perhaps he was tired of me. Now this morning is quite saturated by the feeling of departure, this English summer morning with shimmering sunlight through the early mist, with the sleepy rattling of a lawn mower and the distant clatter of horses' hoofs. There lay my brother's tin pistol on the garden path, I picked it up, took it with me, Jacques spoke to me of Spain, of the Civil War, perhaps he expressed a desire to join the International Brigade. Now, looking back on this morning, it contained a final farewell, but at the time there was some agreement to meet in town, it was all over, no more to go on, I shot Jacques dead as he stood there behind the lowered carriage window. I raised the tin pistol, aimed, and imitated a shot, and Jacques pretended to be hit, threw up his arms and fell backward. The train set itself in motion and disappeared in the tunnel behind the station. Jacques did not appear again at the window, I never saw Jacques again. For a long time I looked for him. He left no trace behind. His name was not contained in the official records. I have often thought about this strange figure, and have sought to interpret it. It contained much that I should have desired, this complete license, this freedom to come and go as he liked, this vagabond's life, in my thoughts I idealized his existence, I dreamed of its extravagance and audacity as I sank back into my old imprisonment. Other things, however, made me suspicious, the impulse in him to make up lies and exaggerations, for instance, or his mystifications and his dressings up, sometimes appearing with a false beard, or with a big pair of horn-rimmed glasses, or with his wrists and forehead bandaged. His uniqueness, it seems today, lay in the very brevity of his appearance. He gave a guest performance. With prodigal intensity he built up a friendship, then when he felt it had reached its peak, he withdrew. He wanted the extraordinary. I was too slow on the ball for him, after the brief flight I lost my strength and could not follow him into his dubious and adventurous exploits and so he abandoned me, his role was at an end. Sometimes I thought, Perhaps I was mistaken, perhaps it wasn't a toy pistol I shot him with, but a real revolver, perhaps I have really killed him, and these thoughts go together with dreams that recur at intervals and in which I am involved in duels with an adversary, or an alter ego, and in which there is only one choice, you or I, and either he will murder me, coming slowly and threateningly closer, with his knife, his gun, or his terrible bare hands, or I will plunge the dagger into his body, or fire my pistol into his dissolving face. After Jacques's disappearance I returned to being a piece of furniture in the communal household, I stood at my appointed place, and when we moved to the Bohemian town in which my father was to take over the management of a textile factory I allowed myself to be shipped with them. There I lay in the evenings in the living room under the table, with the dog. I pressed the dog's head close to me, felt his warm breath on my face and clutched with my hands at his soft coat. You, Harras, I whispered, and the sheepdog laid his paws on my arm and gazed at me with his big, black eyes, and his tongue licked me. From this low vantage I saw my father sitting in the armchair glancing through the paper and my mother at the sewing table, her hand gliding up and down with the needle. On a sofa tucked away in one corner of the room sat my brother with his schoolbooks, while in another corner my sister Irene bent with her short-sighted eyes over a letter. The room was warm and clean, white curtains hung at the window, the books stood tidied on their shelves, the grandfather clock ticked in the hall. I too was thought of as part of the imposing whole. The look of the place had been settled once and for all. The piece of furniture that I was in this home was all polished and put in place and the dirt forever settling down on me forever wiped off. No one ever asked where it came from, this distressing dirt that trickled out of me, no one ever inquired, they just rubbed, brushed and polished, tirelessly, so that the shameless spot was never seen. When my mother looked down at me over the top of her spectacles pain seethed up in me and something within me urged me to crawl to her and lick her hand. I held more tightly to the dog, we belonged to one another in our dumbness. Nothing could be explained. My life was a dull waiting for the catastrophe. My father folded up his newspaper and got up. He said that it was time to go to bed. Each of us slowly worked himself out of his hole. We said goodnight to our mother. She embraced us as if we were setting off on a long journey, pressed us to her and kissed us. Oppressed and embarassed, I took leave of my father. Sometimes in my need for reconciliation I gave him my hand and got nothing but cool, dry fingertips which he hastily withdrew. I crept out of the room and my brother joined me, the dog following. We went out into the bare garden and got caught up in our games in which the lostness and instability of our existence was expressed. While we strolled over the clayey fields and woods of the neighborhood, we were changed into explorers in unknown regions of the world. We came across strange creatures and were involved in dangerous battles. We composed documents that we blackened with smoke and splashed with red paint to show that one or the other of us had been taken prisoner and was awaiting sentence of death. With the help of complex spy rings we discovered each other, liberated each other from the deepest dungeons and out of the hands of the most gruesome inquisitors. It seemed as if there were more reality and topicality in these games than in my work up-stairs in the loft. These games were psychodramas in which we tried to adapt to an emigrant existence, and in my work all was alienation and concealment. My room was in our landlady's apart-ment in the top floor of the villa. To reach my room I had to pass through her hall. The widow lived on this floor that was filled with flower pots and smelled sourly of cabbage. When I came through the door to the flat, she stuck out her gray head from behind the leaves of some plant or out of a niche and stared at me distrust-fully from her close-set eyes. From dawn till dusk she shuffled about, swept and clattered about in her hall, I locked my door and hung a cloth over the keyhole. Only at night was I free from her sniffing around my door. Then I was alone in the rushing quietness of a vacuum, alone with my pictures and my written pages, alone with my books and my music. I muffled the record player with blankets. From an immeasurable distance the music came to me, like a dream of liberation. I stood in my grotto and my hands danced in time to the music. In my blood and in the vibrations of my nerves, in my pulse and my breathing sounded the music. Tears streaming down my cheeks I drank in the music, and then went to the spirit-voices of books, carried on imaginary conversations with the people of the books, they seekers like my-self, and to me the books were secret messages, letters in a bottle dropped out at sea to find kindred spirits. Everywhere, in the most distant cities, on desolate coasts, in the seclusion of woods, these individuals lived and many spoke to me from the kingdom of the dead. This concept of belonging together consoled me. It seemed to me as if the man whose book I was now reading must know of my presence, and when I sat down myself to write, I knew that others were listening for me through the great rushing

noise that surrounded us all. When I saw Haller's name for the
first time on the back binding of a book, a memory was awakened
in me of a head gardener who appeared in a book out of my
childhood. This head gardener, who had lived with his family in
the jungles of South America, gave to the name of the writer
Haller its first depth effect. The dedication on the flyleaf of his
book roused my interest. It came from a friend of my parents,
who had emigrated to China, had there been converted to Bud-
dhism, and later committed suicide. My parents had spoken of
him only in disparaging terms. He had left his family, it was
hinted that he even threatened his wife with a gun. He had withdrawn from everyday life and disappeared. The words he had
confided to my parents in his nervous, scratchy handwriting out-
flowing onto the absorbent paper were, This book is written by a
brother of mine. I removed Haller's book Only for the Crazy from
the orderly row on the shelf, I freed it from its unappreciative
environment and let it speak out in my own realm. Reading
Haller's works was like probing into my own pain. Here was a
blueprint of my situation, the situation of the bourgeois who
wants to become a revolutionary but is crippled by the weight of
established convention. In many ways these readings held me fast
in a romantic no man's land, in self-pity and nostalgic longings, I
could have used to advantage a harder and more cruel voice, one
which would have torn the veil from my eyes and made me rise
and shine. The "I" that I was carrying around with me was used
up, destroyed, useless and had to go by the board. But how could
I get to do that, how free myself from everything that was dragging me down, poisoning and stifling me. Where could I find the
energy. The difficulties were bound to force me more and more
into a corner. There was no other way but the way of disintegration and decay. Changes occurred with infinite slowness, one
hardly noticed them. Sometimes I felt a sharp jolt and then I believed that something had become different, and then the underground waters closed in over me again and hid what I had gained
in mud. Thus I felt my way along until I believed I was on the
track of something new again, and one day something actually
would be there, perhaps I would find firm ground beneath my

feet. When I wrote to Haller it was an attempt to escape my unreality. And I received an answer to my letter. There stood my name on the envelope, I read it again and again. Suddenly I had entered into an inconceivable relation to the outside world. Someone had written my name on a letter, someone believed in my existence and directed his voice to me. I read the words of a living mouth. I was almost indifferent to the meaning of these words. The fact that someone spoke to me was enough. They were the words of an aged, humble craftsman. Perhaps I was disappointed by the quietness and tiredness, the reserve and the suffering in this voice. Perhaps I had expected a signal for rebellion. The voice was too remote for me in its mature wisdom. It spoke of patient work, of slow, thorough studying, of the necessity of some means of livelihood, and of the dangers of isolation. Only much later did I understand Haller's words. At the time I was too impatient. The words were too mild, too conciliatory for me. The words stood on the side of the orderly and the considered. I longed for the other extreme, the extreme of blind self-abandonment to the extremes of the unruly and the instinctive. I longed for it, but did not understand it, I groped in the dark and everything slipped through my fingers. It was decided I should go to Prague and take up an apprenticeship in a textile factory. A room was rented for me not far from the factory. The minute I set foot in this room I knew I would never stay. Experimentally I filled the walls with my pictures and drawings, spread out my papers about me, and then lay down weakly on the sofa, while behind the pane of frosted glass in the door the sounds and shadows of a strange family came and went unsteadily. Next morning I went to the factory to present myself to the Director. The building rose like a fortress in the midst of broad, dry fields. Inside in the workshops the looms hummed in long rows, and the working girls were cocooned in the close, whirring threads. In a small room I made my mission known by shouting above the roar of the machines and men in white coats handed me on to each other until I landed up in front of the Director, from whose words, as far as I could tell, hindered as I was by the foreign language and the ceaseless roar, I thought I gathered that he had to turn me down on grounds of competition, since my father ran a similar factory. Already he had turned away and the assistants in the white coats, having wheeled me around, shoved me off and away out through the screaming rows of machines. Triumphantly I walked past the cocooned weaver girls who turned their pale faces after me, ran across the fields and into my new freedom. What now happened had been long since prepared, it was the moment in which after years of pressure the bars around me fell away. I packed my belongings together and stood with my suitcase all on my own, out on the sidewalk. Haller had given me the address of a man from whom I might expect advice and help. Max B. lived in a boardinghouse near the freight-yard, his room was veiled in dense tobacco fumes and Max lay in bed in a woolen coat with a green scarf around his neck, half buried under newspapers. His slabby, bony face lit up when I mentioned Harry Haller's name. The account of my suddenly and unexpectedly won freedom roused him out of his lethargy to which four years of emigration had reduced him. From the very first moment there was an understanding and trust between us, I who was twenty years his junior, embodied the hopes and possibilities that he had long since given up. I had a future ahead of me and immediately Max championed this future, on the same afternoon we looked up all his contacts who might be useful to me. The editor of a newspaper, a dark, owlish man to whom I showed my drawings, gave me a commission to do illustrations for him, the head of a school of graphic arts recommended me to a professor of the art academy who, after he had studied my work, assured me that I would be able to enter his class. Thus on the afternoon of the same day on which I had set off as I thought to take up employment in a textile factory, I found myself in the light-flooded studio of the academy and my new comrades in their paint-smeared smocks gave me friendly smiles. This upheaval in my life had been accomplished with effortless ease but after only a few hours the old darkness and heaviness welled up in me again and extinguished all the brightness. I had no right to this freedom, I did not believe that it could have been handed to me on a plat-ter, I must have got it by stealth, have sneaked into a preserve where I did not belong. Although the professor attempted in a letter to persuade my parents of my needing to paint, I was filled with feelings of guilt, and foreboding. In the evening in Max's room on the sofa, which had been made up as a bed for me, a swamp fever buzzed in me, my throat, my chest, my head were inflamed by the bacilli of the old, unresolved pestilence, and then Max suddenly came to me, naked, his tall, lean, hairy body glaringly lit up by the lamp on the ceiling and his penis erect. He approached me and in his approach I understood his great need for closeness and tenderness and his helpless attempt to break through the long, killing loneliness. There was nothing repulsive about him, I was only sorry that I could not fulfill his wish. When I refused him there remained no tenseness between us, our understanding for one another had at this moment been only increased. For a long time we lay and talked to each other until I sank into half-sleep, and it was then that I heard my name being called, a long drawn out, icy cry, that cut through the noise of the freight yards, where wheels were rolling on frozen rails, brakes squealing, where the crashings of car couplings being engaged were being propagated from car to car, it penetrated me, a cry in my mother's voice. And my parents became resigned when they got the letter from the Authority, they gave up on me, but nevertheless, with his sense of the practical, my father tried to make it an orderly leave-taking, and I was sent money, given a trial year, by the end of which I was to show I was equal to a painter's calling. Now I was on my own, all to myself, no one to keep an eye on me, no one to fence me in, I could make of my day what I pleased, and so undertake the impossible, to be done with my old self and create an existence of my own. There I stood in the city of Prague and had to prove myself, and I looked for a room in this city, a room that would take me in, in which I could find myself, I walked about in the strange city and the streets were hung with black flags and muted drums were beaten and a coffin was borne to the grave on a mount through the ranks of the silent crowds. There I stand before alien doors, speak brokenly in a foreign tongue, ask for a room, am led by strangers down corridors where the air is stale and stuffy. I intrude upon these strangers, force my way into their apartments, I have never seen these people before, and they know nothing about me and I expect them to give me a room. These fat women, these lean women, these poorly dressed widows, these dolled-up *demimondaines,* they open the doors of the rooms and switch the light on and the light is always feeble so that one does not notice how wornout the room is, and I stand before a dimness of furniture, gloomy shapes which try to look like chairs, tables, wardrobes, beds, enveloped in a smokiness of nightmare wall-paper, and always, somewhere, the big nail sticks out of the wall, the nail on which to hang oneself. Until I finally find a room with its own entrance, a studio, dilapidated, dusty, with sooted win-dows, the ruins of a bedstead, with boxes and planks from which a table and a seat could be constructed. This room appeals to me, it is sick, it is spotted and burst open with sores, it shows me my wretchedness, it shows me the lowness of my estate. So I settled down in the foreign city, I found a lair into which other strangers had crept before me, and which would serve someone else as a flop. In this brief interval I made it livable for myself in my stony den in the middle of a great pile of stone, and surrounded myself with scrawls, hieroglyphs intended to give notice that I lived here, surrounded myself with magic signs, spells, with which I wanted to frighten away the evil spirits of loneliness. I lived for a whole year in this city. The city, with its ranks of streets, its architectures piled one atop the other, its gateways, bridges, and golden statues of my life, and in this framework the long walks and conversa-tions with Max took place, along the banks of the river or on the slopes of the vineyards, in the parks, and in the outer framework lay the great Academy building among trees in which the birds chirped, in this external frame the hours of work passed away in the communal studio, with my fellow students in front of the model or the still life, scraping the brush on the canvas, in the smell of oil paints and turpentine. The inner levels of my exist-ence, however, were enclosed by the room, this dwelling-place in which I could hide. Relieved of my parents and my teachers, I took over the tyranny over myself. Nobody could have been harder and more ruthless than I was to myself. At daybreak I forced myself out of bed and began my work. The lessons at the academy were merely a formal justification for my stay in this

city, my actual achievements were like blood oozing out after torture. I punched myself in the ribs, I spat on my hands and
slapped my face with them, I punished my tiredness and inatten-
tion by depriving myself of food and with all this drudgery it did
finally come about that pictures rose up in me and slowly, tentatively were projected onto the panels before me. Memories of the
surroundings of my earliest childhood re-echoed in these pictures,
interspersed with the impressions and reflections of later years, I
tried to recognize myself in these pictures, I tried to heal myself
with these pictures, and they were full of the leaden heaviness of
my isolation and the explosive glow of my pent-up despair. The
evocation of these visions brought me no release, the visions came
to me as to a drowning man, and the bodily experiments I carried
on beside my intellectual exertions led me to the brink of madness. In the past years I had several times tried and failed to have
sexual intercourse with a woman. A few days before my departure
for England I tested myself with a prostitute. I was still dressed in
mourning after Margit's funeral. I thought now I must prove myself, now I must begin my new life as a man. The woman took off
her skirt and placed herself with legs astraddle over a pail and
pissed into the pail. I did not even try to undress. I gave her the
money and departed. In London I came across a woman who
invited me into her apartment. First of all she sent me to have a
bath, for I was dirty and had wandered around town for some
days in an attempt to break away. She came to me in black, transparent silk. She tried hard to get me going but she had two little
Pekinese dogs lying on the bed who distracted me with their
squeaking and sniffing and their licking tongues. She did not want
any money from me, she wanted me as her lover, perhaps wanted
to pay my way, too, but it did not appeal to me. I ascribed this
failure to my outward lack of freedom, nevertheless sensed it had
deeper roots. Even now, when there was no one to stop me from
bringing a woman up to my room, and no one to disturb us, a
prohibition, a curse, paralyzed me. Outside in the world beyond
there had been kisses and close embraces, I had been gripped by
physical desires, but now in the containment of my own room,
when the naked, bodily acts were imminent, I felt only coldness

and futility. I explored the warm, strange skin, the limbs and joints, the soft parts of the flesh. With the flat of my hand and my eyes I had carnal knowledge of the curves of shoulders, breasts, hips, belly, thighs, and my conscious mind pieced these perceptions together into a concept of woman, but my function as a man was not awakened thereby, I found myself faced with an insoluble task. The woman's movements indicating sexual excitement scared me, I knew that her sexual parts, now heaving up and down, were waiting for me, but I lacked the key to set the mechanism of this union in motion. I tried to find something in the woman's face that could help me to overcome the chasm of strangeness. Her eyes were shut, her half-open mouth breathed heavily. Behind the closed eyes lay the world of another human being, who wanted my most intimate closeness. When her eyes opened and I caught her longing look, I could feel for a second's duration the possibility of entering her, but straight-away the meaning of our being together was lost again in intangibles. My fingers stroked her pubic hair and the lips of her vagina, which opened up between her yielding outspread thighs, I saw the rosy and brownish inside of the wet lips, I imagined the depths that wanted to take me in, yet I felt no enticement, felt only the impossibility of it all. Suddenly I could see Margit's body in front of me, as she had once offered herself to me, and I saw the bones of this body far from me in a hole in the earth and I sprang up and only wanted to be alone and the stranger who had followed me into my lair threw on her clothes and fled in terror. She, who was dead, I could love, I could give myself to her, I need no longer have any fear of her, she asked nothing from me. To her who was dead, I could escape and no one could find out if my love was genuine. Whenever I failed in my attempts with the living, the living woman in my presence, I consoled myself with the dead, the childlike woman of the past. From a living woman I could not hide, in her presence I had to come out of my confinedness, reach out far into an outer world. And that meant being swallowed up, surrendering myself. As a child I had once seen my mother's genitals, she was standing bent over in her nightdress and between her heavy thighs gaped the dark, hair-fringed hole. As then, when I had stared in vertiginous alarm into my mother's great crack, so now my gaze was riveted on the genitals of a living woman of the present, my fingers opened the wet, soft lips, under whose swellings and recesses was concealed the secret of all existence, and if I could penetrate into this sucking depth I would penetrate to the very core of life. In my impotence I looked for women who wanted to be hurt and who put up with the endless preliminaries that always had no result. These women had no names, their faces were blurred, they were merely an *idée fixe* for me, I drew them into my madness, I felt them out and searched them out, and sometimes for a few moments they were like my dead sister, and their faces were surrounded by wire frames and the head was fastened to the neck with screws and tubes and I worked feverishly in this technical confusion to restore the control mechanism that could bring her back to life again and sometimes the mouth moved and sometimes the eyelids twitched and I whispered, Wake up, wake up, and around me in the half-dark room the surfaces of pictures and the boxes and plants and frames stood out and the easel rose up like a gallows, and white papers shone out of the shadows, and then I pulled the naked body from the bed on to the floor and we wallowed in the soot and crawled around between the planks and pots and embraced each other in contorted positions. I could not talk to anyone about it, not even to Max. Once I went to a doctor who in a newspaper ad promised to cure impotence. He sold me a powder that I was to take mixed with soda water. There was no other remedy. There was only hang on or kick the bucket. If I do not kick the bucket, perhaps sometime I will find a woman whose look and gestures, whose voice and caresses, will suddenly break through the layer of ice. And one day I will find out what this opening underneath her body is like, this entrance to life, and I will thrust myself into the silky warmth, I will let myself be sucked round by life's wet, soft mouth, I will burrow into it, and unload a part of my life into the greedy, viviparous deep. My mouth, too, will trace out the opened, mussel-colored lips, my tongue will lap up the sweet taste to the tenderly haired vagina, incredible that I should have recoiled from it before. And then perhaps one day I will discover that there is no

loneliness, that this whole culture of loneliness was only a misunderstanding, only a convention, a lack of fantasy, an impoverish-
ment of feeling, for how can there be loneliness if one can come so
close to someone else, so deeply pervade each other. And this possibility must have existed then too, otherwise if it had not been
there I should have thrown myself out of the window. Max told
me once how in the World War and in the Spanish Civil War he
had heard dying men calling out to their mothers, Mamma,
Mamma, they had shouted. There lay these finished men, perhaps
fallen for something they believed in, and the last thing they
screamed for was the abyss from which they once had crawled.
One cannot live unless one loves this great crack. Oh life, oh great
cunt of life. In the moment of death we scream for you. Such
realizations came with lightning rapidity and immediately afterward I could no longer conceive them. But they left their mark
behind. They occur again. I shout, Yes, that is how it is, and I no
longer know what I meant. Oh cunt of life. Now I can throw my
arms around my mother again, can weep on her riddled body, can
cover her sunken mouth, her decrepit cheeks with kisses, can
stroke her worn hands, can now press close, close to her naked
body, to her sucked-out breasts, to her scarred belly, press between her vein-swollen thighs, close, close to the hole whence I
came. In Prague, in this first place where I wanted to find my way
to freedom, I found only darkness and self-destruction. When my
appointed time was at an end after this year, the pressure of the
outside world had fiendishly grown. In a preliminary practice for
later disaster the sirens had wailed and in the blacked-out city
invisible crowds pressed into the streets with clattering footsteps
and murmuring voices. Here and there shone the dancing glow of
a cigarette, and suppressed shouts and whistles rose up out of the
ebbing and flowing throng. The inhabitants of the city were like
one single widely branching black body, wholly given over to one
single uncertain expectancy. When the siren sounded again we
stood still, as if beneath the rushing wings of some mythological
monster. We stood in darkness in the foreboding of an apocalyptic time. When the lights in all the streets flamed on again all at
once, we greeted them with a thousandfold cry of hope in life

renewed, yet for a long time we had been conscious of lawlessness and disintegration lurking in the streets. And on one of the last days I stood with Peter Kien, a friend from the Academy, in a bright street and we held between us a large picture I had painted, a picture that showed a burning city, and Peter Kien stared up into the air and drew in his breath with a sobbing sound, and I saw a dark mass of rags come falling down from above, and as the rags smacked onto the stony pavement of the street I saw what sort of rags they were. The dark pile of rags had a head, and blood streamed from the head, and the rags were a body that huddled itself together, that waltzed over on its side, pressed knees hard into its belly, and then lay still, stiffened, like an embryo in a great pregnant mother made of stone. People came running from all sides and we held up the burning city to them. Peter Kien's breath came in sobs. Flee, Peter Kien, don't stay here. Flee, hide yourself, you with your hopelessly open face, with your disconcerted staring gaze behind the thick prisms of your glasses, flee before it is too late. But Peter Kien remained behind. Peter Kien was murdered and burned. I escaped. I sent my pictures to my parents, packed my knapsack and wandered south, I found a village by a mountain lake, then I went up to the north where my parents had escaped with their possessions. When I was tramping along the road to the south, it seemed continually as if the dark rag was falling from a great height and I saw above me the open window, high up in a house in the stone city, and I imagined the room through which a living man had just run, I saw the window from inside the room, the blue pool of the window, I experienced the irrevocable decision, the overcoming of the last resistance. Alone with my own footsteps on the smooth ribbon of country road, I rushed through the room, this last room of a life, a red carpet with a Persian design lay on the floor of the room, and in front of the sofa stood an oval table with carved bowlegs, and on the table stood a violet crystal vase, and on the wall hung a mirror with an ornate gold frame and the window could be seen in the mirror, and my rush to the window. I imagined the second in which everything solid vanished, the second in which I rushed up to the window sill and hurled myself out into the blue waters of emptiness. In the very first instant after crossing the frontier from which return was no longer possible, I flew as in a dream, it was as if I could fly upward, light as a bird, I would mount and mount, with outspread arms, how had I summoned up the energy for this leap, whence had I taken the courage for this leap, in the very first instant after the second of the explosion I flew on without gravity in an ecstasy; the air rippled around me, I breathed no more, I was enraptured, my eyes were closed. It was Death that had seized me, it was the power of Death that had taken hold of me in the room and hurled me out of the window, the leap was inconceivable if Death had not become voluptuousness, then a current enveloped me that sucked me downward, suddenly I got no further, the heaviness of the whole world hung upon me, and ever stronger and stronger was the force of the current that sucked me into the depths. Landscapes revolved past me, I heard the beat of my footsteps and felt the falling and the terror at suddenly realizing that it was too late, and then I lay smashed and shattered in the city's stony womb, I rested at the roadside, drank water from brooks and wells, stayed overnight at hostels, and after weeks reached the lake, ran through thickets and down pebbly slopes to the shore, threw off knapsack and clothes, and plunged into the tepid water. I lay on my back, moving my hands and feet only slightly, and around about rose the mountains in the haze of twilight. White villages shimmered out of the violet-green shadows and everywhere bright bells were ringing. It was as if I were floating backward, I hovered in the depths of a vast chalice, whose rim dissolved in the gold dust of the sunken sun. All heaviness and oppressiveness passed away, washed off by the light embraces of the water, absorbed and evaporated in the mother-of-pearl light. Here by this lake I found an intermediate kingdom, here arose the beginnings of another relaxed, almost happy existence. It was an existence that hung from a single thin thread, but curiously enough I found in this outwardly ever more uncertain state of things a tinge of inner harmony. Previously I had felt no contact with the countryside, rather I had felt lost in it, an outcast and abandoned to transience, and only in towns could I feel as if I belonged, but there in

this mountain scenery, these vineyards, deciduous woods and ancient villages pieced together out of rough stones, here in the
mildness of early summer, which would soon become a shimmering tropical warmth, I experienced hours of vegetative peace. I
lost the manic need to be active, and could lie on the shores of the
lake in the sun or in the dry grass of a clearing in the wood without being troubled by a bad conscience. And when I wanted to
draw or write something, I could wait for a long time and medi-
tate beforehand, and drawing and writing were not so important,
I could also leave them be, it was more important that I existed,
that I was alive, and before working I had first to learn how to
experience. I strolled through the thick, dark green woods, and
even though at times, faced by this luxuriant growth and the fragrance of rotting vegetation, a sudden fear rose up in me, this was
outweighed by a desire to explore, a *joie de vivre* under whose
influence I often found myself singing and laughing in utter solitude. And here in a warm, starlit night for the first time I got into
a woman's body, we stood embracing on a balcony overlooking
the lake, and she drew me into her room, on to her bed, and there
was no struggle and no strain, it was effortlessly easy life played
with us and I no longer rebelled against it. Early the following
morning I stood below in the courtyard, I washed my face and my
hands in the trickling water and on my genitals I still felt the
warmth of the inside of the female body, and in the village a cock
crowed and animals were stirring in their stalls, and I straight-
ened and stretched myself in a new self-awareness. But after the
elation came the depression. It was not the daily increasing pressure of the outside world that led to the extinguishing of these
days, the break took place within me, I could not endure in such
brightness. Incapable of living on my own energy, I had to return
to my parents' home. My father had transferred his factory with
the machines and capital to the new country and the accustomed
home had grown up again under my mother's hands in the interior of the new house. I came back as the Prodigal Son, to whom
was offered the grace of a place to stay. A folder with drawings, a
couple of notebooks with notes were my sole possessions. My pictures, which I had entrusted to my mother, were no longer there.

When she was preparing to move, she had carried my pictures into the cellar, chopped them up with an axe, and burned them in the furnace. She explained this destruction as a safety precaution. She had feared that my gloomy, weird pictures would arouse the suspicions of the frontier authorities. She had saved the home. The pictures, an expression of disease, had had to be sacrificed. I returned to this home and I had been robbed of the only signs of my strength. With her own hands she had destroyed the picture world of my youth, the dances of death, the apocalyptic visions, and the dream landscapes. With this destruction she had freed herself from the threat that these pictures had exerted on the orderliness and protectedness of her home. I stood there empty handed like a tramp. I had no other choice but to enter my father's factory. The factory was still encased in scaffolding. Next door in a small green shack the temporary office and warehouse had been set up. Here stood the machine parts and precision instruments, packed in wood shavings and corrugated paper, here stood barrels and cans full of paints and chemicals, and in the piled-up boxes lay the materials that would later be colored and printed in the factory. The cement mixer rumbled the whole day outside in the courtyard, and inside in the hut everything rattled and trembled with it. I sat at my typewriter and hacked down the almost incomprehensible words that my father had dictated. Although I had to invent half of the business letters, everything developed according to plan. Answers came with the mail and were acknowledged, the building of the factory progressed, through the cracked windowpane I could see the walls growing. Agents and future clients appeared, collections of patterns were worked out, contracts signed, while the door was being wrenched open and shut with a crash, while laborers, skilled workers and engineers came in, spread out and discussed construction blueprints, while dust rose in whirls and the naked bulb on the ceiling, fed by the factory's own generator, shook, flickered and from time to time went out. It was a dark time of year with much rain and mist, and it was hoped to have the building finished before the winter. And everything went according to plan. We lived here in the Wild West, but a few yards away from us machines were mounted on to their bases, cables, steam and water systems were laid, a few yards away from us a huge, functional composition in glass and concrete arose, wrapped up in a network of wires and rods. With the first snow we shifted into a new world that smelled of paint and polish and that still resounded to the sound of hammers and saws. The workmen and clerks were inspected and introduced to their new activities by a handful of specialists. In the dyeworks, in the scouring mill, in the finishing rooms and in the printing rooms, in the laboratories, in the room where the colors were mixed, in the pattern room, in the warehouse and in the office everything was set in motion, at first slowly and fumblingly, but full of confidence and enthusiasm. This was my new music, the song of the machines, and statistics and schedules were my poems, I was a workman among workmen, but I was not one of them, I was the owner's son. But I had nothing to do with the owner, so I remained a foreign body among the large throbbing machinery that steadily grew into its melody. I lived in a vacuum between the world of my parents and the world of the workmen. If I had been anonymous and unanchored to my home, I could perhaps have struck up a friendship, a communion in physical work, with a girl perhaps, one of the weavers or a female warehouse clerk, a simple bodily relationship, but that too is a dream, in this dream I deny myself, in this dream I deny that there is only one thing for me, the struggle for the independence of my work. So long as I suppressed this struggle, everything else was bound to be bleak for me, I comprehended nothing of the living conditions of the workers, of their struggle, their problems, for the most elementary thing was not granted me, the chance to carry out my own work. But who here carried out his own work. Sometimes I looked into the organization of this structure in which each of them was cocooned in his movements, but in which no one inwardly participated, I saw these absent-minded faces, these mechanical activities, and the extraordinary lostness and extinction of the lunch hours, people played cards, solved crossword puzzles, and such personality as there was in them dissolved into a shapeless pulp. Here one found a livelihood, one could earn what one needed for the rent, food, and a few pleasures, and perhaps there was nothing more, perhaps this was all, no one seemed to ask for more or at most only a better flat, richer food, and new means of amusement. In this existence, with no chance of starting discussions about problems of self-expression and formation where one could feel concerned about more vital matters, all my personal projects fell victim to the doubt that they no longer had any *raison d'être,* and that it was only diseased selfishness on my part that had ever led me to concern myself with them. Perhaps I lived in this factory as all the others lived, in the mornings I came in with the stream of workmen and carried out my appointed tasks and in the evenings I left again, in the stream of the others, and a dull dissatisfaction and vague dreams filled me, just as all the others were filled with them. By day there was only work, nothing but being harnessed to the production process, by day only this unique, important business of manufacturing fabrics for curtains and clothing, and sometimes this uniqueness and importance took on feverish proportions, as I saw it then, whereupon I experienced in depth the way things were made, how the raw material was swallowed up in the factory's maw and, amid the pounding of powerful machines, proceeded through the stages of its metamorphosis, rolled through vats and drums in which it was prepared, steamed and drained in the wash room, came alive in the dye house where the dye boss's control booth hung like a glass ship in the steamy mist, and was slung forth by rotating metal arms, to be sucked up by rollers with broad metal lips, and then fluttered in long ribbons onto the rubber-covered tables of the printing rooms, where in the tropical heat half-naked workers bent over it and let it drink in the colors of the printed patterns, and now one could already guess their future existence, heavy and gleaming with flowers and butterflies and figurines the materials hung stretched out to dry in the long rooms behind whose windows the sky reflected their colors, then they were snatched into a new vat, dragged through new streams, and made compliant by a hail of blows from little hammers, and then they rolled light and fragrant off the belts and were divided up and wrapped up in rolls and supplied with labels, and many of them bore the names of goddesses and their earthly existences began and they shone in the streets and woods as dresses, they fluttered as curtains from windows, and finally they lay faded and torn on the rubbish heaps at the edge of cities. And we kept on producing them. Ceaselessly we kept on, while outside a world fell into pieces. The war did not open my eyes. The frustrated struggle for my vocation had put me in a state of derangement. My defeat was not the defeat of the emigrant in face of the difficulties of living in exile, but the defeat of one who does not dare to free himself from his dependence. Emigrating had taught me nothing. Emigrating was for me a confirmation of the not-belonging that I had experienced from my earliest childhood. I had never possessed a native soil. I was left untouched by the fact that the struggle that went on outside affected my existence also. I had never come to any conclusions about the revolutionary conflicts in the world. The effort I had made to find some means of expression for my existence had claimed all my awareness. This period was for me a period of waiting, a period of sleep-walking. I spent two years in the factory. I carried out my work in the darkroom of the printing department, where by the feeble red glow of a safety light I developed photos of sample designs, I carried out my work in a little sealed room, deep in the bowels of the roaring factory. Although his wish to see me employed in his field had been granted, my father paid no more attention to me. He never came to me with any questions. It was as if he sensed I would again desert him. The hours I spent together with the family passed in the same atmosphere of estrangement, I sat through one part of the evening in my parents' company as if it were a debt, silently turning the pages of a book or magazine, while on the radio monotonous anonymous voices reported inconceivable events. Out of this period a cry breaks out of me. Why have we squandered these days and years, people living under the same roof, without being able to speak to or hear each other. What sort of disease is this that makes us so dreary, that fills us with such distrust and reticence, that we can no longer look one another in the eyes. And yet this period, which at the time seemed completely dead to me, contained expressions of a secret life. At night in my room or on Sundays, pictures, drawings, poems, hidden expressions of someone unknown and renounced came to life. In the depth of this total isolation there was a quiet deliberation as a result of which each month I put aside money for the future. In the late summer of the second year the break-up began with a violent blow. I had gone into the woods to work. The buzzing of the mosquitoes was like a light drone of bells; beetles and spiders rustled in the dry foliage. I settled down at the side of a mountain lake. I fell asleep, wishing that I might never wake again. I dreamed of my way through this forest. There was the old fear of being lost in the forest, of death in the bog, among the ferns in utter stillness. On a narrow path I encountered a man in a hunter's outfit, a hunting bag and a gun over his shoulder. He went past me and it was as if I had met him once before, a long time ago. Then I wandered along a country road. The road led me through an immeasurably wide and confused life. Again I met the huntsman, he came straight toward me and I had to step aside to let him pass. Hastily he raised his hand in greeting. I came to a lake and let myself drift into the water and out there in the brightness of blurring reflections the huntsman popped up again in front of me, I recognized him and awoke. On a holiday trip many years before as a child I had met him in a wood. There was the resinous tang of freshly felled fir trees, and I twisted between my fingers a small round wooden disk that had fallen from the beginning of a bough of a sawed-off tree trunk. The huntsman appeared and asked me my name. I told him. He said, That's my name too. He asked me insistently where I lived. I told him the name of the town. He said, I live there too. He asked me what street. I named it and he said, I live in that street too. He asked me for the number of the house, I told him, and he said, So we live in the same house. He moved off and left me behind in unspeakable astonishment. With the warning of this dream in my mind I jumped up. I could not interpret the dream but only felt that a change had come about, that my life was governed by new forces. I saw my footsteps in the sand at the edge of the lake. For a moment the vision of these steps that had led me from my birth onward to this place filled me. In a single instant I saw the dark pattern of their track. I recognized it and forgot it again immediately and in fear at my past I ran up into the undergrowth. Birds fluttered out of the trees, the sky was blood-red from the sinking sun. And the uneasiness that had now begun could no longer be contained, after weeks and months of slow inner changes, after relapses into weakness and discouragement, I took leave of my parents. The wheels of the railway thumped away beneath me with their ceaseless hollow drumbeats and the forces of my flying forward screamed and sang in incantatory chorus. I was on my way to look for a life of my own.

II. Vanishing Point

I arrived in Stockholm on November 8, 1940. From the railroad station I rode to Schedin's pension in the Drottninggata, where Max Bernsdorf had taken a room for me. It was a large corner room with brown wallpaper and brown velvet curtains at the window. There were shiny spots on the wall over the high wooden bedstead and on the upholstery of the lumpy armchairs, and black spots stared at me from the scratched wood of the bureau, in the mirror of which I could see myself putting away my bags. Max lived at the end of the hall in a small room with a sign hanging on the door that said: LET SLEEPING DOGS LIE. As four years before in Prague, when I had visited him for the first time, he was lying on the bed, to save his strength. He was half-buried in newspapers and smoking his pipe. Wardrobe, chairs, table were shadowy in a haze of blue smoke. The hand he held out to me was cool and bony, his face emaciated, the skin colorless. His hair had turned gray and only the bushy eyebrows were still black, as if drawn in charcoal. The hand sank back and lay limp in the rustling newspapers. The fingernails were bitten short, the skin around them fretted to shreds. Only a short time before he had been released from the camp where he had been interned after his flight from Norway. They either deport us, he said, or stick us behind barbed wire. There was a lot of big talk, he said, about struggle and human rights, but we, the ones really on the receiving end, were treated like mangy dogs. Anyone with money could buy himself asylum. But the rest of us live on charity, we're not allowed to work. Anger had animated his face. He knocked out his pipe, refilled it, made more clouds of smoke. Above the bed, on a shelf, stood worn paperbacks with English titles, whodunits, political writings, a few volumes of Persian lyric poetry, Hemingway's *The Sun Also Rises* and Aldington's *Death of a Hero*. Behind Max Bernsdorf lay seven years of emigration. For him refugee life was only a time of waiting. He was sweating out his day of return. For him there was still a landscape in which he had roots. He lay in his smoke-filled, dirt-colored roominghouse room and dreamed of a plot of earth he called home, driven from it though he had been. In narrow cubbyholes in foreign places he imagined how it would be back in his Swabian village and its little forest, and the very smell of meadow and mountain was there and real to him. Sweden he saw as an enemy who had attacked his forebears three hundred years ago, with Wotan's horde and the famous torture drink of dungwater. Peevishly he complained about the bad coffee in this town, about the sweetened bread and all the messes they cooked in flour. There wasn't a decent bar in the city, or a café, as in Oslo, where you could sit half a day over a cup of coffee, reading newspapers from all over the world and talking with congenial people. In Oslo he had talked the same way about Prague, as in Prague he had praised Barcelona. Now he was waiting for his American visa, for someone to sponsor him, and once in America he would lie in his hotel bedroom and think about Europe. I listened to him tell about the trouble he was having filling out application forms, how long he had to cool his heels at the consulate. He had to get it all off his chest, vent his own ill humor before he could ask me about my plans. Then the look of a dog who has been whipped and made to crawl faded from his eyes, and my arrival, as it had in Prague, brought back some of his old liveliness.

I myself did not come to Stockholm as a refugee looking for asylum. I came to live there as a painter and, at the beginning, I had the money I had put aside each month while working at the factory. There was no lost hometown for me and no thoughts about going back, for I had never belonged to any particular country. Since Max was not aware of this freedom and insisted on viewing my present situation in the light of current events, I briefed him on the background I had forsaken. My father came

from a Hungarian village. His parents, who had run a grain business there, had been orthodox Jews, whereas he, himself, had
gone over to Christianity as a young man when he moved to Vienna. My mother's people came from Strassburg and Basel, and
among her ancestors had been a peasant leader who fought in the
Thirty Years' War with a pitchfork. During World War I my father had had to serve in the Austro-Hungarian army. He was
wounded by a Russian machine gun and for it decorated and promoted to the rank of lieutenant. He was proud of these distinc-
tions and brought them up on festive occasions. The first years of
my life were spent in the Galician zone where my father had been
transferred and among my earliest memories were marching soldiers in clouds of dust and the Polish peasant women who offered
my mother fat white geese for sale, and bent their broad faces
down over the baby carriage in which I lay to tease me. After the
war, because of boundary revisions, my father received Czecho-
slovakian citizenship. However, he settled in Germany and there I
spent my youth. I became aware of the fact that I was no German
and, on my paternal side, of Jewish ancestry, shortly before the
emigration period. I had been baptized and, as with everything to
do with education, had let myself be carried along, indifferent and
half-numb, through Christian religious instruction and confirmation. My manner of speech had never become identified with any
region, for we often moved from city to city. I was at home in
harbor districts, in fairs and circus tents, wherever thought was
open to change and travel, where the gaze was directed toward
far places. I read about the worlds of Russians and Frenchmen, of
Englishmen and Americans and Scandinavians, and nothing hindered me from feeling at home in thought among them. I felt
kinship with Gauguin on Tahiti, with Van Gogh in Arles, with
Myshkin in St. Petersburg, Lieutenant Glahn in the Norwegian
forest and Fabrizio in the charterhouse of Parma. My suddenly
being ticketed as a foreigner and half-Jew, my being forbidden to
use the new *Heil* greeting, failed to make much impression on me,
since I was indifferent to questions of nationality and race. My
father was for order and the *status quo*. He had no criticism of
nationalism and his wartime experiences had not made him an

antimilitarist. He had even wanted me to serve in the military since he thought of it as a school that might make a man of me. I had never had any contact with radical circles. Whatever revolt I had felt had been directed not against the bourgeoisie, but against constraints hampering my personal freedom. I knew nothing about social controversy and only in art found weapons I could use in self-defense. In art there were no frontiers, no nations. Uli, my school friend, was a citizen of the world like myself. Together we went on exploring expeditions to the libraries, the museums, the concert halls. When I migrated with my family to England, it was just another change of address. I went along with the household without demur, but would just as well have remained, had my father not had the foresight, decisiveness and means to escape the danger in good time. Uli and my other school chums stayed behind. Uli drowned during the occupation of Denmark. His body was washed up on the beach.

Max launched an offensive. Why did he have to go to Denmark anyway, he exclaimed, and ran his fingers through his unkempt hair. You just lay low to save your own neck, he said, in the clutch you ought to have known on which side you stood. I replied that if I hadn't happened to get out in time, I'd have been driven onto the battlefield like all the rest. I carried Uli's picture in my briefcase. I took out the snapshot. It showed a blond young man with smooth strong features and broad shoulders. He was wearing the Luftwaffe uniform. Max examined the picture and then looked up at me in silence. His look said, the man in this picture was your enemy, he would have aimed his machine gun at you and shot you down. I remembered how enthusiastic Uli had been about the Pergamon Frieze in the Berlin Museum and Bellini's head of a Doge at the National Gallery. The veneration of this hard, cold, autocratic face and of the warrior-heroes of Greek sculpture was all part and parcel of the national intoxication with might and bigness. Uli's preference for Greek mythology, classic Rome, Michelangelo's powerful statues had shown me how opposite we were. To me art which celebrated strength and battle was alien. I was attracted by painters like Cranach, Baldung Grien, Bosch,

Brueghel, Klee, Nolde. The Greek and Roman hero cult was a rotten sort of thing. The medieval poetry, the oratorios and masses, the classic dramas and operas were saturated with lies; everywhere were large, sweeping feelings, military leaders, saints, martyrs, all of it was cut off from its original reality and grossly suspect, and even Bach himself subject to distortion. I thought of Dietrich, the musician, who had introduced me to the world of fugues and organ music. Dietrich's home was filled with Gothic art treasures and precious things from China and Egypt. But in this same home, where cultural possessions stared at you from all sides, in a dominating position hung the Fuehrer's picture, and, as at an altar, adoration was paid to the etherealized features and ennobled head of the man with the little Chaplin mustache. You can interpret all art any way you want, said Max. You can falsify everything, twist everything to suit your own interest. But now they are asking only one question: Which side are you on?

I might have been on the other side, I said, if my grandfather in his kaftan had not saved me from it, I might very well have stayed over there where I was. Max came at me again. I must have some inkling of the danger, even living embedded up to my neck in the bourgeoisie. I replied that I had been preoccupied with another "Kampf," another struggle than Hitler's. In the midst of my security I had barricaded myself behind books and pictures. I had surrounded myself with totem symbols, to resist pressures from the outside. During the persecutions, which I became used to from the start, I did not see myself as member of a particular race, but as a kind of foreigner, an alien to the generality whom every pack had to track down and yelp at. It had seemed perfectly normal when, on my way to school, a man came up to me and, like the so-called bolt out of the blue, gave me a crack on the face. During the last days in Berlin I went up the Charlottenstrasse to the Leipzigerstrasse, where my father had his office. In the neighborhood of the French Cathedral I ran into a man coming the other way wearing a brown uniform. On the whitely glowing pavement he came right for me. I dodged him and, as he was passing, he hissed the word *"Kohlrabi"* at me. Only right then, while making this report to Max, did I all of a sudden fully recognize the danger and how great it was. At the same time the meaning of another event also became clear to me. One time I had taken part in a pogrom. I could see the friend we had assailed as if it were yesterday. Judging by appearance and name he must have been a Jew. Inspired by the film *Ben Hur* we had been playing galley slaves in the vaulted cellars of an abandoned construction project. We were sitting on a plank, pulling on imaginary oars. My friend's suffering began when he made me the overseer and I had to swing the whip over him. When the persecutors broke in on us I was only too ready to go over to their side and the galley slave became our common victim. Out of thankfulness at being spared, grateful that this time someone else had been chosen, I joined the party of the stronger and outdid them in cruelty. They were not going to realize their mistake if I could help it. I led the way in dragging the prisoner to the edge of the flooded excavations. We threw him onto a raft, shoved him out on the water and pelted him with chunks of clay. Later, time and again I would see him as he clung fast to the slippery planks, splashed by the yellowish water. I heard him crying out for help, heard my own yells egging the others on, by which means I ingratiated myself with my new allies and tried to divert them from the thought of grabbing me and pushing me out onto the water, too. Recounting this I was unsure where the truth lay, whether our victim had capsized and drowned, an idea long lurking in the back of my mind, or whether, as my memory preferred to have it, a worker had appeared on the scene and come to the rescue. The only thing I saw clearly was that I could be on the side of the persecutor and hangman. I had it in me to take part in an execution. Max would have none of this. Only the sins of youth, he cried. Every one of us at some time or other has been tempted to commit torture. It was just because of things like that, he said, that we become aware of the danger. But today, he said, you are another person. Today you know what side you are on. Max had to believe in this struggle for the right, although weariness often brought him to the brink of throwing in the sponge. He had to believe in a rebirth, for if there were no rebirth, emigration was meaningless. For me emigration did not imply taking a special point of view. I was a stranger wherever I landed. When I lived in England the children in the streets of the London suburb yelled insults at me. In the country where I had grown up and whose language I spoke, I had been called a foreigner. In England they shouted *Fritz* after me. When I went to Czechoslovakia a couple of years later, the country to which I belonged according to my passport, I was again looked down on as a German and for being unable to speak the language, though notwithstanding I still had to do military service there. An officer addressed me in Czech as I stood, hollow-chested, crook-backed and shoulder blades sticking out, at the examination desk. The thought of a barracks existence, of machine gun and bayonet practice, paralyzed me, and there was no need for me to feign psychic instability. I got a deferment and was able to continue my art studies. When Bohemia was invaded and I should have reported to take part in its defense, I was in Switzerland. Here I was put in jail as a suspicious foreigner, but since I was able to show that my family was living in comfortable circumstances in Sweden, they put up with me for a few months. An almost homey mood arose at the police station when I explained that my mother came from Basel, where her father had run a watch factory. Touched, they weighed the possibility of my settling in Switzerland, but I lacked the means for that. I came to Sweden on a valid passport, shortly before the total occupation of Czechoslovakia. I was allowed in because of my being able to fall back on my parents' security.

We talked about how we should act if this country too were invaded. Max had to admit that with all his knowledge of journalism and his political views he had not contributed to any final victory. During the Spanish Civil War he had been a journalist and escaping from Barcelona he had shit in his pants. In the last resort we would have to try to get to Russia by way of Finland, he said, and showed me on a map the route we would take. I had as little time for these considerations as for the thought that had occasionally occurred to me at the factory, that I ought to go to London, and offer myself as a volunteer. I felt no guilt about not participating in the war and showing no solidarity with any nation or race. I had attempted to break my last link and had left my parents' house in order to concentrate on my work. Political and ideological demands were insignificant beside the work that awaited me. During the one and a half years in my father's factory my pictures had been created in a state of half-sleep in the rare hours I had been able to set aside for them. This clandestine painting, with its fragmentary results was now over, and something new and frank was about to begin. That this beginning coincided with the war raging outside did not faze me at all. I made the only decision I could honestly vouch for, at a point where the pressure of not doing it, which continued to be generated by the whole inhibitive nature of my upbringing, had become absolute. I had to break down this menace, disprove the charge of cowardice and selfishness, and have faith in my plans. Max wanted to help me. He conceded the artist a certain right to live in a no man's land. But he expressed these views as a champion of romantic art, which suddenly seemed suspect to me. He compared me to such painters as Runge and Caspar David Friedrich. But at this moment the relationship was stale and obsolete. For a while we exchanged parts. Max Bernsdorf now lay there eyes averted from the world, and I was the one who wanted to participate and come on strong. My painting was active, an expression of life; I wanted to choose it consciously as my alternative to taking part in the war. There lay Max, this big strong man with an angular, stubborn peasant face, broken by not belonging anywhere and long disuse. He was in his mid-forties. It was my twenty-fourth birthday. Everything I had done up to this juncture seemed only so much preparation. The night before, when I packed my bag in my parents' house, it was in the belief my life was about to begin. But this life of mine had actually begun at birth, it was a single, indivisible life, in which there was no way to go but forward. Benumbed by the clatter of the train journey still ringing in my ears, I sat on the edge of my friend's bed, looked through the smolder of smoke toward the window, and heard the rush of cars in the street below.

Max asked me about my pictures. Suddenly the pictures I had done made no sense. I had hardly produced anything during the factory period, I said. Painting cannot be carried on in unreality, it's something done with the hands, down to earth and practical. For painting you need stretchers, canvases, drawing boards, paper, sketchbooks, pens, Chinese ink, oil paints, turpentine and linseed oil, chalk and plaster. Painting is tangible, you can smell it. My painting was a dream. In my hideout something was created and then buried again. Yet Max's questions recalled details from the twilight of the last few months. Although Max himself was bogged down in inactivity and disorientation he wanted to hear about things that were clear and concrete. He rejected all that was dubious and uncertain and wanted to know about events from my everyday life in the factory. He asked for descriptions of where I worked, the city and its surroundings and the people I had met. Even when I was with Max in Prague I had discovered how oppression and uncertainty could disappear, how all things had their form, color, weight and each its name. In his presence the world was simple and matter-of-fact, full of people, animals and buildings. We used to cross the Karlsbrücke, past the weathered baroque statuary, the Moldau flowing beneath us and ahead of us, on the hill, the yellow-golden castle with the cathedral towers. From the little clay houses of the Alchemists' Alley that looked as if they had been baked together we climbed to the vineyards where we sat on a water pipe at the edge of a road building site, and gazed across the city. The cupolas and battlements were bathed in the reddish haze of the setting sun. This sunset hour remembered often held me fast. Then I was relaxed and alert: there were no longer any demands, the blinding light of day had passed, the objects began to glow of their own accord and every sound lay clearly on the air. At the factory I had frequently spent the long late summer evenings in the woods or at the edge of the lake with its many creeks and inlets. The little islands lay black on the motionless surface of the water, and that was how I remembered the evening that war was declared, so still and rapt, with smooth greenish-yellow water and slowly paling sky. I could still

hear the music played after the radio announcements—Orpheus'
Song from the Underworld, an aria interwoven with flute war-
blings. Time had not stood still as I had thought. In the little
industrial town I had gathered impressions, met women, been to
open-air restaurants and dance halls. But I could no longer recall
the names and faces of the women. Max said that in Prague he
had thought me a seducer. He had often been disgusted by how
fast I could cast off a woman. When I told him that none of these
women had slept with me he laughed incredulously. Magda, in a
mountain village near Lugano, was the only woman with whom I
had found tenderness and intimacy, and since then the opportunity had no longer presented itself. But there again the foundation
of the tangible and communicable was lost, and Max wanted to
hear anecdotes. I told him of a girl I had met. Under colored light
bulbs we danced together, sat at a round table and drank lemon-
ade, and after embraces and kisses in the park we arranged an
excursion for the following Sunday. We paddled out in a hired
canoe in the lake, bathed and lay on a rock in the sun. Her body
was ready for me but a large brown birthmark in her armpit repelled me. I tried to forget about it, and as we drifted in our boat
again I bent her face back and kissed it. She had pretty commonplace features, dark eyes and a soft mouth. She was a salesgirl in a
shop, I was a factory worker, we were on a Sunday excursion.
Clouds had towered up and covered the sun. When the storm
broke we dragged the boat up on the beach of an island and ran
up the hill in the rain. Between the trees was a summer hut. It
seemed uninhabited, the door was locked. I broke a pane of glass
and we climbed into the room, where a camp bed awaited us. But
when she put her arm around me I again saw the dark brown
patch, dull as velvet. Her breasts were small and firm, the dark
nipples had contracted with the cold. Suddenly voices could be
heard outside in the storm. It was a release: I could jump up and
pull her out with me. We fled down the muddy slopes to the
canoe. I could relate this adventure and laugh, with grotesque
representations of the way we had jumped up, of the leap through
the window, the rush pell-mell to the lakeshore, though underneath it all lay a fear I still did not dare dwell upon. The factory

too was presented as in a distorting mirror. I saw myself make
senseless movements with a serious expression. What I had found
cramping only a few days before now became a harlequinade.
Engineers and chemists stood bent over lists of figures, scratched
their heads, picked their noses and bored into their ears, rubbed
their shins with their shoes and their behinds with their index fingers as they murmured magic formulae. In the head office I stood
before the managing director, my father: I was inflated with effi-
ciency, with concern that the factory should flourish. I submitted
suggestions for the improvement of technical details in the printing process. He listened to me, nodded, spoke into three different
telephones on his desk at the same time, got his arm tangled in the
cord and mixed up the receivers, while outside in the courtyard
the office boy fell off his bicycle and the letters he was to take to
the post were scattered in the puddles. On one of the last days I
got into an argument with the production engineer. It had to do
with the choice of colors for a sample collection. In a flurry of
accusations and retorts we came out of the printing room on to
the staircase, stopped halfway up the stairs and shouted at one
another. Above us, on the landing, was a row of lavatories. Smoke
rising behind the partition of one of the cubicles proved that, con-
trary to regulations, a workman was taking a break for a quick
smoke. The door of another cubicle stood open, crude drawings of
sexual organs and coarse appellations scratched on the wall. The
machines throbbed in the finishing room below and the concrete
steps vibrated. We shook with anger, roared at each other, and
although we had long forgotten what we were arguing about, we
raised our hands. His face was inflamed and swollen. He was a
diabetic and his blood pressure was too high. His eyes popped out
of his face, saliva spurted from his mouth. He hit me first, then my
hand fell on his chubby cheeks and left white strips that gradually
turned dark red. We were both weeping. Even now tears
streamed from my eyes, but I was laughing. Max took his pipe
from his small nicotine-stained teeth and slapped his knee with
laughter. Then he got up and dressed in the mist of pipe smoke.
He combed his hair in front of the mirror, spoke of supper and the
bottle of wine he had bought to celebrate my arrival and my

birthday. Then, as on that first day in Prague, we went for a walk in the town.

We walked slowly down the main street as the shops were clos-ing, our coat collars turned up, our hands in our pockets in the crush of people, the rumbling traffic, the light of the multicolored advertisements and large overcrowded shop windows. We looked at the window displays and the pictures in cinema entrances, went under the bridge between the two skyscrapers, read the headlines in the evening papers, entered a bookshop, leafed through the latest publications, crossed the square in the center of the city and went to the bend in the river where the white steam-ers, which plied in droves during the summer, were moored in a mist of rain. We walked along the quay past the Royal Gardens and the Opera House and saw, stretching out like a screen on the other bank, the massive terraced palace façade with its sloping ramps. From the Knight's House we went across the narrow wooden footbridge next to the railway bridge, a train trundling slowly past us. And from the station square, where the blue street-cars rang their bells and the windows of the Continental Hotel glowed, we arrived back at the Drottninggata. We were no longer travelers but inhabitants of the city, and when I entered my room it was a room where I could make myself at home, a familiar precinct. I unpacked my case, put my underwear into the draw-ers, hung up my clothes, placed my shaving gear, toothbrushes and soapbox on the glass slab over the washbasin, put my paint-ing equipment on the table, set up the easel and filled the shelf on the wall with books. I had brought Hesse's *Steppenwolf*, Ham-sun's *Hunger* and *Pan*, Stendhal's *Lucien Leuwen*, Voltaire's *Can-dide*, Schaeffer's *Joseph Montfort*, Kubin's *The Other Side*, Heym's poems, Van Gogh's letters and Doerner's book on the technique of painting. Apart from these, a few art magazines, studies of Gauguin, Giorgione, Mantegna, Uccello, Dürer and Rousseau, and the great work on Breughel. I placed the folders with my drawings and the exercise books on the table and leaned my pictures against the walls and chairs. Max came in. He shoved a picture under the ceiling light and examined it, hands in his

pockets, rocking on the soles of his shoes. He nodded, went over
to the table, leafed through the drawings, puffed at his pipe.
These were the leisurely preliminaries for further examinations.
When we went to eat and I had put out the light, the room appeared for a second before I closed the door, interspersed with the
numerous broken reflections on the windows opposite, with swell-
ing glimmering patches crossed by arms of light. I followed Max
into the dining room, where the guests had assembled. The boardinghouse was inhabited for the most part by émigrés: I heard
German, Czech and Danish. At our table sat Herr Blei and Herr
Cimbal who were both there on business. Herr Blei was narrow
shouldered, meticulously dressed, pale and neat; Herr Cimbal was
large and vivacious, with his skull bald on top and a dented nose,
and next to him sat his Swedish friend, a pained expression on her
face, her dark hair knotted in a tight bun on her neck. This meal
was like all the subsequent meals we took in this room. We sat
here together, each of us torn from his past, many worried about
relatives left behind in occupied countries, many who had barely
escaped persecution, many robbed of their closest friends and relatives, all worried about how hard it was to get a job, of making
ends meet on meager allowances, all waiting for news, discussing
the situation and making prognostications. All these faces submerged after meals in their own worlds and when they reappeared we would greet each other, exchange a few words, sometimes jocular, sometimes hopeful if the newspapers had favorable
reports. We were anonymous to one another, recognized one another only as survivors of a common catastrophe and waited for
peace when we would again pass each other by without a sign.
There were moments in this communal existence when I guessed
something of the character of the people with whom I sat at table.
There was the weariness in Blei's face, his pursed lips, the way he
stooped as he carried his heavy case of samples across the landing,
and his forced smile when asked how business was going. There
was the change of expression in the face of Cimbal's friend: sometimes she laughed, she let her hair down so that she suddenly
seemed girl-like, and the rumors of some severe physical disability
with which she was afflicted could no longer be believed. New

guests appeared, others suddenly vanished, and coffee was taken
as usual in the hall, in wicker chairs between the potted plants
listening to the news from London. After the time signal some
remained behind for a while, reading newspapers, playing cards,
or bent over a chessboard. Max and I went back to my room.
Before the electricity was snapped on the room presented itself
again with its shimmering expanses of light and its rotating reflections. Max had brought the bottle of wine. He uncorked it, filled
two glasses and we clinked them. We stood face to face in the
middle of the room, slowly raised the glasses and drank. Then
Max turned to the pictures and drawings. He knew what my
painting had been like at the beginning and had seen something
in it with which he felt akin. Setting up one's pictures was to settle
and secure one's existence. The number of painted canvases
amazed me. And that was without the larger ones which were to
be sent on to me later in a packingcase. In my spare time, sometimes just from sunset to nightfall, I had painted and drawn and
written the manuscripts that lay in a folder. The pictures stood
there in their dark glassy colors and expressed something pent-up
and expectant. They depicted vital situations in which there
lurked a certain menace. They represented the climate of certain
suburban streets; and the scraped, blackened walls, the puddles
with their oily shimmering water, the cracks and blotches on
stones were full of significance. The shape in a doorway exuded
force. Rooms with threadbare carpets in the muted light of a window, faces popping up in a railway station or in the foliage of a
hothouse seemed almost intelligible and then receded. Parks, gardens, courtyards with figures between the trees, tried to warn and
evoke. Max asked about the source of my themes. He lifted up a
small portrait of a woman and we searched it for the impulses that
had produced it. The face reflected ideas of my adolescence, a
time of daydreams and romantic inspirations on evening walks in
Berlin, along the avenues of chestnuts, acacias and lime trees, in
the thick scent of the blossom, with tears in my eyes, my heart in
my throat; it held memories of my dead sister and the masklike
face of Katherine Hepburn. I know what you mean, said Max.
Those faces are like fetishes. I sometimes recall the face of

Michèle Morgan in *Le Quai des Brûmes*. When I reached Paris on my flight from Prague, I imagined meeting her, but of course nothing ever came of it. Our life is made up of relationships like that. *Le Quai des Brûmes* expressed our position, it was the great film that marked the end of a European epoch. The part of Michèle Morgan was our last dream on the eve of annihilation. Faces are images. Your pictures, he said, with their commonplace, often banal figurations, arouse a stream of thought. The bridge behind the park reminds me of the Karlsbrücke, except that it leads in an interminable perspective to the horizon; the paths originate on the banks of the Moldau while the stream has become an ocean, the Pacific Ocean, and the golden shimmer on the water makes me think of the Golden Gate I have seen in schoolbooks. The figures stand between the tree trunks as though they were playing puss-in-the-corner, and behind the bushes a little boat can be seen with colorful pennants on the mast. It looks as if it were rigged for departure. It seems to you that you must have been out of your mind when you were painting them, but your existence is caught fast in these pictures. At that Max drew a little wooden box from his pocket. He opened it and I saw that it contained the brightly colored counters of a game. We sat on the floor with our wine glasses, Max emptied the box and we made the round disks go hopping over the carpet.

After two decades I am trying to recreate a picture of the Stockholm of the first years of the war. But in my search for the paths that we once trod the image of a new, growing city forces itself on me. At that time we could still find parts of the city in which the atmosphere of earlier centuries was to be sensed. Today there is hardly a block of houses left where the façades have not changed their appearance, hardly a street or a square that conforms to our first impressions. Only here and there do I come across a gateway, a courtyard, an embankment wall, lying like fossilized remains in the city of today. And as the city has changed so have I. I look in amazement at a picture taken of me twenty years ago by a street photographer near the zoo on the square by the circus building. We are standing next to one another, Max and

I. I am wearing a long overcoat with a belt and a felt hat with a broad floppy brim. Max has on his narrow dark coat, its sleeves too short, and his bowler hat, and he has a pipe in his mouth. We are staring expectantly into the lens with wry smiles. The iron dragons' heads on the balustrade posts of the steps leading up to the circus are long since gone. Vanished, too, those old-fashioned, laughable aspects which at the time we assumed as a matter of course. Our thoughts, feelings and opinions, have altered, a thousandfold; written down tentatively twenty years later, they are no longer verifiable, for the only witness who could contradict me, the I of yesteryear, has weathered away, dissolved into my being. By writing I create a second life of fantasy where everything that was once blurred and uncertain assumes a false clarity. I walk through a city where I have lived for twenty years and participated in its development. I walk through the now vastly increased traffic, along torn-up streets, past glass skyscrapers, through the noise of pile drivers and pneumatic drills, the rattle of cement mixers. From the station I look across at the new buildings, the scaffoldings, the overpasses and widened streets. The Hotel Continental with its *art nouveau* ornamentation, its sinuous stucco, its heavy draperies behind the vaulted windows, has been demolished. All around lie the tunnel entrances of the newly constructed subway and the bus stop islands amid a forest of traffic signs. New bridges and broad urban motorways stretch across to the old town and the southern part of the city. The narrow wooden gangway next to the railway bridge with its fence that rattled whenever a train creaked past, has made way for a modern construction. You can sit on clean stone benches and enjoy the view across the river, the south bank of which is airily festooned with lights at night. Where dark paths once lay below the Knights' House there is now an incessant stream of cars on broad, asphalted thruways and across the sluice rises a traffic interchange on many levels. Only the iron framework of the iron elevator that goes to the top of the south bank still stands, like an old-fashioned monument in front of the shining blocks of newly erected business buildings. All around the southern part of the city excavating machinery clatters, warning signals and explosions resound. Modern blocks of flats overshadow the last of the old houses awaiting their destruction, with cracked and peeling whitewash and mournful windows. Arterial roads stretch along the quay walls of the Klara Canal, where there were once secret paths, boathouses and workshops and the half-sunk hull of an abandoned brig. And just as the narrow courtyards and alleys are blown up with giant gasps in the center of the city and the streets lash out with impudent thrusts and tear down towers and walls, so the outer suburbs spread and stretch, dust rises in thick clouds and blocks of buildings proliferate over the fields and woodlands and multiply into monotonous new rows of blocks, marooned among railway viaducts. A city of progress, of riches, a young, fresh city, renewing itself after having escaped the destruction of war. But there was still evidence of a quiet city, of more provincial aspect, with streets where Strindberg had wandered between bourgeois façades. We looked up at windows behind which we could imagine his face with its wicked, bristly beard. On our walks we came to know all the various parts of the city, in the late autumn, in the winter, in the spring thaw. We went past the developments near the airport to Rasunda, at that time a little town in a rural setting, now invaded by industrial buildings and functional cooperative apartment houses. From the south bank of the city we climbed up to the seventeenth century wooden houses with their overgrown gardens, their barns and courtyards, and on to the Hammarby docks, where bare cliffs and woods had once formed the city boundary. We strolled through the deserted regions behind the Karlberg Military Academy and the wild wasteland at the bend of the river, now built-up and inhabited by a new generation. We spent hours in the zoo and in the Skansen park among the bears, the sea lions, the elk and the wolves. We leaned on the brass rail in front of the polar grotto in the Zoological Museum. In a curiously smoky light, as I like to think I remember it, were hunters doing battle with polar bears. I clearly remember seeing the animal's raised paws before me, the hunter aiming his gun to shoot, and the other hunter lying wounded in the snow. The grotto is still there, unchanged. I go into the low dark room, behind the glassy walls of which is an East Greenland ravine, gorgelike. As I thought, the light is dim and flickering, like the light above the pictures in the peepshows of my childhood. But there is no sign of a dramatic battle. In the foreground lies a slumbering polar bear, a few birds are nesting in the cliffs, on either side a white hare sits listening, ready to leap away, while a polar wolf creeps up on it; primeval tree trunks loom up in the middle of the ravine, a few shaggy bison behind them. Dry grass and moss grow in the sand of the valley that opens out on the Arctic Ocean in the background. Profound peace and complete timelessness prevail. Supported by the brass rail I gaze into the landscape in the uncertain light. Max stands next to me, as motionless as I, then I hear him give a sigh of admiration. We go up the winding wooden stairs into the rotunda where all around a panorama of the northern animal kingdom is shown in elaborately constructed woods, boulders and swamps, between rocks and hills, by mountain tarns and on the seashore. Slowly we move about within the ring of this illusion of Nature, coming to a halt again and again at the rail, held by the different views. We begin to speak of the relationship between these waxworks and my pictures. Even in the museum of the city where I had lived as a child the showcases had impressed me with their groups of African tribes, the orangutan family, the stuffed crocodiles, snakes and birds of paradise. As I lay in the attic in front of my landscapes constructed with clay and twigs and populated with lead soldiers the pictorial element was already there, the spellbound unique situation. And later I derived my colors from the fairground booth, with the stereoscopic effects and the magic lantern slides.

Confronted by my largest picture, of an open-air concert, I thought of the effect it had had in my parents' house. I can't look at it, my mother had said, when I was working on it in my room. Once she came in with my sister who turned and asked why the faces in the picture looked so ghastly. People did not look like that, what sort of faces were they? My mother answered: Oh, don't ask so many questions, how should I know. My sister did not ask me. It was as though I were not there. She saw me among the concertizers in the garden, sitting at the harpsichord with a

twisted look on my face, the inmate of a lunatic asylum. Now I
stood with Max in front of the picture and we discussed how such
a picture could be produced in a bourgeois household, the development of a rebel characterized by constant friction and disagree-
ment. Everything he is offered arouses his displeasure, he flees
from the waves of warmth into a self-elected frigidity, he rejects
security in favor of uncertainty, preferring indigence to comfortable well-cared-for rooms. Characteristics asserted themselves
which were like chemical reactions wherein no fusion could occur,
only bitterly reeking, seething separation. With the help of a few
sketchbooks, from my first years at school, preserved among my
manuscripts, we looked into the various stages of my development. To begin with we saw the face of Jackie Coogan in Chaplin's film *The Kid.* I could hardly read or write then. I knew nothing about art and literature, but this figure presented a mirror in
which I could identify myself. In Jackie Coogan I saw myself
rushing across the street, clambering up walls, in patched trousers
several sizes too large, and with long hair and a rakish sports cap
set askew. In a garden sandpit I convinced my playmates that
Jackie Coogan was a close friend of mine. Two years later I came
across Douglas Fairbanks in *The Thief of Baghdad.* I opened the
book full of sketches of episodes from this film. The title page was
embellished by a picture of the star cut out of a newspaper and
colored with crayons. He was half naked, a red cloth on his black
curly hair, golden rings in his ears and, as he laughed, he displayed his strong white teeth. Framed, numbered and outlined in
pencil there followed events which never ceased to haunt me. The
Thief of Baghdad dived into the depths of the ocean and came to
a treasure chest. He opened the chest and an octopus appeared.
He struggled with the octopus, thrust his knife into its belly and a
black cloud oozed out. He found the princess in the underwater
cavern. He rode a magic horse and flew through the air on it. He
crept into the Sultan's palace and searched for the princess. He
overpowered guards and warriors, annihilated armies and conjured up new armies. In a moment of breathless tension he
pressed the dagger into the naked back of Anna May Wong, the
Chinese slavegirl. Then there was the great scene in the palace,

and I had set down its various climaxes in one panoramic view. Below, at the right of the hall which I gazed down on, were two empty chairs and an empty table; in the middle of the room the Sultan was enthroned, surrounded by his counselors, and from his mouth issued the decree: Lash him with whips and throw him to the apes. On the left could be seen the Thief of Baghdad, his arms tied behind his back, surrounded by men with raised whips, and, further down, between the open walls of a bedchamber, was the princess in a long transparent gown. I once wanted to live like the Thief of Baghdad, I wanted to overcome all obstacles wildly and adventurously, to laugh at mortal dangers, to defeat all enemies and to find the treasure chest, to release the princess and win her for myself. Later, when I had already discovered books, painting and music, I saw Murnau's film *Tabu*. There the cheerful boldness of the Thief of Baghdad had given way to the unattainable, and I was constantly musing over the final scene when the hero swims into the open sea after his abducted beloved and sinks ever further back behind the boat until, overcome by exhaustion, he drowns, and finally only his hand is sticking out of the water.

In his urge to discover permanent roots and coherence Max wondered whether my parents or ancestors had had any artistic bent. I knew only of one remark my father had made: that in his youth he had often gone to the opera in Vienna. As a relic of this period there hung over his desk a lithograph of the opera house in a rainy evening mood, people under umbrellas rushing to the entrance, lines of hansom cabs driving by and festive street lamps reflected in the damp cobbles. This picture reminded my father of hours of artistic enjoyment. The sensitivity with which he tested the textiles and inspected the designs were also symptomatic of an artistic nature. I noticed his elegant fingers gliding tenderly and expertly over the fabrics, scratching and picking at them. Before marrying my father my mother had been an actress for several years and all the playbills showed that she had taken leading roles under Reinhardt. She was a tragedienne, a striking figure with her tall body, dark eyes and black hair. She used to tell how, in a mystery play in which she was the abbess, she had to let out a scream. She said that she found the exact pitch of this scream with such accuracy each time that the members of the orchestra used to tune their instruments to it. In the heyday of German theater she had acted with Moissi, Kortner and Bassermann. Murnau had been one of her closest friends. She kept letters and drawings from him and she gave me a head in clay he had sculpted and painted. The head, which looked like a self-portrait, stood for a long time in my room. I saw him as my ideal father, after my mother had once hinted that she might have married him and I thought that one day this stranger would understand me. The photograph of the last scene of *Tabu,* with its selfless departure, hung over my bed as the focal point of a collection of reproductions cut out of newspapers and magazines, representing Florentine gardens, figureheads from galleons, knights in tournament armor, parrots and tropical plants, Giorgione's "Three Philosophers," Dürer's "Melancholia," Altdorfer's "St. George and the Dragon," the eagles and devils of the Isenheimer Altar, Balinese gamelang players and girl dancers in a Negro ballet. There was no response in our house to the precious objects which I had found, and with which I hid myself in my room, bristling with African spears, Japanese masks, South Sea daggers and dried swordfish. My father's brief passion for Mahler and Wagner had passed. My mother's need for self-expression had been stifled. Books were bought and read, but only the fashionable works that belong on any middle-class bookshelf. The odd exception that found its way in by mistake to these respectable bookshelves remained unopened. On the radio only light music was permitted, and the few phonograph records that were bought consisted of a couple of current hits, operatic tunes, one movement from the Moonlight Sonata and the *Thieving Magpie* overture. Many pictures hung on the walls, flower paintings and oil portraits, color prints and etchings, but not a single work that displayed any force or individuality, or suggested a personal choice. Like the furniture, the curtains, wallpaper and carpets, the vases, glasses and cutlery, everything came from the big clearance sales. To Max I disclaimed membership of a family just as I had disputed my membership of a nation and a race. Only in friendship or a love affair,

or in my encounter with works of art did I desire to find any sense
of kinship.

Max suggested that we pay a visit to Anatol, a painter we had
known in Prague who, after his flight, had settled down here. Anatol was a few years older than I. Before me he had attended the
same class in the Academy of Arts, had by then already achieved
recognition and commented with gentle sarcasm on my old-fashioned style. I remembered an exhibition of his paintings in his
studio in Prague. His colors were mainly glazed and golden. His
works consisted of signs from the Cabala and astrology, geometrical forms and dotted lines, as well as individual parts of the body
which were magically expressive. I felt that he too borrowed from
the Old Masters, but that his compositions which had been influ-
enced by Bosch, Arcimboldo and Monsu had become contemporary as a result of his study of Chirico and Chagall. We went into
Anatol's room, in the basement of a large apartment house. Beyond the window the heads and umbrellas of passersby moved
unsteadily past in a smother of driven snow. The little room was
crammed so full of pictures that we had to stand by the door at
the edge of the bed. The narrowness of the room was my first
impression: it was impossible to move. Anatol stood in front of us
between the bed and the cupboard near the chair that he used as
an easel. On the chair lay tubes and brushes and newspapers
thickly smeared with paint. Anatol was thickset and broad-shouldered, his neck short and powerful and his face round and all big
planes, with heavy, rather mournful features. He was bald from
his forehead to the middle of his cranium, on top of which, in the
harsh light of the bulb hanging from the ceiling, a circular depression was outlined. His ears were small and underdeveloped. His
thin red hair curled at his neck and temples. In the nicotine-
stained fingers of his pale fleshy hand he held the cigarettes he
chain smoked, although he was periodically convulsed by fits of
coughing that colored his face dark red and drew tears from his
eyes. The pictures stood stacked on the wardrobe, on the chest-of-
drawers and against the wall. A small table by the window was
covered in drawings and colored sketches, bottles, glasses and

boxes. There were bundles of painted papers on the bed, too. Anatol showed us a selection of his pictures. He knew where every picture was. He lifted it out from its pile, leaned it against the chair, and showed us how he had developed from his years in Prague up to the present. The golden tone soon disappeared and decorative pastel colors, soon broke through the varnish. After seeing a couple of canvases we had quite forgotten the size of the room and by the time we left we were no longer even aware of being cramped. The walls had been overpowered, the sense of confinement was meaningless. The pictures, some of them in large formats, were full of visions from the world of a fugitive. In the last Prague period the compositions were permeated by a heavy melancholy, full of ideas of transience and destruction, full of departures and premonitions of disaster. In the abstract spaces, reminiscent of alchemists' parlors and torture chambers, were heaps of objects partly like pieces of furniture, and partly like figures, automata, machines or architectural fragments. The feeling of spatial closure was there, the hallucinations were taking place under a roof. Details stood out from the shapes or fixtures—an hourglass, a cog wheel, a pair of compasses, a wall clock with a swinging pendulum, a fish, a burning candle, a woman's weeping face, a striding foot, a table leg, a door, a gate, a fragment of a landscape, a playing card, a goblet, a pair of tongs, a knife, a baroque sculpture—and all of it brought Prague to mind, a medieval, golemesque Prague. In the later pictures, which had been painted after the flight, space had opened up. There was no longer any support or protection; it was all in the open. The figures had become more human, not through acquiring limbs and features but because of their pain, their heavy burden. They had lost everything mechanical. The organisms of the pictures consisted now only of feelings and thoughts. You could identify the thoughts with objects of everyday life: they were like the bedclothes, frying pans and chamber pots of the refugees. The feelings were represented by whirling splashes of color, quivering heaps of dots or swarms of wedges. That night in the boardinghouse I was still haunted by these pictures. The pictures had risen above the absurdly small room in triumph. They lived in the pres-

ent. Their painter stood in a crumbling world. He neither hid nor
spared himself but delivered himself up: he stood in the rain of
ashes. His face, his leg, his arm appeared momentarily in the
whirl of ruins. Pale and obsessed he stared out in the direction of
flight, probing the chaos with his gaze. He was the Wandering
Jew: he belonged to a race and stood by the persecuted while my
pictures lay under thick bell jars in a vacuum. There was a violence about Anatol's pictures: they ripped the world open. My
paintings covered it over and kept it secret. Through the rumble
of traffic in the street below I heard another rumbling, of waves,
motors, tank-trucks, marching feet, there they marched in the dust
of the roads, tired, dirty and moving against them, in endless columns, with wagons and cattle, with sick and dying, with groan-
ings and screamings, came the refugees, and there were the va-
cantly staring faces of the old, the faces of mothers bent over their
children, and villages burned, woods and fields were torn up by
bomb bursts, there was a howling in the air, a whistling, bursting,
audible in foxhole, in cellar, in bunker, and I tried to imagine how
it was to lie amid shelling in the fields, in stony places, inside the
steely armor of a ship, how it was to lie penned in among the
pipes and wheels of a submarine, as water poured in, as I had
seen it in old film epics, as the water rose, as the head still lay free
between water and bulkhead, and the water reaching the mouth,
I tried to imagine it, we had played it as children, in the coalbin
down in the cellar, and I tried to imagine how it was to crawl
away to safety in the woods, in the shell-riddled city, I had seen it
in the newsreels, and I had pretended to do it in play, crawling
through courtyards and streets, imitating shots, being wounded,
letting out death cries, and everywhere was a creeping up on one
another, a shooting of one another, we had been prepared for it at
school during recess hours, we were even allowed to hold the
chattering cartridge belt of the machine gun ourselves, and then
we were taught the art of taking cover, of tracking others safely,
taught the art of bayonet-sticking, only I had not learned enough,
I had sneaked off, evaded the teaching, had taken off and hidden,
and there they crawled away at each other, and next it was hand-
to-hand combat in the name of the great and sacred cause, knife

in the throat, in the bowels, thumb in the eye, it had to be learned, one had to know how it was done, where the stab is most effective, down in there with the bayonet, then up and out, slitting the belly open with bluishly slippery bowels welling out, and the bag of stomach, full of grits, I tried to imagine how it was, sticking a knife into a living body and hearing the crunch on bone, and I tried to imagine how it was to get a knife in your own ribs or in your own throat, I tried to imagine how it felt when the blood rushed out of your own throat or when your own abdomen was a ripped wet mass, how it was, the fraction of a second in which the bullet struck your own head, and again anticipatory images sprang to mind from films and books, of operations with pocketknives without anesthetic, of firing squad executions and hangings, and I thought of my father, how he had experienced such things, lying in a clay shell hole with a belly wound, I stood in my boardinghouse room in Stockholm, above the evening traffic rush in the Drottninggata, and tried to understand what the others out there must have been through, what others had endured, bound together in the madness of a common fate, I saw them crawling along toward each other, the brave ones, friend and foe, cannon fodder of changing ideals, saw how they murdered each other, how they made common cause so as to fall upon others, with whom they in turn again compacted, to set upon new adversaries. All I wanted was to defend my flight, my cowardice; I did not want to belong to any race, ideal, city or language, and I wanted to see strength in my detachment alone.

The incessant pressure from the menace, the faint horror that we constantly carried about at the back of our minds, was part of our life. I stood by the easel in my room and painted and when Max asked me what I would do if the enemy invaded the country I could not think of an answer. I would certainly do something, I thought, I would try to escape or defend myself, I would sneak away or let myself be killed. In my work, too, I lived in a vast unbounded space. I was open to all possibilities without ever committing myself in any one direction. Anatol came to see me and his criticism no longer contained the condescension of senior-

ity and success. He was full of sympathy and interest, singled out
the positive qualities in formal details but demonstrated in broad
vigorous gestures the changes he had in mind. He remolded the
pictures which, in his view, did not seem to belong to our age, he
adjusted the proportions, indicated expressive contours and distortions with his wide emphatic thumb and suggested I use
brighter colors and work with rougher textures, larger surfaces. In
the beginning painting had been a simple, matter-of-fact accomplishment. Pictures had come about without my having to search
for them. I had drawn, painted and written in harmony with my
thoughts and as naturally as breathing. There had been no other
laws of style and form than the urge to come as close as possible
to my inspirations. I had lived in my withdrawnness, a contemporary of Breughel, had lived on imaginary medieval farmsteads
and monasteries, among strolling players and the tinkling of the
leper's bell. Max felt that my inturnedness was connected with the
lack of a natural developmental background, but this also I had to
disavow. The only milieu I had wanted was the one I created for
myself, I had been allowed to cut out and make the most of it, or
die in the attempt. But what was coming out of me now in pictures was something that could not be conjured away. Leaving
the family had not led to the creative explosions I had expected.
On the planes of my paintings arose only the dirt and scrap of the
shining visions that could arise out there in the city. The lamp I
had screwed on to the easel shone hard and sharp over scratchy
smeared lines. I closed the tubes of paint and washed the brushes,
and in my mind I started a conversation with Max. What I
wanted to say was just as formless as the pictures. The words that
sprang to mind explained nothing. Beneath them lay an inarticulate stammer. But there was an exact term for every vague idea
that haunted me, everything that had happened could be communicated. There was nothing that lay outside the realm of the
comprehensible. The greatest adventure was to produce an
unequivocal, exact world. I wanted to sweep away the mystical,
which was nothing but ideas half thought through, feelings half
thought through, feelings half felt, and experiences feebly evaded.
Everything can be explained, I wanted to say, as I betook myself

to Max Bernsdorf's room. My existence, my origins, my death, eternity, for all these there is an explanation, otherwise life could not go on, I can place my faith in all things, when I am wide awake all things are understandable, even though my intelligence may not be equal to it. Everything is given, I need not put on an act, need not rack my brains, it is enough to hang onto the objectively real, on what presents itself to me, on what I can lay my hands on. That was what I wanted to say but the words would not come out; it was like a flash of lightning, like a brief convulsion, and I went through the hall where a few guests still sat discussing the latest radio reports. I heard Max talking behind his door. He sounded excited. A woman's voice answered, I stopped and listened. Their words seemed to be reproaches and accusations. There was something breathless and pleading in the woman's voice, but it could suddenly become dangerously hard. Behind the door lay a hidden world belonging to Max. I wanted to see him there, in that world of his, and I knocked. After a short silence Max opened the door, his face pale and distraught, and let me in. The woman, who was standing at the window, turned toward us. She was tall, slim and angular, with dark eyes and broad prominent cheekbones, and a cloud of parted black hair. She was wearing a dark blue sleeveless dress. Her arms were thin, the hands big and worn by work. Her whole appearance radiated nervous tension. Her mouth twitched and she tossed her hair back violently. Max picked up books and newspapers at random, put them away again, rubbed his hands and sheltered behind his pipe. As he scraped it out, filled it, lit it and puffed the smoke out he regained his composure. This is Erika, he said. In the woman's face was an expression as much as saying, be on my side, inviting me to betray Max. Wildly she pulled on her jacket and overcoat while Max, his face pale, went up to her and begged her not to go. You know I must go, she said, put lipstick on her mouth and dabbed powder on forehead and cheeks. Max clamped his teeth on his pipe. Breathing heavily and bringing out her words in fits and starts Erika spoke of a friend who was waiting for her, and when Max put out a hand to hold her back she burst into an affected laugh which rose a whole octave. Flaunting her victory, erect and swing-

ing back her mane of hair, she left the room enveloped in a sweet
poisonous scent. On several occasions I gained an insight into the
duel Max was fighting with her, and each round ended with her
triumphant exit and Max Bernsdorf's humiliation. Right up to his
departure for America he courted her and even hoped that she
would later follow him to New York. Erika was hardly older than
I. She had followed the man she lived with into exile. I once saw
her with him in the street. He was blond and boyish and she hung
laughing on his arm: her gait and voice were childish and there
was nothing of her other self which she revealed to Max. When I
returned from this encounter I went to see Max, pacing his room,
lostness written on his face. I could always tell from his face when
he had met Erika, and now, from his impatience and restlessness,
I knew that he was expecting her. He sometimes had to wait for
hours before the telephone call that ended with her refusal. There
he sat among the palm trees outside with a chalky blotchy gray
face and listened to her talking, talking endlessly. He would then
get up with a deep sigh. This here was something to be grasped.
These conflicts had human proportions. The war took place in a
world of giants and demons, but these were events in everyday
labyrinths and impressions could be retained, while events from
the scenes of the war remained inconceivable. Hoderer's face was
also close and clear. It had the agonized expression of someone
gasping for breath. Hoderer had fled from Berlin. He was a doctor
and had been director of a Social Welfare clinic. Like other
émigré doctors and scholars he was not allowed to practice. Because of chauvinistic arrogance and fear of competition foreign
workers were only permitted to do routine clerical work. His
gradual spiritual asphyxiation was expressed by the asthma that
had caused him to lapse into inactivity. Hoderer's face swelled in
his fits of coughing, the veins in his neck stood out, his skin turned
blue and drops of sweat rolled down his temples. Although his
eyes popped out of their sockets and saliva trickled down his chin
his face never lost its composure and patience. His wife and
friends used to ignore the attack. She merely handed him the
leather bag with the syringe. The conversation continued and no
one looked at him as, with trembling hands, he broke the am-

poule, filled the syringe and stuck the needle into his arm. While the others overlooked his ill health I could not take my eyes off him, and his eyes met mine with an expression of sympathy and experience, as if it were I who was in need of help. In such circumstances my neutrality was indefensible.

Now my ears are free to hear; I can remember words addressed to me at that time, cries meant to wake me up, voices telling me that other people were there, none of which got through to me in my endless, shapeless conversation with myself. We met Else on the hills of the Skansen Park, by the sea lion basin. We stood in the snow, breath steaming in the cold air, the pointed heads of the sea lions poking through the lumps of ice, their glistening eyes laughing, their nostrils snorting. Else stood expectantly at the lower edge of the basin. Max nudged me, whispering encouragement, and I went up to her in the crunching snow. Then she came with us to the stand where mulled wine was sold. After we had drunk the sweet liquid we walked to the tropical house and interpreted the cries of the white cockatoos, who mocked us with shrill screams, hello, hello, how goes it, hello, hello, still with us, still on the ball, hello, hello, tomorrow's another day. In the evening Else awaited me in her room. The fire was burning in the tiled stove. There was wine. The flames behind the open door of the stove lit up the bed. The body of a woman I had never known even existed until today lay there for the taking. As I undressed and lay down beside her I had the old idea that it was impossible to embrace a strange body and penetrate it. I looked into her face; her mouth was curiously curved, like a Javanese dance mask. She knew nothing about me, but she waited for my kisses with a smile on the corners of her lips. She put her hand on my skin. This was the simple, matter-of-fact kind of thing I had to get used to. This was the physical world, which was my home. Else knew the rules of the game. I tried to guess them. We had chosen one another so as not to spend this evening alone. By touching each other we could become convinced of our proximity. Where we came from, what we did was meaningless, we did not need to talk, had no need of the values we gave to our lives. In our freedom we had met by chance, we chose the community of this night and caressed each other's skin. We felt each other all over. The radiations of the other skin penetrated my skin, the frontiers of one's own perception dissolved until everything became mutual. Our movements were slow, devoid of lust. All thoughts and secondary considerations had been banished. There was nothing but delight in the texture of our flesh and nerves. Only once, briefly, was I overcome by a sense of alienation and for a second I saw myself in union with the other body, her thigh lying over my hip, my penis enveloped in the softness of her womb, but then I lost consciousness of myself again as I met her half-closed eyes and felt her gasps on my mouth. Later, when we washed under the shower in the bathroom, there was already something of the normality of a routine involvement in each other's life. Else offered me her home, her constant presence, she fried eggs and bacon in the kitchen, boiled some coffee and tried to get some dance music on the radio. For the first time since my escape I saw that I was living my own life, that I had nothing more to do with the forces which had shaped my adolescence. But at night, as Else slept next to me, the possibility of contentment disappeared. I thrust back her arm which lay heavily on my chest. She sighed deeply in her sleep and tried to embrace me again, to hold me tight, then sank back close beside me in animal-like confidence. But I backed away from her, lay on the edge of the bed and looked across the room, the furniture faintly distinguishable in the glow from the stove. The massive sideboard, a family heirloom with superstructure, columns and pinnacles, in the semidarkness looked like the front of a Gothic cathedral. The lamps had silk shades. The lid of the piano was up and sheets of music lay open so that she could play to me. There were no books, only a few magazines. Numerous porcelain figures adorned the window ledge, the table, the top of the stove: little dogs, kittens, ballerinas, a white doe. On the floor was a speckled carpet which Else had bought on installment. In the dark stood a sewing basket with some needlework on it. She would darn my socks; I would sit next to her and watch her knit. We would listen to light music on the radio; she would tell me about the latest events in her office; I would read the papers. There she lay beside me, a stranger, breathing calmly and evenly. The alarm clock jangled, Else got up, drew the curtains and, through the window, past the snow-covered trees, I saw the gravestones of the old Jewish cemetery. I went back to the boardinghouse in the whirling snow. The warnings of the snow shovelers rang out everywhere, lumps of snow were shoved off the roofs and burst dustily in the streets. Muffled pedestrians stamped along between high walls of snow and the cars jerked slowly forward with clanking chains on their wheels. I tried to tell Max, who was lying in bed in his room, something of my night's experience. I pictured to myself this play of bodies, that had come to pass without real knowledge of each other, without questions about each other's backgrounds, that for one night had achieved an independent value of its own, that had actually signified no more than the discovery of zones of the skin, of the blood's warmth, of the nerves' excitability. The fact that we knew nothing about one another added to the charm of the game. This lack of knowledge lasted for a few hours, but then the anonymity faded, we had defined each other and the next step was a confrontation of our words and thoughts. Only now could one ask whether the prerequisites for mutual understanding existed and whether we could see each other again. Because the second time the body alone would not be enough, and sympathy, devotion and passion could only come about when the other's thoughts, aims and way of life were attractive. Max claimed to see signs of contempt in this way of looking at it. He said it would never be possible for me to love if I expected my partner to understand the art of the fugue, or be able to read Joyce. He cited Van Gogh, whose maturity as a painter went hand in hand with his openness toward afflicted and humble people. He reminded me of Van Gogh's life with the prostitute. I saw this as self-flagellation, a kind of religiosity, a self-sacrifice that Dostoevski had also glorified, and in which people had clung fast to each other in darkness. Max charged me with coldness, and in it lay the same accusation he had expressed about my refusal to take a political stand. I wanted to turn away from meltings of the heart, from self-surrender and crawlings back to the Cross, to resist the pressure toward hypocrisy, toward conformity, but the narrow, smoke-

filled room suddenly lost its tenability, the possibility of orienta-
tion vanished and for a few seconds I did not know what city it
was from which the monstrous surf-sound of the traffic was coming up to me. I felt weak at the knees as I returned to reality. Max
lay in bed, huddled in his faded green dressing gown, and smoke
rose from his pipe. Among the newspapers lay pieces of paper
with scribbled verses, dictionaries and a few tattered volumes I
had already seen in Prague, English translations from ancient Persian, the epics of Firdausi, written in exile after he had escaped
from the Shah's threat to throw him before the elephants. For
years Max Bernsdorf had been working on an imitation of this
work.

His seat on a plane to New York had been booked. He had been
given his visa, and had taken it grimly and mulishly, with the
remark that it had come a year too late. The exhibition of my
pictures which took place shortly before his departure was not
intended as a manifestation of my presence in this city but rather
as a parting gift to Max. In the old Exhibition Hall in Brunkeberg
Square, with the old stalls of the vegetable market which have
now long since made way for the geometrical platforms of the bus
station, I hung my pictures in the pillared balustraded room—
now a showroom for electric stoves and refrigerators. After hanging the pictures I stood with Max in the middle of the room. His
narrow brown coat was open. His hands thrust in his trouser
pockets, he swayed gently on the soles of his shoes. That evening
our recent disagreements were over. In the past weeks Max had
become Else's advocate. She was expecting a child from me and
as I did nothing about it she turned to him, and he prescribed
home remedies, also took her to bed, with the fatherly explanation
that violent coition might still induce menstruation. She is expecting a child: you are the father, said Max, gripping my shoulders
and shaking me. I did not ask what she was doing about it. I
turned away from her face with her mouth frozen in a permanent
smile, with her eyes which wanted not to accuse but to forgive.
That evening we stood amid the encircling pictures, in none of
which was there any sign of possible breakthrough and direction

to the future, the whole tenor of them led to only one conclusion. Even before showing my pictures to the city I was fed up with them. They were worn out and stale. Max pointed to one of the earliest of them, a little study of moss and fern leaves. This picture meant most to him, he said. I saw how far I myself had grown away from this picture and how impossible it was ever again to achieve the stillness and composure of this piece of miniature craftsmanship. I took the picture off the wall and presented it to him, and it was as if a draft of fresh air had broken through the gap in the row of pictures, and a bubbling and a rushing pressed in, and behind the thin taut skin of the pictures lay a chaos, where there were no signposts, only a raging and screaming, a despair which the painted figures rejected with gestures of horror. Max fell silent, and reproached me no more. We stood here like travelers after we had walked a piece of the road together, separation was imminent, and I had to go it alone in my search for the absolute. The parting was more final than I had ever imagined, for to me it meant being done with a process the goal of which had been self-destruction. I was born during a war and I was trained for the next war, I told Max, and I must reject all this if I am ever to succeed with another piece of work. Max reminded me of the power he saw stored in my pictures. With the uncertainty of a new life in New York before him, a life that would lead him into dingy hotel rooms overlooking back courtyards he thought of my future work.

Dürer portrays the Prodigal Son wringing his hands in entreaty among pigs crowded about the trough. The yard is enclosed by sheds and barns with planks stacked against the walls. The son has returned to the castle of home. He kneels in the muck with the pigs, who grunt as they grub in their feed. He raises his hands and asks forgiveness for the presumption of his attempted flight. By returning he acknowledges that he has done wrong and that those who stayed at home were right. He humbly waits for the good father to come out of the house and lead him back to the table his good mother has laid. The face of the Prodigal is full of hope for forgiveness. Father and mother appear, raise the son from his degradation and take him into the house, where all the lights are burning to celebrate his arrival. His old room is ready for him, the bed is made, a bath has been prepared for him to wash his grimy body. That night he lies in the soft covers while out on the landing the grandfather clock with its sunlike face strains and chimes the hour, creaking, grinding and rattling the heavy chains so he feels he has never been away from home.

The exhibition in March 1941 had consumed my last savings. Nothing had been sold, there were few visitors and the critics' attitude rejective. The pictures were packed away in boxes and only the world behind them existed. I lay in my room and was left alone. My brothers and my sister were on the verge of escaping from the family. From my hideout I was aware of the disintegration going on in the various parts of the house. There were the so-called frank discussions in grinding voices, which were supposed to teach a lesson to my sister, who had found a man she wanted to marry. And when all the admonitions, common sense and assurances that it was only for her own good that they were imploring her had no effect, and my sister was not prepared to give up her unfortunate choice, the voices gradually became shouts and exclamations of horror. Once I was startled by a clatter. I ran down the stairs and saw my sister lying among the broken crockery in the dining-room and in the door my mother's face a mask of speechless horror. That my sister should have stumbled over the threshold and dropped the tray of glasses and plates instead of putting it on the table was, in my mother's opinion, a violent assault on her home. She buried her face in her hands, swayed and reeled. I dragged her to the sofa and sat her down. As my sister, her tear-streaked face telling of quarrels in the kitchen before her fall, swept up the pieces, I sat next to my mother, and cooled her brow with wet towels. Through the window I could see the gardener in the twilight digging up the fat black earth between the raspberry bushes. On other days I realized what was happening to my brother Gregor. What in my case had bored and grubbed its way slowly to the surface, expressed itself in him sharply and ruthlessly. My years of effort had had their effect on him and stimu-

lated him to rebel earlier than I had. Even when he was only
sixteen he stayed out for days and nights at a time and I heard his
savage answers to my father's questions with satisfaction. But
then I witnessed a scene that I wanted to forget, words I wish I
had never heard but which existed and could no longer be denied.
I heard a din in my brother's room, I went out on to the landing
and listened to him and my father behind the door yelling at each
other. They were both running around the room. My father
panted and tried to grab hold of him but Gregor tore himself free.
Chairs were being knocked over. Then my father shouted twice:
You bloody Jewish lout, you bloody Jewish lout! Outside lay the
farmyard and the grunting pigs and in the house Abraham was
damning his own race.

  During the day I was again working at the factory but several
times a week I spent an hour in the morning under analysis which
was to last for the next few months. I decided to do this after
reading about the death of the poetess Karin Boye in the newspaper. She had taken an overdose of sleeping pills and had frozen to
death on a hill in the outskirts of the town, leaning against a cliff,
looking out through the bare woods on to the lake with its islands.
During the last years of her life she had lived with a doctor who
resided in the town and whose psychoanalytical writings I knew.
Baahl was a pioneer of this science and a controversial personality. I called on him in his old house by the municipal pond. The
walls of the room where he received me were covered with books
and pictures. Ivy glimmered in the sun in front of his windows.
Baahl sat in his armchair like a Chinese sage, with white hair, a
little white beard, narrow eyes surrounded by wrinkles and sensitive hands, his fingertips touching meditatively. I lay on the sofa
and attained a freedom, a relaxation at the depths of which I felt I
was being rocked in a swing. We spoke first about Karin Boye,
whose tiny face, painfully alert and framed by black hair, I knew
from photographs. In her last book, *Kallocain,* the "beauty drug,"
she had described her vision of the future. But she had not been
able to awaken from the nightmare of the present. Her awareness
of destruction had become too powerful. Her personal conflicts

were insoluble and in a doomed world she foresaw her own downfall. London was being shattered by air raids, Virginia Woolf had killed herself, Yugoslavia and Greece had fallen, the pass of Thermopylae broken, the English troops defeated; rumors about mass executions and concentration camps had found their way across the frontiers, refugees were streaming in from Norway and Denmark, waves of suicide spread through the conquered Baltic states and in screaming speeches the German Fuehrer promised that the decisive moment would soon arrive. How could one work under such pressure? Was not every written word, every color set on canvas a presumptuousness in the face of suffering for which there was no longer any bound. Baahl sat in front of me with the resignation of the past master. His life was fulfilled and full of ripeness, while I was struggling to find a catch hold to hang onto. I expected no drastic transformations, no electrifying discoveries, all I wanted was a careful analysis and comparison, wanted to recognize relationships, wanted to know what had happened to me. By being directed at someone else my words were submitted to constant scrutiny. It was a monologue that made me alert, and which, in slow circlings and underminings, clarified much for me. In this provincial industrial city, whose atmosphere was shot through with mistrust and marked devotion to work, the hours in Baahl's office were a relief, and yet even here there was a reluctance, a feeling of inferiority and helplessness. The experienced old man in the armchair accepted everything I said. Nothing would have shocked him, and yet he seemed to belong to my parents' world rather than to my own world of entanglements. When I expressed hatred and scorn for my mother and father I sensed from his indifference that for him these were only my illusions, and that he felt great solidarity with the established, the ambitious and hard working, those who maintained a house and home. He listened to me and condemned nothing, but behind his endless patience seemed to lie the expectation that I would some time find my way back to an orderly existence. In our conversation it was not only the world of dissolution and the world of serenity that confronted each other: the stranded Central European, driven about by crises, wars and persecutions, was con-

fronted by the native of a peaceful country, a man deeply rooted
in the natural setting of his homeland. Baahl led a life of seclusion: he was an expert on birds, fish and plants, on folk stories and
old songs, he was a singer and lute player and a secret poet. He
sat back in his armchair and listened to me with all the experience
of a city doctor whose office had witnessed the afflictions and
grievances of countless people. I was no stranger, no undesirable
alien in this room. I was accepted unreservedly. But sometimes I
noticed that I could go no further, that my words no longer
reached him, I sensed a fever and decay within me which I could
not communicate to him, because I believed he could not understand it. At these frontier posts he tried to simplify my life as if he
wanted to abrogate its dangers and inner strife. But perhaps I was
mistaken, perhaps it was only I who shrank back before danger.
At times I could express nothing more. Then I felt as if I had not
said anything, as if I had chatted about things with which I had
long been familiar. And in the ensuing silence he would take up
his lute and sing me one of his songs. I understood that he wanted
to comfort and calm me, but to me he seemed naïve, I grew furious with such a childish gesture in the face of my desperate pre-
dicament. I could not abandon my revolt, but lulled myself into a
mood of treacherous conciliation, and saw in his naïvety the
naïvety of the sage, firm in his belief, who sings a paean of praise
in the hour of need. Here in Baahl's room I tried out the new
language for the first time, the language of this country, in connection with my own feelings and impulses. The experiences of
another milieu, connected with the sounds and peculiarities of a
childhood tongue, lost their originality and bloodiness, my notions
could not stream forth freely, but were controlled, worked over,
translated, and by the time they were uttered were far from their
source. Baahl tried to re-create an elementary father-son relationship, but my mistrust was too great and his confidence was too
much like a faith healer's gesture. He believed that my uneasiness
could be alleviated if I could learn to breathe deeply and evenly
and relax my body by Hindu meditational precepts. And when he
tried to show how uninhibited he was and, with a somnolent look
on his face, demonstrated the banality of masturbation by unbut-

toning his fly and playing with his limp, shrunken little penis, this childish, almost absurd gesture revealed to me the enormity of the gulf between the master's seclusion in this small town and my own wilderness, and when I broke off our consultations, I was still faced with the bulk of my dread.

At home my mother would anxiously ask what this analysis actually was, and whether I had to tell him everything. She looked at me blankly as I told her something about it. But in the end she assumed with a pained note in her voice that I had of course placed all the blame on her and that all she could now do was to go up to the attic and hang herself. For the first time I understood how vainly she brooded, alone in the large house, and how inexplicable the loss of her children was to her. I replied that no one was guilty and with an anxious look she stared straight ahead. No less comprehensible were the confused words with which my father cursed the misfortune that had driven him into exile. I saw him on a Sunday morning as I stood in the bathroom shaving. He did not dare to step naked into the bath but kept on his pajama bottoms. I saw him lying in the warm water, the pants floating around him, hiding his genitals with the circumcised penis he had never let me see.

When I returned to Stockholm I kept my post as pattern designer and committed myself to supplying the factory with a certain amount of work each week. In my new room in an apartment house on the south bank of the city I awaited the moving van with my furniture and packing cases. The house was on the cliffs and through the window I could see the wide sweep of Lake Mälar, the peninsula with the wharfs and the silhouette of the inner city on the other bank, the Council House tower crowned with a cupola, the tall campanile of the Town Hall, the copper roofs of the Knights' Island, the pinnacles of the Klara Church and the iron tower of the old telephone exchange. Tugs were moored at the pier below the harbor installations, stones were being unloaded and stacked, and cranes hauled sand out of the ships' holds and shook it out on to high, pale yellow heaps. From the dockyards came the sound of metal saws and riveting hammers. I stood in my new room, with nail holes on its bare gray walls, with the smudges of strange hands and heads and the shadowy outline of vanished objects. The floor was worn down by the steps that, year in year out, had gone from door to bed, bed to table, table to stove, stove to window. This room now had to contain my steps. I would walk about in this room, shove back my chair, work, clear my throat, cough, sneeze, talk to visitors. In the adjoining rooms the other tenants would hear me and if they pressed their ears to the wall they would make out the creaks of the mattress and whispers at night. While waiting for the movers to arrive I took possession of the room, in a corner of which stood a white porcelain stove, and whose ceiling, at its borders, was decorated with a stucco ornament. When my belongings arrived and I had opened the front door and returned to the room it was already my room and it accepted the objects with which I was going to live. The bookcase, the bed and the chairs were carried in, the easel and the drawing board were set up, the cases and boxes opened. Spreading out and distributing this inventory was an activity I had often undertaken, in my rooms at my parents' houses, in hotel and rented rooms in various cities. Surveying my possessions I sought resistance against the strangeness outside. I set up a camp and fortified it with my property. Even if the room had been in a desert, abandoned to destruction, I could still set up around me the objects I prized. Arriving in some chance room I erected a provisional home for a shorter or longer period until the next departure. There was something adventurous about traveling, arriving and traveling on. Even in hotel rooms for a single night I tried to deceive transience and achieve security by unpacking a few books, a drawing block, a writing pad. All the things in this room had passed through my hands and many had been created by my hands. Each thing had its significance. I set up the pictures and arranged the drawings. There were the large works, with a great deal of black, dating from my time at the Academy, studies of models, the face of my friend Peter Kien, his aquiline profile, the professor's Kirghiz face, the shadowy features of Hanna Pickova with the dark straight hair. There were the small pen-and-ink

drawings in old masters' style of my journey south and the rapid
sketches of the factory, the dye house with its steam, the printing
rooms with long strips of material, the courtyard with the barrels,
the smoking chimneys and, in tiny writing, there were often indi-
cations for colors and hymnic captions. There were notebooks
with my attempts at writing, which contained beginnings, initial
statements that would never reach a conclusion, for the reason
that there was no conclusion, only an unbroken streaming and
flowing. There were the letters stacked in bundles and the books.
The order in which I placed the books in the shelves corresponded
to an inner consistency that had increased over the years. The
books were stacked in groups according to when I had read them.
Behind each worn, stained volume I could find a world of my own
thoughts. The titles, the colors, the ornamentation on the spine
evoked particular experiences. The row began with the collected
works of Hesse, bound in light blue. The gilded curves were interwoven with memories of my rooms in England, northern Bohemia, Prague, Tessin, and my parents' houses, while within, on the
pages, lay the dreams and fantasies of my adolescence. The mar-
gins were filled with scribbled notes and marks. Next to Hesse
were Hamsun and Stendhal, followed by the red volumes of Dostoevski's *Brothers Karamazov, Crime and Punishment, The Insulted and Injured, The Devils, From the House of the Dead, The
Idiot,* and *The Dream of a Queer Fellow.* Then came Rolland's
Jean Christophe and *Liluli* with Masereel's woodcuts, Wasser-
mann's *Etzel Andergast, The Maurizius Case, Christian Wahn-
schaffe* and *Kasper Hauser,* along with an old volume of Daumer's
Revelations about the Foundling. Then *The Devil's Elixir* and
Murr the Cat, Stifter's *Late Summer, Studies* and *Colored Stones,*
the India-paper edition of Büchner, Kleist's short stories, *Don
Quixote, The Notebook of Malte Laurids Brigge,* Heym's poems,
Green's *The Dreamer,* Walser's *The Tanner Children.* Further
along, *The Man without Qualities, The Magic Mountain, The
Counterfeiters, An American Tragedy* and *Berlin Alexanderplatz,*
Canetti's *Auto da Fé,* Céline's *Journey to the End of Night,*
Wilde's *Epistola,* Conrad's *The Shadow Line* and *Heart of Dark-
ness,* Zola's *Nana* and *Savage Paris,* Galsworthy's *Forsyte Saga,*

The White Peacock, and *Sons and Lovers* by D. H. Lawrence, Jahnn's *Perrudja,* the short stories of Stefan Zweig, *Pelle the Conqueror* by Andersen-Nexö, and Kierkegaard's *Diary of a Seducer.* Only for two books in brown bindings, *The Castle* and *The Trial* could I find no room. I had received the books from Peter Kien in Prague and had often skimmed through them and tried to read them, but always lay them aside again. Suddenly I was receptive to the opening words of *The Trial.* Someone must have been telling lies about Joseph K., for without having done anything wrong he was arrested one fine morning. This was the book I read that first night in my new room. All that I had read previously receded into the background. In all the books that had revealed their world to me so that I might identify myself there had always been some chance of retreat—into mysticism or a concept of beauty, into an idyll or illusory love. In all these books I became aware of reservations and escape clauses that no longer existed in Kafka. Here all the trimmings had been peeled off and the I of the book stood there naked and defenseless. Even if this book presented me with a rich store of new images, the essential virtue of this confrontation was to provoke thoughts of my own. So now, while reading *The Trial* I became keenly aware of the trial in which I myself was entrapped.

When living in Prague, the city where Joseph K. fought for his life, *The Trial* was too close to home for me to recognize its meaning. All I experienced was impossibility and no way of escape, though seemingly I was given every freedom. Every month I fetched my allowance from my father's representative in his office, where rolls of material from the factory filled the long shelves. From the dark storerooms I looked out into a courtyard surrounded by tall housefronts. In the windows opposite half-dressed women could be seen putting on make-up or shaking out their bedclothes, shrill dance music came from the basement door as it was flung open and drunks staggered out. Herr Fried, my father's righthand man, was one of the forces whose workings I had not yet seen through. White-haired and thick-set, he pressed himself against me and whispered incomprehensible accusations and threats into my ear. Prague, this frontier city between East and West, with its sombre buildings, its heavy baroque vaults, was an ideal place to shelter my marginal existence and, in Kafka's descriptions, I could identify my own path through streets and gateways with stairs leading up to the chanceries of prosecuting counsels and powerless lawyers, through the palace courtyard and into the cathedral. My thoughts hovered over my experiences in this city and the deeper they penetrated the heavier was the unassimilated element that lay in them. I had fled and the people I had met there remained behind. My fear of real intimacy had made these faces unrecognizable. Hanna Pickova's face faded into the shadows of my evening studio: not one of our words could be found again, only a brilliance in her eyes and the shadowy suspicion of a long walk along the banks of the Moldau. I recalled one gray dawn in a garden before I went south. It was the garden behind the villa where Anita Kahler lived. Anita was sitting next to me on a white bench, in a white dress, after a party. Streaks of mist hovered over the meadows, her dress rustled, her hair shimmered red in the early light. I could barely feel her touch or her breath on my mouth. And in her parents' house where I had once visited her Lucie Weisberger stood between a highly polished sideboard with flower-filled crystal vases and porcelain jugs and a clock ticking on the wall. This world, where I still belonged a few years ago, had been plundered and crushed underfoot: its inhabitants had been driven out or imprisoned. I had escaped and Peter Kien had remained behind, living a distorted life. From Theresienstadt I received a note from him, crossed through with a blue and pink pencil, bearing the insignia of an eagle with outstretched wings. His note seemed curiously peaceful, as if he were writing from some holiday resort where he had taken his books and paints. He spoke of the blossoming cherry trees outside his window and of a letter I had sent him before the war from my village on Lake Lugano: it had accompanied him like a talisman—a worn, crumpled piece of paper and I could no longer recall what it said. He also mentioned Lucie, who lived near him in another street, as if this fortress were a country village. Only his address, High Street 228/2, made one suspect that these were barracks. I tried to recollect Lucie's face and I briefly remembered her soft, childish features: suddenly this face and her vague form became a challenge. I felt as if I had deceived and deserted her and I began wearisome attempts to obtain her release. In spring 1942 there still seemed to be a chance of getting into contact with the enemy administration through the Foreign Office. I collected money, offered to marry Lucie Weisberger, wrote to her and received letters in her hand. At first my requests were acknowledged by the various offices who referred me to other offices, as if an appropriate administrative body really did exist. My petitions were never refused, but in the end they remained unanswered and after a final announcement from Peter Kien that Lucie had moved on to some unknown destination and that he too would soon be moving, there remained only the ultimate silence.

You don't yet know what sort of opponents you are dealing with, said Hoderer. And yet the camps already existed when you were living there and when you passed through Berlin with your Czech passport in the last winter before the war and clouds of smoke hung over the city, the night with the beautiful name of the Crystal Night had just taken place. The purpose of your survival may be to find out where the evil lies and how to fight it. You are still burdened with the ballast of your bourgeois origins. You know it is all rotten and doomed to decay, yet you do not dare make a clean break with it. Your attempts at work will be in vain as long as they do not contribute to the struggle to remold society. If you cannot commit yourself to us you are lost. But I mistrusted all bonds, all shared ideas: I was still unable to look for broad perspectives and political allegiance. I had to stick to the little fragmentary pictures that reflected my own experiences. Only in these pictures could I find out how I was part of my age; everything else had to remain scaffolding. I saw myself on the school playground many years before, in the dried-up ditch behind the toilets, hidden behind the leaves of a water hemlock weed. It reeked of urine and tar and the bitter juice of plants, and up on the playground my enemies were looking for me. They shouted my name, banded together, and the ringleader peered everywhere. I cowered in the thick stalks of the plants, and behind me, on the railway embankment, a train rolled slowly past, the passengers standing at the open windows. This memory was still vivid, although it neither purchased my freedom nor put me on an equal footing with Peter Kien and the others who had been persecuted. Compared to the excitement with which Hoderer followed the events on the various scenes of the war my imprisonment in the sandbox was totally insignificant. Nevertheless, while Peter Kien and Lucie Weisberger perished, I looked back on the time when I was shoved into the dark damp hole, on how the sunlight flickered in the cracks of the planks in front of me, and how I saw the plank ripped away and Friederle's German shepherd appeared, with its shiny white teeth. I thought of the terror which gave me the strength to shoulder my way through the thick roof of sand, even though such strength was mere impotence in the prisons where Peter Kien and Lucie Weisberger lay. I had nothing else to report; I had not been driven out on to the battlefield or into the torture chambers. I sat in a secluded room and tried to explain something to myself, with the only material at my disposal. If I were once to succeed in noting exactly what had happened to me, it could become a part of the events on the border of which Hoderer and the other vigilant selfless ones were standing.

To get to the words which I had learned in my childhood, words which still seemed worth writing, I had first to force myself away from the language I heard and used every day. My thoughts were full of it, I saw it written everywhere, and I made notes in it. I tried to find my way back to the old language because I controlled it in all its details and because it was connected with my basic impulses. And yet something alien and repellent soon appeared in it; the words I wrote lacked all resonance, all connection to the thoughts I wanted to express. I was made to realize that the things I wanted to say could not be said once language ceased being a natural means of exchange: only now was I conscious of the break I had effected by emigrating. I lived in another country's linguistic milieu, into which I had been accepted on an emergency basis, where I could now make myself understood, but where I was far from having mastered the refinements of the language, and where I was looked upon as an emigrant from a foreign way of life. However, the land I had been driven out of was at this time more hostile than any happenstance place of exile, and when I wrote something it was not necessarily in the assumption that someone might be listening to me, the idea that I might be turning for help to someone else, rather it was as if I had to hide myself, as if no one was permitted to hear my words. I saw that it was impossible to express oneself on a remote and desolate island. In such a situation only inarticulate cries could be used. At first I looked for help in books. Here was the language I wanted to speak, and all around me, among the émigrés, were others who had stood by this language and tried to disconnect it from the events of their country of origin and continued to treat it as an independent agent. But my dialogue with books became somehow artificial. It was often directed at authors long since dead, or, if they were still alive in their various hideouts, even their words betrayed the hopelessness of the situation. A few Olympian spirits were no longer approachable, so deeply were they anchored in the tradition of the language which they had taken over with such self-confidence that they lent no ear to my doubts. Others, like Hoderer, went in for an ideology, and I could learn from their sharp, matter-of-fact, language. But what I had to tell them did not interest them. Moreover, I had nothing complete to show them. My writings were still at a formative stage. Until now I had only managed to produce small disconnected fragments and there was little enough originality in them: they were mostly based on the books I carried with me on my travels. I wanted to start writing at the very moment when it was becoming clear to me that I no longer possessed a unitary language, and that it was getting to a point where I could also make use of a South Sea idiom if, by chance, I had landed in Tahiti. I did not believe in a return to the land of my origin, and I could not imagine ever finding individuals or groups, with whom an understanding was possible. All I found were my persecutors and they had given me their answer long ago. If I wanted to have it out with them it would have to be in a soliloquy, and for a while I continued this monologue in a

vacuum. I described a Sunday breakfast. My father was eating his
fried egg and we children were watching him. With his egg he
consumed a crisp roll which he dipped with his fork, piece by
piece, into the brown butter sauce. If on this particular morning
one of the children were to be honored with his special attention
and rewarded for good behavior during the week he would hand
one of these tidbits to him. When, after several attempts, this description still did not succeed, I tried to translate it into my present language. There were immediate difficulties of vocabulary—
and I was none too sure of my spelling or my syntax. I groped for
idioms and had to look them up in the dictionary. Nevertheless it
seemed to me that this stuttering, this mutilation of the language
was more appropriate than a routine account in a language I
knew only too well. The places where the events I wanted to describe had occurred were far away and had become foreign to me.
So even a foreign language might suit them. Every word must be
discovered through an adventurous search and the scenery that
developed in this way often took on surprising and novel colors.
After a period of indecision I believed that this expedition, which
was slowly progressing, was more meaningful than sticking to the
outdated forms of expression that had until now seemed natural
to me. This also resulted in my rejecting the old books, in trying to
forget their sound, so that I read works only in the new language.
I had lived in this country for three years; I was able to live here,
and compared to past experiences, this country was no worse than
any other. But my dreams showed how few inner links there were.
Here there was no question of permanency and an ordered use of
language. My dream dialogue contained a mixture of all the lan-
guages I knew. English and Czech and a smattering of French
were natural to me there, and when I woke up the witch's brew
bubbled on. There were moments when I tried to evade the conflicts, when I tried to allow all the nations within me to speak in
turn while I scribbled down the words as they came, automati-
cally and regardless of syntax and sentence structure, a deposit for
all corners of Europe. While I was actually writing this seemed a
solution, this was my expression, one vast formless fermentation, a
cacophony, a whirlpool of suggestions that appeared for an in-

stant and then vanished again. Yet I was never able to read these
unbridled fantasy words, these sentences which came pouring
down like an avalanche. If they had any meaning they showed me
nothing but my own decline, and that I knew about already; they
brought no solution and interpreted nothing. These free-flowing
monologues often had a magical incantatory effect and seemed to
contain a dark poetry, but then I would become mistrustful of
these seductive underground words, of their tonal magic, all too
easily achieved, all too easily scattered to the winds, as the expressive power of dreams often loses its substance upon awakening.
The distortions and disguises could be iridescent and lure one
with their exotic colors, they could spur me on or remind me of
past riches, could set raw material in motion. But they were not
enough, the treasure chests that loomed up in dreams never
sufficed; they disappeared and left only emptiness behind. The
hieroglyphics had to be understood and that was the difficult part,
calling inner experiences by their names and putting everything
where it belonged. It was easy to run riot with symbols, but often
impossible to bring to light the facts that lay behind them. Always
when the bewilderment and bogged-downness of the adolescent
years came over me, I landed back in this opaque art, and convinced myself that a strength lay in hallucinations. But this art
was never dangerous. It only teased me and flattered me. Its extravagance might have appeared audacious, but it left everything
in its place, untouched. It might appear bold in its excess, but it
left everything just the same as always. It could become a weapon
only when everything I wanted to express had been tangibly
translated back into the reality out of which it had penetrated into
my being.

Painted images, as I had earlier busied myself with them, were
now too static, too bounded, too closed off for me, too much tied
down to a single, immutable situation. They were segments, windows, glimpses of my peepshow and at their best they could still
evoke heroically the uniqueness of a single moment. I had taken
them over from a world where the meaning of such signposts was
still credible; but now even their weight, their frames, the cases in

which they had had to be packed, seemed ridiculous. At the most
they made sense only on the long strips of paper I had used so I
could roll them up and carry them along in my knapsack. I
stretched out these strips of paper all around the walls of my
room, and I occasionally turned from the writing I did mainly half-
lying on the bed, surrounded by books, works of reference and
notes, to painting, with Indian ink, watercolors and brushes close
at hand. Preparations for painting and drawing had to take no
time: the meticulous preliminary treatment of the materials,
grinding the colors and mixing them with oils, which had previously been part of the work, a craftsman's ritual which seemed
to make my intentions lasting, were now impossible. Even rousing
myself from the meditative state of thinking in images was sometimes too much, and so the phenomena before my eyes lost their
clarity. The house where my room was located was quiet in the
daytime, since all the other tenants, except for the retired sailor
who slept dead drunk in his room, were out at work. In this silence, broken only by occasional noises from the shipyards and
the pier, I wrote with my notebook on drawnup knees and my
back supported by cushions; and when the words had passed
shapes would appear, first as patches on the retina consisting of
colored dots, then gradually expanding into shapes, objects,
figures. Before the images faded I often examined the activity in
the photographic darkroom of my eyes, directed my pupils to the
window so that its brightness and spars of shadow penetrated the
lenses, then closed my eyelids and laid my hand in front of them.
The negative appeared and changed into various tints according
to the color of the sky. By briefly blending new images I could
vary the reproduction in the interior of my eye or develop it into
a clear positive. Sometimes the crosswork of the window stood out
in a brilliant red against the black background, sometimes blue on
a red surface, sometimes the color of the crosswork shifted to gray
and black in a violet area; and when the dazzling ball of the sun
was added, sometimes in the late afternoon, these effects were
often enriched by circling lights, jetblack stars and other slow-
moving ornaments. I frequently waited a long time for these vis-
ual events, and only when I had reached a state akin to half-sleep,

where my thought process was shut out while my consciousness was still awake, did they appear. Chiefly at dusk and often at night they were projected in front of me, and out of a shape moving in the dark there emerged something, a woman in profile, running on the spot with ultra-rapid movements, with billowing clothes and smoky hair, staring straight ahead, her mouth wide open. And then in her place appeared an old man, turned toward me, hobbling slowly along, leaning on a shepherd's crook and draped in layer upon layer of skins that fluttered around him. I could take such an impression with me when I went to the drawing board. The old man's face with its glittering white stubble might be conveyed, and then other faces grew from it, piling on top of each other in their transformations, until they lost all human features, became stones, plants, animals, crystals, curious tangles of shapes, and, in the course of months, my room filled with these friezes, and, when I had finished painting them, I placed them high up on the walls. There was no purpose to the pictures any more than to what I had written. They were only exercises, a sort of inventory: with them I indulged in an extremely refined sort of idleness in which my only concern was to process these pictures which possessed the curious ability to become phosphorescent under the force of my imagination in the dark. Only occasionally, when Hoderer, Anatol or other friends visited me, were they subjected to criticism. Anatol, who worked untiringly and obsessively, trying to keep abreast of the *avant-garde* of modern art, and who was only content with a masterpiece, sought in vain among my paintings for some work of lasting value, and sometimes I felt from his look that he thought I was insane. I myself admitted this insanity to him, I recognized it, it was part of me and I did not care where it might lead me. The danger of losing myself, with which Anatol had reproached me, was not yet discernible; I had lost neither the sense of time nor the consciousness of my daily tasks; I continued to earn my living by designing, spent hours at a stretch painting the Turkish pavilions, the ladies in crinolines, the garlands of tulips and the caravels. I traced them, prepared the individual color schemes for the printing patterns, carried them to the post and spent the rest of

my day on my investigations, as useless as the games I had once
played in the attic and cellars. Amos, a Latvian painter, showed
more understanding. Amos achieved brilliant textural effects in his
pictures and drawings. The many levels of his complex personality
were represented in the technical richness of his woodcuts, where
a single sheet would often be cut from as many as twenty blocks.
From indolence he hid his true self in decorative exteriors and
Anatol said of him that it was a pity he did not bring out in them
his own experience of life, which could be read in his distraught,
sharp features. He judged Amos by his own exacting standards,
according to his own merciless demands which made even his
own private life miserable. He turned away from Amos, who
could manage only virtuoso arabesques and would only be satisfied if he made a big splash. Amos worked according to his mood
and with relish. He slept late, he read, he went to the theater, ate
well and always sat in his warm studio full of the latest books and
magazines with a beautiful woman, a different one on each of my
visits, often young and girl-like, gazing at him in admiration. All
thought of distress and persecution had been banished from his
studio, not because he had not experienced it, but from a desire to
extract only pleasure from life. This was evident even from his
hands: the nails on his sensitive refined fingers curved forward
like claws, as if they wanted to snatch something up. The success
at which Anatol aimed was a hard-earned success purchased by
staking his whole life on it; the success that Amos expected was a
triumph of taste, the result of carefully calculated effects, with the
application of all the finesse of the latest artistic devices. The pur-
poselessness of my work and the fact that I scarcely felt a need to
display it repelled Hoderer. For him who had subordinated himself entirely to the practical problems that had to be solved art
had also to have a utilitarian value. I asked him why art was not
allowed to develop under socialism and reminded him of Vertov,
Eisenstein, Archipenko, Meyerhold, Vassilyev, Tatlin, and Maya-
kovsky whose revolutionary works had been decried as decadent
and formalistic. Other tasks were more important, said Hoderer.
The country first had to be armed, and today we see how correct
that policy was. The war was already inevitable even then and

private interests had to take a back seat. I do not wish to live for the future, I said. I am living today. I don't want to have the war forced on me like an obligation and to have a guilty conscience because I have escaped. Is it not true that those in power are always on their guard against freedom of expression, I asked. The socialists did not forbid art, they merely made it harmless, they stuck to the tradition of plush and velvet and gold frames. For whom were the experiments of the 'twenties carried out, Hoderer retorted. For all those who wanted to think, who wanted to change their lives, I said. Hoderer countered: When all is said and done it was never more than just another form of amusement for the upper crust of the bourgeoisie. Only the rich could benefit from it. Only they could afford to read books, to go to the theater, listen to music or look at films and pictures. The growing threat could not be contended with by this form of art. And yet it persists, I said, and it will survive the collapse, it is stronger than petty bourgeois obstinacy, treachery, stock responses, militarism and chauvinism. I had only just begun to study the works of that decade. At that time I had had to come to terms with my adolescence and had absorbed only a few disconnected ideas about recent artistic discoveries. I had heard of the Bauhaus, had read secretly the forbidden magazine *Der Querschnitt,* had heard the music of Stravinsky and Hindemith, *The Threepenny Opera* and *Mahagonny.* But the 'twenties had not yet provided me with this field of experiences in new painting, new music, new language and drama; the 'twenties were only colored neon reflections in the damp cobbles of the Kurfürstendamm; they were a few suggestions, heard but barely understood; and yet all of this could have been mine already, all this daring and novelty, while I trudged to school each day with my satchel under my arm and learned Schiller by heart. Only now did I realize what the authorities had been hiding from me; I discovered Dadaism, found out about Huelsenbeck, Ball, Arp, Schwitters, studied the works of Picabia, Duchamp, Tristan Tzara, Raoul Haussmann, Max Ernst, read about the films of René Clair, Eggeling and Richter, saw Schlemmer's figures for the Triadic ballet, read Klee's essays and diary, Tollers' and Kaiser's drama, engrossed myself in the paintings of Kandinsky, Chirico, Miró, Dali, Tanguy, Magritte and in the poems of Jarry and Apollinaire. I read Gertrude Stein, Freud and all the magazines about the literature and art of that time which I could lay my hands on in the libraries. Everything that had been attacked during that one decade still existed today, just as vigorously as ever. The pictures and sculpture, the plays, dances, films, fiction, and music were not isolated but embodied values which one could continue to develop. You know, I told Hoderer, I have never dared call myself a painter. The term seems to have something slightly disreputable about it. When I was called up in Czechoslovakia I wrote self-employed as my occupation on the questionnaire. That of course merely confirmed the impression they already had: that I was mentally retarded. Only now am I beginning to maintain that my painting and writing is work, even if, for the time being, I must give my detractors the satisfaction of knowing that I am achieving nothing with this work. They will tolerate you, said Hoderer, for you are part of their luxury. They think you are picturesque and they will make money out of you. They will make you dance: you are their court jester. You do not endanger them. They would drop you and cast you out the moment you dared attack them. Until then the radicalism of your art is merely self-deception.

And yet as he said these words there was an expression of weakness in Hoderer's eyes. He spoke of the future of socialism, of freedom of expression after the final victory, but in his face was the premonition of a doubt. His illness constricted his breathing more and more. He put up with it; it was insignificant beside the vast struggle going on outside. But when, a year later, he committed suicide, I saw his face in front of me as it had been during our conversation. In spite of his harsh attacks he had looked at me full of understanding and there was something terrifying about his tolerance, his self-control. He never expressed any bitterness about not being allowed to practice. Without irony he accepted the fact that he was finally appointed to a minor post in a medical advice bureau after the victory of El Alamein, when sympathies in this country swung toward the Allies. After his death in the spring

of 1943, when the danger of invasion and annihilation had decreased for us and we could already think in terms of the final
victory, I thought of the look in his eyes, which no longer contained any belief. This look was broken. During an asthmatic attack he omitted to give himself the injection. He suffocated.
Shortly afterward Karel Kurz, a refugee German sculptor, also
killed himself. He hanged himself in his studio near my flat, where
I had often visited him. Kurz, too, was an active and practical
man, his body was sturdily built like the figures he hewed out of
stone and carved out of wood. His drawings displayed a generous
confident touch, his voice was calm and composed and he attacked his problems of form with the straightforwardness of a
craftsman only concerned with imitating nature as closely as possible. He listened to me calmly in the large basement room filled
with sculptures, while beyond the broad windows sparrows chirp-
chirped in the bushes along the river banks. When I had worn
myself out talking he would lay aside his hammer and chisel and,
with a glance in my direction, would go into the kitchen and return with bread and sausages and a mug of steaming chocolate.
While I gulped down the warm drink he said: Do you feel it
going into your blood. Your face is already taking on color. I
could not get over him and Hoderer choosing death. Both men
seemed to belong to the future which was now being fought for.
That they should disappear when fulfillment seemed almost
within their grasp cast a shadow on the struggle: it was a bad
omen. The finished sculptures and still more the unhewn blocks of
stone and heavy lumps of wood that stood waiting outside in an
enclosure in the bushes had surrounded him with an atmosphere
of determination and resilience. I looked for signs that might
throw some light on his despair and, just as Hoderer's illness had
long since paved the way for his self-destruction, so now it
seemed to me that the nervous twitch with which Karel was
afflicted was an indication of his inner tension. His face had been
periodically stricken by convulsions, a wheezing noise burst from
his nose and his mouth jerked to one side as if it had just been
struck. These were the results of being alive in the First World
War.

I had not seen Else for a year now. Perhaps a child of mine was there. I went to see her in her old flat, stood for a while at the door, listening for a baby's cries. All was quiet. The child lay in the cradle asleep. She had been suckling it. It was my child. The father was standing at the door and within the family was waiting. I rang. Steps approached. For a few minutes we stood facing one another in silence. On the clothes hook hung a man's coat and jacket. Else asked me in. At the table, in front of the remains of supper, sat her companion. The fire was burning in the hearth. There was no child. After a short awkward conversation I left. In my room I collapsed over the drawing table. Warm salty water smudged parts of the leaf-tendrils I had been painting and it took the rest of the night to touch them up.

Apart from my efforts to learn the new language I made other attempts to adapt myself during this period. Although I knew that I could no longer attach any meaning to such concepts as allegiance or residence for a few years I gave way to endeavors that would provide the illusion of a settled way of life, a home of my own and a family. Even though these attempts were beset with doubts from the very beginning I nevertheless carried them through until it was quite obvious that none of them were tenable. I had abandoned Lucie before my efforts to have her released had failed. It became ever more apparent to me that I myself did not believe in rescue. With my petitions and declarations to the administrative authorities of the enemy I had merely temporarily relieved my burden of guilt and given Lucie some spark of hope. I forgot her and only years later did I think of her whom I scarcely knew, with whom indeed I had been connected in a delusive way. I tried to imagine how she had borne within her the hope of rescue and how she regarded me, her supposed rescuer. And I tried to imagine the moment when she gave me up, me the betrayer, but the hardness and coldness of this moment were unbearable. While she was being robbed of everything, I was deceiving myself with the delusion of a permanent home and property. There was nothing more I could do for Lucie; I had never been able to do anything for her and had at most increased her suffering by pointless hope. Now I knew nothing more of her existence and did not want to know anything more of it, but I shut myself off from this fate for which I too had been destined, but which I had escaped through no act of my own, and I had long since betrayed Lucie, the prisoner condemned to death, with a live free girl, an inhabitant of this city. Edna's family had lived in the city for four generations. The patriarchal villa where she lived with her mother near the zoo had been frequented by the writers, painters, publishers, bankers, and art-collectors of the turn of the century. Inside the vast house, adorned with turrets and towers, reigned the silence of a mausoleum. When Edna crossed the colonnaded hall and opened the little side door in the main entrance she held her breath and, in order not to frighten the ghosts who dwelt in the shadows of the niches, she tiptoed up stairs creaking with old age to the attic, where she had had her own room from her earliest childhood. In the large rooms along the landings naked goddesses could be seen through open doors in the diffused light of windows overgrown with palms, magnolia and vines, sunk in thought or with arms outstretched among the foliage of the potted plants, the draped tables and mastodontic sofas. However carefully one trod, the crystal prisms in the chandeliers would tinkle softly. Edna's mother lived with her books and correspondence in a bedroom with drawn curtains and little round family portraits hung in the blossoming boughs of the wallpaper. Her ailing face, lit by a lamp with a small, rose-colored silk shade, shimmered amid the pillows of the tall mahogany bed as she listened to the trickling and whispering sounds inside the walls. In Edna's room her old toys still lay among the painting gear, the nursery pictures hung over the narrow white bed, and in the corner stood the dollhouse with its miniature furniture, its tiny cups and saucers and its occupants with their minute painted porcelain faces. The only person physically present in this house was Cecilia, the old cook, who had been there at Edna's birth. Waddling and corpulent, her face black in the twilight, she looked after the kitchen and served at mealtimes. No one dared speak to her once she had started on her murmurings. One waited patiently until the invisible shapes with whom she was conversing, to whom she listened and nodded, had

vanished and she had returned to her task. We ate in silence off a
venerable tea set and Edna was careful not to clatter the knives
and forks for fear of arousing the disapproval of her ancestors,
who looked down at her from their banished past on the walls. In
the garden, under the tall broad trees, she came across the traces
of her first walks at every step. Her name was cut into the bark in
a childish hand, faces grimaced from the bulges in the trunks; the
shaggy, boisterous troll who lolled about in the coalbin at night,
peeked up the shaft of the cellar stairs, and in the sand she would
step on marbles, sometimes bringing to light a glassy sphere with
varicolored threads in it. She lived in the atmosphere she had
been accustomed to from the beginning of her life. Near the garden, behind the high wooden fences, lay the adventurous regions
of the Tivoli Gardens with the garish cupolas of the merry-go-
rounds, the flagpoles of the fun-fair booths and the scaffolding of
the switchback. In the summer months the tootling music, the
screams and laughter and the sound of shots from the rifle ranges
could be heard until late at night, and on the square in front of
the circus tent she still came upon the figures of her mythology,
the photographer with his box camera plastered with pictures, the
gypsy girl who sold balloons, the warty old sausage vendor at her
booth and the lion tamer in shiny black boots, red morning coat
and a whip under his arm who stepped out on to the perron and
winked at her. She was still fascinated by the big ads, all humpy
with blisters of paste, at the circus entrance, with the lions and
tigers, elephants and prancing white horses, the sea lions balanc-
ing on balls and the tightrope walkers and jugglers. Below the
garden, between the shed and the moored barges, lived the old
sailor in his houseboat, with his tales of distant lands, and in the
house next door was a hermit, rumored to have castrated himself
in his youth with a pair of garden shears. Although she had spent
a year traveling before the war it was as though Edna had never
left her native city. She was not so much sheltered as isolated and
in this isolation her character had merged into the world of her
origin. There were no disturbances, no dangers, and there had
never been anything to check her in her games or flights of fancy.
Her uniform continuous ways and her old childhood atmosphere

still surrounded her. What she represented in her pictures and painted clay figures were the experiences she had grown up with; here she was still the child in her hiding place, listening to the occupants of the house, the guests and neighbors. And with the keen observation of a neglected child she saw the absurdity of these posturing figures; she caricatured everything she observed at a distance, that could alienate and frighten her. She made it innocuous and laughed at it. So I met her in a corner of the Academy of Arts where she had settled down to work, laughing among the naïve pictures, the little toylike sculptures which portrayed her world of enchanted cooks, children's nurses, teachers, dogs, cats, grandmothers, cousins, little brothers and sisters, generals, admirals, witches, harpists and ducat-collectors. I too became an inhabitant of her saga. I was the vagabond, the Homeless One, and she let me into her forests and lakes, populated by magpies, woodgrouse, elks, princesses and crowned fish. Her father, who had married again, appeared in her fairy tales as a lobster walking upright. It was with amusement that she watched me meet her father, as he stood before me, stiff in his shell, his face looking up, dusty with lime, swiveling his jaw and sharpening his claws. In his human guise he was a paleontology professor and head of the Natural History Museum and his house was a meeting place for scholars, diplomats and high-ranking officers. Distrustfully he scrutinized the starveling who had fled from the homeland of venerable intellect and great culture, and whose villainous intentions he had already guessed.

In spring 1942, when the river was still frozen over after the severe winter, Edna walked with me over the ice, which was glittering in the sun. I pointed to the tall red building on the rocky slopes of the south bank and through the thick lenses of her spectacles she tried to distinguish the windows of my room. Her eyes reflected the light blue of the sky and her laughter was a part of the clear air, the radiant light, the blinding reflections from the ice. From my window we looked down on to the path we had just taken and the tracks we had left in the snow. There we had just walked through the park and climbed the steps of the wooden

stairway that led up to the house; we saw the path and our foot-
prints, and now there was a provocative mockery in Edna's laugh.
She was like Botticelli's Flora and the blouse that peeped from
under her buttoned-up jacket was sprinkled with tiny flowers. Her
voice had a childish eagerness about it and between our kisses, as
I stripped off her blouse, she talked on about the view of the
towers built by her forefathers, the rows of pictures on my walls
that she wanted to look at, the disarray in the room through which
we had been edging from window to bed, the dance we performed
as we did so, like the mating dance of the woodgrouse. When I
removed her glasses her face became helpless; she looked for a
chair where the glasses could be put within reach and then everything was ready for taking a new strange unfamiliar body to bed.
I folded back the blanket, helped her to remove her skirt and
underwear, scattered our clothes with ridiculous movements all
around the room, and then we lay naked next to each other, having arrived from somewhere in order to touch and enjoy each
other to the full. Still her whispered words, her eyes half shut, her
face smiling with its myopic expression, her legs drawn up to her
belly, her hands pressing defensively against my shoulders, and
my uncertainty in the preparations for this game of lying with her,
the question whether we would succeed in fitting the parts together, the fear of failure, the wish to forget, and her voice warning me to be careful, her half-obliterated words, something about
her virginity or semi-virginity, something about a man who once
hurt her with his finger, and then the climax was near, was already
about to come, and we clung to one another in this amazing intimacy: the slime of generations already on its way, a stream of
countless little heads, countless whisking little tails, our heirs, the
guarantors of our posterity, and for a second I lost consciousness
and returned too late, to anxious questions, calming, consoling
lies. Perhaps I wanted to tie her down even then, the sheltered native, but did not dare to when her pregnancy had become certain.
Lucie was still vividly present, as was the hollow mockery of my
attempts to free her. No less present was the advance of the German army and the prospect of further flight. My luggage had to be
restricted to the bare minimum, and a doctor came to our aid. He

was a Hungarian émigré who had previously been in charge of a large gynecological clinic and was now obliged to continue his practice in a friend's kitchen. He was not allowed to treat natives, nigger that he was, but only his equals. I gave him a picture by way of fee and he came to my room and performed the abortion out of necessity, out of humanity. He sat on the edge of the bed, broad-shouldered, gigantic and bald, and unpacked his bag. He spoke in a friendly soothing way in his lilting Magyar voice while I put the water on to boil. Edna held my hand when she had to raise her legs and suddenly, with a deft sure movement, he introduced the long sharp instrument; Edna's fingernails bored into my hand, a short high-pitched cry burst from her throat, and then it was all over. The doctor patted her playfully on the cheek, sat for a while chatting with us, told Edna to stay in bed, prepared us for hemor-rhages and left. But the next day Edna's mother forced her way into my room, not as an accuser, not to condemn me, only with her silent melancholy power. She wanted to free her daughter from the evil that had befallen her and while Edna dressed, as awkwardly as a scolded child, she sat in her black coat on the worn-out kitchen chair next to the door, her hat under a veil. The sound of riveting hammers droned up from the shipyards.

For the summer holidays I rented a hut in the woods near a farm, but before I moved in there with Edna, I worked for a month on the hay harvest. For my daily stint I received food, a place to sleep in the hired man's room, and a little pocket money, which the farmer still seemed to think was too much for a for-eigner. I had no right to ask for more; I was the lowliest person on the farm and with the age-old blindness of the humble I slogged at it the hardest. Before sunrise I cleaned out the stalls and wheeled the barrow out to the dungheap. I poured the swill in the pig trough and groomed the horses. I acted as if I were used to handling horses, but the horses realized my ineptness and, whinnying, squeezed me against the plank walls. By day I was in the field and swung the hay high on to the cart with the pitchfork. At mealtimes I sat at the lowest end of the kitchen table and picked at the swill with which the stable boy and the milkmaids were satisfied. The milk had been skimmed to a watery blue; the meat was full of bones, gristle and sinews; the old potatoes were musty and studded with black eyes. Apart from the over-boiled turnips there were no vegetables, and salads seemed unknown. The ersatz coffee was thin and bitter and was drunk with stale rye bread, while, instead of sugar, a tin of saccharin was placed in front of us. As we sat at the table the farmer, a lean gaunt man with steel-rimmed spectacles, prowled around us and killed the fat bluebottles with a swatter. In the parlor next door with his wife he ate splendid meals, drank beer or whole milk with them, and used cream and lump sugar in his fragrant coffee. I had read about farmhands in the old Swedish agricultural system, and some contemporary writers had themselves grown up in this proletariat. There were no longer any serfs, the farm laborers belonged to the agricultural workers' union, but the old spirit lived on in this farm and no one protested against it. The maids were housed in a windowless barn and the tiny room I shared with the hired hand would have been unfit for a horse. The walls were cracked and covered with cobwebs, the stone floor was cold and damp, and the broken skylight had been patched together with newspaper. The hired hand's possessions, consisting of a Sunday suit, a pair of shoes and a shirt, lay preserved in a suitcase, and there was no table with a letter or photograph. A bottle with a dripping candle stuck in its neck stood on the floor. There was no electric light. The hired man slept in the shirt he wore in the day and during the month I spent on the farm he did not once take it off. On a stand was a rusty washbasin that we did not use. I washed under the pump and the hired hand, whenever he did wash, used the tap in the pigsty. My attempts to make him aware of the bad conditions met with dull resistance. The old foreman who lived in a room by himself gave me a hostile look whenever I hinted at any criticism. The maids only giggled: they seemed to know nothing and never to want to know anything. And yet the farmyard was not far from the capital and the Labor Party was running the country. It was as if, after all the upheavals and renovations in society, the country had again become dormant. A revolution had never taken place, the workers had once been granted all their rights and that was that. There was no call for any further protest. I said to the hired man, The farmer eats new potatoes, juicy meat, butter and sauce and our grub is worse than pigswill. He only pulled a face, shook his head, and looked around in embarrassment in case my inflammatory speech had been overheard. I asked him whether he could not ask for a room fit to live in, whether he did not need a table and a chair. He looked at me blankly and answered that his room was good enough for him. To my question whether he ever read a book he said he had no time for that, that was not for him. The country was rich, it had been spared the war and had a reputation for high social development, and yet there existed this benightedness, this reluctance to face changes, this primeval situation prior to enlightenment and culture. As I had nothing to lose, one Saturday, after a sparse lunch at which the ersatz coffee and ersatz sugar again stood on our table, although our ration cards with sections for coffee, sugar, butter and meat had been handed over to the farmer's wife, I went to the farmer's room. There I took the sugar bowl, the butter dish, the coffee pot and the cream from the table and carried them back to the kitchen. I spread my bread thick with butter, poured some coffee, helped myself to sugar and milk, while the stable boy and the maids stared at me speechlessly. Even the farmer could say nothing. He got up and followed me and stood behind me gaping. His wife appeared at the door and stood there in silence. I lit a cigarette, smoked and drank my coffee and no one said anything because there was nothing to say. The stable boy and the maids did not dare take any coffee or milk. I knew what was going on in their heads, and finally they came to the conclusion that I, as a foreigner, did not understand the local conditions and that there was no place for me there. On the last day of my stay the farmer's son was at the farm. He had come home on leave from military service, was wearing his uniform and had his gun with him. In the morning in the stable a shot had gone off while he was resting the muzzle of the gun on his foot. As he had been standing on a rotten piece of flooring the bullet went straight through the foot, no bones had been damaged, and that afternoon he returned from the local military hospital with a thick bandage around the flesh wound. He slung the gun over his shoulder again and wanted to go out hunting on the lake in the evening. He asked me to row for him. I took my place on the oarsman's plank and he sat opposite me in the stern, stretched out his bandaged leg and lay the gun across his knees. Several times I had to push aside the muzzle of the loaded gun which pointed in my direction. Midges whirred across the surface of the water, the sky was red from the setting sun and the wood loomed up black and motionless on the banks. The blades dipped into the water, rose slowly, dripping. Then a shot rang out, there was a rush of air in my ears, the hair on my temples was singed. A cloud of smoke rose from the gun. The oars were raised, rings of falling drops spread all around in the water. I remembered once having read that you never hear the shot that hits you. I felt my head while the farmer's son stared at me, gaping. The echoes still resounded. And now everything could lie in deepest silence, deepest darkness. In this eternal night the colors of the sky, the humming of the midges, the falling of the beads of water would continue. Despite the deepest night within me the water would reflect the red of the sky, the cows would low in the meadows and in the orchard the apples would glint on the trees. Slowly the boat drifted to the shore. I walked into the luscious green of the forest and along the path toward my hut. The echoes of the shot still resounded over the countryside. On the following evening, as we sat in the glade in front of our hut, Edna and I, this moment of absolute silence would sometimes recur, the moment of contemplating the final departure, and then in the leaves and in the sand the worms, spiders and field mice rustled again, birds and squirrels pecked and chirped in the trees, and in the depths of the wood the twigs cracked under the hooves of an elk. For Edna the sounds of nature were familiar. As a child she had spent months each summer in the country; she was familiar with the blueberry thicket, with the silent black forest tarns, with the hills and crags in the birchwoods; she sat melted together with forest and field, with stone and sky, and she could sit so still, so much a part of the foliage, the grass, the earth, that I could walk right past without ever see-

ing her and then she would hoot at me like an owl, or startle me
with a snake-hiss. Her naked sunburnt body stood long-limbed
among the ferns. She used to bind her hair and hips with birch
leaves. She offered herself to me on the moss or in a bed of anem-
ones. She wanted to make love on the ground, in the grass, with
beetles and grains of sand trickling all around her. I was just a
stray city-dweller here in her wilderness. The corn in the fields,
the juicy grass, the fading leafage on the forest floor did not evoke
fertility or the course of the seasons, but had for me only the odor
of transience. I could not come to terms with this nature, could
neither describe it nor draw it; I could not take any interest in the
spiders and the constant humming of the midges and, when I
woke up in the morning, I lay deafened by the shrilling of the
birds. Edna had long since disappeared, she bathed in the lake
and sunned herself on a warm rock while I sat inactive at the
table in the hut with a book or a writing pad, listening to the birds
whirring past and gazing through the window out into the dense
greenery whence came the distant tinkle of cowbells. I was distracted by the speed at which insects shot past, and by my medi-
tations about the ants filing along the window ledge in endless
columns, coming from somewhere and disappearing somewhere
else. As Edna strolled through the bushes, singing and humming,
talking to the animals and calling all the plants by their right
names, I thought of the stone cities, industrial suburbs and harbor
districts where I felt at home. I went to the barns at the farm,
chatted with the hired man or just sat quietly in a corner behind
the barn, where I could survey a small self-contained world. The
longer I stayed there the more important this place seemed to me,
fenced in as it was with rotten, gray boards, and within its con-
fines the dungheap, the tool shed and the privy. The shed was half
fallen in, and crooked rusty nails stuck out of its board walls. The
privy door hung askew on its hinges and a bundle of long bean
poles was stacked in the corner next to the grindstone. Behind the
stall was a pigsty and I saw the snuffling damp snouts of the pigs
between the planks and heard their feet rooting in the slush and
their prickly bodies rubbing against the wood. Whenever I

stopped here I felt as if I could stay here forever. It was a place of banishment, of damnation, a place that reminded me of a picture that Swedenborg had drawn of hell.

I could attribute it to the war and to the despair on which Hoderer and Kurz had also foundered, I could ascribe it to the inability to work that sometimes overcame me, but basically it was the wish to give myself up to banishment and damnation that drove me to the woods again in the winter. I had seen advertisements in the streets for forestry workers and because this was the last thing I would be any good at I presented myself at the labor exchange. The man behind the counter looked doubtfully at my hands, but as men were needed in the forests, he allocated me to a group just about to depart. I received the necessary equipment: long underclothes of coarse brown wool, a padded jacket of medieval cut, a pair of boots, a protective cap with earflaps, thick gauntlets, a Swedish bow saw, a backsaw, an ax and a bark spudder. I took the clothes with me, packed my rucksack at home and completed my last pieces of work. Before turning out the light I stood in the doorway with my rucksack buckled up and looked at the room that had sheltered me for a year. The room looked dreary, full of dead objects with which I had lost all connection. Later, on the journey and in that forest at the back of beyond, this room sometimes came to my mind with its gray walls, its bed, its bookshelves, its stacks of pictures and drawings. In the waiting room of the labor exchange I sat down with my fellow travelers. Our movements had adapted themselves to the clumsy crude articles of clothing. We sat bent forward on our bench, with heavy shoulders, our arms on our knees, spitting on to the wooden floor and every now and then uttering some gruff comment. The fire crackled in the iron stove. The hard hands of the men tested the saw blades, the cutting edges of the axes. They got the feel of an ax or a notching iron by its handle. They knew their way around with the tools. They knew the forests. They talked about woods easy and hard, of woods in which trunks grew up straight and clear as a candle, and of woods all clogged up with undergrowth, into which you had to crawl through briers and broken rock to get

at the tree. They looked out toward the forests with brows, eyes
and mouths worn with weariness and deprivation. We received
steaming black coffee in tin mugs. Playing cards were produced.
The greasy dog-eared cards were thrown down on the table with
regular insistent movements, the spectators leaned on the shoulders of the players and bent over them in leaden solidarity. The
foreman came and shouted at us to break it up. The gear was
loaded into a truck, we climbed into it and drove through the city
to the railroad station. The shop windows and bright ads shone
through the falling snow. The city sank back behind us in snow
and we clustered together in the smoky railway compartment.
The skat players had put a suitcase on their knees, the cards were
slapped down. Two men hooked their index fingers together and
measured their strength; they panted and tugged and their faces
turned purple. Another was already known as a joker and his
every word was received with roars of laughter. Single words
emerged from the murmured conversations. Kinds of work were
named, work sites, wage rates. The words smacked of coal, wood,
oil, iron, sand. A match fired up over the bowl of a pipe. Smoke
was sucked in and puffed out. Lights twitched past the windows.
The wheels of the train hammered, whirred. One man, who had
been a ship's stoker, mentioned the word Valparaiso. A hand
scratched a bare hairy chest. A mouth devoured a piece of bread
spread with herrings; a herring tail hung out of the mouth, on the
tongue lay a piece of parsley. Many fell asleep, stretched out their
legs, breathed heavily or snored. Roaring and singing the train
drove north. Toward morning we alighted at an out of the way
station and, in the thickly falling snow, between snow-covered
trees, we waited for the narrow-gauge railway. Huddled together
we leaned against one another in the light drizzling flakes, half
asleep as we stood there, blinking through the snow on our eyelids, breathing through the snow on our lips. Noiselessly the train
appeared in a flurry of snow. We lay on the wooden benches and
stretched out on the floor and beneath us rattled the wheels, the
cogs and gears of the world, beneath us the axis of the world
creaked. Then on the truck that burrowed through the ice with
clanking snow chains, ever deeper into a landscape of white

mountains and forests. In the twilight we were transferred to a sledge, a flat open ferry that led us over the frozen swell in the evening. Nothing could be heard but the tinkle of the horse bells and the scrape of the sledge runners. The first stars shimmered, soon the sky crackled and scintillated with them. A star in front of us grew larger and turned into a window. We entered the hut where a woman stood by the hearth poking the fire. The long table was set with tin plates and the woman, a primeval figure, served us large steaming dishes. We shared this living space with the cook. We were twelve men on the two-storied bunks and the woman lay behind a plank screen in a corner. The air was a hot paste. The rough blankets stuck to our bodies. I climbed out of the rustling wood shavings of the mattress and went out in front of the hut. As I was pissing I saw Orion diagonally across the horizon, his sword girded. Smoke floated up from the chimney and the trees bore their burden of snow. Although I was dazed with exhaustion and heat I could not fall asleep. I stared into the glowing stove and heard the sleepers sawing at the trees of the forests. They had the feel of the tools in their hands. Their arms and back muscles were used to exertion. They had shoveled coal, blasted rocks, built roads, laid railway lines. They were at home in the forest and at home in this night. Toward morning the cook's body stirred. She crept out from her wooden screen, stumped across to the stove, and threw logs on the flaring embers. The water in the kettle began to simmer, the bacon to sizzle in the pan. With creaking joints and yawning the stuffy air out of their lungs the men got up from their bunks. Bodies in underclothes staggered muddily out of the shadows, slipped trousers and jackets on, pulled on their boots and seated themselves at table. No one washed. The carbide lamp buzzed. The cook served steaming potatoes and beans; bacon swam in a fatty gravy on the tin plates. It was still dark when, led by the foreman, we set out to work. The bow saw on my back, the ax stuck in my belt, I carried the pad saw, the shovel and the notching iron in my hands; Indian file we trudged through the deep snow, the saw blades hooked on to our clothes. The snow forced its way into our boots. Sometimes the ground beneath me gave way and I sank up to my chest in snow. As I crawled out the ax would get stuck between my legs and the bow saw slipped down over my arms. We burrowed our way uphill. Our clothes were encrusted with ice and snow. Sweat ran down our bodies. When we reached the hill the morning began to dawn. At the edge of the forest the work areas, their boundaries marked by notches in the trees, were distributed by lot. Everyone had to cut himself a ten-foot branch from the bushes on the slope, by which to measure the lengths into which the felled tree trunks were to be sawn. The foreman showed me how to saw the tree. He shoveled the snow aside, sank down on his knees and drove the saw with regular effortless movements back and forth. In a horizontal groove close to the roots it penetrated the wood. When the trunk was half sawn through I realized the purpose of the little iron wedge we had been given and which hung on a string around my neck like an amulet. The wedge was driven into the crack by a blow of the ax and so prevented the saw from getting jammed by the weight of the tree. The foreman explained to me how the felled tree was to be stripped, reminded me to see that the saw blade did not warp, and left me. The remaining workers had spread themselves far and wide along the edge of the forest. They could not be seen through the snowed-up undergrowth, only the rasping of their saws could be heard and the first crash of a felled trunk. Snow flakes fell softly, tinkling lightly. I soon had to use both hands in order to force the saw to and fro. The blade was constantly about to bend. When it was stuck fast in the wood I beat the wedge further in. With my foot pressed against it and straining all my muscles I succeeded in loosening the blade, but after a while it stuck a second time and the wedge had again to be driven into the crack. A groaning sound suddenly burst from the trunk as if a vein were torn and a tremor could be felt in the wood. Half lying down I made the saw rush back and forth, sweat streamed from all my pores, the blood hammered in my temples and I panted in time with the movements of my arms. There was a splintering sound in the tree and I saw the crack widening. I remained lying down and carried on sawing while the trunk slowly heeled over, erupted at the base and descended in a cloud of snow. With a rumble it crashed down, the branches bor-ing deep into the snow. The tall jagged prongs of the shattered tree stump sprang to and fro whistling, and splinters of wood whisked past me. The hacked and mangled stump, the disgrace of the novice, must be sawn off smoothly. The deeply scarred notches on the trunk would mean a deduction from my pay envelope. I had to provide unblemished trunks, other people looked after the firewood. The lopping of the trunk was done partly with the ax and partly with the saw. In order to get at the base of the branches I had to climb on to the trunk. Legs spraddled out on the smooth bark, I tried to get a footing, and raised my ax for a swipe. I missed my aim and the swing of the ax brought me down off the trunk. Branches, I found, could hold me fast and attack me with sharp points. Snow seeped through my sleeves and collar into my shirt. My attempts at removing the branches continued. I climbed on to the trunk, slipped off and climbed on again. The blade of the ax remained stuck in the base of a branch and had to be jogged loose. The ax skimmed past the trunk, brushing my shoe and my knee. I gradually succeeded in removing the branches from the trunk and the green sprays spread out at the side of the trunk smelled of resin. After falling off time and time again, after lunges in the air and a few cuts that sank deep into the soles of my boots, I leaned back exhausted against the stripped trunk. When I stood still in order to eat my bread and drink hot coffee from the thermos bottle ice crystals formed on my wet clothing. I saw the notches I had sliced into my boots and I imagined I had hit my foot and would bleed and freeze to death here. My work mates were far away. The sounds of the saws and ax strokes drifted through the falling flakes. You must keep moving or you'll freeze, I thought. I was so exhausted that I sat on the trunk and for a while forgot the danger. Half asleep I found myself recalling an experience I had had in England. Friends had invited me on an excursion to a stud farm. They had asked me if I could ride and I had said yes, although only once before, as a child, had I ridden on a broad-backed circus hack. Now a highly strung horse pranced beneath me. I lost the stirrup and clung on to the reins, but I succeeded in keeping to the rear of the party so that no one noticed how I slipped in the saddle and steered with my feet in the air. We trotted through a wood toward the fields. I held the reins taut and the horse lashed out with its head to dislodge me. A thunderstorm was gathering in the sky and it began to rain. At a violent peal of thunder my horse bolted, leaped sideways off the path and galloped across the plowed fields. At first I gave the horse free rein and then steered it in a broad circle back to the path where my alarmed friends were waiting. When I reached the path I jumped down like some daring experienced horseman. After a short rest I remounted and now we trotted through the drizzle. I sat relaxed at an even trot and adapted myself to the rhythm of the horse. Suddenly it flung its head back and hit me under the chin with the close-cropped brush of its mane. Stunned, I rode on until one of my companions cried out and pointed at me. My shirt and my jacket were soaked in the blood that ran down my neck. I felt no pain, only a weak exhaustion. I wrenched myself away from the image of my silent bleeding. My clothes crunched with ice. My hands were stiff. Snow had settled on my shoulders. I flung my arms across my chest and stamped up and down to warm my feet. Soon I was again hanging sweating at the trunk and sawed it to pieces. In the afternoon when it had begun to get dark and the others were knocking far away with their axes, I worked at the trunks with the bark spudder. My body was a steaming pumping machine. My back glowed. With wide blows I shoved the spudder under the bark of the trunk lengthwise. Under the layers of bark the smooth white wood with its spicy odor came into view. Without a pause my body moved to and fro. The spudder laid bare the flesh of the tree. With the hook on the back of the iron I turned over the logs. When the foreman's whistle announced the end of the first working day, the treated wood was gathered up into a pile. I stacked the tools together and covered them with fir twigs. The workers appeared out of the gray dusk of the forest and set off home. In a whirl of snowflakes we slid downhill. The hut was our home. The woman had prepared food for us. We called her Sister. Her broad prehistoric body was taboo. Some joked with her and asked her about her sweetheart, but she did not answer, did not even smile. The evaporated sweat mingled with the steam from the cooking range. Our mouths watered, we sniffed expectantly. We threw off our wet clothes and shoes. Our skin was hot, our muscles burned. The odor of wet wool hung thickly on the air. We sat at the long wooden table, in underclothes and socks, leaning back in heavy lethargy. Delayed members of the group stumped in like great ice birds, the snow still swirling around them. I felt the satisfaction of accomplishment. Bacon and potatoes were served. I ate as I had never eaten before. I felt my body taking in the nourishment and digesting it; I felt the nourishment spreading through my body and weighing it down. Someone said, after a meal like that you have to pry yourself up with a crowbar. Over coffee the playing cards were produced. The skat players gathered in one corner; the spectators bent over them; copper coins clinked on the table. Others leafed through a pile of old weeklies. I too took one of the magazines and read of luxury yachts and hotels on the Riviera, of a poor orphan who became a millionaire, of helpful St. Bernards and of a surgeon who fell in love with a nurse. There was no other literature. No other literature had ever been written. We read the yellowing pages stuck together by remains of food; clumsily we worked the words out letter by letter as other generations of the banished had done before us. Here and there a conversation started. I heard something about someone who knew someone who could spit in some special way. He spat without spitting his cigarette out at the same time. Imagining the method of spitting occupied me for a while. Then I became absorbed by a long calculation of my wages which made it clear that at my present rate of work I would not even be able to meet the costs for board and lodging. Each of the others had already accounted for a whole row of trees. At night as I lay on the straw pallet I was again unable to sleep. Behind the screen the wood shavings creaked under the woman's body. The glow from the stove smoldered in the dark. The air was a mountain. We lay in the mountain through which we had to gnaw our way to the land of Cockaigne. The mountain was made of beans, chewed potatoes and bacon fat. My fellow travelers lay exhausted in the mountain and snored, their noses and throats full of beans, potatoes and mashed bacon. The sleepers murmured and rattled and calculated, they snored

and sawed deeper into the mountain. The next day my muscles
burnt in wound fever. Wrists were swollen, hands full of blisters.
We again made our way through the snow. In the gray dawn I
dug out my tools and crept up to my second trunk, dug and burrowed into the wood, sawed, slashed and bit my way into it, felled
it, threw myself over it, sweating, steaming, cursing until again
the odorous naked flesh lay in front of me. The crystal bells of the
snow sounded incessantly. In their fine monotonous tinkle I overcame my trees. Every movement stabbed and burned in me. Furi-
ously I attached the saw, wielded the ax and thrust the spudder
under the bark. My sawteeth and ax-bit glowed. I was far behind
the others. Their ax blows, the scrape of their saws could scarcely
be heard through the mist of snowflakes. From day to day the
snow rose higher. Sometimes the gale helped me with the felling.
Obsessively I worked away at the tree lest it be wrenched apart. I
lay at the foot of the trunk that leaned over me, my consciousness
had been transferred to the trunk, I felt its weight on the saw
blade, I sensed the tension in the wood, sensed the bursting and
whimpering, and sometimes in the gale I had only started to saw
when the trunk began to fall and I was still sawing as the trunk
with whipping twigs crashed down beside me. A couple of men
lay in the hut with fever; one was suffering from frostbite in his
foot, the other just lay and howled and was mocked by the rest of
us as a malingerer. The sick were sent back to the city while we,
the survivors, continued the struggle. Primeval horses came and
dragged away the felled trunks into the valley. The horses, swimming in snow, looked like sea monsters with their black long-
maned heads, their glittering eyes and snorting nostrils. The drivers came from Niflheim; they were clothed in shaggy furs and
their faces were hidden under encrusted beards. They let out incomprehensible guttural noises and slept at night against the
flanks of their cart horses. Every evening we sat around the table.
The skat players slapped the cards down and the pages of the
magazines rustled in our hands. Our voices faltered sleepily. We
were like saws and axes learning to speak. Our voices uttered the
word movies, or the word dance, and eyes were sucked into inde-
terminate distances, and only when someone waggled a hand in

front of them did they tear themselves loose. We laughed at the
jokester when he went out to the privy and said, I'm at the office if
the phone rings. The idea of a telephone here, at the end of the
world, always provoked laughter. We would shout, hey, Long
John, phone call for you, and then we would double up with
laughter. Only on Sundays did visions of another life stir in us. On
Sunday we lay on the bunks and spread ourselves out and
stretched and yawned and listened to the dreary humming of the
flies at the window. In the emptiness and inactivity of Sundays
we stole sly glances in the direction of Sister, who sat dumbly at
the table and laid out cards for herself, bending her dark face
with the broad cheekbones and slanting eyes. Monotonous as the
humming of the flies our thoughts circled around her heavy
breasts and hips. A few went on skis to the nearest villages, several hours away, to sit there a while in the café reading newspapers and listening to the radio and came back in the evening
more exhausted than after working in the forest. We sat at table
and brooded, enclosed by the woods. The snow lay over us. Our
lips moved, whispering and murmuring, working out our week's
wages. The flies buzzed at the window panes and pencil strokes
on greasy pieces of paper were totted up. I saw the austere worn
shapes sitting around the table, saw the faded colors of their
clothes, the graining of the table top, the notches in it, the blue
coffee pot with its patches of rust, the pipes in the ashtray, the
tired hands folded. The fever I had at the beginning had passed. I
was wide awake, and saw myself as one among the workers of this
Siberia. I had got used to the hut and the work and my other need
now returned. And again I met with resistance and rejection from
my companions and with a dull mistrust of any change. I had
suggested that we be sent books, but no one wanted to read
books. They made disparaging remarks about books and said
mockingly that books existed just for stay at homes and book-
worms. I had books sent to me. I offered them some to read, but
they barely leafed through them. They let me read without making fun of me because I had shown them that I could work as they
could, but they shook their heads and asked what good it had
done me. They could not understand either why I should sit writ-

ing in a notebook and sometimes sketched. They would have despised me if I had not gone out with them in the mornings into the forest and emerged from it again with them in the evening. When I spoke of the lack of the most elementary prerequisites for comfort and hygiene and said that the grub was only provided in order to keep us quiet, they looked at me suspiciously and replied that they earned good money, better than many others. They had no complaints about their country's government or social system. Literature and art did not exist for them, because they had not even begun to seek conditions of life fit for human beings. They thought it ridiculous that I should wash after the first few days of exhaustion. When I was gargling one of them pretended the sound made him sick. They regarded dirt and sweat on the skin as a warm protective layer. They lived by casual labor and the concept of further education was unknown to them. But they knew much that I did not know. They knew all about the quality of tools, they could distinguish the various types of wood, they knew the names of shipping firms and building companies, they were well informed about the most varied methods of work and wage structure. I wondered sometimes what they could hope for from life and what could make them happy, but I obtained no information about this. They told of drinking bouts, of the number of bottles of schnapps they had consumed, and of the price they had had to pay for the bottles, but their faces did not light up as they spoke. In their descriptions of places of work only the everyday practical details were mentioned and their expression betrayed no personal involvement. These subjects of a rich land that had been spared the war still lived extremely primitive lives. Like the hired hand or the dairy maids at the farm they suffered from the day laborer's sense of inferiority. The fact that they were free workers did not entail any sense of involvement with the goods they produced. They worked indifferently, only thinking of their wages. They had their trade union and believed that their power was thereby insured. It never occurred to them that they had been cheated. They shared the traditional view that culture and art were luxuries. They had become accustomed to a hard crude language because it fitted in with the hard crude work they were

forced to do. When for a short while they got drunk everything
that was latent and dissatisfied in them came out and they lum-
bered about and shouted, started fights and lashed out, only to
sink finally into imbecile stupor. And when we then sat in front of
our bowls, slumped over them, smacking our lips, drinking noisily,
and leaned back and belched and wiped our mouths on the back
of our hands, and then waited for the night, they bent over their
playing cards or tattered magazines, I over my notebook, scribbling away with a pencil, the slight difference in our cultural
background, the greater awareness which, I believed, made me
differ from them, vanished, and the night was the same for all of
us.

In my room in the city I could see these men who expected
nothing from life and took the day as it came. Even now I was at
pains to get to know them. Why did the play of colors of a sunset
or the blinding night sky or this gently singing fall of the snow-
flakes mean nothing to them? Why did they shrug their shoulders
disparagingly when I tentatively pointed out a detail that had impressed me. And what did I then see different from what they saw
in the white smoke from the hut chimney, in the dented pots on the
table, in the shaggy black horses, in the ruddy gray of the dawn
over the snow slopes, in the movement of hands with playing
cards, in the primeval face of our cook. That I took time to im-
press the appearances upon myself and be aware of them, was
this not merely the result of my old bourgeois security and leisure.
Could I not stand for a long time at my place in the forest and
gaze at the stack of tools, because ultimately the results of my
work were a matter of indifference to me, because it made no
difference to me that I scarcely attained even a minimum wage
and that I had lost an hour of working time. Did this sheltered
feeling not lie in my blood, in contrast to my work mates who had
grown up in poverty and had from an early age to contribute to
the breadwinning. And what was there in my image of the smoking chimney, the stack of tools, the card game, the horses swimming in the snow, that was not in the image which the same
things presented to my companions. Smoke was smoke, horse was

horse, snow was snow and nothing else. I saw the things, groped after their forms, noted them down, described them to myself. They too saw these things, but to them they were self-evident, they were not worth consideration. The chimney smoked because there was a fire burning in the hearth, the horses were there in order to drag the wood down to the valley, snow fell because snow had to fall. To observe and note down what I experienced was my work. For me things only obtained a value when I made them clear to myself. The others simply lived with the things. I knew why many periods were gray and dull: in these periods something lay in front of my senses and dulled them. These periods were dead, even though I was still there. I was just like all the others, then, in a colorless commonplace existence. I looked into the faces in the city. I rode in a tram and all the faces stared blankly ahead. We drove over the high span of the West Bridge. The sun was sinking and the rays squeezed out behind extensive black-red- and gold-edged banks of cloud. Fan-shaped violet strips of cloud floated into the greeny-blue sky and the sun's rays broke into the windows of the prison buildings below on the island. A golden glow filled the hall behind the bars and inside a giant shape with a lion's head sat leaning forward. Slowly we glided past this spectacle and I felt as if I must shout out: Why don't you look at what's going on. Look at these colors, this light. But by that time we were already engulfed again in the shadows of the street canyons and not a face had turned around. And anyway, what else was there to say but that the sun had set.

I knew no more, after all, than the clerks on their way home from their offices, workshops and stores and, if sometimes my senses were so unfettered that it seemed I was seeing things for the first time, on the other hand the limitations that would again crop up, and which no one else paid any heed to, had a stultifying effect on me. Whenever I seemed about to achieve something, some obstacle would suddenly arise and I would have to discard and break off whatever I had at hand. I fought against these limitations and when I succeeded in removing them in one place I slumped back again, understanding neither what I had gained nor

what these limitations actually represented. Kafka had stood before this wall, a wall against which he finally battered himself to
death, running against it again and again, though it was no higher
then himself. This wall consisted of laws handed down, and all I
needed to do was take one step sideways to stand before an open
place. But to do this I first had to get rid of the chimera I was
lugging along with me. In the biographies of painters and writers
I searched for hints as to what they had achieved at the age I had
now reached. Nothing more could be discovered from this than
the fact that some had arrived at usable material in their early
years while others only came to it later. There were the youthfully
successful, and there were those who discovered what they
wanted to say only in the middle of their lives. Many showed
from early on a clear and definite line while others had to look
long before finding anything convincing. There was something
puzzling about the integrity, the ever sharp consciousness of the
great masters. How was it possible to produce this certainty and
this endurance. And how had they overcome the forces that must
also have appeared before them to hold back. I studied the openings of their books. Many books opened with conscientious intro-
ductory passages in which the reader was prepared for what was
to come. This type of opening gambit seemed tenable and it was
moreover, possible that some further development might arise
from it, but it was also possible that only uncertainty was hidden
beneath it, a strained desire to establish something still indetermi-
nate and obscure. Others plunged straight into their subject matter and opened with a few bold strokes. This method seemed convincing; it was exciting but it was possible that beneath it lay
despair that would later make everything that had been expressed
confused and irrelevant. In one book it was the firm structure that
was attractive, in another book it was the meditative and mysteri-
ous element that allured me. Every opening—whatever form it
took: restrained or determined, concise or circumstantial, aggressive or defensive—every opening was the result of long prepara-
tory pressure. Every opening was a decision that had grown out of
contradictory considerations. The manner in which the decision
expressed itself, the way in which it was carried out, showed the

essential character and way of life of its writer. My openings constantly came to a standstill and were destroyed by doubt. Every
time what I achieved seemed a falsification. The words were
there, trying to construct something out of a material devoid of
shape. The uncertainty from which I started and in which I tentatively recorded points of view in regions where there was no question of paths or any indication of definite shapes in the landscape,
deprived me of the confidence that I needed in order to concentrate on a particular theme, a particular technique. There was no
established style, no unifying medium, writing and drawing could
equally well have merged into music or dancing. The only purpose in the work was movement, circling around and illuminating
a few moments as they arose and before they disappeared again. I
started off from my doubts, my contradictions, the constant argu-
ments for and against. At that time this indecision was often ex-
hausting. I did not see the vast and varied potential in this, the
possibility of a total art, in which the convention of specialized art
no longer existed. I was only constantly aware that something was
exhausted and out of date. Even the books, which some time before had an irreplaceable meaning for me, suddenly seemed like
so much unnecessary ballast and, in a fit of asceticism, I packed a
suitcase full of them and took them to a secondhand dealer. I may
have seemed to myself a murderer carrying parts of a corpse
around with him in the tram, and I may also have had to pluck up
my courage and to explain my actions as a necessity in troubled
times, when everything superfluous has to be cast overboard. I
stood in the bookshop like a traitor with my open suitcase as this
block of thoughts and feelings held between the pages of the
books, this past reflecting my journeys, my stays in various cities
and countries, was laid bare under the purchaser's appraising eye.
Secondhand books in German were not much in demand. The
dealer's cellars were crammed with discarded volumes from the
libraries of émigrés. The dealer took out the works and stacked
them up as if he were working out the transaction by weight and I
beat a hasty retreat with my thirty pieces of silver. I had retained
only a handful of books which I could not dream of parting with:
Klingsor, Steppenwolf, the volumes of Kafka, *Hunger, Pan* and

Van Gogh's letters. When I gave up my room, too, and settled in
an empty summer house that I had found in a suburb I read Van
Goghs' letters again. They were part of this sudden breakaway,
this vagabondage, this constant traveling. I had read them for the
first time as a seventeen-year-old in England and in my first man-
uscript I had identified myself with Van Gogh. It was a sort of
diary in which I portrayed his existence which had become my
own, from his stay at the London art dealer's to the pistol shot in
his chest at the edge of the wheat field. I now journeyed into my
own Borinage. I shared poverty and isolation with Van Gogh and
I wanted to possess nothing beyond the bundle on my back. At
night in the half-dilapidated house I lay on a mattress on the floor
and by day I covered the walls with pictures. In the autumn of
1943 Edna came to see me. Returning from a visit to the doctor
she leaned out of the window and called down to me in the garden, through the foliage falling from the decaying cherry trees,
that she was now certain. Once again a chain reaction had been
produced and in the woman's womb a life was forming generated
by me in the twilight among the stacks of pictures. An apocalypse
surrounded the germ of a new human being: the semen had
flowed out, and lay engulfed in the uterus, grew slowly, developed limbs, surrounded by my pictures. The pictures were taken
and spread out in an exhibition, these volumes of pictures, of picture surfaces, stuck together, stuck one on top of the other,
kneaded out of shape, handled out of shape, in part many layers
of transparent paper, in part interspersed with writings, or with a
series of cutouts from reproductions of finished works of art,
colors in paint or torn out of bright papers, and the forms and
objects, sometimes arranged catalogue-fashion, sometimes any
which way, now gave an impression of photographic precision,
again one of a confusion of lines and smudges. This whole attempt, this discharge, easy to tear up, burn and throw away, represented the inadequacy of my means, made it clear that language
and picture were no longer enough and were merely refuse. And
yet there must be some other element in this obsession which en-
abled me to attack the devaluation and dissolution of everything
familiar, for if there were really nothing more to grasp I would

also have nothing further to say and I would accept lethargy that often seductively came upon me. But it was satisfying to wring a few more hieroglyphs out of the catastrophe, and I was still a creator so long as I could describe to myself the destruction and disintegration.

In our new apartment, which we had rented to await the birth of the child, I was often overcome by a satisfaction in being able to take part in a debacle, in being able to see what was going on and to feel that I had not yet been choked off. Even if I lay crippled in the mire, as I sometimes imagined, at least the activity that then took place could not be argued out of existence, and even though every symbol and every text might seem questionable to me, they were nonetheless recorded, and to the extent that I reacted and expressed myself I was still part of an inhabited world. Once at night I jumped up and woke Edna because I had come to what I thought was the epoch-making conclusion that after destruction and dissolution one could start again with the simplest elements. In these months before the birth of the child we spent the best part of our marriage, in a single room apartment constructed in modern economy style, and through its concrete walls signs of life from the other occupants hummed, hissed, crackled, cracked, moaned, creaked and rumbled. Individual cries, and every now and then a groaning and a droning, stood out against the noise of the music and chattering radio sets, the sinks and the water pipes. Lying in a warm bed, we listened to the evening's entertainment of rows and reconciliations, transmitted to us from the farthest corners of the house and amplified by the megaphone-like ventilation system. At night, when a curtain of silence had been drawn across the walls, a disembodied bawling, clattering or snoring would penetrate with super-clarity into our room more distinctly than ever. We woke up and laughed, threw glasses at the wall, put on music, danced, and then to a tom-tom knocking from all sides I lay with my ear on Edna's naked belly listening to the movements of the child. In the late afternoon a narrow strip of sunlight seeped through the window making Edna's hair shine golden red. She sat at the easel and spun away

at her picture dreams, laughing about the figures that she conjured up in front of her, and speaking to them in a whisper. Her
distended body curved forward. Sometimes she sat for a long time
and listened to the life growing within her. Her mouth smiled.
The light glittered in a tear in her eye. In front of her in the green
of the picture there arose the garlanded midsummer pole. Children danced around it. Elks, hares and capercaillies with divided
tail feathers peered out of the forest. The child moved in the belly
of the pregnant woman, he kicked and tried to get out. The invasion troops had been hurled on to the beaches of Normandy. With
my brush I worked at the stalks, blossoms and leaves of the
clothes patterns, made up the technical reports and traced the
individual color schemes, while on the special news bulletins ac-
counts were given of the battles, the losses, the advances and de-
feats. On Midsummer Night's Eve the labor pains began. In this
night before the holiday music blared out everywhere from the
loudspeakers and people were singing in the streets. As we lay in
bed in a close embrace we rocked to and fro in time to the street
musicians. In the early dawn of this bright night we went down to
the car that was to drive us to the clinic. It was two in the morning, the sun was already rising from behind the roofs. I accompanied Edna into the examination room. She had been given a short
linen smock to wear, sat on a high upholstered stand and from the
room next door we could hear the screams of a woman in labor.
Then the doctor came and showed me out. It would last a few
more hours. I waited below the hospital at the edge of the site
where the marquee and the booths of a traveling circus had been
erected. The animals morosely came awake in their pens. A few
dark-skinned figures, half asleep, emerged from the caravan, pails
clinked, a baboon was led out of his cage and tethered to a stake
in an enclosure. The ape sat erect on his blue behind and looked
about him attentively, with jerky movements of his head. Several
times I went up to the clinic, but Edna's hour had not yet come. I
sat on a slope in the grass and watched the ape in the growing
heat, playing in a bored way with his thin, red phallus. In the
paddock the ponies stood shooing flies away with their tails. Acro-
bats practiced their art on a rope. The traffic on the wide road out

of town had increased, families were driving out to the country, accordions were being played in the gardens, and children were dancing around the flag- and leaf-bedecked poles. The sun was high in the sky. A new human being was working his way out of the womb, fatty, with eyes gummed shut. From the dark warmth he reached the light. He was swung into the open by his feet, the doctor gave him a spank, he let out his first scream, his umbilical cord was severed, his body washed and swaddled, he received a number and a name, and had to find his way around out here on the outside.

I can see myself leaning on the balustrade of a terrace; behind me in the dusk on the wide river the white steamers are returning from the rocky islands with thudding engines and a wave of music, fast motor boats rattle past, and screams and laughter waft across from the pleasure gardens. In front of me is the open door of the flat we have rented; Edna is sitting by the light of the lamp, drawing, painting, modeling her figures and in its bed lies the child, our child: it sleeps, stirs and wakes up. Above the house, between the dark chestnuts, rise the towers of the villa where Edna's mother lives, its weather vane standing out clearly against the pale sky. I lean on the wooden balustrade, smoke a cigarette, hear the noises of an evening in late summer, and look for all the world like a man who has his place in a home and a family, a city and a country. I try to retain this image. I see myself entering the flat. The rooms are furnished with Edna's furniture, her pictures are hanging on the wall, her colorful little statuettes populate the tables. I look for signs of myself in this flat, impulses or expressions that might betray my presence. There is a child, there are the child's hands, the child's feet, the face with its eyes taking in their first impressions and the mouth forming its first noises. There is nothing to show that I have bent over this face, to make it aware of my existence, nothing to show that I have taken up the light body and carried it in order to show it that it was under my protection. I try to find some clear proof that Edna is my wife. I still have memories of her body, of her long smooth limbs, her pink nipples, memories of her movements as we embraced, but

they are vague: they do not convey the idea of an everyday asso-
ciation. I can discover no conversations in which we revealed ourselves, even though days and nights, months, a few years have
prepared us for it. The terrace to which I now return is clearer
than the interior of the rooms. It is possible that Edna is coming
out behind me, that we are now both standing at the balustrade.
It has grown dark. The sound of shots from the shooting gallery,
the shrieks from the roller coaster, the pipings from the merry-go-
round have died down. Now in the stillness of the night an occasional screech from the peacocks on the heights of the Skansen
Park can be heard. On such nights there would have been much
to say; we might have been able to confront each other with our
different worlds and reconsider them, but there is no trace of any
words. I do not even know if we ever took the trouble.

We had been invited by Edna's father to a family celebration.
It was the first time I had been allowed into their house and from
the room where the relatives were gathered he beckoned me into
his study. He shut the sliding door and we stood facing each other
on the Persian carpet between the tall bookshelves. First of all he
said that it was unseemly for me to talk familiarly to him: I should
call him Professor. It was also out of place for me to express opinions about the way the house was furnished, as I had done on
entering. Since I could not remember having done so I contradicted him and this led to a complicated argument even before he
had broached his real subject. He then said that he wanted to try
to consider me as a member of the family, but that it had to be
pointed out that this was due to the force of circumstances and
that he still condemned the manner in which I had seduced his
daughter and forced my way into her social milieu. In his pre-
amble he repeated what had been obvious to him from the very
first time he heard of my existence: that I was a pariah, a stray
mongrel who wanted to gain a foothold in the fleshpots of the
upper classes. But he could not help recognizing the fact that the
situation in the autumn of 1944 was different from that of the
spring of 1942—I no longer even belonged to the mob of refugees
and stateless immigrants but had recently become a subject of this

country and the king had certified it for me on a document. That, said the Professor, was also why he wanted to see me today in his family circle. I replied that it was only my father whom I had to thank for my naturalization; he was welcomed as a factory owner and employer and without him I would not even have been allowed across the frontier. The chalky skin of his face screwed up and his little lobster eyes glinted. I went on to say that for me my naturalization was a mere formality and that I still belonged to no country. He retorted that my remarks merely confirmed his opinion of me and for a while he continued to harangue me about my duties as a family man and a subject. While he spoke my eyes glided over the rows of books and deciphered some titles that excited my imagination—*Dynamic Geology, Geotectonic and Stratigraphic Geology, Physical Geography,* the study of the first living creatures—then I looked at the bronze group that adorned his writing desk. It consisted of a scantily clad Diana whose outstretched right foot was resting on its toes while her left foot swung far back in flight and her right hand, raised high, aimed a spear at a lion who crouched before her, his right paw ready to strike. The Professor had now stopped talking and seemed to be awaiting my reply. His large carefully washed paleontologist's hand was raised in front of me, the index finger outstretched. I asked him about the mythological background of the sculpture, as I had never heard of a struggle between Diana and a lion. For a moment it looked as though he were going to slap me across the face with his expressive meaningful hand, but then he let it drop and stood stiffly, leaning back in his hard shell. After a few concluding words of contempt he set himself in motion, strode toward the door and slid it open. Meanwhile, in the drawing room, the family had been making arrangements for a house concert. I remained standing in the doorway of his study so that during the performance I could look at the books that had aroused my interest. The Professor's wife firmly beat out a few notes on the grand piano and his fourteen-year-old daughter, Edna's half-sister, tuned her violin with pizzicato plucks and scrapes of the bow. After a while it turned out that the scrapes on the violin and the vigorous pummeling on the keyboard, from which a few fragments of melody could occasionally be identified represented a sonata, and the notes, over which the performers bent with such obvious effort, had once been devised by Mozart. The violinist stood stiffly in her white tulle dress, her white stockings and buckled shoes, with a white bow in her braids, fiddling jerkily. The pianist in a low gold-shimmering gown, nodded in time with her swinging earrings, counted and tapped the soles of her shoes on the floor. All around, in the armchairs and sofas, sat the audience, the ladies in evening dress, the gentlemen in black or uniform, with medals or insignia of high command; only I stood grayly at the door. I had taken a voluminous book from the shelf and was leafing through it, reading here and there of primeval eruptions and inundations, the formation of oceans and continents, ammonites, the first mammals and deciduous trees. From the drawing room came the noise of applause. I replaced the book and went to join the guests. Edna's brother Alfred came up to me, gave me a confidential slap on the shoulder, and expatiated on my painting which he did not know but about which he had, however, heard. He was going by a few reviews in the daily papers of my latest exhibition; from these it appeared that my work was nothing but a revival of long since abandoned Central European trends. I studied Alfred's face. It was narrow, with an unhealthy pallor about it, like his father's face but without the concentrated strength. His blond hair hung in curls around his high vacant forehead. His wife, Johanna, who had joined us leaned against him and gazed at him tenderly, asking me whether I thought he looked like Leslie Howard. A roar of laughter resounded behind us. It was Jörg, Edna's cousin, sitting in a deep armchair with his legs outstretched, exploding with laughter. From all sides people turned to look at him. Jörg was the black sheep of the family, he had no regular job, had even taken a stab at being a writer. Jörg again laughed encouragingly to me, then drew himself up to his full six feet. Glasses were now handed around; Jörg, who emptied his glass in one draught, immediately grabbed a second one, thereby earning a withering look from the lady of the house. The chatting voices clustered together to repulse the embarrassing attack of laughter, but it hung in the air. A man in a general's uni-

form, with a white trimmed mustache, turned to me and asked me
when I would be doing my military service which was obligatory
now that I had acquired Swedish nationality. I answered that because of psychic injuries I had been exempted from this superfluous activity. Again Jörg let out his barking laugh from deep in his
chest and the general was just about to bellow at him when the
doors of the dining room opened and the hostess summoned her
guests to table. We took our places. Candles were burning in silver candelabra. I was assigned to the lower end of the table. Next
to me sat Edna's half-sister, the violinist, and opposite me sat
Edna and Jörg. Now and again Jörg bent over to Edna, whispered
something in her ear and exploded with laughter, at which the
hostess's face scowled her pained disapproval. I praised my neighbor's playing and this made her blush. I asked if she had other
interests as well, and, lowering her eyes, the corners of her mouth
primly drawn down, she said that she hoped after finishing her
studies to work in the Natural History Museum. Apart from her
school work and her music lessons she was interested in her collection of shells. In her room she kept over a thousand different vari-
eties, catalogued and arranged in boxes. The general rose from his
place of honor next to the lady of the house and began to make his
after-dinner speech. He held up a glass of wine for a toast and the
guests all stood up; only Jörg remained seated, leaning back as if
he were asleep. Those nearest him prodded him, but he did not
seem to notice anything. A murmur spread round the lower part
of the table. Alfred rolled up balls of bread and pelted Jörg with
them. Finally the disturbance spread to the head of the table and
the general too discovered the sitter and interrupted his speech to
shout at him angrily. When Jörg still did not stand up he replaced
the glass overflowing with wine on the table, ran to Jörg, seized
him by the ears and screamed: Stand up, you lout! At this Jörg,
giggling to himself, slowly and shakily got to his feet. So the family ceremony could be continued and the toast drunk.

Even now I sometimes meet Jörg in the street late at night. From
afar I recognize his Herculean figure. The laughter, with which he
greets me, resounds through the gullies between the houses and

every time I am in his company the city takes on the appearance of a wilderness, a stone desert. His booming laughter, punctuated by violent belches, comes from a prehistoric epoch, and Jörg, expanded to giant height, uttering wild guttural cries, eons old, wanders around, lost in the debris of later civilizations. Stand up, you lout. We shout to each other, and then we walk a stretch together and inform each other of the events in our day-to-day lives, divorces, remarriages, new divorces, work begun and then broken off. We come to the conclusion that basically nothing has changed, and that at most we have become a little more furrowed and weather-beaten by the winds that blow through the passages of our hunting grounds. It is usually he who embarks on one of his chaotic monologues which replace his unwritten books and in which the confusion of his life finds expression. He is loaded to bursting point with material and his disclosures have point and weight, but he lacks the ability to organize them, gets lost in rage, hate and belligerence, never manages to work loose from his entanglements, and escapes, when he can take it no longer, into the delirium of a drunk. Sometimes I saw him as an example of the great loners of this Nordic world, people who, amid the coldness of the social forms, the reserve, envy and hatefulness can never develop, who always dream of a land where it is warmer, where people are more open, but who never muster enough courage to look for this other land, who remain trapped in the ice because they are too heavy and are themselves already saturated with ice. Whenever I met Jörg, and when, on an empty square or at a dreary street corner, I took leave of him, and his laughter and his last belch died away among the dark ravines, the city became completely alien to me and I did not understand how I had been able to live here for so long, but I myself had already become too heavy to believe in other better cities.

My studio was on the top floor of a large apartment house on the Fleminggatan, which at that time was still served by the No. 11 streetcar line. Along the broad street were the undertaker's windows, with splendid caskets, urns and catafalques, and above the shoemaker's and the glover's hung large golden shoes and hands, swinging and creaking in the breeze blowing steadily from the open river to these northerly suburbs. From my windows I could see the Saint Eric's Hospital park, where the white smocks of the doctors fluttered along the paths between the damp black trees. Screeching and clattering, the blue streetcars rolled past and with a whooshing sound the doors of the red buses at the bus stops opened and closed. I would often gaze down on the street for a long time. At the hospital gates brakes were often jammed on as cars ahead in the line of traffic came to a sudden halt there, and pedestrians ran back and forth across the roadway. Ambulances lurched into the entrance, its barred gates opening noiselessly. Visitors came with flowers, patients appeared with limbs in plaster casts and leaning on crutches. Men accompanied pregnant women to the long low buildings of the maternity clinic and groups of mourners gathered in front of the chapel at the far end of the park. Looking over the long straight road in either direction I saw the traffic streaming toward and away from me. The chances of accidents could be calculated from a considerable distance. The swerve took place at the very last moment, but sometimes the cars' fenders scraped each other with a screechy sound, a pedestrian leaped aside with a cry, stumbled and pitched forward, or a motorcycle lamp shattered with a splintering of glass. When someone had been knocked down and injured, which happened not infrequently, there was always a moment of arrested movement, as at a play. The incident with all its force struck a hole in the even flow of events and later, long after the injured person had been taken to the first-aid station, and a patch of blood on the curb still bore witness to his injury, the spectators stood dumbly in front of it as at a sacrificial altar. Every day by streetcar I covered the long distance from the zoo to my studio. With me traveled clerks to their offices, civil servants to their chanceries and tradesmen to their businesses. Through their work they had a direct relationship with the city, and their faces, which still stared blankly in front of them in the swaying streetcar would soon be animated by the interplay of supply and demand. Sometimes I drew sustenance from this early morning ride, I became engrossed in the activities of my fellow passengers who gradually left the car and hurried to their work just when I too finally reached my work, in the increasing traffic, as the shops and offices were opening. Like them I was at my post all day and even if no one asked me to contribute, I still wanted to see some value in the things I produced. There was no fruitful exchange of ideas about technique, problems of form and possibilities of artistic development. Anatol was too self-absorbed and Amos was too indolent to find any pleasure in such conversations. Hoderer and Kurz were dead and the local writers, painters and critics whom I met did not know what to make of my attempts. Even my correspondence with Max was of no assistance. He was living in his hotel room overlooking a back yard in the Bronx, cursing America, longing for Europe, now and again translating a few verses of his ancient Persian and waiting for the long postponed day of his homecoming. I felt indifferent to his grove and his exiled Firdausi, just as he was indifferent to my ideas about the possible means of representing an explosion. Edna, who was close to me every day, knew least of all about what was going on, at the most laughed at the strangeness of my pictures if by chance she ever saw one, and for her I was only an ornament, a complicated caricature, a form run wild, something she often consigned to hell because I paid no attention to her, the household, or the child. And in her, too, I saw only a superficial weaver of images, saw only the fairy tale figurines she had set up all about her for her own protection, and I never moved closer to her, even our embraces never led to a melting together. And with all this there lurked behind my work a constant feeling of danger, a feeling it could not go this way. I knew this kind of work was for me, and that other forms of activity were unthinkable for me, I did only a minimum of textile designing, and tried to live on the rare sale of a picture, on the proceeds from an illustrating assignment, the fee for a published piece of writing, or on returns from a little volume of prose pieces, I tried to make my point of view clear in my work, chose to believe that my pictures and writings were signs of the events in which I was participating, but again and again it seemed as if I would never make it. For this too I had explanations. It was tempting to regard the work as a game of chance, to realize that

everything was only put down for the time being, and that everything stood for something else, something impossible. This something was the dangerous part. This something was the actual collapse, of which I had had forebodings at Max's departure on the
eve of my first exhibition.

Such a collapse would have been an absurdity, as it appeared to
me. But just the same I could see it lying in wait, a towering,
shapeless mass of a thing, and then I would shove it away from
me and just let it be there, a precondition of my work, an inherent
condition of life itself, even the dangerous part of it, which was
not diminished by its immanence, I accepted, and in the awareness of the menace of its proximity the work became only more of
an adventure. In the nights—and at the beginning of this last winter of the war I spent more and more nights in my studio—my
resistance sometimes flagged, and I got close enough to the lurking mass to touch it, a mass which had a viscous, elastic consistency, which always gave, always pulled back, which could be felt
but not taken hold of, and exploring which made my flesh crawl.

In the mornings I looked in the mirror to see if my hair had
become white, but it did not lose its color any more than I went
out of my mind feeling out the sinister form. Through these expeditions I enlarged my field of vision but maintained my puritani-
cal self-control. So great was my trust in my powers of dispassion-
ate observation that I toyed with the idea of putting myself right
inside the formless shape and savoring it to the full, not as a collapse but as an unknown lawless part of myself. However, I succeeded in advancing no further than into a frontier region.

I stood on the river bank opposite the castle and watched
people throwing pieces of bread and crumbs from paper bags to
the ducks and swans gathered below on the ice. Although there
was nourishment to excess the birds squabbled over every crumb,
snatched the pieces from each other's bills and chased one another, screaming and shrieking, while the people, many of whom
had unbuttoned their coats and removed their hats in the prema-

ture warmth of the sun, laughed. A line was untied from one of the iron rings and thrown up onto the bows of the steamer, its screws twirling violently backward, whereupon it began to heave its way through the creaking breaking ice floes. The white steamer, the light blue sunny sky, voices and footsteps, the ringing of a streetcar, the ships' hooters, distant hammer blows, all these things aroused in me thoughts of summer and of travel. On the steps of the National Museum office workers sat sunning themselves during the midmorning break, the faces of the young girls were bent back in an expression of devoted self-abandonment, their eyes tight shut. The imposing palace façade on the island of the Old City lay in shadow and behind me on the Nybro Square rose the vast hotel, brightly illuminated by the sun with the dazzling golden crown adorning its roof. I walked over to the canopy that extended from the main entrance out over the pavement, stood still for a while, looked at my watch, walked up and down, peered around as if I were looking for someone, and finally stepped through the door that the porter was holding open for me. The rays of sunlight fell through the high windows of the entrance hall and spread over the settees and tables. Here and there sat guests, drinking coffee, leafing through a newspaper. Newly arrived travelers followed the bellhop who carried their cases to the elevator, while others, about to continue their journey, were paying up at the reception desk. Telephone calls were announced, books bought for the journey, people walked chatting toward the broad glass doors leading to the dining room and came out of it, red-faced and replete. I walked slowly around in the lobby, keeping a lookout, and then sat down on a sofa near a dark-haired woman. I crossed my legs, leaned back, let my eyes wander up and down the room and at times rest on the woman. At first her features were severe and reserved, but suddenly they relaxed as she raised a book from her lap with her left hand and opened it, while with her right hand she undid the bun into which her hair had been tied. Her hair fell at the same time as the book was opened, glinted in the sunbeams and fanned out, and then, as she bent over the book, the surge of her hair flowed down over her shoulders. Fascinated by this sight, I had thrust my hands deep into the gap between the upholstery of the seat and the armrest, and I now felt, with the fingertips of my right hand, a flat object which, judging by the shape and feel of it, must be a wallet. Carefully, lowering my eyes from the woman, and slowly and indifferently keeping a lookout, I drew the object between my fingers from its recess and secreted it unobserved in the spacious pocket of my overcoat. Then I lit a cigarette, got up, strolled through the hall looking at my watch, glanced around once again and left the hotel through the door which the porter again held open for me. I did not succumb to my desire to take my prize out of my pocket and examine it until I had reached the park, at the Nybro Bay. The wallet contained no identity card and no monogram, and it was crammed only with bank notes of various high denominations. With this unexpected possession, which I had perhaps taken over from a con man who was being pursued, I continued my walk along the avenue beside the river. I crossed the roadway in front of a big gray building, with balustrades and balconies molded, as it seemed, out of some sort of clay. I went in through the gateway and walked along the red velvet carpet in the middle of a broad stairway between the dazzlingly white marble walls streaked with reddish veins and blotches, up to the dark-grained door of the Embassy, pressed down the copper latch of the door and proceeded to the waiting room where I took a seat on the soft leather sofa by the smoking table. I drew the packet of cigarettes from my pocket, lit a cigarette, left the packet lying in front of me on the black table surface studded with a white wedge pattern and began to leaf through the illustrated magazines laid out on the table. I did not engross myself too deeply in the pictures, so that I could still observe the people coming in and out. The people who went through the door all had a purpose in mind, some business or other. Many of them carried attaché cases under their arms or the inner pockets of their jackets were swollen with papers. I studied the cut and patterns of the gentlemen's suits and the ladies' clothes. The gentlemen mainly preferred dark materials, sometimes pin striped, and with these they wore white shirts with stiff collars. In their ties they liked a red or a blue, and often the glittering pearl of a tiepin. From their breast pockets peeped

the smooth tip of a white pocket handkerchief. No signs of wear
and tear could be detected on their collars or cuffs. The cuffs and
the hems of their jackets were equally flawless. The suits, dresses,
blouses, jumpers, coats and hats of the ladies offered a rich variety. The costly materials were often supplemented by items of
jewelry, rings, bracelets, necklaces and earrings that sparkled gold
and silver. Bracelets, in loose sequence one over the other, or set
with spangles, tinkled softly in time to steps that were inaudible
on the soft carpet. The ladies' hats often looked like exotic birds
whirring past, little forest animals with bushy fur or uprooted
sprays of leaves and flowers. One lady sat down to wait in a deep
armchair by the smoking table. Under cover of my newspaper I
observed the ankles and joints of her feet and her toes which
stirred under the thin leather hide of her shoes. She rocked her
foot up and down, so that the shoe with its sharp high heel slid
back and released her heel. Leaning back in my chair with the
magazine in front of me I smoked my cigarette and, when I had
finished it, I stubbed it out in the ashtray and lit another. A recep-
tionist who had given me several piercing glances as she walked
past now came up and bent over me to ask in a voice which had a
wheedling, melting quality, whether she could do any thing for
me. Her face was carefully covered with foundation makeup,
powdered and rouged, dark streaks emphasized the almond shape
of her eyes and lengthened them with an upward curve. She had
mascara on her lashes and eyebrows, and a metallic violet on her
lids. Her lips were painted a bright red and contoured with a fine
darker stroke. I replied that I was only sitting here waiting and
looking at the magazines. After standing irresolutely for some moments she turned away and disappeared into one of the numerous
rooms that led off from the waiting room. My attention was now
caught by the picture of a soldier, naked from the waist up, sitting
in a jeep between two medical orderlies. He sat bent forward, his
face at an angle, looking as though he were holding his breath. A
thick arrow was lodged in his back. In the background was a tropical landscape. I was not able to imagine the situation of the man
in the jeep for very long because a gentleman who was standing
next to me kindly requested me to follow him into his office. I put

down my magazine, closed it, pocketed my cigarettes, for a moment regretted not having a revolver with me in case I had to shoot, got up and followed him to the door of his office. He let me in first and offered me a chair. The neatness of his desk top was perfection. In the right corner next to an ink pad and a rubber stamp holder, sharpened pencils of various colors were spread out together with a fountain pen, a paper knife and a pair of scissors. On one side of the table there was a box with neat piles of correspondence parallel to which lay a ruler and a magnifying glass. On the other side of the table, in a wooden container, were a few books, and from their gold-embossed titles I realized that they must contain customs regulations and navigation laws. In the middle of the desk lay the large green rectangle of a blotting pad with leather edges. The gentleman had sat down at the table opposite me and requested me to tell him the purpose of my visit. His voice was expectant and polite, anxious to be of assistance. I explained to him that I was spending my time there only in order to read the magazines. Wrinkles radiated across his brow from the bridge of his nose. He said that I would be able to find the magazines equally well in a bookshop or a library and he seemed to expect other revelations. I explained to him that for my hour of reading I had also chosen the comfortable seating and the atmosphere of elegance and worldliness that prevailed in the waiting room. His face now lost the last vestiges of willingness to be helpful, he got up and showed me out without any polite phrases. Down in the street I went past a row of cars parked at the edge of the avenue. Tentatively I pressed some of the door handles. When I found one door unlocked I climbed in, pulled the door to behind me and sat in one corner of the front seat. It was a large new car with an upholstered dashboard. I leaned back in the seat, supported my face in my hands and looked out into the street. Cars, with their drivers and passengers, glided over the wet asphalt, and pedestrians strolled along the pavement. The activity outside, where everyone was making for definite destinations, increased the enjoyment of my tranquillity. When the door was suddenly wrenched open and a man bent over me violently with an angry exclamation, seized me by the shoulders and shook me, I acted as if I were just waking up. I remained seated and looked up into his face, which was staring at me. On his upper lip quivered a mustache. After a while I explained to him that I had almost fainted and had by chance found the car door open and sat down here to rest. He surveyed my clothes and when I begged his pardon for the liberty I had taken he asked me where he might drive me. I asked to be dropped in the center of the town and on the short journey I sat silently with half-closed eyes while my chauffeur steered the gently roaring car with confident movements. When he stopped he asked me whether he should not rather take me to a doctor or a hospital, but I only shook my head, opened the door, bowed and thanked him. I went to a bookshop on a square in the center of town and skimmed through the volumes in the foreign department. I took a few books down and went with them to the shelves where the technical publications were displayed. I placed the books I had selected on a ledge and covered them with a few voluminous scientific and medical works. In one of these I came across a section on the training of military surgeons throughout the ages. Reproductions showed how, in earlier times, operations had been conducted. Hands under stiff cuffs elegantly severed the wounded limbs with knives. The directions for a leg amputation showed how the sexual organs were fastened to one side and the femur cut out of its socket in the pelvic girdle. The face of the patient was given individual features, with a large twirled mustache, and showed no signs of pain. In another work that I had taken from one of the shelves after changing the books several times and alternating the positions of the books I had borrowed first, I found a picture of the development of electromechanics. In an illustration from a chapter on research in sound oscillations a man in a lab coat was shown on the balcony of a house. Below the house was an avenue with lopped trees, children playing, a dog and a nursemaid with a baby carriage, and across the avenue stretched wires that extended from the scientist's head to a windowsill in the foreground. On the sill was a plate with a couple of flies and an arrangement of stoppers and membranes. The caption underneath the picture explained that the vibrations made by the flies' feet on the plate were transmitted along the waves to the investigator's earphones. I took this work, which contained many other reproductions of acoustic experiments, of distribution of energy in magnetic fields and prismatic dissections of light rays, together with the books I had chosen first. I took a newspaper out of my jacket pocket, again picked up the books I had taken first, thumbed through them, and finally chose one about the spread of the drug traffic. I placed the newspaper on top of the scientific work and the book on drug traffic on top of the newspaper, took this packet in one hand and in the other hand the books I had put on one side and went with them to the shop assistant. These last I laid on the table next to him, while I kept the work concealed by the newspaper in my hand and handed the book on the drug traffic over to the assistant saying that I wanted to buy it. After I had given him the money I told him not to wrap it up and placed it on the outside of the newspaper next to my hand. He asked if I were also interested in the other books I had put on the table. I leafed through them once more and then said that this time I only wanted the one I had. Keeping the scientific work under the newspaper and the other book openly displayed in my hand, I went slowly past the bookshelves, turned once again to ask the assistant about a magazine I knew was out of print, lingered in the front of the shop to skim through a book on display and revolve the metal paperback stands and then, in my own time, went out into the street. Back at my apartment I made myself something to eat. The unwashed crockery had been piling up in the kitchen. I set a pan of water to boil on the gas stove. From the pantry I took a paper bag of potatoes and a can of meatballs. I placed a handful of potatoes in the pot and sat down at the kitchen table with my scientific work. On the table was a red oilcloth. The walls of the kitchen were painted yellow. From the ceiling hung a frosted glass lamp globe. Above me, in the corner next to the crockery cupboard, the works of the electric meter were humming away in their black container. A wheel with a red stripe rotated slowly under the dial, the last figure was moving almost imperceptibly upward. I stood up, went into the studio and into the bedroom to see whether a light was on. Only when I came back to the hall again did I notice a crack of light under the lavatory door. I put out the light, made sure the meter had stopped and then returned to my book, read about the movements of cloud masses and the discharges of storms, stood up now and then, and poked at the potatoes with a match. The mail slot in the front door flapped open and a folded green card was thrust through. I picked it up. It was a printed matter, its text directed at myself and other householders and housekeepers. In words that could hardly restrain their enthusiasm the manager of a chemical firm, who in turn referred to the recommendation of a well-known chemist which was supported by analysis, recommended to me a new substance for washing both dishes and articles of clothing. From the description of the qualities of the washing powder it appeared that its cleansing power excelled the cleansing power of all the washing powders previously launched on the market and that, sparing the skin from harmful materials, it dissolved dirt and fat without a trace. I read the notice through once again. Large red letters at the bottom of the card promised the delivery of a free packet on surrender of the coupon. I spread out the handbill on the noticeboard above the table and went to prepare the meatballs. To open the can I used a tool consisting of a metal plate with a cutting tooth attached. I pressed the tooth into the lid close to the rim of the can, fitted the semicircular section underneath the tooth into the protruding edge of the can and sawed through the lid by levering the opener with my right hand while my left hand turned the can toward the cutting edge of the tooth. I shook the meat balls into a frying pan and warmed them over the flames. The window panes were steamed up: I had to switch the light on. The potatoes were ready. I took a bottle of wine out of the cupboard, uncorked it and poured myself a glass. As I ate I read the book next to me. Toward evening I went out again. I climbed down to the bank of the canal where the boat sheds and workshops lay in darkness. Across the rails of the freight yard a brakeman's light was blinking and trains with lighted windows rumbled past from the suburbs to the station or from the station to destinations far beyond the towering blocks of houses. A large, decked-over barge lay at the bank, half-sunk, hatches nailed down. I unloosed a boat belonging to the city from its mooring stake, got in and shoved off. There were no oars, I found only a plank, with which I steered the boat as it slowly drifted down the canal. Packs of ice scraped and bumped against the boat and the water slapped against the plaited rushes on the bank. The wings of the hospital suddenly appeared from behind the bare trees; lights were on in every window; in the operating theater, too, they were still at work; shadows moved behind the milky blue panes. I neared the bridge joining the two banks high over the strong walls between square watch towers. With the help of the plank I steered the boat under the arch, the stone blocks of which trembled and rumbled with the traffic. On the other side of the bridge the water extended. To the right lay heaps of rubble and a deserted factory, to the left blocks of flats at the edge of an avenue. The waterway divided and, maneuvering with the plank, I let the boat drift into the broader arm. Here gardens came down to the left bank, with dark houses half hidden in the shrubbery, and to the right, behind a railed-in courtyard, lay the extensive buildings of the barracks. The steps of a sentry crunched in the rollered sand. The water was deep black. I drifted out into a lake where I allowed the boat to follow the movements of the water. Gently it swung around, drifted stern first for a while, and was then again turned by light ripples so that for a long time it seemed to lie motionless in the middle of the water, while all around lay the silhouette of the city twinkling with lights, until I noticed that a bank was gradually edging nearer.

But then it hit me from behind, surprised me with its onslaught, something that had nothing to do with playful experiments, but which declared itself in a solid blow that made me crumple. It came so unexpectedly that at first I did not believe it. Just a common stitch in the side, and I breathed deeply to get myself in hand again. But it sat on my back, clung on to me and could not be shaken off. I then realized how unfamiliar was this body with which I lived. I tried to listen in to the organism and to imagine my intestines, and I did not even know how the various parts fitted in with one another or how they worked. I did not know the number of bones in my spine and ribs, or the shape of my heart and stomach: I could not locate the gall bladder or the kidneys and saw only a vague complex of shadowy tissues, tendons, veins, —heaving, thumping and full of liquids. This complex was myself, with this I presented myself and walked around and my head was only a small observation tower. I had been attacked in a mean, underhand way and the attack came from my body, from inside myself; I was still stunned by the blow that had shaken the lower part of my stomach and I still regarded it as an eruption of the spleen, but then it began again, radiated over my back, hips and abdomen and delivered another blow that stretched me out on the bed. I lay on my side with my legs drawn up, not daring to move while, to play safe, I gave a groan at every breath in order to appease the hostile powers. The room stood out in front of me with a hitherto unknown hardness and sharpness. Chairs, table and easel were driven into the floor, steel structures with glittering edges of light and deep black cast shadows. A crumpled piece of paper had become a giant formation on the floor, nails, tools and balls of fluff were no longer commonplace objects but appeared unique and incomparable. The groaning that I listened to for a while struck me as peculiar. What are you groaning for. I asked. Again I believed that I would now be able to get up again at once as if it had all been my imagination. It was quite impossible for me to be overcome by such an attack; I had been working as always, in fact the work had been progressing better than ever: I had managed to achieve ever greater continuity. I was simply exhausted and would have to rest for a while. The pressure in my back is not worth thinking twice about, I thought, and stretched out my legs. At once the cramp in my abdomen punched me again, my knees shot back to my stomach, the strange sounds forced their way out of my throat without any action on my part. My brain assembled its various pieces of information, tried to locate the source of the pain, and my acquaintance with medical text books led me to conclude that it was the appendix or the kidneys. Cautiously I felt with my hand over my back, around my groin, and then there came the frontal attack, a general offensive. It felt as if everything were about to fall apart. I heard myself moaning and screaming, whether I wanted to or not, and convul-

sions forced their way up to my stomach, stinking sour slime
welled up through my nose and throat. I just managed to bend
my head over the edge of the bed and vomited on to the floor. I
lay like this for a while, the saliva dribbling from my mouth; then
I worked my way from the bed, reeled toward the door, heard
someone whistling in the street and footsteps going away at a run
and the rattling and ringing of the streetcar and brakes screeching
at the stop. In the lavatory I clung on to the water pipe, bent over
and vomited again, and the rusty red color of my urine showed
me that changes of which I was no longer in control had taken
place within my body. My body had overpowered me and was
dictating its terms. In my room the odor of my vomit rose in
waves toward me. I got to the window and opened it. A white
ambulance with a red cross drove through the gate and halted in
front of the first-aid station. On the back of the telephone direc-
tory was the number to call in case of emergency. I took the receiver off and began dialing, then replaced the receiver. You can
clean up the vomit, I thought, and walk to the hospital and regis-
ter yourself. You don't need an ambulance for a stomach-ache.
But I did not get far, and soon found out what it feels like when
your legs will no longer hold you and you simply crumple to the
ground, moaning, teeth chattering. Later I crawled on my hands
and knees through the room between the vertical posts, pulled the
telephone down and dialed the number. Then I dragged myself
out into the hall, sat on a kitchen chair and waited for the
stretcher-bearers. When they came they took a poor view of the
fact that I could sit up. If I could sit I could stand, and if I could
stand I could walk. But because they had brought the stretcher
with them they loaded me on and bound me to it. In my weakness
it was a gratifying sensation to be carried four stories down the
winding stairs. I had given myself up, others were carrying me.
Well packed under the woolen blanket I swayed past the windows behind which lay the ravinelike courtyard, over which, at
first, towered the cupola atop the city hall, this presently giving
way, as I swayed along, to garbage pails, clothes fluttering between clothes-posts, the one bare tree and children playing ball.
People had collected on the pavement and were watching the

stretcher with me on it shoved into the ambulance. Through narrow transparent strips in the frosted glass window I saw the façade of the house with my window still open glide past and swing
back, then came the electric trolley wires of the streetcar line and
already the black boughs of the trees in the hospital park brushed
past us. The ambulance drew up, the door was opened and I was
carried out again through the doors swinging open, through corridors where steps echoed and there was a smell of medicine, to a
room where I was set down and placed on a stand. The bearers
left the room. The white enamel paint on the walls gleamed. Here
stood a metal chair and an oxygen tank, a blood transfusion stand,
a glass cabinet with flasks and boxes, a wheeled table with basins
and instruments, and a pail with a lid which could be raised by a
pedal. In the undulating window panes the red surface of buses
slid past and the flowing black shadows of the passengers swung
to and fro. With all this there was a rhythmic beat of footsteps
and a humming of motors. After a long wait the doctor came, took
down details of my identification, and in the telling I completely
forgot I had a wife and child. I was rolled into the basement,
bathed and then delivered into the ward. In the course of the
afternoon female assistants in white coats came to draw blood
from my arm or sucked blood from my fingertips in which they
had pierced a hole with a needle. Castor oil, swimming thickly in
a beer glass, was infused into me. Then I lay on my side on the
wooden bench in the washroom and a ward orderly held a tin
container up in her hand out of which water gurgled into my intestines, I sat bent over in the cubicle. Another man sat in the
cubicle next to mine, and we sweated and groaned and dis-
charged ourselves, bubbling and farting and surrounded by the
stink of our own disintegration. The next morning the same proce-
dure was carried out once again, after which I was wheeled
through long corridors into the X-ray department. Only my body
existed, and its revolt had been made the subject of scientific investigations. I lay on the table under the X-ray apparatus and the
doctor pressed about on my arm to find the vein in which to insert
the injection. The vein tried to avoid the jab of the needle and he
had to bore the cannula into my flesh several times before he

found it. A violet liquid was inserted into my arm from the large needle and left me nauseated and panting for breath. During his manipulations and while he was waiting for the liquid to penetrate the kidneys the doctor talked to the nurse about the military hospital of a provincial town where he had spent a few years during his military service. He mentioned the shortcomings he had encountered there and the possibilities of improvement. Then he came to speak of the town library, which he had found ill-equipped. He listed the various classics missing from their collection, the nurse listening admiringly to this display of culture while a wooden belt with an inflated rubber bladder beneath it squeezed my abdomen. From the X-rays it was evident that a stone was lodged in the kidney at the top of the ureter. During the following days attempts were made with long maneuverable instruments to reach the stone from within through the genital and urinary system. But as the hooks and tweezers could not reach the stone, an operation was decided upon. I was laid out on a table in a greeny-blue room and above me hung the silver operating lamp. Everything that I now observed seemed ludicrous. Cutlery was wheeled up on a little trolley, knives, forks, and spoons, the table was set, napkins were placed around me, and the doctor, too, tied a napkin about himself. Again the needle bore into my arm and I was told to count. The counting tickled my throat, giggling I counted, lying on the festive board, in the dazzling silvery lamplight between glass containers, tubes and an incomprehensible array of machinery. I still heard someone counting, someone of whom I knew nothing more, and there was this greeny-blue, this metallic greeny-blue, and it was not so funny any longer because this greeny-blue meant that I had to go away from everything, away with you, out you go, you're through, and I wanted to scream, but I could not scream because someone was still counting and then I dissolved in the greeny-blue vapor.

Now I knew of what this stone consisted, this sharp-edged prickly foreign body. Now my own knowledge went to work to investigate this crystallization of undissolved material. The attacks on my abdomen, the painful treatment of my ureter and bladder,

the tyings-off and the ominous manipulations awakened ideas out
of the earliest period of my existence. At first I was born through
my mother's mouth, but that could not be right, for it was her
phallus that bore me. Under the blanket I carried on the game of
giving birth, and my bed stood in the kitchen next to the cooking
stove where Augusta, our housekeeper, was hard at work. My
knees loomed up in front of me like mountains and the music was
already playing in the subdued light under the blanket, the music
that was part of this game. My inside produced the music while I
gave birth. I drew a little lead figure, the shape of a pharaoh, out
of my foreskin. But that was not the way children were born
either. My mother had a wound, an enormous wound between her
legs: thence it was that we fell out. And the fertilization took
place in a reddish mist, in a squealing and moaning that I could
hear at night coming from my parents' bedroom, and in this mist
whirled minute tadpolelike creatures. Sometimes my mother took
me to her when I had been crying a long time. I was allowed to
sleep next to her bed, between her and my father, and I snuggled up close to her into the hollow her body had pressed into the
mattress. I want to come to you, I called, and there I lay beside
her, pressed close to her, and her face, resting in her hands, was
bent over me. And suddenly I understood why I had come so
close to Magda that time in her little house on the southern lake,
why shyness and strangeness had disappeared. She had taken me
to herself, had seized me and embodied me in herself, in the opposite direction to birth. Suddenly I was inside her and something
that had been broken off long ago was pieced together again, a
reunion was effected. Earlier, in the mythical remote past, we had
groped about in the dark. In order to represent a woman we had
to make believe, a friend and I, and in turns one of us clamped his
penis tight between his legs so as to look like a girl while the other
made the movements of coitus, and in the evenings we spent
hours walking and reveling in sex-talk. We lived in a fever swamp
of uncertainty. In a corner of the garden I initiated my sisters into
the infamies of sex. We called the game *behind the hut,* after the
spot where it took place. There my sisters had to lift up their skirts
and let themselves be fingered by me. When they wanted to see

my penis I stuck my hand under my belt and wagged my index
finger at them through my fly whereupon they rushed off screaming. These games left me with an almost suffocating sensation in
my throat. At meal times my sisters would ask with perfectly in-
nocent expression whether we could play *behind the hut* later,
and a red glow sprang to my cheeks, and then they giggled and
asked me why I was blushing. Sometimes they asked me why I
was red even before saying anything, and then my face burned.
Even a glance from them, or a stealthy smile, made me blush.
This sitting there in fear of being found out, this constant dirty
conscience, was what I called the shits. The shits, the big shits had
me in their grip. And because of this I wrote out one hundred
times copybook fashion, as a punishment: I must be a good boy
and not disgrace my parents. What had lain within me thick and
pregnant during such hours, with a paralyzing compulsion, now
broke out into the open, snarling, grimacing and croaking the
words mockingly. I painted into the blue exercise book: I must be
a good boy and not disgrace my parents; and my laughter became
uncontrollable at this hundredfold faultlessly written sentence and
I took the exercise book and flung it at the door which my mother
at once wrenched open. This was the world of madness and I could
alter it, I no longer had to be burdened with it, it had been cut
out of my body, it had only eaten away the happy childhood years,
but I could find other years, could discard humbug and burst into
the laughter of contempt that had once previously been restrained.
In the schoolroom I was standing in the corner, smelled the cold
plaster of the wall and heard the class humming behind me. I
collected saliva on my tongue, stuck my tongue out and let the
spittle run down the wall. After all, who were these teachers or
these schoolchildren who had driven me into a corner and had
forced a wave of protests out of me? What were these complaints?
Was it not the teachers, the parents, the sayings of the wise, the
tablets of the law that complained through me? Was it not the evil
premonitions, the reproaches, the fears, the threats of others, that
I gave back, chattering away like a parrot? Slowly I began to
recover from the anesthetic. I saw the old tormenting spirits mul-
tiplying still further, but I tried to get a devilish pleasure out of

them, I could make fun of them, abuse them, pull away the chairs from under their behinds. In the blue glow of the night lamp I saw how they rose like shadows from their beds all around the ward, how they crept up to one another with great white bundles on their backs. This was the night in a children's home, the first night after my arrival. They wanted to throw the bundles over me, it was their form of greeting with which they wanted to test me. In the morning after being delivered up to the home I looked through the window into the street and witnessed a procession outside. It was the wounded from the war who were marching by with banners and slogans; they walked on crutches and hobbled along with wooden legs, they had black bandages over their eyes and empty sleeves tucked into their pockets, they were pushed in wheel chairs and carried on stretchers. Many trembled continuously and threw their heads back and forth, many wore uniforms and steel helmets, and all had medals on their chests, Gottfried, my stepbrother, who had accompanied me on my journey, had gone home to the family who no longer knew what to do with me. I was alone in the dormitory at night, in the bluish glimmer of the night lamp. If they should come with their pillows I was on my guard. Someone rose out of his bed, stood in his nightshirt leaning against the edge of the bed and splashed into the full-bellied glass bottle. I had to suppress my laughter for my abdomen was plastered with lint and below the incision was a glass tube in my skin through which the pus was drained. Where are you now, you pillow bearers, I called. What has become of you and what has become of your crippled fathers. I have escaped your threats, I have outlived you, I thought, and I sank back into a doze in the consciousness of triumph.

Then, in the spring of 1945, I saw the end of the development in which I had grown up. On the dazzlingly bright screen I saw the places for which I had been destined, the figures to whom I should have belonged. We sat in the seclusion of a darkened room and saw what had up to this moment been inconceivable. We saw it in its full extent, which was so vast we would never be able to comprehend it in our own lifetimes. A sobbing could be heard and a voice called out: Never forget this. It was a miserable senseless cry, for there were no longer any words, there was nothing more to be said, there were no declarations, no more admonitions, all values had been destroyed. There in front of us, among the mountains of corpses, cowered the shapes of utter humiliation in their striped rags. Their movements were interminably slow, they reeled around, bundles of bones, blind to one another in their world of shadows. These eyes in the skeletal skulls did not seem to grasp that the gates had been opened. Where was the Styx, where the Inferno, where was Orpheus in his underworld, surrounded by the rippling trills of flutes, where the great visions of art, the paintings, sculptures, temples, songs and epics. Everything was reduced to dust and we could never think again of looking for new comparisons, for points of departure in the face of these ultimate pictures. This was no kingdom of the dead. These were human beings whose hearts were still beating. This was a world where human beings lived. This was a world constructed by human beings. And then we saw them, the guardians of this world: they had no horns, no tails, they wore uniforms and they huddled together in fear and had to carry the dead to the mass graves. To whom did I now belong, as a living person, as a survivor? Did I really belong to those who stared at me with their immense eyes, whom I had long since betrayed, or did I belong to the murderers and executioners? Had I not tolerated this world, had I not turned away from Peter Kien and Lucie Weisberger, and given them up and forgotten them? It no longer seemed possible to go on living with these inextinguishable pictures before my eyes. It no longer seemed possible ever to go out again, into the streets and up into my room.

And yet I made it. I had gone out again with the other living people, other inhabitants of the city; I had walked around in the streets, my tears had been overcome and my vision had cleared; I had breathed, spoken again, laughed, read books again and looked at works of art. I had lived on in the continuous presence of these images. These images belonged from now on to the existence of all of us, never to be thought away again, and often they made every word spoken, every line drawn, a lie and a mockery. For a long time I bore the guilt of not having been one of those who had had the numbers of devaluation branded on their flesh, of having escaped and of having been condemned to be a spectator. I had grown up to be destroyed but I had escaped destruction. I had fled and had crept into a hole. I should have perished, I should have sacrificed myself, and if I had not been imprisoned or murdered or shot on the battlefield I had at least to bear my guilt; that was the least that was demanded of me. I heard the voice of the dead Hoderer. Now that the danger is past you dare to look at something that existed for a long time, the existence of which was known to you. Now that nothing more can happen to you you dare to open your eyes. But your suffering is in vain, you are not worth the horror that overcomes you. And on that day in May, when the bells rang and confetti fell from the windows and we danced in the squares of the city and embraced one another, in the middle of this delirium of liberation, in which forbidden bottles of wine were openly being handed around and the ponderous stolid people of this country for a few brief hours sensed other possibilities of life, I heard his voice again. You are acting as if you had won the victory, he said mockingly, but you have had nothing to do with the victory. Everything runs off you; you are a parasite, a fellow traveler; others have done the fighting for you, and will carry on fighting for you, while you sit comfortably at your writing desk and contemplate the misery of the world. I wanted to defend myself by asserting that I had never chosen anything but my flight and my cowardice and the arrogance of my detachment but he only smiled. What do you want then, I cried. Must I despair because I was not murdered. Must I kill myself as you did. Even this did not perturb him. You do not need to kill yourself, he said, for you are one of those who die out and fade away through their own indifference. What am I to do then, I asked. But he did not answer any more. Whose side should I take. No answer.

In his own way Hieronymus had made a decision which was the final answer to all his doubts. Efforts to achieve a total view, to become committed to the world situation, the problems of responsibility and of international solidarity, this was all twaddle to him, not even worth a thought. He had completely withdrawn from the world of bankruptcies and of new hopes in order to dedicate himself entirely to the gigantic structure of his work. Originally a mathematician by profession, a constructor of adding machines and an expert in national economy, he had given up his job in a bank, his house in a smart part of town, his car and all the other trappings of a well-ordered existence and had settled in an old workshop where the concrete bases of dismounted machines still stood. One could still see the former elegance of his stained and threadbare clothes and although his face was hollow and shaded with gray stubble, it retained an air of mundane superiority. Poverty, hunger and sickness were not merely accepted as the price he had to pay for his freedom, they were for him necessary components of his experimental work. The work on which he was engaged was only a sideline and was actually doomed solely to decay, for what interested him above all else was the capacity to last, and he thrust this ever more into the farthest reaches of possibility. Since he had been ticketed as having a nervous ailment, from his earlier place of employment he received a small disability pension which gave him the necessary minimum on which to live. I met him when he was about fifty years old and when his work, which was destined to remain incomplete, was still in its initial stages. And yet he had been working on it for many years, and systematically collected the material for it and in so doing had neglected more and more his profession, in which he was regarded as a leading authority, until it came to the final break with the old way of life. The work that slowly accumulated under his hands was the construction of a book. He did not write it from words that he thought up but built it out of fragments he had discovered. The collage that emerged on the giant sheets of paper contained countless little units that he had cut out of the mountains of old books and magazines that turned the room into a furrowed landscape. The walls were filled up to the ceiling with cardboard boxes which he had gathered from shoe shops and in which he preserved the stacks of raw materials. Each of the boxes was labeled. His card index contained fragments from all the aspects of everyday life which were to be dealt with in his universal book. Arrival at a station. Preparations for the journey and destinations. Conversations in the train. Moving into a new apartment. Foodstuffs and the preparation of meals. Ways of eating. Conversations at mealtimes. Furnishing a room. Activities and events in rooms. Occupations in offices, workshops and factory halls. The construction of machines. Conversations between technicians. Articles of clothing and conversations about clothes. Accidents in the home. Accidents at work. Events in the street. Conversations in the street. Various sorts of faces. The composition of families. Rows in apartments. Conversations about the weather. Children's games in living rooms. How children find their way about outside. Interiors and exteriors of school life. Barracks and barrack squares. The use of weapons. Conversations with superiors. The structure of the body. Symptoms of disease. Methods of cure. Sleeping together in bed and other places. Conversations between lovers. Old age. Birth and early infancy. Scenes of war and military consultations. Statesmen's speeches. Social institutions. Various forms of architecture. Staircases, cellars and attics. Rocks and sand. Canals and sanitation systems. Gardens and parks. The peculiarities and instincts of domestic pets. Gatherings of people. The concept of panic. Looking for work. Conversations in shops. Transitions from one room to another. Suggestions for experiences. Court hearings. Glimpses into prisons. The latest results of scientific research. How one behaves on one's own. From such and hundreds of other groups Hieronymus chose single words, sentences or paragraphs, cut them out, plastered them with glue and pieced them together into liana-like convoluted statements in the most varied styles. Outwardly too, from the type faces, these fragments from newspaper cuttings, popular novels, detective stories, scientific and technical works, magazines, catalogues and advertisements provided an inexhaustible abundance of variations. The sentences were closely pressed one against the other, forming one single solid block on the page. Only here and there were illustrative supplements let into the text. They were mainly sections of reproductions, as in a puzzle: a hand, a foot, a face, an animal, a

household article, sometimes spreading out over a series of lines
with a building, a panorama or a view of a room. He himself did
not add a single line to his book, and yet he was creating a work
that in its content, no less than in its volume, was to make all other
books superfluous. When I called on him in his room he gazed at
me like an alchemist who has just succeeded in making gold. His
gray hair was tousled and his face was haggard from lack of sleep
and malnutrition. The only piece of furniture in the room was a
narrow bed without a mattress. He slept on a blanket on the bare
bedspring. He boiled coffee or warmed up canned foods on a
primus stove. In the course of the year which he was still able to
spend in freedom I became involved in the slow advance of his
work. As he read the newly evolved lines to me, the expression on
his face changed in accordance with the various sorts of text. His
features could crumble and vanish, they could tighten, tremble,
twitch or crease into a laugh. The laugh was predominant. There
constantly occurred combinations of incidents so surprising that
we had to burst out laughing. With his harsh and grotesque juxta-
positioning of invented words Hieronymus transcended the limits
of personal thought. He compared himself to an electronic apparatus that reacted to impulses. The writer, who sat dejectedly at
his typewriter or even scribbled away with a pencil in an exercise
book and tried to puzzle out his own thoughts, was for him an
obsolete phenomenon. It was unnecessary to rack one's brains for
formulae. Everything had already been said, only the finished
components needed to be grasped. When he was attacked by
toothaches or fits of giddiness, when he suffered from colic or
other effects of food poisoning appeared in his body, he accepted
it with a superior laugh. He tugged out the rotten tooth, dosed his
cramped stomach with alcohol, lay rolled up in bundles of newspapers and waited tensely for what would happen next. It sometimes happened that neighbors, who had heard cries and blows
from his room, rushed in. They would find him unconscious and
bleeding, his body bearing every sign of a violent assault, but no
perpetrator in sight. These states, which were the results of long
sleeplessness, often induced by brandy and narcotics, were espe-
cially valuable to him. He was, however, reticent about the ex-

cesses that took place there and at the beginning I still accounted
for them as schizophrenia or epilepsy. But gradually I saw that
they could not be explained by either psychiatric or medical diag-
noses. He simply lived in a reality from which everyday criteria
had been removed. When I asked him what had happened to him
as he lay across one of the concrete pedestals, as battered as a
shipwrecked sailor, he said that I must wait for a few days, then
he would give me the answer in the form of a text he had com-
piled. Such a text, which he would read to me, might contain an
extraordinarily detailed description of the furnishings of a room in
which something of the monstrosity of his journey dawned on me.
He was contemptuous about the researches of depth psychology.
He saw psychoanalysts merely as the representatives of the pre-
vailing social order, a new caste of priests from whom one received absolution after confession. The analyst simply represents
another authority, he said, and the patient, whose neurosis has
developed through conflict with authoritative society, has here to
be trained to adapt himself through new conflicts of allegiance.
The world he encounters is the same as the one against which he
reacted with his so-called disease, but instead of realizing that in
his resistance, his hatred, his turmoil there lies the best he has to
offer, he suddenly becomes soft and knuckles under. Because he
cannot summon up the strength to rebel, he seeks solace in his
supposed collapse. Before a court that has subordinated itself to
the existing laws he launches his Jeremiads, while the analyst, sitting behind him in his comfortable armchair, puffs away at his
pipe, thinks of beefsteaks and earns his gold from every minute
that the patient lying on the sofa babbles away in his impotence.
What do you think an analyst could tell me? Return to your bank
and your stylish flat, drive around in your fast car and construct
adding machines. What do you think this gentleman, experienced
in the working of the mind, would make of my work? Brought up
on the classics he could merely find a bottomless fatal disease,
interesting at most as material for research into insanity. He
would have me locked up, for he would realize that I was past
being tamed or made serviceable to the community. Later I

thought about these remarks and I understood that he must have realized what awaited him even then.

In his studio, in a corner between the piles of books, there often sat a ten-year-old girl. She played with a cat, read and sketched, or did her homework. Most of the time she was so silent that I did not notice her. Sometimes she sat hidden behind cartons and mountains of newspapers, and appeared soundlessly when Hieronymus called for her into the darkness. For a long time I had no idea where she came from. She seemed to be a neighbor's child, who sometimes came to visit him. As he himself never said anything about her, and as she hardly ever greeted me and never talked to me, I did not inquire. She was tall and boyish and her blonde hair hung down smoothly. She had beautifully regular features. Soundless though her movements were, there was never any suggestion of stealth in them: she went through the room proudly erect, with a floating gait. Later I saw the expression in Hieronymus' eyes when he gazed at her long childish legs as they strode around among the piles of books. I also saw how he kissed her on the brow or on the cheek when she entered or left the room, and I saw the gesture of her hand on his arm, the light lifting of her hand toward his throat. Her eyes only seldom met mine, and then a glow of jealousy or contempt lay in them. Only when he knew that I understood what was going on between them did Hieronymus speak to me about her. He had found the little black cat in front of his door. It was mewing and as no one took any notice of it he brought it in. The cat remained with him. Some weeks later the girl stood in front of his door. The cat belonged to her, but she did not ask for it back: she only wanted to visit it. So she came for an hour, for an afternoon, for a whole Sunday. She sat quietly beside him. He worked while she read, drew or bent over her school books. He discovered that she lived with her mother, brothers and sisters in the house next door. They were refugees from Poland. The mother worked in a factory. The girl's reticent nature was a constant provocation. She it was who sought him out. She had cunningly inveigled herself into his

isolation and awaited his first caress. I knew few details of this
relationship which lasted for a year, right up to the time when he
was arrested and sent to the asylum. I only picked up occasional
hints which suggested passion and devotion. He mentioned a trip
with her in the summer. They had taken rooms in a hotel by the
sea. She was regarded as his adopted daughter. Her mother too
had agreed to this trip and it remained uncertain whether or not
she had seen through him. For her it was a relief that he had
taken to her daughter and that he invited her out and paid for her
clothes. He described the dignity with which she appeared in the
hotel. She had an assurance about her, as if she had never lived
anywhere but in large hotels. The staff spoiled her and stood
ready to gratify her every wish. She had special dishes prepared
for her, ate mussels and snails, snipe and Chinese soups. She was
the affectionate daughter who strolled arm in arm with her step-
father on the esplanade. She was so young that no one suspected
that behind the locked door of their room she could be his mistress. She wanted to play like a young animal; she was a weasel, a
marten, she bit him and he had to catch her. I asked him what he
could talk to her about and he merely looked at me uncompre-
hendingly. With one's lover one can talk about everything, he
said. There is no difference of age between us. She has more to tell
me out of her life than I her out of mine. She knows more than I
do, understands more than I do. She gives me what I have never
found in any other woman. Again I brooded a while over conven-
tional objections and reservations. I wondered whether the girl,
still a child as far as her age was concerned, could be injured by
this relationship. But then I saw that he was the only one in danger. She obtained all that she desired. He had taken advances
from his pension and was himself near to starvation. He even
suffered when he saw her with her playmates, with her admirers,
and she was woman enough to let him see that she had swarms of
admirers. Sometimes, when I visited him, he drew me to the window and looked down anxiously into the street where the girl was
walking up and down arm-in-arm with a fourteen-year-old boy. I
saw him going to pieces more and more and giving ever less
thought to the danger that was hanging over him. He knew that

his companion would not betray him, but the slanders of the
neighbors, the insinuations of her school friends would slowly poi-
son her and put her under pressure which, in the long run, she
could not support. Sometimes I felt he wanted to be taken away.
He was indifferent as to what would happen to his great unfin-
ished work. The time he had spent with his child lover made up
for all that was to come. During the last months, before they came
for him and even brought a strait jacket which he smiled at scorn-
fully, he no longer touched his book. The final result of his isolation—that society should destroy him—was still to come. He
waited nonchalantly while the dry glue crackled in the pages of
his book, accepting the idea that the work would rot and decay in
some dustbin.

Many insights into other people's existences can be so sharp and
cut so deeply into one's feelings and thoughts that they become a
part of one's own life. So Anatol appeared to me in his studio after
I had not seen him for a long time. He sat in front of me, broad
and heavy, his fleshy hands on his knees and his large round face
as if carved in plaster. I thought of him as I had met him on my
first visit to this city, thought of the energy exuded from him and
his pictures. Even now this energy still existed, but it had been
warped, it no longer animated his face, it was under control; the
heavy pouting lips hardly moved as he spoke and the words came
out without sound. At first he spoke about his wife's slow death, of
his guilt, of all he had omitted to do. Jarmila had followed him
from Prague, had accompanied him into exile and spent the war
years with him. After a year's separation he was again living with
her and the child who was now four years old. But it was not only
Jarmila's incurable disease that had this paralyzing effect on him;
his work did not seem to be making any headway either. What he
had achieved in his first years here had only been superficial success, he said. During the last years of the war people had hypo-
critically pretended to be interested in his art, had acted as if they
welcomed the refugees who had landed here, but now they were
mum and he was no longer allowed in any official exhibitions. To
my question whether he were not exaggerating the importance of

this struggle for recognition he merely shook his head. Your name had to be brought up all the time, he said, otherwise you were forgotten in the rat race, in these constant reshufflings. It seemed to me that, in his efforts to hold his own in the front ranks, he had lost sight of himself and that his pictures had lost something of the glowing intensity they had previously had. He may have implied this himself when he said that during the last ten years he had been working under continual pressure, a constant strain, that everything else had fallen apart and his pictures contained only impotence and terror. Suddenly, as I watched him sitting in front of me, so exhausted and embittered, I recalled what he had once told me of his childhood. His mother, who owned an inn in Slovakia, used to tie him up in the evenings to the leg of a large table to keep him from being underfoot. The table leg, the corner of the table, the candlestick on the table, the burning candle, the clock ticking on the wall, the ghostly room supported by beams where he was imprisoned, the clinking of glasses, the laughter of the customers in the tavern, all these things had been present in his old pictures. He spoke of Jarmila's suffering and I saw her face looming up out of the pictures all around, or fragments of her face, her weeping eyes, her mouth. He tried to shift on to someone else, on to Fanny with whom he had lived for a year, a part of the burden he bore. I had to bend down close to his heavy plastery face in order to catch the words that were forced out of his almost motionless lips. Jarmila was dying now that he had returned to her. Fanny had disappeared but his thoughts still revolved around her. And his work had become sterile: he attributed that to the country, this country where he had to remain a foreigner, this hygienic mean-spirited land where there were no discussions and exchanges of views about art but only disfavor and silent condemnation. He had to leave this country before it was too late, before it had poisoned his own powers of expression. He had to come to terms with a threefold break—the failure of his life with Fanny, the end of his marriage, and the end of his attempt to gain a foothold in a new country. But I know I'm stuck, he said, I've got too many possessions, I just can't take off and begin again somewhere else. He lit a cigarette and held it close to his mouth in the

nicotine-stained fingers of his broad white hand so that a curtain
of smoke welled up in front of his face. Through the smoke I
heard indistinctly the slow and monotonous flow of words from
which I formed an idea of events that I tried to tally with the
account I was hearing. The hotel room that Anatol mentioned became, for me, another hotel room; with the speed of lightning,
interposed details from familiar hotel rooms combined to form
this room where I imagined Anatol for a purpose that was really
my own purpose. Anatol spoke of a letter among the heap of papers and books on the table of the hotel room where Fanny lived.
The shape of the table, the objects on the table remained in Anatol's story just as vague as the rest of the room: he saw only the
letter. Fanny's hotel room, the room of an authoress in transit.
There stood the table, too small, full of manuscripts, notebooks,
odd sheets of notes, a few books in English, her open handbag, its
contents half emptied on to the papers, lipstick, powder puff,
purse, British passport, crumpled letters and articles of clothing
everywhere, on chairs and on the unmade bed, for Fanny used to
lie in bed until the afternoon, and Anatol had come into this room.
Fanny had telephoned, asked him to come to her, but now that he
was there she was not in the room. The Anatol conjured up by my
imagination bent over the table. Anatol, who was sitting in front
of me behind his smokescreen in the muted afternoon light, had
experienced something similar: when no one answered his knock
he had entered the room, and, disappointed that she was not there
waiting for him impatiently, had gone to the table, driven by the
desire to find something out about her or to discover some token
of feeling for him. He was uncertain of her, as always; she had left
suddenly, suddenly returned. And then he saw the letter and immediately recognized the handwriting. It was Caspari's. I knew
Caspari's books and I had heard Fanny speaking of Caspari. He
was her literary mentor: she had said that without his criticism
she would never have attained conciseness and concentration in a
language that was not her own: an immigrant from Germany she
had had laboriously to learn English. With the clairvoyance of
jealousy, Anatol smoothed out the letter and deciphered the
words he feared and from which he could not tear himself away.

Perhaps he guessed more than he could make out, for his knowledge of English was patchy and inadequate, but he understood
the sense of the term *Beloved* and he gathered that the writer was
speaking of the hell in which she was living with him, Anatol. She
should try to get away from him, he wrote, and then mentioned
her diary which she had let him read. Anatol looked up: for a few
seconds his face appeared between the wisps of smoke with a
tortured ugly expression but still plastery, not like the face of Aha-
suerus, the Wandering Jew, as I had seen him before, but a face
filled with selfish suffering, a face before the Wailing Wall, a face
whose hard flat surfaces could not conceal a sullen bid for sympathy. She had made a page in her diary out of him, he said, had
sacrificed him to her diary's pages, had made a distorted image of
him, the noble one, the judge, while she was letting him support
her, while he was buying her every cigarette she smoked in bed.
He carried on with his litany, in which Fanny lay in bed, smoked,
read, wrote letters and diaries, while he had to grind away to
support Jarmila and the child, had to pay the rent for the studio,
the flat and the hotel room, and the tax inspector was threatening
him with the sheriff. And then the air of pettiness and avarice, the
look of having been insulted in his face half-veiled in smoke,
passed away and I saw that what tormented him was part of his
painted visions, and that it was perhaps more important than being driven into exile, genocide, or the total destruction of cities,
for here was the tangible, here were the communicable experiences of persecution, mistrust and deception, here existence was
enacted, in the breakdown of human relationships, in the lies, in
half-truths, in lack of self-confidence. Behind it lay the other thing
that was common property; it penetrated everything, but the only
tangible things were the cigarettes that he bought for Fanny and
that she smoked leaning back in the cushions, the only visible
things were her double game, her reluctance to share the conditions of his life. What was visible was that she sprawled about in
bed all day, and in the evenings, when he was tired after ten
hours work, got up, refreshed, and wanted to go out, that she
wanted to go to a restaurant, to talk and have people around her
and that she expected him to pay. I saw Fanny coming in with her

dressing gown loosely slung around her, her powerful breasts visible under her nightgown. She wanted to embrace Anatol, wanted to get at his throat as he put it, and that seemed more like a premeditated murder than a spontaneous greeting. He dodged away from the stranglehold, and still clutching the letter, stretched it out toward her. He became the hero of a cheap novelette in the costume of the 'eighties: I saw his full beard, the tails of his morning coat swinging back and forth, the spats over his shoes. Large gestures, accusations, cries like: What sort of letter is this. The woman's reply: It's an old letter, you've no right, my letters and so on, renewed exclamations: You promised me, and so on, and in response replies, hand on heart, I could never cheat on him, I have him to thank for everything, and the hotel room has changed now in appearance, too, there are heavy draperies hanging at the windows, bound with cords, a chandelier sways over the table, the walls are studded with gold-framed mirrors in which the couple, reflected over and over again in unending perspectives, strides toward each other and in this interminable multiplication one can see him tossing her the letter with the words: It's over, once and for all, it's over. And she leaps at his throat again with the words: Stay with you always, and his answer: How often have you said that. And her answer: Realized my mistake, need you, and his answer: Caspari too. And her answer: Don't bring up those old stories again, and his answer: Old stories. *Beloved, Beloved,* Hell, get away, diary, come when you like, go when you like, it's all over, enough. And then he turns around in all the mirrors and in the mirrors within the mirrors, and he seizes his top hat and his walking stick and slams the door behind him, leaving the woman by the table in a negligee wringing her hands. And yet this was no parody. This illustration of a hotel lounge had nothing to do with the hotel room that Anatol left. For him this hotel room was clearer than it could ever be for me: it was the room of a final leavetaking. It was a cheap untidy little hotel room, and Fanny, with her erratic panic-stricken movements, stuffed everything into the suitcase, clothes, letters, books, manuscripts, while Anatol ran to his studio and shut himself in. Chain-smoking and surrounded by the increasing darkness Anatol sought

his way further back into the past history of this departure. As
early as Christmas, Christmas 1945, he had wanted to separate
from Fanny. She had spent half a year with him, lived off his
income, smoked his cigarettes, constantly dinned into him that he
should get a divorce. I don't believe she ever had any intention of
marrying me, he said. She simply wanted to take away my last
chance of retreat. My studio was at her disposal, I wanted to live
with her, but I could not leave Jarmila. She was already ill at the
time, and I could never have given up the child, Fanny was free;
she could travel when and where she wished; her second book
had just appeared in England and had been a great success, but
she did not contribute to the housekeeping. She wanted things
handed to her on a silver platter; she thought it beneath her dignity to write an article or ask a publisher for an advance. When I
did not want to go out again in the evening she called me a tedi-
ous petty bourgeois. I should have liked to talk to her about my
pictures; I wanted to review the day's work, wanted to hear how
my pictures affected her, for she had an eye for these things and
knew what I was aiming at. My pictures are related to what she
told me about her books, but she would only bother about them
when she felt like it. At that time, in the autumn, I was often
working for ten or fifteen hours a day. I still believed in the great
exhibition—but it had bad notices and flopped. I could have done
with Fanny's moral support then, but she no longer liked being
with me. There was too little variety, too little social life, too few
parties, and one day she disappeared, wrote to me from Ham-
burg, her birthplace, from the ruins, telling me about the nice
officers of the occupation army in whose hotel she was living,
wrote also that she could at last work at her book again, as if it
had been my fault that she had not finished anything recently. She
did not inquire after me or my pictures. I did not answer. On
Christmas Eve the telephone rang. From the receiver Fanny's
voice rang out through the whole flat. Jarmila had just lit the candles on the Christmas tree and when she heard the voice she went
into the kitchen. Fanny said she was in town, she was on her
deathbed in a hotel and I must go and see her at once. I implored

Jarmila to forgive me for leaving her for an hour. She wept in the kitchen, the child clung to me and screamed, and when I arrived at Fanny's she was lying in bed smoking, said she was already feeling better, she had just had a severe colic and had to go to the hospital the next day for an operation. They took a few gallstones out of her and she settled down again with me in my studio after I had paid for the hotel and the hospital. For a while Anatol seemed to be overcome by Fanny's presence. His words could scarcely be heard: I had to edge even closer to his face that looked bluish in the twilight. For him she was present in this room, there in the corner, behind the stacked pictures, but invisible to me. The wide sofa was made up as a bed; she lay on the pillows, her nightdress taut over her breasts, a cigarette in her mouth, reading or writing. The pictures, their colors and forms no longer distinguishable in the darkness, stood around in the long narrow room like the walls of a labyrinth. I saw nothing but the turmoil of these dark surfaces, whereas Anatol could have gotten up and walked over to her. He had forgotten Jarmila and her slow death, had forgotten that he had cast Fanny out, for a moment, while his words tried to express something about this departed spring, and once again only found some banal phrase that did not explain anything. But then, when it was agreed that it seemed possible to live together that spring, or as Anatol perhaps said, to build up a life together, it revoked itself, it was not a success. He had stayed away from his home for months, was well on the way to sacrificing his wife and child, and suddenly he realized that she could not stay with him, that she would leave him when the spirit moved her. She traveled light; a little suitcase and a handbag was all she needed: tomorrow she could travel to London, or to Paris. She had friends everywhere; publishers and translators awaited her new books, and the idea of her lack of commitments, her lightness, only made him the more melancholy and before she said anything about an impending journey he was already accusing her in his mind. And again the bitterness returned. She had only come to him in winter after the operation in order to rest, to convalesce with him. It was comfortable and convenient to be

looked after by him, to allow herself to be cared for and worshipped by him, while at the same time he acted as a model for
her diary in which Caspari, her master, could participate. When,
in the early summer, she traveled to England, he returned to his
family and swore to himself that from then on he would only live
for his wife and child. It was then that he discovered from the
doctor that Jarmila would scarcely be able to outlive the summer.
When Fanny now reappeared and telephoned him as if nothing
had happened and as if she expected that she would again be able
to spend a few months at his place, he too was tempted for a
second by the desire to give up the past, to betray all that was
diseased or dead, to strike camp and to begin a new life in London, in Paris, and then he landed up again in the same hotel room
he had entered at the beginning of his tale, under the influence of
a brief insane hope. Then the letter, the return, sitting in the
studio behind the locked door, and just as he expected, the bell
rang and he knew that it was she who was standing at the door,
and he sat motionless and listened to the bell ringing again and
again. He got up carefully and crept out into the hall, listened to
her walking up and down outside, heard her open her suitcase,
take out a book, light a cigarette, sit down on the stairs, then, after
a while, get up again and ring and thrust up the tin flap of the
letter box and call his name. I know you're there, open up, she
called out. I saw her mouth in the slit, he said. She must have
been kneeling down. I'm staying here till you open up, she called.
And then she sat down again on the stairs. Anatol knew she was
quite capable of living there for weeks, she would settle down in
front of the door, would sleep in her coat and appoint someone to
fetch her meals for her. She has got people everywhere who are
only waiting for a chance to answer to her beck and call. And then
he told me, and as he did so I could distinguish his face in the
dark as a pale ball, how he crept back to his studio, carefully
locked the door into the hall, telephoned the nearest police station
and asked the constable to free him from someone who was besieging the door to his flat. Then he went out on tiptoe and a little
later he heard the policeman arrive and, after a brief exchange of
words, lead her away.

A couple of days after my meeting with Anatol I met Fanny. She said she had been spending a few weeks with friends in town and was on the point of traveling on to Paris. The French translation of her book had recently appeared and been well received: she had a handbag full of money which her publisher had sent her. She asked me if I needed anything, pressed a few notes of larger denominations into my hand before I had time to answer and, since we had embarked on a discussion about our work, accompanied me to my flat where I warmed up some coffee and spent the afternoon with her. I knew she would talk about Anatol and would want to find out something about him from me, and she soon came out with her first question: when had I last seen him? I said that it was a long time ago and then I heard once again about this leavetaking, from Fanny's mouth, the mouth Anatol had last seen in his letter box. He came to my hotel, she said. I was in the bathroom and he took the opportunity to rummage around in my handbag. He found an old letter of Caspari's Why can't he leave me in peace about Caspari. I need Caspari for my work. After all, he has Jarmila and the child. But he never had the guts to break with his family. He held the letter in my face and shouted at me. What on earth does he want? He made me leave from sheer disgust and yet I came back to him and wanted to live with him. When I see him among his pictures I feel how much I am bound to him. There he regains his power. The ghostly quality in his paintings sometimes depresses me, but I am fascinated by them. To me it is as if Anatol must possess some of the qualities of these pictures. But he remains as stolid and dull as a stone. I am constantly making fresh efforts with him, but he always repulses me. For weeks at a time he doesn't say a single word. He is sulking about something, at a party I may have spoken to a man he did not like. He believes that when I talk to a man I go to bed with him. I let him get the better of me at once, the very first time I visited him in his studio. He always rubs that in, even now. And he is right: it was the stolid inert force with which he threw himself on me that impressed me. I wanted to come closer to him. I have tried to get him to talk. I once succeeded, when he told me something about his youth, the inn, the brothel, the nightly din at home, but I could get nothing further out of him—there he sat like a block of wood. I only sensed what was dammed up behind this hardness, behind this thick immobility. He got frightened when I wanted to touch him there. I am inquisitive by nature. When I love I want to deliver myself up, I want to talk about my experiences, even about Caspari, but I had to learn to be careful about every word so as not to wound him. I understood, he has been whipped fundamentally and has his tail between his legs so that he gives out that air of rocklike immobility. And sometimes a rift gapes open. Then he flies into a rage and insults me with the most vulgar expressions which he learned long ago at the inn. Not that it matters to me where the insults come from: they are directed at me and the slaps he gives hit me. I hit back. We stood in the middle of his huge studio, so huge, fifteen yards long, like a dancehall or a barn, and let fly at each other. He could not imagine that a woman would want to stay with him. Jarmila was a mother for him. I wanted to be his wife. I thought that if I were to stay by him he would be bound to thaw sometime. But he just cowered there, dumb and stupid. He gnaws away at something or other. After a few days' silence he was quite up to saying: You once said such and such a thing. What did you mean by it? I have no idea what he is talking about and laugh at him. And again, these nights when he sits next to me without a word in the room with the pictures. This endless silent accusation. What on earth is he accusing me of? After all, I am with him. Surely that ought to satisfy him. What does it matter if Caspari was my sponsor, if I talk about other men. I am with him, in his bed. Recently, before I went away, I was quite dazed, quite gutted: I could hardly move, I can see him sitting there. We only had two chairs in the studio, we were sitting there in front of the large open hearth where a fire never burned, behind us the room with the pictures and Anatol, dumb and lowering, his shirt sleeves rolled up and a large knife in his hand with which he scraped at his arm. Not a word, just this scraping away with the knife. I believe he was a devil for me, a regular spook. When I was together with him everything within me that was vicious and poisonous came to the surface. I became crude and stupid. And he,

what did he see in me? A pedlar, a whore. He had to call a policeman for help. I was waiting in front of his door. I knew he was at
home, I could hear him. Then someone came up the stairs and
said I must move along. The policeman was a young fellow, he
blushed when I looked at him. He took my suitcase and carried it
for me as far as the street corner. I wanted to invite him to drink a
cup of coffee with me but he was not allowed to do that: he was
on duty. In Paris I could have gone into a bar with him. Her face,
which often changed expression as she spoke, now took on sharp,
almost masculine features; now, as she meditated, appeared old
and witchlike; and now, as she stood up laughing, became childish and venturesome. In her thoughts she was already in Paris, in
a summer Paris. You must come to Paris, you must visit me there,
she said, and Anatol was forgotten, she no longer asked about
him. And when she had gone and I wanted to look at the money
she had forced on me it was no longer there. I had hung my jacket
over a chair and while I was in the kitchen she must have taken
the notes back.

Jarmila lived until the autumn of 1946. The funeral service was
celebrated in Greek-Orthodox fashion. The mourners stood in the
pews and watched the manipulations of the two priests. The dead
woman's relatives received little burning candles, and even some
of the closer friends who were not members of the family had a
candle pressed into their hands. They stood there awkwardly with
the burning candles, while the priests performed the ceremony.
One priest had a long beard, the other a clean-shaven bony face
and glasses. Both were dressed in golden robes. The priest with
the glasses wore red bands over his robes and swung a censer with
incense on a chain. The long-bearded one opened the proceedings
with some rapid gibberish. The other interrupted with his bass.
There ensued a duet between them which was developed by a
group of singers composed of three female and two male voices
on the dais. Each of the voices could be clearly heard in its timid
sallies. The voices were not sure of their tasks and tried to find
support from one another. The tenor was the best acquainted
with the chant and as he sang the loudest the lack of training in

his voice came across the most clearly. The stony echo in the chapel contributed a consoling muzziness to the sparsely interspersed embellishments of the litanies. The singers sang and sometimes, when the five voices, after tentative beginnings, had found their way to harmony, they seemed, as they mingled with the echoes, to be imitating a Gregorian chant. The priests once again recited and intoned their incomprehensible words, the voice of the bearded priest unctuous, the bespectacled priest grinding and monotonous. As they spoke and sang the priests took up various positions in front of the catafalque that contained the coffin. They beat their fingertips against their chests and the priest with the censer in his hand made clouds of incense billow up over the coffin. Sometimes the two priests stood next to one another at the foot of the coffin and sometimes at the head, sometimes one stood at the foot and the other at the head, and sometimes they stood opposite one another at the sides of the coffin, ceaselessly talking and singing and accompanied by the voices on the dais. Then the priests walked around the coffin several times in rapid succession and every time they passed the altar they bowed down, dabbed themselves lightly on the brow and tapped their fingertips on their chest. Anatol wiped his face with a large white handkerchief. Then the bearded priest remained standing in front of the altar while the other took up his position at the foot of the coffin, violently swinging the censer. The priest at the altar concealed his intentions behind his broad-sleeved robes. From his movements it looked as if he were cleaning his teeth. The choir sang lustily and one began to suspect that the ceremony was nearing its end. The priests, however, again began to run around the coffin, to overwhelm it with their incense, to speak and to sing and to thump their chests, and the choir gathered its strength for new variations. After the bearded priest had once more taken up his place at the altar and had once more returned to the coffin and had read out of a thick book with gold-ornamented binding, whereupon the other priest had uttered a short mooing noise, they had suddenly had enough. The priest with the glasses quickly took the candles from the hands of the assembled mourners, blew them out, clasped the bundle of candles in his huge bony hand and ran off, followed by his bearded companion. Six men appeared walking in step, clad in mourning coats and with top hats in their hands, lifted up the flowers and wreaths, carried them out, came back in step, in a single movement placed their top hats on their heads before the coffin, seized hold in unison of the black straps lying underneath the coffin, raised the coffin and carried it out. Slowly the mourners followed the coffin, which was now pulled on a cart by the six men along the path to the grave. It was getting dark and rain swirled across the expanse of the cemetery. The cart came to a halt at the grave in front of a plank-supported wall. The bearers raised the coffin and climbed the black ramp with it. They lowered the coffin, three on each side, into the depths. The figures of the bearers showed up clearly in black against the misty rain. Near the grave stood Anatol and his daughter. The remaining mourners stood around in a wide circle singly or in couples on the damp down-trodden earth. The priests once more stepped forward, over the grave, murmuring and singing, then the bearded priest, with a long-handled shovel, threw sand three times on to the coffin and, after he had squeezed Anatol's hand, disappeared among the trees, accompanied by his bespectacled colleague. Anatol climbed the step to the edge of the grave, thrust the shovel into the sand, threw the sand down on to the coffin, handed the shovel to his daughter who, climbing the step next to him, emptied the shovel and the sand thumped dully on the coffin. Friends and relations climbed the step one after the other, stood there for a few moments, glanced into the pit with its sides draped in black and at the depths of which the coffin was visible under the flowers. It was obvious that one might slip on the wet soil at any moment and fall into the grave. Anatol stood to one side next to his daughter. Everyone went up to him and squeezed his hand. Then they all stood isolated in the increasing darkness. Anatol's friend Vladimir came forward and made a short speech. Jarmila's beauty, he said, lived on in the many icons the painter had made of her. Anatol stood in the drizzling rain, his head bared, square in his black coat, like a figure of granite.

Only now, in the summer and autumn of 1946, did I begin to
grasp something of the essence of the previous decade. The pattern by which I had lived was still stamped in my blood. Although
there was no longer any exile or flight, although I was the subject
of a land that had been spared the ravages of war, I could not free
myself of the idea that I no longer belonged anywhere. During
the war I had adapted myself to these conditions of life and I had
thought of the future as a fruitful non-allegiance in which I
should be able to feel at home all over the world. But now that
the war had been over for more than a year new hostility was
accumulating, free and unrestricted travel remained a Utopia and
I had to decide on a permanent residence, a new point of departure. Everything that I had undertaken since my exile had had to
take place as something consciously provisional, constantly threatened with dissolution, which was natural in such a situation and
even allowed one to construct a philosophy of life from it. This
mode of living had served me as an excuse for everything that was
half-finished, everything that was unsuccessful, in my work no less
than in human relationships; but it was no longer adequate, I was
no longer threatened and persecuted and even the threats and
persecution I had experienced had to be re-evaluated. I had experienced them only indirectly, in a consciousness under the spell of
fear, I had suffered no physical want, and only in thought had
repeatedly created a substitute for the banishment to which I felt
myself condemned. I had to kid myself along in this fashion, since
it seemed to me it was all I was good for, and ridding myself of
this compulsion means paying for it with guilt. All this suddenly
became evident in all its senselessness and hollowness, just as the
whole war now stood out in all its absurdity, and seemed to be
nothing but a prelude to more wars. In my conversations with
Max I had tried to show him that I wanted at any cost to avoid
any part of the challenges of madness and with Hoderer I had
spoken about the impossibility of finding salvation in a political
system. I had turned against self-denial and self-sacrifice, and yet
I had found nothing to replace it but bewilderment. The sole
truth seemed to me that I could only represent myself: but who
was I, laden as I was with dirt, with crap. When I thought back

on the course of my development, all I could see was this rubbish
heap of useless, life-hostile ballast that I had let myself be burdened with, and only a tiny spark glowed somewhere in it, and
this spark was myself. I was almost thirty years old and this
seemed to me to be an age at which I must stand on my own, in
the full possession of my powers, faced up to fruitful tasks. I did
not want to admit that Hoderer was right in saying that I belonged to a dying species, that I was doomed to decay, I had
survived the existence of the fleeing and the persecuted, a rotting
existence which I had not wanted, an existence full of misunder-
standings and deceptions, still permeated my movements and gestures, many of my impulses and thoughts, yet I could still seek a
new place to make a stand. At the time this was the same for us
all. After the paralysis had gone we had to find some regeneration.
Max Bernsdorf tried to find his way back whence he had come.
He had to wait for a year before returning to his little wood and
his village, he had still to work on the authorities for a year and
now he was hindered by his political past, his radical opposition
which had driven him to flee the country, and he had to vegetate
in his hotel room and seek refuge with his ancient Persian poet
before finally, white-haired and robbed of the best years of his
life, being again allowed on to the soil from which he had once
been banished. The trip I took to the land of my birth awakened
no wish in me to settle down there again. The strangeness that
confronted me was all the more upsetting since every word I
heard had such a familiar ring to me. It was a reunion in a dream,
a dream in which everything was recognizable, in which everything lay open and bared to view, but which was shot through
with a monstrous disfigurement. What I found was ruins of
houses, in which I had lived, and one undamaged house in a big
garden run wild, but what was there was not worth restoring to
use again, it was fit only to be accursed through time and eternity.
Anatol, too, broke loose after Jarmila's funeral. He settled in London where he had the chance of a retrospective exhibition. Perhaps he had hoped to meet Fanny again, but she remained in
Paris where a year later she died from a blood disease, in her last
hour surrounded by large hideous beasts. I heard little more from

Anatol, but discovered only that he was gradually achieving his aim and could now participate in the international art market with his pictures. His works, which I encountered occasionally in the pages of art magazines, showed an ever increasing hardness and coldness. Amos accepted a teaching post at a California art school, where he marked in his diaries what child's play it must be to write one's autobiography, as easy as writing down a dream. And yet he never got around to it. In the openings of his books there was an immediate compulsion, a suppressed element. He had never been able to renounce his father, and for women, too, he had never felt anything but his inadequacy. He had stared his eyes out at the wall, at the barricaded door, and had allowed himself to be treacherously murdered. But here, from the red and green book, revolt against every authority came upon me. There was no longer any superior force. The book began at a point where all superior force had been overrun. The news came from the same world in which Kafka had perished, the mechanically anonymous world of annihilation, only experienced in a more intense, a more brutal and feverish way. But it had all been surmounted by a device which seemed extremely simple, but which could only be attained when the decision to surrender oneself up completely to this world and to give up every possibility of retreat was carried through. With Kafka everything was permeated by his terror of contact. His pain was in the intellectual sphere: he portrayed the battle of ideas, conflicting feelings. He found himself on a hopeless search for the closeness of others, he dreamed of a community, a reprieve, a reconciliation, and constantly he had before him the unattainable, the impossible. In this other book, however, the dazzlingly bright world of daylight prevailed where body struck against body; here they snapped their fingers at the idea of community, and guilt and respect were so much dead wood. The hierarchies of offices, the all-embracing laws were smashed, and free life began in a fertile chaos. Everything was tangible and possible—and sex, which in Kafka lay dimly in the background, assumed a tropical luxuriance. By exposing everything that was concealed and recognizing nothing but one's own voice, obeying nothing but one's own desires, a new Primitive

Man, a giant, appeared in the midst of a corrupt civilization which was longing for death. It was still as a worn exhausted European that I looked into this world of wild hunger for life, and I was still made dizzy by the possibilities that lay before me. But I had already sprung up in consternation as I had once done a long time before when, in a theater I saw someone just like myself was to be shot to the moon by a great basilisk of a cannon. Little Peter was put into the cannon's thick mouth, a figure with gold stars on his cloak lit the fuse. I sprang up in nameless horror at what was about to take place, could not be restrained, got to my feet and stood with baited breath, hands cramped on the rail before me, and when the bang came the floor vanished from under my feet and I flew along with the other little boy up into limitless firmament.

When Fanny had left for Paris I often thought of our conversation which led to her account of her life with Anatol. We had started by talking about our different opinions on the process of writing. For Fanny this process was a game of chess which had to be conducted according to specific rules. She set up characters who had to go to their destination along a preordained route, and in so doing had to be assailed and impeded by other characters. The individual characters, however, who had their own names, ages and appearance, were filled out with material from inner events for which Fanny did not account. Nothing out of her conscious personal life was used in it. What was known to her from her private reality no longer had any interest for her, it had been lived and superseded and only in what she invented did she see an expression for her deepest experience. She did not write to clarify these experiences, to restore inner relationships and to understand herself better, but only in order to sense the tension and joy that occurred during the slow incarnation of her characters. She refused to see in them symbols for her own endeavors and her only wish was to see the game she had devised for herself played out. The more surprising and confusing the material with which she loaded her creations and the more contradictory and improbable their essence became, the better it was for the game and the more

attentively the characteristics had to be drawn. I could think of no
rules for my own work. Playing with imaginary figures seemed to
me like an artifice, an emergency measure. I had no desire to di-
vide myself up into fictitious personages and let my affairs be conducted by advocates, but wanted to find the thief, the grocer, the
thug, the hypocrite, the do-gooder, the apathetic and a thousand
other disguises within myself. We want to do exactly the same
thing, said Fanny, only when I sit down to write I have a firm
basis while you tear the ground away from under your feet. In
your attempt you discover just as little about yourself as I do in
mine. However much expounding and explaining you do, you
don't become any the wiser. After all, you'll never change yourself
and you'll always make the same mistakes. I have long ago given
up trying to improve myself, for the whole of this examination
merely leads to the morality of improvement. You want to see
yourself as an indivisible whole, want to recognize everything
within you, but I think you are deceiving yourself. Just because
you don't have a good idea of yourself, you brood and poke
around in your nature. If you really get a clear perception of yourself, you will leave yourself in peace, you will let yourself exist as
you are without asking in what way your machinery functions.
Only then will you be capable of every task you set yourself. I
answered that I could not see my work as an independent mechanism, my work was part of my everyday life. I could not imagine
isolated works of art, only immediate expressions of the present,
of a continuous change and re-evaluation, and because of this, for
me, there was only a diary, notes, sketches, the various stages of a
picture, perhaps mingled with improvisations of a musical or dramatic nature, but never this crude chunk of a novel, a rounded
picture. You are not in love, she said suddenly, you should find a
woman you can love. Somebody subsistent. Then you could think
up an enduring book, a good, solid picture that would last. Then,
before asking me about Anatol, she spoke of my marriage that
was no longer a marriage, although I still tried to keep up appearances from fear of confessing my failure. If you could accept
yourself, said Fanny, you might even make something of this marriage. You have a wife with whom you can spend the night, you

have a child who can teach you all sorts of things, you have a secluded studio where you can do whatever you like, and yet something is wrong. Where is the mistake. I tried to talk my way out of this, said something about a curse that prevented me from living in a family, something about my inability to compensate for what was rotting away inside me, asserted, with the falsity of the words ringing in my ears, that I saw in my work a means of achieving clarity and objectivity, but Fanny merely bared her strong white teeth in a laugh. I wanted to explain even more. I wanted to point out to her that she herself, in her relationship with Anatol, had proved the impossibility of living with someone merely on the basis of a decision, that this demanded mutual understanding and consideration which was rarely attainable and was usually replaced by an empty routine. But she broke in and said that she did not believe these justifications of mine. You do not resolve one single conflict in your marriage at your writing desk. If you get no fun out of sleeping with your wife and you don't even enjoy throwing a plate at her, and if you get no pleasure from letting your child ride you and gallivanting around the garden with her, then there's nothing for it but to separate. It's hard on the child but in the end she too must make the best of it.

My daughter was two years old when I took her to my parents. My mother wanted to look after her. Now that her own children had left her the house had become too empty. On the way from the station I drove past the factory to bring my father home from work. It was a long low building at the edge of the street with brightly lit windows, roaring machines and steaming chimneys. The workers were still busy in the printing rooms, hanging up the long colorful materials to dry. Below in the offices lights were being turned out; only in the head office was the dazzling neon light still on, and my father's shadow, surrounded by the shadows of his engineers, could be seen on the opaque wavy panes of glass. With the child on my arm I went in to the room and he looked at us with a brief flicker of pride and joy. The engineers greeted us. Mr. Politzer, the head printer, knew me from the time when I worked in the factory. Pattern designs were spread out on a table. Next to them lay sketches of ideas, art reproductions and photographs. The new collection was mentioned. Politzer lifted up a color print of Klee's "Wood with Yellow Birds" and asked me if this picture could not be used as a pattern. Politzer had a dark Babylonian face with a sharply defined bluish jowl, heavy eyelids and a broad nose, his nostrils running in chiseled curves. My father asked me approvingly whether I could execute this design. He laid his hand briefly on my shoulder and I was again drawn into the conversation about new compositions. There were reproductions of old coins and coats-of-arms, of fossils and lizards, of lions, bulls and dragons, of helmets, castles and pennants. There were Chinese woodcuts and African stone drawings and reproductions of paintings of Braque, Picasso, Cézanne, and Matisse. Everything could be put to some purpose. Everything could be transformed into textiles. Here was a color harmony, a treatment of surfaces, there the mannerism of a brush, the expression of a line or a form. In the Klee composition the birds had to be left out and the sickle-shaped trees and heart-shaped leaves emphasized. The whole thing could be overlaid with a silver sheen. Oriental motifs were very much in demand. Balinese sarongs had to be launched on the market and the batiklike effects brought out in the printing. And here was a color photograph from an American magazine: it was a possible theme: the leaves of the trees merely had to be executed in the manner of Rousseau but with the colors of Matisse, but making the whole thing a little more vigorous, lighter and airier. There was also a requirement for abstract patterns. In the following year an increased demand was anticipated for modernistically overlapping triangles, quadrangles and circles. During the discussion at the table I looked around the room. On the large desk the incoming letters lay in trays; there were telephones and loudspeakers which from time to time emitted a clicking sound and a voice asked questions which were answered by my father or one of his colleagues with a movement of the head. Several times the door opened and a foreman, a printer or a clerk came in with a note, a list or some oral message and there was an incessant soft humming and vibration in the walls. Over the desk hung a por-

trait of my father in an imitation French baroque frame, painted
in sickly colors and looking like a colored photograph but at the
same time totally unfamiliar, with an artificial smile on his lips.
Whenever my father turned toward me I sensed his pride and his
joy at our visit. He tenderly patted the child's cheeks, then he
pulled out of his waistcoat pocket his silver watch with the en-
graved starfish, seahorses and snails, and let the lid flick up. It was
time to drive home for supper. When we came out of the factory
he took my arm. He became smaller, more bent and shriveled, but
still bore some of the authority that had been evident in his office.
He said that he felt his best when he was up to his ears in work.
But as we walked across the road to the parked car I noticed how
tired his steps were. He supported himself on my arm and said
with a laugh: I'm getting old. On the way home I asked him what
he thought of doing after he retired in a few years' time. He
answered that there would be enough work to do: he would still
have to run the sales department and show his successors the
ropes. For a few seconds I sensed his old bitterness and disappointment at my not having joined him, but his need for sympathy was the stronger and he tried to adapt himself to me. He said
he would do a great deal of reading: all these years he had
wanted to read but had seldom managed to do so; above all he
wanted to read art, historical and scientific works. He had recently discovered a fascinating book about deep sea diving and
wanted to find out more about it. We drew near to the house in
the outskirts of the town by an open field next to the lake. It
loomed up darkly, surrounded by its garden hedge. The light was
on in the ground floor windows and at the kitchen window stood
my mother. We opened the garden gate; my father lifted the flap
of the letter box and looked in. The evening paper lay in it, he
took it out and banged the flap shut: the sound reminded me of
the time when I had been living at home. My mother came to
meet us on the threshold of the kitchen. She hugged and kissed
me and took the child from me. I stood at the edge of the top
step; my father was standing below us and for a moment it looked
as though we would crash down on top of him. Inside the house
the uneasiness of everything that remained unspoken imposed it-

self on me. My mother took me into my old room that had become
the spare room. There was new furniture in it and the walls were
freshly papered. Have you only brought your briefcase asked my
mother as I unpacked my pajamas. Haven't you got a toilet case
she asked, as I unwrapped soap, toothbrush and shaving gear
from a piece of newspaper. In the dining room the table was laid.
As always my mother had prepared the meal herself. She had no
servants. From dawn to dusk she was busy with the housekeeping.
What else can I do, she said. But the stairs make me tired: with
my legs I can't manage them any longer. The food was heavy and
lots of it, I soon had to undo my belt and felt drowsy and replete,
even though I had not yet tried the sweet and the cheese, and
coffee and cakes were still to come. We drank the coffee at an oval
table with a lace tablecloth in the room that had always been
called "the ladies' parlor." Here too was the large radio of stained
walnut. My father had turned on the news and the announcer's
voice boomed out through the room. Although the round corner
sofa and the deep armchairs were thickly upholstered and piled
with cushions it was uncomfortable. The arms of the chairs in
which my parents had seated themselves were too steep and the
sofa's curved support poked into my back. The table was too close
but could not be pushed to one side since otherwise everything in
the room would have been out of place: the carpet, the little table
with the tall porcelain lamp, the sewing table with the open
drawer, the footstool, the tall carved chair with the Gobelin patterned cover which my mother had embroidered herself after old
English patterns. Moreover, the opposite edge of the table was
wedged tight against my parents' knees. My mother sat embroi-
dering. As it glided up and down the needle added a red thread
to the decoration picked out with a little blue cross on the cloth.
My father had opened the newspaper; the news was over, now
came the weather report and the shipping forecast. I scrambled
over the arms of the sofa to turn off the radio. When I had sat
down again my mother said: "Well, now, tell us what you've been
up to, how you're living." I tried to make my voice sound as non-
chalant as possible. I'm working on a book, I said. Pity you didn't
stick to painting, said my father, and shook his head. So you've

switched over to writing. He had now lost the tautness he had possessed in the factory and had slumped down: the padded shoulders of his jacket had been pressed up at an angle, there were deep shadows under his eyes. You were so good at painting, why on earth did you give it up, he said. With that, he drew a wallet from his pocket and took out a faded carefully folded newspaper cutting with a review of one of my exhibitions. He read out from it a few complimentary sentences. He shows that to all his friends, said my mother. After a pause she added: It really is a pity you aren't painting any more. Can you live by writing. What are you writing now. Is it something heavy no one will want to read. I held the cut crystal glass with the sweet red wine in my hand and between two gulps I heard an echo of the same old complaint that had long ago been leveled at my painting. Oh, forget it, Mummy, my father said from the depths of his armchair. My mother got up, fetched a bowl of fruit, a bowl of nuts, a bowl of sweets and placed them on the table next to the tart and the pastries. She urged me to eat. Do take something to nibble at, she said, and put a piece of chocolate in her own mouth. Every now and then she would take a spoonful of cream tart. I merely refilled my glass. My father said, with an attempt at a joke: You're pretty good at drinking. That brought my mother round to the subject of her friend Ruth who had visited them some little time back. The amount that woman drinks! said my mother, and my father concurred. She took to drinking during the war, said my mother. She starts off early in the morning with a whisky, a whole glass at one gulp, and then she takes the bottle wherever she goes. Wherever she is she's got the bottle. Not that she gets drunk, but she loses all sense of order. She wants to talk all day long. She can't understand that I have to get on with the housework. Papa comes home and the meal must be ready. When I say: Ruth, I really must start cooking, she says: But we can have some sandwiches here in the kitchen or fry a couple of eggs. She doesn't know your father! What would happen if I were to say to him: Go into the kitchen and cut yourself a slice of sausage. My father cleared his throat in embarrassment. So there she sits in the kitchen, said my mother, and stops me getting on with my work. She wants me to spend the

whole time sitting with her and talking and smoking while she
fugs up the room and drinks. But that's why she came to visit you,
I said. To sit with you and talk. All the same I can't let the house
go to rack and ruin, cried my mother. Isn't one's friend more important than one's house, I asked. That may be the way you live,
she retorted violently, that may be all right with you, but it won't
do here. I have to live according to my own standards. If I don't
do one day what has to be done, everything goes to pot. My father began a short absent-minded humming. He could have been
clearing his throat but he was humming, two or three notes,
scarcely even the beginning of a melody: it was his signal to take
a pause, a signal indicating emptiness and fatigue. How would
you manage without me, said my mother and sat bolt upright.
She enthroned herself in her chair with a wounded but dignified
expression, wetting with tongue and lips the end of a new thread,
pushed her spectacles forward on her nose, screwed up her eyes
and stuck the thread through the eye of the needle. No one can
really appreciate the work I do, she said, and her face took on an
expression of bitterness and anger. Her mouth had fallen in and
her thin lips were tightly pursed, hard lines ran down from the
corners of her mouth. Her hands tidied her sewing. The large
aged working hands were swollen with gout, but well cared for: a
sapphire glittered next to the heavy golden wedding ring with the
wave-shaped ornament. The gnarled little finger crooked, the little finger that knew everything. How did you like the book I sent
you for your birthday, I asked to change the subject. Very much,
she said at first, nodding her head, but then she enlarged on this:
All the same, the hero was far too complicated for me, someone
who's always got to get mixed up in awkward situations. It's certainly very subtle and sensitive, but it's all too dreamy and vague
for my way of thinking. That sort of thing doesn't appeal to me.
I've got both my feet on the ground. I replied that dreams too
were real, but I knew how pointless this reply was: it could only
lead to fresh quarrels. But it was as if we were hexed, whatever
we even touched was flammable and underscored our opposite-
ness. I've never had much time for dreams, said my mother. Do
you remember, she asked my father, how when we were just mar-

ried you were always coming to me with your dreams. And even then I said: Leave me alone with your dreams, I've got no time for them. With a cough my father again quietly hummed his little signal. Why do you just sit there saying nothing at all, she said, why are you so mum. Again I thought up a new question in order to avoid a silence. I asked what had become of a former acquaintance. I lit a cigarette from one of the full metal boxes, refilled my glass and waited for an answer. He committed suicide, said my mother. Must have been insane of course. Before he did it he smashed up everything in his workshop. Just the same at home, broke up all the furniture. I asked after someone else. Did they know about him. And the answer came: Him. And the answer came, he's a lazy bum, a load on his father, no good for any kind of work, or at least pretends not to be, and no wonder with such a dumb father sending him money every month, but in any case he can't be quite normal, he has his room full of gadgets, with wires and electrical stuff, a terrible blow for his parents, best not to bring it up at all. Then she suddenly leaned across the table and said: Your way of life sometimes makes me so uneasy. I'd like you to have firm ground under your feet. What do you actually live on. I get so worried about you. I just don't understand. I have done everything I could for you, what have I done wrong. I replied that the mistake was perhaps that we had never talked to each other, that we had never had an opportunity to do so. She looked at me blankly for a while. My father's face was gray, his eyes half closed, his thin white hands with their prominent blue veins were fussily folding the newspaper. Bringing up six children, said my mother, that's quite a job, it doesn't leave much time for talking. My father heaved himself out of his chair. He replaced the newspaper in the newspaper rack, took up a few books which I had been leafing through and had left lying on the table, and put them back in their places on the bookshelf. My mother, too, got up, placed her embroidery in the drawer of the sewing table and carried the cups and saucers into the kitchen. Up in my room I lay awake for a long time. From the hall came the slow dragging tick of the grandfather clock: every quarter of an hour the old clockwork strained with a rattling noise and clatteringly gathered its breath between the trembling discordant chimes. From their room I heard my parents groaning in their sleep like the wounded on a battlefield.

The next evening my mother appeared in full regalia. She had been invited to a hen party. Her face was white with powder, her mouth a black line. The long damask gown crackled with its crinoline, the jacket with the high collar and the huge puffed-out sleeves glittered with gold embroidery. A diadem set with pearls was stuck in her hair, heavy ornaments hung from her ears and about her throat. I've only got a few scraps left for today, she said as we sat down to our meal. The scraps comprised cold roast, potato salad, crab, canned vegetables, sausage, scrambled eggs, peaches, pears, various cheeses, coffee and pastries. Actually I shouldn't be going, she said, but I can hardly refuse: I'm one of the guests of honor. Most of the women there are pretty simple people, downright common in fact. But it would look bad if I didn't go. I am sitting at the head of the table, between the Mayor's wife and the wife of the bank director. When she was gone my father turned the radio on for the news. I went upstairs to my room to wait until it was over. The announcer's voice boomed through the house. My father called me. I'll be down straight away, I called back. I lay down on my bed. I had eaten too much. I felt lousy. The announcer spoke of statesmen, threats of war, trade agreements, new bombs and sporting events, static crackling sharply amid it all. I got up. It must be over soon. Undeterred by the bursting sounds and the crackling the announcer spoke in an impersonal voice about the weather. Then came the shipping announcements and a police message: they were looking for an elderly man who had escaped from a mental home, dressed in blue linen trousers, a blue linen jacket and no hat, who was probably wandering around in the forests. Then there was a sudden silence. The radio had been switched off. I got up to go downstairs. As I left the room my father came up the steep narrow stairs from the kitchen, resting his arms on the banister in front of him, and the face he turned to me had for milennia been resigned to grief. The stairs creaked under his slippers. With a sigh he pulled himself up to the edge of the landing and went silently past me in to his bedroom. I went after him and asked if he wanted to go to bed. He did not answer. I stepped into his room and asked if he were tired. As he began to undress with his back to me he said: Now that you've been here a couple of days instead of spending the evenings with me you leave me sitting down there on my own. I answered that I had merely been waiting for the end of the news. Simply went upstairs without saying a word, he said. He was now standing in his underpants. I turned away and went one step back on to the landing. Round about on the walls and down the broad staircase hung pictures that I had painted while I was still living at home. The clock behind me ticked and groaned. From the bedroom I could hear my father's dry rasping cough. I again crossed the threshold of the room. My father was sitting in his pajamas at the edge of the bed. Slowly he let himself sink back, his raised legs close to one another, and drew the blanket up to his chin. I sat down in the chair next to the door and spoke to him across the plains of the carpet. A pity we always have to misunderstand each other, I said. That's all right, he said. No, it's not all right at all, I said. Forget it, he said. I'm tired too, the work at the factory is a strain and I have a lot of worries. Yes, there are always problems, I said. My own work is only making very slow headway: I'm working on a book, but it is difficult to deal with the things that matter to me. My father's eyes were shut, his breath was already gripped by sleep. I sat for a while by the door, then I went into the room where my daughter was sleeping. I sat for a long time by her bed.

The next morning my mother said: I don't know whether I'm coming or going, I just can't concentrate on a thing. I have heart trouble at night and last night Papa wasn't well either. I sat at the kitchen table with my coffee. My father was already in the factory. In an hour I would be leaving. My mother packed some food for me. She folded the brown wrapping paper with the same care that diapers are folded. She tied up the parcel. Then she sat down with me at the table and took up the half-finished carpet which she was stitching. The carpet was for my apartment. A work that

lasted many months. In every free hour she sat and counted out
the bright threads of colored wool and stuck them into the fabric
with her needle. The glasses had been pushed down on her nose.
In the corner of her mouth she held a cigarette. The ash grew and
fell. I should have liked to give you a bottle of wine to take with
you, she said, but where wine's concerned your father is so peculiar. He locks it up and lets no one get at it. After a while she said:
The other night I felt so ill. Papa was off on a journey and I was
alone in the house and suddenly I was paralyzed, I couldn't get
out of bed, couldn't even reach out my arm to the phone. It lasted
an hour. I could hardly breathe. And the house was locked up.
That was the worst of it, that the house was locked up so that no
one could get at me. I have thought about it constantly since
then: the house being locked and no one being able to get at me.
In the cold morning light her face was saggy, her mouth slack and
sometimes hung open as the muscles gave way. After a pause she
leaned over and looked at me over the top of her glasses and said:
What have you got against me. I groped for an answer. Uncer-
tainly I said: Perhaps I still sometimes see you as I used to see
you. As a superior force. I only want to do what's good for you,
she said. I must feel that people need me. Otherwise life has no
meaning for me. I am so happy that you are leaving the child with
me. I saw that, maybe to please me, she was wearing on her finger
the ring with the blue turquoises I had bought for her years ago at
the Caledonian Market in London. I know of a dream you once
had, I said. The night after I gave you the ring you dreamed it
was magic. You only needed to turn the ring on your finger and
say: You too, my prince, and all your wishes would come true.
Yes, that was a strange dream, said my mother. Then she looked
at the white clock on the wall and said: I think it's time to go. I
said: But the train doesn't leave for half an hour yet. It's better to
leave in good time, she said. It's a long walk and you never know
that the level crossing gates won't just have closed when you get
there. It takes ten minutes to the station, I thought. But I stood up
and put my coat on. My mother put a packet of sandwiches and a
few apples in my briefcase. Then she hugged me. I said good-by
to my child, and went down the gravel path to the garden gate. At

the gate I turned around. My mother was standing with the child
in her arm in the open kitchen door. We waved. I shut the gate
and slowly went down the street. I turned around once again. My
mother was still standing in the doorway. We waved once more.
Then the house of dark brown wood disappeared behind the
trees.

On the 8th of November 1946, my thirtieth birthday, I met
Cora. On this day I opened an exhibition of my paintings in a
town in the west of Sweden. The evening before I had seen her on
the stage of the theater. I did not yet know her name but just saw
her close before me behind the footlights in a plain dark dress,
and nothing existed beyond this face, a pale severe face surrounded by dark hair. Hieronymus would have been able to fill
pages of his book with descriptions of Cora's appearance and the
disturbance of my feelings; out of his collections he might have
been able to come up with the colossal material to do justice to
her voice, her mouth, her movements, material in which everything was expressed, too, about my wishes and my expectation.
Even the following day, as I stood among my pictures, among the
visitors and the representatives of the local press, the face was still
branded on my memory. Asked something by someone, not understanding the question, nodding distractedly and staring into the
crowd of people, I saw her coming down the narrow steps into
the basement room. I walked across to her, greeted her, she returned my greeting with surprise, I stayed next to her, did not
move from her side, showed her my pictures, heard the lilting of
her voice, breathed in the fragrance of her shining black hair, had
her lips, her dark eyes, her broad black eyebrows close before me.
I left the exhibition with her, I talked to her incessantly, I did not
know what about but just talked in order to keep her next to me,
in my infatuation, and now and again she emitted a long drawn-
out astonished noise with her deep voice. And then we sat at a
table, I held her hand and coffee and pastries were set down before us and I was talking and then we were sitting at another
table and meat and vegetables and wine were placed before us,
and I was talking and kissed her hair and her throat but she only

answered with her sounds of mockery, incredulity, of darkly explosive laughter. I accompanied her to the theater and sat again under the footlights, saw her mouth, her eyes before me, she was near me, I had already touched her, our eyes had met, yet she lived up there in a trance, and I could still feel this feyness when I walked up to her in the dressing room to take her away. She seemed to have forgotten me, was surprised that I had come and did not understand what it was that I wanted of her. She walked along beside me like a sleepwalker, then we sat down again at a table surrounded by whirring clattering noises and drank wine, and I spoke and her answers were sluggish and evasive and I urged her to follow me, but she was tired. Tomorrow, she said, tomorrow, and then we walked again along the dark streets up to the edge of a park where she lived in a large house with her parents. To break off then, to separate was inconceivable for me, but again she said she was tired and had to sleep. I hugged her, kissed her, it was inconceivable to release the softness of these lips, to withdraw my arms from this body, there was no resting place, no ending, we flew away, my old world had fled, all that existed was this flight with her, but she fobbed me off with tomorrow. When tomorrow. Tomorrow morning. No, we have rehearsals all day. Tomorrow evening, after the performance, and she had already opened the door and was disappearing up the stairs. For the next night I had booked a room in a hotel outside the town. Cora had brought a little suitcase to her dressing room, a shabby little case about the size of a school satchel. Her coat too was the coat of a schoolgirl and she wore children's shoes with worn down heels. The day had been one endless expectation and now, as fulfillment seemed within my grasp, the vague and indecisive aspect of her replies was borne in upon me. We sat facing one another, alone in a compartment of the suburban train. For me this journey was something absolute, a turning point in my life, while Cora seemed as indifferent to the trip as if it were a school excursion. The wish to renew my life was still so strong that I thrust aside any shadow of a doubt, I held her hands, I kissed her. I talked to her, and her answers had as before a cooing, lightly amused tone, something like the sounds one makes to a devoted animal while gently stroking its coat. Even in the room of the large hotel, hidden in the woodlands and now empty and out of season, when we lay naked on the bed, the contrast was obvious between my rapturous frenzy and her reticence. She did not respond to my caresses but merely tolerated them, and when I had long kissed and savored every part of her body, when I constantly returned to enjoy to the full her loins, her breasts, her mouth, her armpits, behind her knees, her fingers, her toes, her neck, her hair, her navel, it dawned on me that I was holding a phantom in my arms. But then I drew her so much the closer to me, sucking at her breasts, her throat, her ears, with my hands on her knuckles, her ribs, her collarbone to prove to myself that she was made of flesh and blood, that her skin lay on my skin, her lips on my lips. In the morning we went through the hotel park, damp with mist, and along the woodland path; I had given up talking, we walked arm in arm, and I saw that the hair on her temples was already streaked with white. This sign of her aging, that stood out in contrast to the childishness of her clothes, filled me with tenderness and the uncertainty that had arisen during the night disappeared again, till only the desire to cling to this other life remained. In the weeks and months that followed, when I constantly had to recapture for myself the hours of being together with her, I thought I detected hints of a more friendly attitude on her part, but these hints were contradicted by the way she averted her face or by the noncommittal shrug of her shoulders. I was living in Stockholm again, but at the end of every week I took the express train to visit her, awaited her in her dressing room, heard her astonished gutteral greeting, hoped that she would sometime express pleasure at my being there, hoped to hear sometime from her the words: Stay here. And my appearance there was always an intrusion, she did not know how to deal with it and when I left she merely gave a whispered sigh of surprise, as if she had only just become aware of my existence. I visited her in her room at her parents' house. The fact that she still lived at home with her parents, although she carried on her work with all the strength of self-sufficiency, also belonged to this picture of withdrawnness. I had to wait in this room for her, but I could not bear being alone in it, nothing here bespoke the creature I had once seen on the stage, whose figure and movements, whose voice and expression, had had such a deep effect on me that they seemed to have changed my whole life. This room, in the house with furniture that suggested prosperous security, had an air of impersonal strangeness which frightened me. I ran to the theater and when she found me in her dressing room, her look was pained, it seemed to be asking why are you chasing after me, and again all possibility of understanding had passed. The intervals between my visits lengthened, but after each disenchanted departure again and again I had the illusion I could find in direct contact the rich and glowing life expressed on the stage. I could not believe that it did not exist, that it was only acted, I could not forget the experience in this face, could not shake off the deep resonance of this voice, but had to admit that it was beyond my power to set it free.

More than ten years later I met her again. Traveling through the town where she lived I saw her name on a playbill. I called on her in her dressing room. The play was over; she had appeared in her mask, her costume as a queen. Attired in a crinoline, with a leaf-entwined shepherd's crook in her hand, a high powdered wig on her head, a large gold-glittering ornament about her neck, her mouth and eyes coarsely outlined, she turned toward me in slow incredulous recognition. Her voice had not altered but her face, after the make-up had been removed, showed signs of age: tired wrinkles had formed around her mouth and eyes. To hide the gray she had dyed her hair a reddish color. Again we sat at a table opposite one another and a dish was served with wine, and again I heard the short, forced laugh out of her throat, meant to express amazement when I told her that once I had thought it impossible to live without her. But this time my delirious impression of a mad plunge forward was not there; this time I was simply someone passing through, making noncommittal conversation, this time there was no compulsion, there were no demands, and as I accompanied her to her flat I understood that I would have been able to win her if this noninvolvement, this unurgency, the unde-

mandingness had been natural to me. As she lay next to me she
told me that I had alarmed her by my persistence and repelled
her, and for a while it was as though the long time that had
elapsed since our first meeting had vanished, as though the moment of renewal were there again and as though I knew how to
manipulate this renewal, as though we could find each other in
this night, in this hotel, out of town, in the woodlands, in this first
meeting. And again I lay against her naked body, against this
body that I would follow to the death, and in this night the aging
of this body was revealed: it was leaner, the ribs and hip bones
protruded hard, the breasts had sagged, her cheeks were hol-
lowed, her skin had been eaten away by make-up, the enamel of
her teeth had yellowed; and this was all part of it. In the eternal
embrace our hair would grow white and our skin become like
parchment and our teeth would fall out and our limbs grow
crooked from arthritis, and the embrace would never come to an
end: this embrace was a single obsessive feast. For one whole
night I lay next to her, on a short stop in a journey; tomorrow we
would again be far apart and for the first time I saw her in a
detached way, not in my imagination. I saw this aged schoolgirl,
this tired tragedienne who had carried all her passions, all her
beauty on to the stage and had led her life there in a world of
appearances. There she had acted the love of which she was capable, there she was the adventuress, mistress, comrade, sister,
mother and monarch and now I found out, with her large face
distorted by nervous tension close by me, how she had suffered
under this dichotomy and what agonies every role had cost her. In
this night's stay, just passing through her city, she confided in me.
We were relaxed, I wanted to achieve nothing, and she did not
need to defend herself, and because I no longer loved her illusory
existence, in which she had been unapproachable and from which
she had never been able to give me an answer, but saw her as she
was in this night, without glory, violated, weakened and yet still
childlike, she could talk in her dark searching uncertain voice
about her existence, about her substitute existence on the stage, an
existence in which no success, no fame could extinguish in her the
feeling of failure. Our encounter was exorcised and freed of

drama. The delirium had burst into emptiness; I no longer needed to make my approaches in the frenzy of impotence. We lay on our sides facing each other, her lean leg lying across my hips, and so we talked, smoked and occasionally drank a gulp of cognac and caressed each other. We were aware that we could experience this trust only a single time; this night was an exception and its precondition was a complete refusal to make claims on one another. At break of day I left her room, this little girl's room, with a few books and records, with a radio and family pictures on her writing desk, and she waved to me from the balcony: she had never waved to me before. As I continued my journey in the train impressions of the trip we had made after our first night together came back to my mind: six vast factory chimneys had glided past the window one after the other, and in the field a horse had followed us with great leaps and a flowing mane.

On the evenings when I understood that I could no longer return to her, Cora's face with its Arabic profile appeared in the tangle of lines on the drawings. From my present studio in the same city where I had lived twenty years before, I looked into the room where I had stood twenty years before working at large, crackly sheets of paper, in the bluish-white light of the lamp, scribbling away with my pens and brushes and trying hard to retain something. I picked moments out of spans of time in which hours, days, weeks, months were swallowed up, I sought footholds in the flowing and running, in the ceaseless change, I conjured up objects, facts, surrounded myself with them, in order to butt head on against them to test my ability to take it, I confronted myself with faces and words to see where I stood, to obtain a statement from myself which would let me know who I am. In my current state of being I pictured to myself the completely alive moments which had always been overwhelming, which had never let themselves be exhausted, whose challenges I had never been able to fulfill and which always set off new resonances in me. The first night with Cora returned to a constantly renewed present and changed ever more completely, and perhaps the obsession of this night only came over me later, when I had long been alone.

Only Cora knows how I was as I lay beside her naked in the hotel at night. Only Max knows how I was when I entered his smoky boardinghouse room and he still sees me as I appear on the strange and distorted photograph taken by the circus. There is always a too late when one writes, a substitute for something lost. I spoke with Max when he was far away, in his New York hotel room, and when he was back in his little wood and was no longer like the Max Bernsdorf whom I had known from our days in Stockholm. Hoderer's voice was close to me only when he was already dead, and I came to terms with my parents' voices only when they themselves lay turned into ashes in the earth. When I stood in the snow-covered forest in front of the stacked tools I felt only exhaustion after the walk there and indecision in face of the day's work ahead of me. Later this moment became weightier and more comprehensive. I saw myself standing in the driving snow-flakes and the moment had already adopted a timeless quality: I would stand here forever, abstracted in isolation and faced by tasks that could never be fulfilled. My freedom to alter these moments in accordance with my inspirations is unlimited. Like a blind man I can enter the room where Max was lying in bed, and from the swirling gray I can evoke a cupboard, a table and the curtains at the window; I can imagine the palm tubs in the hall and Erika in her blue sleeveless dress; I can conjure up forms, colors, smells, movements and attribute truthfulness to them even when everything was different. Only Cora, Max, Else, Edna, Hoderer and Karel Kurz saw me as I really was, as I stood opposite them and expressed myself in front of them. Only the survivors know these single valid unalterable moments: I myself rushed on, away from them, in my flight, burdened with my inadequacy and my guilty conscience, half-dead and half-blind under the rubble of prejudice, contaminated by a milieu and an upbringing. Only in the immediate present, out of moments now transformed, do I peel from its rind the idea of freedom of action, of relating responsibility to events concurrent with it. I see Peter Kien and Lucie Weisberger again, clearer than they were in Prague, on their way to destruction, I see them already bearing the imprint of what is to come, Lucie's soft, childish face still unaware in the

security of the polished room and yet with premonitory shadows
about eyes and mouth, and Peter Kien, in the atelier of the Academy, humming a duet with me at the window by his easel, see
him that day of the Austrian Anschluss when the man threw himself out the window and landed on the pavement in front of us, I
see Peter Kien's helplessly staring look from behind thick lenses,
this look which already encompassed Theresienstadt. I sketched
away at Cora's picture until the blackness of the lines became
thicker and thicker, and her face disappeared in the blackness,
and when I met her again ten years later the confusion of lines
lighted up and the past melted into a clear present. At that time in
spring 1947 I ran out on to the country road, ran around for a
whole day in the drizzling rain, stood somewhere in a village by a
hedge where the boughs of a large bare tree stretched far out over
the road, turned around, and wandered back to my room: and
later came the impressions of this mindless, monotonous walk in
the drizzle, images surfaced, I saw my littered rooms, drawings all
strewn about, saw myself leaving the room in a curious garb, with
high boots, my trousers tucked into the tops of the boots and a
raincoat over my leather jacket, its leather collar turned up over
the coat collar, was aware of my regular steps that seemed free
from the force of gravity, heard the cars rushing past, saw myself
running across wet, black plowed fields and on to the platform of
a country station, saw myself in the train, in the hot crowded
compartment, in my twilight state, while a man sat opposite me
leafing through the catalogue of a mail order firm. Ceaselessly the
reproductions of tables, beds, chairs, lamps, cups, plates, glasses,
keys, cutlery, pots, vases, dolls, rocking horses, hats, skirts, coats,
trousers, blouses, shirts, shoes, combs, brushes and umbrellas
flickered past, this inflation of objects with their stated prices,
until the train stopped and I got out and walked on. And this road
was a continuation of my hike from Prague to the South, through
the valleys and over the mountain passes. There arose images of
nights spent in hostelries, of a room I shared with a traveling bas-
ketmaker. I can still hear him spitting and rasping in the night,
and when I left, in the early morning mist, the peasant led his
large horse toward me on the road. I can hear the jingling of

the harness, the scuffing of hooves on stone, the chafing of the hooves against the stone. I see Magda as she came toward me to embrace me, a quarter of a century ago; I see her bed, the open door on to the balcony, the lake, the mountains outside. I hear the music coming across from the Italian shore, the shrill hasty trumpet blasts, and see Magda's face, the scar on her forehead, the left eye curtained by a wave of ash blonde hair. Magda is still as young as she was then, and my sister too, who died thirty years ago, has grown no older: she is sitting on my bed, in the room in Neu-Westend, a twelve-year-old girl a few days before her death. She has her hands folded and is smiling at me, and on the paper I do a charcoal drawing of her and then hang the picture among the other pictures on the wall, between the Thief of Baghdad and the final scene from *Tabu* and then the picture follows us on all our journeys, hangs in my parents' house in England, in Bohemia, in an industrial town in the west of Sweden, and then the household is again split up, its possessions strewn to every wind, and perhaps the piece of paper is still lying around somewhere with its blurred charcoal strokes, in a suitcase or a trunk. Moments that lie far back assume a dazzling brightness, become overpowering, and I must go into them again, in the present, and again I see myself abandoning my daughter at the house of my parents, and in a dark transaction giving my child to my mother and her turning the magic ring on her finger to the enchanted formula. I see Else at the edge of the sea lion basin, hear the awkward words of my advances, and see her responding with a smile, and Max stand teetering in the crunching snow and from these advances came a child that was never allowed to live. And Edna lies with legs drawn up beneath the hands of the doctor: she felt the pain, I felt only the pressure of her fingernails in my hand; and Cora sits once more in front of me, on the stage, as Lucie in Sartre's *Men Without Shadows,* in her dark clothes, with her sleepwalker's face, and I stare at her in fascination, as my father had once stared up at my mother on a stage. And I plunge on again and for years, a whole decade, new moments are superimposed, new experiences, and I sound them out, distort them, use them for my present purpose, search them for the tracks that led to today when I am bodily present, here in my studio, looking through the window out over the city.

Here lie the remnants of earlier epochs, geological strata, which bear the imprints of images and signs. In the bookshelves, dominated today by Beckett, Miller, Genet, Michaux, Sartre, and Brecht, the old volumes that I brought back from the cellar of the second-hand bookdealer—when the final stage had been reached and any further expression had seemed impossible, when there new messages reached me, were opened and answered. The old volumes, that had served their time and been thrown away and then reappeared after the shipwreck, and were washed ashore with me, still stand there. Among the new voices that were again to be heard, which continued to speak despite the catastrophe, the new messages reached me, were opened and answered. The old volumes still stand there like deserted stations, many of them burned out, robbed of their contents, and their words, which had once gripped me, have become incomprehensible burbles, while others are still alive and fresh: *Mysteries, Hunger, Pan, Steppenwolf, Klingsor.* Everything that was literature had faded, only here and there could a few sentences be salvaged and entered into the great book of thoughts. In the demand for truth only the most intimate personal statements were valid. Diaries, case histories, reports from prisons deprived novels of their force: little pieces by Arp, Max Ernst, Artaud, and Giacometti overshadowed *Green Henry* and *Henry of Ofterdingen,* but it was possible that in the course of constant re-evaluation these remote dream images would again be readable, just as *Gulliver's Travels, Candide, Pantagruel, Robinson Crusoe* and *Moby Dick* survived alongside *Ulysses,* just as *Wozzeck* stood up beside *Molloy, Michael Kohlhaas* beside *Melanctha* and *Wuthering Heights* beside *Maldoror* and *Nadja.* In this present lie the deposits of past moments in the stacks of papers, the hieroglyphs of which I try to interpret. How was I then, in the spring of 1947, in the chaotic room among the drawings, the sheets of paper, full of abortive openings, notes and sketches, many of which can no longer be deciphered. Where did I stand, what did I want to say. Here in these papers lie the crys-

tallized moments, but they give me no clue, I cannot build up my
present on them, they are communications from a stranger. What
happened that afternoon, when I left the room in a sudden overpowering desire for change and ran down into the city.

Cora was lost, my marriage had failed, nothing had come of an
attempted reconciliation. A mountain of rustling crackling paper
remained behind in the room. Nothing had been made to last by
these papers. I stood in a square in the center of the city, in a
sharply outlined space lit by the sun in the middle of a crater of
shadow, the pages of a torn newspaper fluttered across the main
street in the gusty wind. Irresolutely I went to the travel agency,
stood for a while in front of the window, then walked in and only
when the assistant behind the counter turned to me, only after a
brief glance at the colorful posters on the walls, did Paris occur to
me as my destination. That same evening I boarded the train and
in the early light two days later the suburbs of Paris loomed up
through the smoke and the soot. I was standing in the corridor of
the express train, still dazed from the night I had spent sitting in
the crowded compartment. Next to me stood the two musicians
and their fingers, which during the journey had plucked at the
strings of their guitars, now strummed and danced upon the window pane. The one with the pale effeminate face opened a street
map, while the other with the huge jowled chin bent over it and
we discussed where the cheapest hotels were to be found. Between these fellow travelers, who suddenly stood beside me like
two jailers, I walked out into the city. The city of mighty con-
querors. The vast living mass of city, its air pierced by the cries of
newspaper vendors and the rattle of the old-fashioned green
buses. Here, on the steps outside the railway station, facing a
broad avenue, I confronted them, all of them, the great minds
that had left the signs of their existence here. Then I was led off
by my companions into the shafts of the métro, stood with the
other passengers in the clattering carriages in the odor of singed
dust and stale breath, in the buzz of a foreign language. We
moved into a hotel behind the Panthéon, near the Place de la
Contrescarpe. I unpacked my suitcase in my first room in Paris,

laid my writing pads on the table, looked through the window at
the façades opposite, heard the tinkling of guitars from the next
room and from the narrow street below, heard voices and steps
and runs up and down the scale on a Panpipe. Dark stained carpets, yellowing lace curtains, a dressing table, a washstand, a
bidet, a double bed. And outside, the city that wanted to be conquered, the city full of promise. I stepped out into the stream of
people, walked along the boulevard, among youthful open faces,
among smiling glances, among the tall proud figures of Africans,
walked through the parks, into museums and libraries, sat on the
terraces of cafés, and instead of winning any of this new life for
myself, from hour to hour I lost more of myself until even my own
name became uncertain to me, until, sitting in a wicker chair at
the edge of the street, I no longer knew in the whirr of voices
which language was mine. The language that had surrounded me
for the last few years had evaporated, its words slid out of my
grasp, here in this melting pot it was washed away from me,
which showed how loosely it was attached to me and how little it
had meant. Everything that was not firm, that was not a part of
me, was flooded out, all the trappings fluttered off like leaves,
trickled or ran away from me: I sat in my wicker chair, in the
cauldron of movements, and what I had attempted to articulate
during the past years frothed and whirled away. It had only been
a lisping, I no longer knew to whom I had addressed myself and
where I had got the idea that it could reach anyone. The words
were no longer correct, they were not even sufficient for the simplest communication. I had again to start afresh, in pidgin
French, stuttering, lying in my wicker basket at the roaring edge
of the street. It still seemed to me as if I had left behind pictures
and pieces of writing, but they could no longer be recalled; it still
seemed to me that countless attempts had been made in all directions, attempts with the most varied tools, in changing materials,
changing forms, attempts in which a choice of possibilities was
explored, but they had all fled into aimlessness, there was nothing
more there that I could have shown this vast city. People bent
over me, stretched over me, shouted words at me, talked about
me, laughter buzzed to and fro and I could not answer, could not

participate in it, could only cry out the few phrases I had picked up: *Garçon, encore un café, l'addition, s'il vous plaît.* This was the moment of explosion, the moment when I was hurled out into absolute freedom, the moment when I had been wrenched loose from every stay, every allegiance, released from all nationalities, races and human links, the moment I had myself wished for, the moment when the world lay open before me. Now I could prove who I was, what sort of I it was whom I had borne with me through all the years of flight, whom I had saved from annihilation on the battlefield and in the gas chamber, whom I had projected and for whom I had wept. Now the moment had come when I could explain to what purpose all this labor had been expended and what I expected. But the freedom was so great that I lost all sense of scale. I had not won freedom, but had been condemned to it, and only one perception was there, of primordial evil, of not belonging, of being forsaken. No one asked about me, no one expected anything of me, no one scolded me, no one threatened me, no one wanted to know about my plans or my origins, I was left unmolested in my wicker basket and people talked over my head with words I did not understand. I was in the middle of a maelstrom, incapable of speaking or of walking; my life was useless, I had not even lost something because I never possessed anything. I could display no wounds, no scars, because I had taken part in no battles, I had nothing to report because I had experienced nothing—I was merely an infant taken too early from his mother's breast and set down on the sidewalk.

Until late one afternoon I found myself again under the trees of the avenue on the embankment in the middle of the Seine, and I was restored to my true dimensions. I was standing still, watching boats sail past; I saw the reflection of the setting sun on the tip of the Eiffel Tower, knew what I was called, where I came from and where I would travel on to, although I found there only something temporary, a roof over my head, and this was no longer a mere vagabondage, but a decisive movement across the earth's surface. I was resident in a country, I had spent a few weeks in Paris, my money had run out. I would return here again sometime, to visit exhibitions, go to the cinema or the theater, or perhaps even come with my own works, perhaps travel here sometime with a mistress, walk with her arm-in-arm along the avenue, live with her in one of the hotel rooms where it was a sin to lie alone in the wide bed. And the avenue along which we would walk was already there now and the hotel room stood ready, even though it would be years before we moved in. What the Seine showed me this evening was not a way, or a knowing, I had gained no conception of this existence, had no plans for it, I felt only the clearness of the air, felt how I was standing there and breathing and that I had emerged from the derangement into which the shock of freedom had thrown me. The freedom was still there, but I had got a grip on it, it was no longer a vacuum where I lay in a nightmare of anonymity and where all designations lost their meaning: it was a freedom in which I could give everything a name. I had only changed my point of view. I had once more tasted to the full the fear of independence; I had allowed myself to fall and given up all the views and all the endeavors that composed my identity, and now I stood here under the trees of the Allée des Cygnes, and this was a simple fact, I stood between two poles which had been there from the very beginning, the pole of the *Thief of Baghdad* and the pole of *Tabu,* the pole of irrepressible life and the pole of transience. The freedom was absolute: I could lose myself and I could find myself again in it, I could give up everything, all endeavors, all allegiances, and I could again begin to speak. And the language that now asserted itself was the language I had learned at the beginning of my life, the natural language that was my tool, that now belonged to me alone and had nothing more to do with the land where I had grown up. This language was presented whenever I wanted it and wherever I was. I could live in Paris or in Stockholm, in London or New York, and I carried the language with me, however light I traveled. At this moment the war became a thing of the past and I had survived the years of flight. I could speak, could say what I wanted to say, and perhaps someone was listening to me, perhaps other people would speak to me and I would understand them. Everything that had happened was still there, but we could express our views about it, nothing needed to be hidden any longer. And I could buy myself paper, a pen, a pencil and a brush and could create pictures whenever and wherever I wanted. And when it was hard to find the right words and images this was not because I did not belong anywhere and could recognize no possibilities of communication, but only because many words and pictures lay so deep down that they had first to be long sought for, handled and compared with one another before they produced material that could be communicated. That evening, in the spring of 1947, on the embankment in the Seine in Paris, at the age of thirty, I saw that it was possible to live and work in the world, and that I could participate in the exchange of ideas that was taking place all around, bound to no country.

THIS BOOK WAS SET IN

CALEDONIA AND PISTILLI TYPES,

PRINTED AND BOUND BY

H. WOLFF BOOK MANUFACTURING CO.

IT WAS DESIGNED BY

LARRY KAMP